*Books by Skye Lewis*

LIFE FULL OF EMOTIONS – INCIPIENT EMOTIONS

LIFE FULL OF EMOTIONS – RECURRING EMOTIONS

LIFE FULL OF EMOTIONS – RELENTLESS EMOTIONS

LIFE FULL OF EMOTIONS – JOURNEY FULL OF EMOTIONS

LIFE FULL OF EMOTIONS – FINAL EMOTIONS

RAVEN'S PHOENIX

THE DOME CODE

THE ISLAND TRIALS

*skye-lewis.com*

# THE ISLAND TRIALS

A YA science fiction/dystopian novel by Skye Lewis

Published by Amazon and Brave New Books

First published 2025
Published in this edition 2025

Text copyright © Skye Lewis, 2025
All rights reserved

Skye Lewis has asserted their right under the Copyright Designs and Patents Act 1988 to be identified as the author of this work.

The moral right of the author has been asserted.

Set in Janson.

The Island Trials is a work of fiction. Names, places, and incidents either are products of the author's imagination or are used fictitiously. Any resemblance to actual persons, living or dead, is purely coincidental.

Book cover design by Coach K.

Every effort has been made to obtain the necessary permissions with reference to copyright material, both illustrative and quoted. We apologise for any omissions in this respect and will be pleased to make the appropriate acknowledgements in any future edition.

This book is sold subject to the condition that no part of this book shall not, by way of trade or otherwise, be reproduced, stored in a retrieval system, transmitted, be lent, re-sold, hired out, or otherwise circulated without the publisher's prior consent in any form or by any means of binding or cover other than that in which it is published and without a similar condition including this condition being imposed on the subsequent purchaser.

ISBN: 9798307393529

*For my cat, who was always by my side.*

*For Keegan, who has been my ride or die.*

*For my family, who never stopped believing in me.*

*For all of you, I'll be eternally grateful.*

# CHAPTER ONE

Low light shined on a bed wheeled down the depressing hallway, two men dressed in full-body, air-supplied, yellow positive pressure suits on each side of the creaky bed. Following the white LED lights embedded in the ceiling, scientists and orderlies were passing by; their sensible shoes squeaking on what once used to be pristine tiles. Various dimly lit signs hung above the doors, one of them was labelled *RESTRICTED*.

One of the men pulled a credit card-looking key card out of his pocket, inserting one end into a horizontal slot above the doorknob. With a quick beep, the heavy door ground open. Once through, the man pressed the button, causing a series of bolts to click into place in the two inches thick door with metal cladding.

The other waved his ID badge at the security camera, opening a small side door. They wheeled the bed inside the TC, a BSL-4-levelised laboratory. To the right were centrifuges, freezers of different temperatures, and incubators, to the left six privacy curtains hanging from a track on the ceiling.

They wheeled the bed next to an electronic machine sitting on a cart with odd wires leading from it, attaching one of the IV solutions to the patient, gluing data-collecting wires to his chest which came through the neck of his hospital gown.

"Any news on the preliminary samples we got back to the lab to ascertain why the mutations present so deadly to him?"

"No, sir, we just wheeled him back for further observation."

A thin man with sallow skin walked forward, emerging from the shadows. He pushed his round glasses back on his nose, examining the patient's file.

"The transmission rate shows that the mutation has multiplied, which collides with the initial data."

"Great." The scientist sighed, looking over at the young male patient. "We should propagate the sample further."

"No offence, sir, but isn't our goal just to catalog it?"

The scientist looked over at him, taking one of the blood samples that they extracted earlier. "May I remind you that our lab results will provide us with more definitive data? I won't let *protocol* stand in my way."

He hovered over the boy, his *research.* He walked over to the table and studied the blood in a petri dish beneath a large microscope. Next to him were his reports and charts all scattered across the surface. He picked up a stack of papers bearing the deciphering of the audio log listened to earlier.

"Check the storage unit for me. Mister X should've left some samples he collected earlier, and some syringes with *Serum C.*"

One of the men who wheeled the boy in nodded and left. He read the analysis report in the meantime, having destroyed the decryption key provided as instructed.

Having been given the Serum, he extracted it from the syringe and added it to the blood, watching it combine to confirm his hypothesis.

"$R_0$ is between 1.2 and 1.6." He wrote it down, smiling sheepishly. "Fascinating. Guess Mister X was right after all."

Figures emerged in front of the dome-shaped lab, observing the guard. The key card they needed to break in hung from his belt. They were hiding behind multiple piled-up crates on the main loading dock. To their left were guards hauling crates back and forth to a ship while a scientist barked orders, overseeing the process. To their right was a series of large tents and labs, tucked away at the foot of the hill. The lab had been hard to find, hidden behind the mountain in a hidden valley near the coast. The crates in front of them caused an obstructed view to fully observe the research lab nestled near the woods.

One of them peeked around the corner of the crate, watching the guard idling near the entrance. Looking back at his leader, he received the nod. He pressed the button on his handheld radio. A loud, wailing alarm pierced the air and echoed through the valley. The scientist got flanked by two armed guards upon hearing the alarm, being prod forward to safety.

Their leader stood on top of *The Pulse,* their best advanced armoured truck out of the array of formidable war machines in their fleet, equipped with ballistic glass and steel, gas tank protection with nylon armour, dual ram bumpers, and run-flat tires. Their finest reinforced vehicle to withstand bullets and heavy artillery.

"I hereby command you, my military endeavours, to ensure the order's safety," he ordered, looking at the guard with the key card heading their way.

One of the figures nodded and pulled his mask over his face to maintain his anonymity. He sneaked towards the guard, moving around the crates like a ninja. Approaching the guard from behind, he pulled out his combat knife and seized his head, pulling it back. The knife went into the side of his neck at the base, pushing it through his carotid artery into his windpipe, killing him instantly. He pulled the knife back out and watched the body slump to the floor, then took the key card.

He signalled to his leader that he retrieved the card, then moved forward to reach the lab.

As soon as he entered through the door, he let out an audible gasp at the state-of-the-art equipment decorating the lab. It seemed way more valuable than their makeshift science equipment. He ordered himself to focus, studying the laboratory with a focused intensity. He fumbled through a few documents scattered across the table.

"Their cells are decomposing at an accelerated rate... That's not good." He took a picture with his phone, then flipped the page. "The internal musculature details are missing... That's odd." He took another picture, then stopped, staring at a file. "Rate of spread for disease... single strand... experiments... what's all this?" He touched the young girl's face, mesmerised by her beauty.

He gritted his teeth in barely contained rage, knowing what they had done to her.

"What are you doing in here? Who let you in?"

He turned around to stare at a young female scientist, holding him at gunpoint. He sidled over to her until his bulletproof vest stood against the barrel. "I'm confident we'll... *devise* a solution to our current situation. If you put the gun down."

She scoffed, not lowering the gun an inch. "You think you know it all, hm? But his lack of scientific knowledge will get those kids killed. It prevents him, and you, from seeing the holistic picture."

"Our holistic picture? As if yours is squeaky clean. Science isn't that different from our belief."

She opened her mouth to retort, but his radio crackling to life interrupted her. *"What's taking you so long?"*

He looked at her, slowly moving his hand towards his belt, taking the radio out of its holster. "I'm on my way." He put the radio back where it belonged, looking at her. He walked towards a map pinned to the wall, tapping the centre of it. "You see this? We've got this lab surrounded. If you even *try* to shoot me, they'll pierce you with bullets you've never seen before."

She sighed, lowering the gun. "What do you suggest I do then? Just let you go unscathed?"

He chuckled, walking closer until their bodies were pressed together. "Easy. I knock you out, and we go our merry way. No bullets fired, no deaths."

"How can I be sure you're not lying to me?"

He left no space between them, pulling her even closer to his body. "You're just gonna have to trust me."

She rolled her eyes, shaking her head. "You're very stubborn, Jack."

"*Jack*? What happened to calling me Jackson?"

She chuckled, standing on her toes to kiss him. His stubble beard burned pleasantly over her skin. His breath wafted over her lips as he whispered. *"I never stopped loving you."*

She sniffed his hair; a musky scent filled her senses. She sighed softly. "Times have changed." She pulled away, turning her back towards him. "Go ahead, do what you must."

He grazed a quick kiss on her cheek, then knocked her out cold. Once her limp body hit the floor, he noticed a rolled-up paper tube not too far from where she had landed. He unfurled the paper tube to reveal a heavily annotated map. He smirked.

"I knew you'd help me."

He stared at the details providing clarity in understanding the data, removing the ambiguity and confusion he and his fellow men had experienced for weeks. Satisfied, he left the lab, but not before he had made sure she was left behind comfortably.

The bright light of the laboratory faded behind him as he sneaked back towards the shadowy tree line of the ravine where he had left his fellow men behind.

Giving the leader the map, he patted Jack on his shoulder. "Good job, lad. Seems like we'll finally bring those kids home. Where they belong."

He nodded and saluted, then watched the tent-like structure situated next to the laboratory. For some reason, he couldn't remember the tent having been there when they first arrived. While the others received the orders, he walked closer to the tent-like shaped construction.

He crept inside, finding old, rusted machinery stored away. He scanned every nook and cranny, realising what they were.

"Crap... They're trying to *cure* 'em."

His thoughts were cut short when a hail of gunfire lit up the tent. A volley of bullets blasted the tent cloth, forcing him to throw himself onto the ground.

*"The guards opened fire! Requesting immediate air support!"*

His radio crackled to life for a split second, then it was cut off, leaving nothing but static. He forced himself back to his feet and rushed out, reloading his semi-automatic weapon.

"Alec!" he yelled, watching his younger brother standing amidst the gunfire.

He tackled him to the ground as bullets tore through the bushes, shredding the leaves. Splinters of wood flew everywhere, and he threw himself on top of him to shield him.

Branches came down, yet the bullets shattered them into sawdust before they could severely injure anyone. The blasts from whatever advanced weapon they were using echoed all around Jack, forcing him to cover his ears. It was deafening, and it surely would cause tinnitus.

The rumble of engines then filled his ears. Looking up, he saw two motorbikes coming right at them, bearing two guards clad in heavy armour. They revved their engines, lifting two tricked-out automatic shotguns. They opened fire on Jack and Alec, the bullets ripping through the moss and fallen leaves.

Jack pulled his brother to his feet and ran towards cover, hearing rapid gunfire behind him. Then, it halted.

Jack peeked around the thick bark of the tree, looking at three of his fellow men holding their semi-automatic weapons, smoke coming out of the barrel. He smiled at them as their bullet shells clattered to the ground, then heard a quiet shudder coming from his left.

He stared at his little brother's shirt soaked through with blood.

"Alec... no..."

He crouched by his side and lifted his shirt. Several ragged punctures that oozed dark blood became visible, and Jack gasped loudly.

Sweat glistened on Alec's forehead, his breathing ragged. He clenched his jaw against the pain as Jack tried desperately to stop the bleeding, applying pressure to the wounds.

"I need tweezers," he told the three men standing behind them. None of them moved. "I said that I need tweezers!" he yelled, saliva flew from his mouth as he did. "And find me some bandages!"

One of the men left in a hurry to get him the medical equipment he needed. The other who stayed behind took out a clean handkerchief, beginning to tear it into smaller pieces.

"You need to sterilise it before you can do anythin'," the one staring said. "But there's no way we can get boilin' water around here."

"Give me your bottle then."

He offered him his canteen.

Jack took it and wet a piece of the torn-off handkerchief given to him. "Any soap here? Or alcohol?"

"Would grain alcohol work?" the guy sitting next to him asked.

"Whatever. Just find me *anything* to clean it with."

He nodded and left, leaving Jack behind with the staring guy. He could barely see what he was doing and commanded him to use his flashlight. The staring guy sighed, shining his flashlight on the wound.

"*Bloody hell...*" Jack muttered, looking at Alec whose eyes were filled with fear.

"I'm dying, aren't I?"

"No, of course not," Jack answered, laughing a little. "Remember that I promised to take you to that weird-looking place with machines that people used to play games on? With those built-in weapons that have zero actual ammunition?"

Alec nodded slowly, shivering. He shuddered when Jack touched his wound to put pressure on it.

"That's where I'll take you once we're back at the base safe and sound, *okay*?"

Alec nodded again, his eyelids drooping. Jack knew he had to hurry. The first guy who had left came back with the tweezers, giving them to Jack.

Jack pulled out his knife, the very one he had used to kill the guard. When the other came back, he urged him to sterilise the knife and tweezers, then to clean the wound on his brother's abdomen.

He meanwhile prepared the suture kit so he could immediately stitch him back up once he had removed the bullets. There was no exit point, so the bullets had to still be inside.

The guy that brought the tweezers gagged, running away to throw up. He couldn't handle seeing blood. The other assisted Jack, while the one staring before kept holding the flashlight up.

Jack made an incision, hoping that the bullet hadn't gone too far in. If it had, and it had hit any vital organs, there was no saving his brother.

"There," the one assisting said, pointing at a glint of metal close to his intestines.

Jack picked up the sterilised tweezers, moving his hand deeper into his stomach to extract the first bullet.

Alec tried his best not to scream as he was being operated on without anaesthesia. He looked a little woozy, his face gaunt.

Jack had removed the three bullets that had pelleted him, cleaning his last wound. He then began to stitch him up with the prepped knotted suture. The guy assisting bandaged his side, while Jack slouched back against the tree, exhausted. The guy settled Alec onto his back as he lay asleep, passed out from the blood loss.

"If I didn't know better, you could've fooled me saying you're a surgeon," the guy said, clapping him on his back.

Jack showed the slightest hint of a smirk, shaking his head. "Don't cheer yet, mate. He's not outta the woods yet."

The guy nodded, offering him a flat metal flask.

Jack opened it and sniffed it, laughing. "Seriously? Hooch on the job? That stuff's sixty years old if not older."

"So? Doesn't mean it's bad."

Jack shook his head, then took a sip. He didn't even grimace as he swallowed it. A sudden volley of gunfire erupted once more. Jack looked at the two guys readying their weapons. "Help me get him on my back!"

The two guys did as they were asked, hoisting an unconscious Alec on his back.

"Go, we'll cover you!" one of them yelled, to which Jack nodded gratefully.

He ploughed through bushes, stumbling over tree roots to bring his brother to safety. Then the gunfire behind him stopped abruptly.

He turned around, watching as the two guys that helped him earlier didn't even make it to cover. A line of bloody holes ripped open along their torsos; both of their lifeless bodies fell to the ground.

He stared in disbelief but was soon forced to move on as another round of bullets tore through the bushes around him, a panicked glance shown on his face while manoeuvring through the thick canopy.

A sudden sharp pain hit him in the shoulder, and he collapsed.

"Jack! Jack, *wake up!*"

A slap to the face made him startle awake, looking into the panicked eyes of the girl he had knocked unconscious earlier.

"Easy, you lost consciousness due to the shock from your wounds. But they don't look mortal."

He groaned; eyes glazed over. Clutching his arm, he noticed the blood staining the leather shoulder pad of his uniform.

Time stood still as he looked over at where his brother was, a clean shot through the head. He could care less about the blood that was seeping down his shoulder where the bullet had pierced him.

"Alec!"

He scrambled to his brother but was too weak to reach him. She carefully pulled him to his feet, wrapping his uninjured arm around her neck.

"Come on," she said, determined to take him out of harm's way.

"No! No, he's my little brother! I can't just leave him!"

He tried desperately to reach him, but she didn't budge. She looked around for a means of escape, and the only way out seemed to be jumping into the ocean.

"Listen to me, Jack," she said, cupping his face in her hands, "I'm *not* abandoning you again. I did that once before; I'm never doing that again."

It was quite the steep drop into the ocean, but it was better than staying there and risking getting shot.

Despite Jack's efforts to still try and reach his brother, she forced him along with her, then pulled him along as she crashed into the water.

She looked at Jack bobbing beside her, struggling to keep his eyes open. Multiple bullets pierced the water while she swam towards him, watching in horror as yet another bullet hit his other shoulder. Blood clouded the water around him, blood she wished she wouldn't have to see.

She swam towards him and grabbed him beneath his arms, trying to dodge the bullets piercing the dark water. She started kicking towards the shore, breaking the surface with great effort.

She gasped for air, looking up at the cliff they jumped from. The guards that had opened gunfire on them had disappeared, giving her enough time to swim towards the shore.

Pulling him onto the sand, she immediately fell to her knees to press both hands against his gushing wounds, trying to stop the bleeding.

He coughed up water, still conscious, which was a miracle at this point.

"Viv..." he said weakly, watching as she looked around, searching for a safe spot to tend to his wounds.

"Shut up," she said, looking at him, "you spared my life. I'm trying to repay that favour."

She helped him back to his feet, supporting him as he wobbled on his feet. His arms hung limp, blood seeping between his fingers once the blood had run down his arms.

Leading him over towards a cave, she struggled to make him walk along. He was way taller and heavier than she was with his armour. Taking it off piece by piece, she tossed it all in the sand, not caring if he needed it or not.

They reached the cave, and he sat down against the rocky wall, watching her kneel beside him. She ran back to the ocean to fill her flask with water, then ran back to him. Using the ocean's water, she washed the blood away as best as she could to examine the wounds more closely.

"Looks like they both went through cleanly, I see two exit wounds," she said, putting on her glasses.

He chuckled softly, then grunted. "I wasn't looking forward to you digging in my shoulders the way I did with my brother's stomach."

"I'm so sorry, Jack," she said, looking at him. "I know how much you loved him."

He groaned loudly when she applied pressure to his wound. "Your *people* took him away from me..." he said, hissing.

"They're not *my* people," she said, taking a lighter out of her pocket. "I just work for 'em."

He scoffed, then noticed the lighter. "You kept it..."

She nodded, holding the lighter beneath her flask to heat the water. "Of course, I did. It helped me remember what I'm fighting for."

"Then why do you think *curing* those kids is the right answer?"

She sighed, ripping up a piece of her lab coat into strips, soaking them while pouring the boiled water. "Neither of us has the right answer, Jack. None of our beliefs does 'em right. Only they can." She turned to him regretfully. "This is gonna hurt."

She poured the water on the first wound, and he braced himself against her, clinging to her shoulder. His fingers dug into her skin to transfer his pain to her.

"You know I can't do that, not anymore," she said apologetically, hearing him hiss in pain. "I gave it up for science."

He pulled away reflexively once she washed the deeper parts of his wound. He shook his head. "You can't let 'em cure those kids the way they've *cured* you."

"You would've used me the wrong way if I hadn't," she said, a single tear escaping her eyelid.

"That's not true, we—"

He groaned in pain once she moved on to his other wound. Yet the cleaning worked the way she had hoped it would, nodding with gratification once she got a better vantage point. No bullet fragments remained.

She held her palm to one of the wounds, keeping pressure while retrieving a makeshift bandage, slowly winding the strips of cloth around the wound. She pulled the two ends of the cloth strip tight, tying it off.

He drew in a sharp breath at that motion, to which she apologised before moving on to his other wound.

He flexed his arm, gingerly testing its range of motion. He shuddered and winced, knowing he wouldn't be able to defend himself, or her.

"How about I kiss it better?" she asked teasingly.

"Is that your medical prescription, doc? Will that heal me?"

She chuckled, moving forward to gently kiss his bandaged shoulder. "Maybe."

She finished with his other arm, moving to sit next to him. He leaned his head against her shoulder, sighing deeply. "I'm sorry I nearly jumped outta my skin when you poured the water."

"I would've done the same, I think."

"Let's not test that, I prefer to keep you unscathed." He saw the red mark on the side of her head, feeling guilty. "How's your head?"

"It's fine."

He moved his hand up to touch it, yet she met him halfway, her hand grabbing his wrist. She pushed his hand away.

"Can I ask you a question?" he asked after an eerie, awkward silence.

"I can't really say no, can I?"

"What does CRISIS want with those kids? What's the *cure* you're giving 'em?"

"You know I can't answer that."

He made her turn her head his way, their eyes locking. "I know you'd never go on board with 'em acting as a pharmaceutical company. I know it's just an appearance to hide your science-related scheming."

"It's not a scheme…"

"Then explain what it is."

"In the eyes of the current leadership, President Goldlib and Samuel's, we appear to be the city's most advanced company in launching a medicine program that's set to repair what we've done wrong. We're cooperating with Timothy, their Head of Science and Medicine, to keep providing the *cure* to fix all *aliens* and Squad members."

"But?"

"But… CRISIS is now operating under Mister X. And no, I've never met the guy. He's this mad scientist who's trying to push science to its limits, no matter how inhumane the tests are."

"So, you're—"

"Trying to stop 'em from the inside. They've made this new serum, *Serum C,* and if what I've read is true, those poor kids won't live to see another day."

"A spy?" He chuckled. "Never pictured you being one."

"There's a lot you dunno about me, Jack." She sighed. "My brother's one of 'em. One of the kids they're performing tests on…"

"What does the serum do, Viv?"

"It—"

A bullet whizzed past them, far too close for comfort. It ricocheted off the wall with a shower of sparks. Viv looked up at the black-clad guard looking down at them, shaking his head.

"I knew you were a traitor the second you walked in, Vivienne."

"Listen, it's not what it looks like," she said, holding her hands up.

But he didn't listen, shooting her straight between her eyes. Her lifeless body fell into Jack's lap, who drew his gun at the guard.

"You're gonna pay for that!"

His finger squeezed the trigger, and the guns went off with a crack that seemed to stop time. The cave was deathly still, the air raw and buzzing from the deafening gunshot.

Two still-smoking guns lay on the ground, both Jack and the guard left behind with a hole in their heads.

Jack's eyes stared unseeing right at Viv. His thumb managed to push the button of the small device he held before the cave was blown up by dynamite.

# CHAPTER TWO

Nothing but darkness surrounded the honey blond male, coming to as he woke up from what felt like the longest slumber he had ever experienced. His head was pounding, and for a moment he thought he was blind.

One bright light shining directly at him forced him to cover his eyes, noticing he was being kept in a holding cell. He saw a figure standing in front of the light, a looming shadow that overpowered the male.

"Who are you?" the male asked, blinking rapidly, "and where am I?"

The figure stepped forward, until he was right in front of the bars. The male gasped at the figure's face. Half of his face bared flesh of what used to be his skin, the other half nothing more but wires and prosthetics. Half-robot, half-inhuman.

"You're in a convertible auxiliary lab, one I've made for... more volatile experiments," the man spoke, his voice iron, almost chilling. "You're quite convertible yourself, aren't you?"

The male backed away in one of the corners, shaking his head. "I... I dunno what you're talking about."

The man got even closer, holding a syringe in his hand. "I'm sure you do."

The male swallowed, then realised something. "Where's Viv? She... she was the one looking after me."

"Don't worry, Andrew, she's safe and sound upstairs. She had to take your *samples* from the storage area."

"Which samples?"

"Blood samples, cheek swabs, pheromones. Lymphatic fluid."

"Lymp—" He gasped. "You're not a cyborg, you're..."

"Dr. Cretin. Yes, the one and only."

The male gasped and disappeared, turning himself into a plant. Dr. Cretin smiled, observing this first-hand. "Fascinating... You truly are capable of shapeshifting."

"You made me this way! It's your fault!"

"Just a mere... *addition* to what we originally planned with you."

He opened the cell door, standing to the side, making way for the male to run outside if he pleased. Yet nothing happened. Dr. Cretin laughed. "Atta boy. Follow me."

Out of the shadows, the male made himself visible again, walking after Dr. Cretin. They walked through one of the makeshift chemistry labs, one to uphold the reputation that they were indeed a simple pharmaceutical company now and had distanced themselves from their previous status.

They ended up in the biology lab, data shown on various monitors scattered around the walls of the bright room.
"Andrew, it's so lovely to see you," the older lady who worked closely with Viv said, looking up from a file she was busy reading.
"Hello, Mrs. Husion."
She took him to the drug discovery lab hidden behind the biology lab, access only via the key card. It was a lab similar to the one Jack had found only a few hours earlier, yet this one bared their greatest secrets.
Upon entering, Andrew was mesmerised by the enormous chair waiting for him in the middle of the room. He tried turning around but was met by Dr. Cretin blocking his exit. He forced Andrew forward, pushing him into the chair. He put the leather restraints around his ankles and wrists, and another around his neck.
"Let me go!" Andrew yelled, struggling against the restraints.
From each side, a robotic arm came his way, a tiny needle protruding from both. He tried with all his might to break free, but the needles found their point of entry into his temples.
He gasped loudly, feeling a buzzing sound in his head, something electrical.
Mrs. Husion pulled up the scans when Dr. Cretin joined her in the room.
"His gene splicing is beyond anything I've ever seen," she said in awe, staring at the red lines on the screen.
"How's the virus design coming along?" the Doctor asked, clearly not as impressed as she was.
"You can't seriously consider infecting him with the disease, Doctor. He's already got something inside of him that I can't explain. Injecting him could possibly kill him."
"That's precisely the point. He's our super soldier experiment, don't you see? If he were to die, we've got a reason to bring him to the dissection room to get an actual look inside."

Mrs. Husion had clearly gotten quite attached to Andrew, same to Vivienne. She knew Viv was down in the morgue, and she would be damned if she let that happen to Andrew too.

She knocked over a flask with Reactive, a chemical agent that could cause a chemical hazard, watching it get mixed with water.

With Dr. Cretin distracted, she pushed a button to get the needles away from Andrew, rushing forward to undo his restraints.

He practically fell into her arms, and she tried to help him stand. "Listen to me, Andrew, there's a little lodge not too far away from the facility. Take this." She extracted a key from her personal keyring, slipping it into his hands. "Stay there until I come find you, okay?"

"But..."

She hauled him towards the lift, scanning a special key. "Whatever happens, don't go off until you reach the ground floor." She pushed him inside, and the doors closed.

He bypassed all the floors, shooting straight for the top. In this case, the ground floor. He ended up in what CRISIS used as the point of entry lab, *the wet lab*. In the eyes of the public, one for preclinical drug discovery. For them, *hell*.

He saw the vials ready for the tissue collection, looking at the animal facility they had designed to uphold their lie. Every normalised pharmaceutical company had a room for testing, the room filled to the brim with shelves of cages.

He heard the mice squeaking in their cages. Despite it being the most sterile lab space of the facility, it didn't stop him from gagging. The smell was excruciatingly disgusting.

He noticed the specialised bin for biohazardous waste and walked over to it, hoping to find something he could use in case of a potential threat.

Hearing a door open directly behind him, he was forced to hide, hiding in one of the lockers keeping the scientific protective clothing near the entry location.

"Let's skip the nitty-gritty and cut to the chase," he heard a male voice say.

"I've spoken to the lads working in the engineering lab. They've stopped fabricating the weapon parts," a female voice answered.

"What? Why?"

"Our priorities lie elsewhere."

The man scoffed. "As if. Our guards were at the weapon testing range this morning, and the guns backfired on 'em. Several got hurt. We can't just abandon the only way to protect ourselves. We need to upgrade our firepower."

"I know. I've tried to convince him this isn't the way to conduct a masterplan."

"What about robotics and cybernetics?"

"Same story, really." She went over to what Andrew could only describe as something close to a refrigerator. She pushed a button, to which a robotic arm pulled out a dispersal cartridge from the big hole in the middle.

"Is that *Serum C?*" the male asked.

"Reinvented and recalculated with the newest determination of molecular identity and structure."

It was made clear to Andrew that the refrigerator he referred to was, in fact, an NMR spectrometer. Or at least a smaller version of it. The hole was the sample-holder, hidden inside a very strong magnet.

"What did the diffractometer say?"

"The usual. The structure of the material we've used reacted weirdly to the beam of radiation of the particles we let it interact with."

*What the bloody hell are all those words? How am I supposed to make sense of any of this?* Andrew thought to himself.

At this rate, it seemed like he would never get out of there. Desperate to flee and get to the lodge as instructed, he began thinking of a plan to distract the two scientists. His eyes landed on a big red button, presumably a fire alarm.

*No, stupid idea. You wanna leave the building in stealth, not in a body bag.*

He scanned the room further, hating that it was windowless. All he could see in the nearby vicinity were piles upon piles of paperwork waiting to be filed, week-old cups of coffee that seemed like an experiment itself attracting bacteria, and a litter of used vials and syringes nesting beneath the refrigerator.

The female looked at the utilitarian clutter about them and sighed. "We should really fix this mess. If Mister X were to see this—"

"He won't come here. We don't even know his true face or voice. There's no way he'll ever set foot in here."

"Still, it doesn't hurt to clean a bit."

She walked closer to the locker Andrew was hiding in, and upon getting closer, she smelled something unusual. Clearly,

Andrew hadn't showered in weeks, and it could be smelled from a mile away.

She waved the male over to her location, pointing at the lockers. "You smell that? Smells rotten."

"Don't tell me that gal put in another decaying body..."

The air inside the locker hung heavy and cold. It pressed down on him like fathoms of icy water as he struggled to breathe. He couldn't stand the pressure of that silence.

He wanted to stop breathing altogether, thinking it made too much noise. Yet the frantic thrum of his own heart seemed unbearably loud. Even more so while being in that still situation.

His forehead was drenched with sweat once she opened the first locker, and he knew she would soon open the one he was in. *The third.*

His breath came in heavy pants when she opened the second, readying himself to jump out on her. Her hand reached for the knob, and he watched with bated breath as it slowly opened.

An alarm blared. *That's not the fire alarm, is it?*

"Attention. Subject V has escaped. Harbouring or aiding this fugitive will be punishable by death. Don't approach the Subject, don't put yourself at risk. Report any suspicious activity immediately."

"Not again." The female grabbed her tranquiliser gun. "This happens *way* too often."

*Too often? More escaped before I did?*

He watched them leave the room and waited for about two minutes before he deemed it safe to get out of the lab.

He heard the conveyor belt further down the hall, for some odd reason remembering that sound. He had vague memories of being given a tour once, and it also reminded him that there was an exit point near the loading dock.

Heading over there, he hid behind three stacked crates as three guards rushed about. They were clearly looking for *him.*

"Attention. Facility lockdown initiated."

He looked behind him, watching the roll-up doors closing on their own. He observed the guards, calculating how much speed he needed to time his escape right.

Then he just bolted, taking the risk that he might get shot at. But everything was better than staying put in that hellhole.

He dove towards the roll-up doors getting dangerously close to being locked, and at the last second, he slid right under it, ending up outside. The rain pelted him with cold droplets, faster and faster, until it was a downpour. It soaked through his clothes within seconds.

He watched the glass of the pharmaceutical factory; the rain pelted the glass in what could only be described as thick rivulets, making it impossible to look inside. He looked at the woods looming behind him and made a break for it, hearing the wailing alarm behind him. It faded into the distance the deeper he headed into the woods.

Twenty minutes later, he hadn't come across anything that looked like a lodge. The torrenting rain washed away the mud, water dripped from his eyelashes, rivulets trailed down his gaunt jaw.

The unrelenting rain, the night sky, it all faded with each step he took as he grew more and more exhausted.

Leaning against a tree bark to regain some energy, he stood there stiff-backed while the rain kept pelting him, dripping down his soaked form. He needed to find shelter, and *fast*.

He tried walking forward yet was met with resistance coming from the east. A harsh, howling wind tried to stop him from reaching shelter. On top of that, the dense vegetation ahead of him didn't make things easier either. He had no knife to carve through it, and was forced to walk around it, which slowed his progress even further.

He stumbled through the woods, seeing light in the far distance. *I've found it.*

He could see the contours of the lodge through the dense vegetation and began inching closer.

After what he could only describe as the longest trek he had ever experienced, he finally reached a cluster of large wooden buildings nestled in between the trees. Despite a few of the windows being broken, and the weeds having begun pushing through the wood, the structures looked remarkably sound.

The pine branches swayed in the harsh wind, dropping specks of rain droplets on him as he moved closer to them. *Strange. Wasn't it supposed to be one lodge? This can't be the place.*

His blood ran cold when a loud bell rang out through the woods. *Is that an alarm bell?* Looking down at his feet, he noticed a tripwire. *Crap.*

It took only a matter of seconds before he was surrounded by unknown men and women pointing rifles and crossbows at him. He slowly raised his hands in the air. "I come in peace," he said, stammering.

"Who sent you?" an older man asked.

"Mrs. Husion."

He then lowered his crossbow, ordering the others to follow his example.

"Follow me," he said, making the crowd disperse.

Andrew crossed the path towards the man, propelled by some unseen force. Was this man forcing him to walk? Was it something inside of him that caused him to just obey? Whatever it was, he felt himself jostle against several of the people staring at him. And yet it didn't stop him.

# CHAPTER THREE

Upon entering, he saw a haggard bald man leaning on the doorway across from him, glaring at him, eyes hot with anger. He jumped and whirled around as the door closed forcefully, swallowing hard.

*What did I just walk into? Is this a trap?*

Behind him, the same older man from earlier readied an arrow, nocking it, just in case he would try anything funny.

"So, you must be Subject V. The last one missing."

*Missing?* "I was missing?"

The old man behind him laughed cruelly, something that sent shivers down his spine.

"Is that supposed to be *funny*? Is it *funny* that I have no idea who you people are and feel like I'm about to get murdered?" he asked, sounding angry. Though his confident expression faltered as the bald man came closer.

"Listen, you're gonna have to get used to some new faces and names around here, kid. And yes, we may have strange customs and hints and half-truths that you can already sense going on around you," he said, getting closer to his face, "but you'll thank us eventually. You know, for saving your life."

He snapped his fingers. Before Andrew could fathom what was happening, he was grabbed roughly on both sides, manhandled by two older men who shoved their crossbows in his face, shouting at him to not put up any protest.

Despite Andrew's small efforts to not give in, they tightened their grip on his arm, forcibly dragging him backwards. He succumbed to their strength, no longer putting up a fight. *What good does it do to resist anyway?*

They dragged him towards a warehouse, slamming the door shut behind him. He heard the bolt of a lock slide closed, trapping him inside.

He didn't dare to move for a good whole ten minutes, until he decided that if there had been a murderous beast inside, it would've eaten him by now.

He stumbled in the dark, cavernous space, tripping on something that clanged loudly once it skittered across the floor.

*Crap, that must've attracted someone, if not something.*

Light flooded the space, causing Andrew to shield his eyes from the sudden light entering his pupils. Adjusted to the light, he noticed the maze of shelves filling the room, stacked high with nothing but junk.

An earth-shaking *bang* came out of nowhere, debris clattered down from the shelves due to the impact. He darted behind a crate for cover, making himself as small as he possibly could. Broken wood and metal rained everywhere, forcing him to duck back behind one still-intact shelf. Another loud *bang* rocked the very foundations of that shelf. In the heat of the moment, he grabbed a pan and wore it like a helmet, telling himself it was either that or something smashing his skull.

He heard bolts clattering down from the shelves, knowing one would come loose soon. As he tried to get up to avoid injury, a wooden beam from the ceiling suddenly crashed down onto him, trapping him beneath it.

Hearing shouts outside, he forced himself to scream silently, tears running down his face. His leg caused a burning sensation throughout his whole body, and he was almost certain that he heard a snap. No, he *was* certain. He *felt* it.

*Crap... Double crap... Triple crap!*

He tried freeing himself, pushing against the wooden beam. It wouldn't give. He let out a frustrated groan, praying silently that no one had heard that.

Outside, he heard rapid gunfire, one of them belonging to a machine gun. He couldn't tell the brand, but he knew it was a newer model. He just *knew*.

*Whatever's happening out there, it's a massacre.*

Trying again, he pushed with all his might, until he somehow managed to wiggle his leg free. Looking at it, he noticed how severely swollen and bruised it was in combination with the odd shape his leg seemed to have.

*Is that... is that my bone poking outta my skin...?*

The sour taste in his mouth made him gag, the acids in his stomach slowly found their way towards his throat. He had never seen a broken bone before, but it was horrifying enough to cause acid reflux.

At that point, he realised how quiet it was. *Too quiet.*

Listening carefully, he told himself the coast had to be clear. At least to try and make his escape. Whoever these people were, he couldn't trust them. That much was clear.

Forcing himself up, he stumbled about the room, trying to find something he could use to bind his leg with, and something to lean on. A smaller piece of wood, presumably from the same beam, seemed as good a thing to use as any. Ripping off a few strips of fabric from his shirt, he began attaching the wood to his leg as well as he could.

Out of the corner of his eye, he noticed a crowbar lying on the floor. Picking it up, he felt a sticky substance sticking to his hand, but didn't care enough to pay attention to what it could be.

Using the crowbar as a means of moving forward, he went over to the door, though it was still boarded shut. Looking around, an idea came to mind as his eyes fell upon a crate, and a plank placed against the left wall. Stumbling over, he managed to drag the plank towards the lock, carefully fitting the makeshift lever against it.

*I hope this bloody works.*

Lifting the quite heavy crate with great effort, he dropped it onto the plank, watching it break in half.

He sank to the floor, trembling and shivering from the pain, and a possible fever, almost catatonic with fear of dying there. He clutched the crowbar tight to his chest, as if it was the last thing he would ever hold.

He saw the light reflecting onto something that had to be metal out of the corner of his eye, something that had to be sharp enough to use to regain his freedom.

Using his arms to move himself towards the object, he left the crowbar behind, reaching what appeared to be a knife.

*Maybe I'm not so bloody cursed after all. Maybe someone's watching over me.*

Grabbing the knife firmly, he dragged himself towards the door, barely able to reach the lock from the position he was in. He wedged the knife into the lock, pushing to try and pry it open.

*Come on... Come on!*

A click sounded, filling his body with relief and ecstasy. He pushed the door open, only to find all the people he met before thrown onto a pile of bodies.

*They're all dead...*

It felt like hours had gone by, but it had really only been ten minutes when he had thrown up. He sat against the wall next to the door, staring at the bald man with his eyes still open. The day had been one desperate situation after another, and he felt exhausted. His body felt as though it had been chewed up and spat out. Overcome with emotions, he took the crossbow the bald guy had been aiming at him minutes before he heard the gunfire. He took a bloody arrow off the floor, touching the sharp end of it, looking at his skin.

*Maybe this is better for everyone. Maybe this is better for me.*

Before he could hurt himself, he felt someone grab his leg, screaming from the searing pain that person caused him. Looking down at whose filthy hand was gripping his leg like that, he noticed how badly wounded the person was.

"Help... me..."

"How? I dunno how!" he said, trying to free himself from the stern grip. "I'm not a doctor!"

The bloody guy coughed, pointing at a white-looking box above his head.

"Aid..."

Andrew knew what he was getting at but had no way to reach it without hurting himself even more. Looking at the arrow in his hand, and the crossbow not too far away from him, he had a brilliant idea come to mind.

Nocking the arrow, he turned his body sharply to have a clear shot. Closing one eye, he focused on the target. Forcing all the strength onto the bowstring, he breathed in. Steadying his breath, he let go, exhaling once the arrow hit the first-aid kit.

It hit the floor with a loud bang, falling open as all its contents spread out over the floor. Andrew forced himself over to it, using his arms to drag himself forward. Reaching it, he grabbed what he thought was necessary to try and save the guy, though he knew it would be a lost cause.

Making his way back, he began applying pressure onto the guy's wound before attempting to clean it, working fast to try and stop the bleeding. For as far as he still could.

"How's that?" he asked the guy, binding his stomach with the bandage. "I dunno if it really helps much, but..."

"It'll do," the guy interrupted him, scooting over to the wall next to Andrew.

Both were breathing quite heavily, relying on the tiny bit of air that came in through the holes shot in the walls.

"They promised, you know," the guy said, swallowing with great effort. "The Government? The new President? They promised."

"Promised what?" Andrew asked, not having the faintest idea what he was going on about.

"Humanitarian aid. They said they'd sanction the military for humanitarian purposes. Now don't act like you haven't heard about that, boy."

He felt himself caught in the man's gaze like a helpless rabbit in a snare, yet he truly had no idea what the man was going on about. He swallowed convulsively, searching desperately for space to breathe.

"My brother bribed the Government to stop implementing their *so-called* effective aiding measures. And you know what the funny thing is? He swore he was all for protection, hated violating any kind of national and international laws. Guess who caused a battle of futility to spring? *He did*. The Government's withdrawal to help us left a path of destruction."

Andrew's brows furrowed in groggy confusion, watching as the man's eyes struggled to focus on anything. He knew he was fading, trying to spill as much information as he possibly could before he would draw his final breath.

"Who's your brother?"

The man slowly turned his head. His glazed-over eyes raked over Andrew's face, lingering on the tiny, jagged scar on his jaw. Andrew's warm brown eyes met his.

"You know him as *Mister X*, but I know him as—"

A bullet pierced the man's skull, and his blood ended up on Andrew's face. A shocking wave of heat rushed through him, his skin slicking with cold sweat. He began to feel nauseous; his heart rate was increasing. His mouth produced extra saliva from the incoming stomach acid, and as his face went pale, he threw up the remaining acidic bits his body was living on.

"We've found a life one!"

He looked at the squad of soldiers aiming a submachine gun at the dead bodies, wearing dark grey clothes with armour plates covering their chests. He couldn't see their faces covered by non-see-through helmets.

He was attuning himself to their every movement, looking at the dark blue cladded uniform who walked out of the knot of soldiers shielding him.

*Is he a cop? Why would a cop be amongst soldiers like that? Where's their general?*

"You okay, kiddo?" the uniform asked, kneeling in front of him.

*He shot a guy who told me the Government wasn't providing any humanitarian aid. What do I call this then? It doesn't make any sense...*

Every bone in his body told him to suspect the man, but for the moment, he was just glad he had survived. He commanded one of the soldiers to gently lift Andrew in his great arms and take him to the Xopper. Providing him with some painkillers, he slowly drifted off into a deep sleep.

The van rattled beneath Andrew as he woke up, rubbing his eyes.

*How long was I out for? I thought we were in a chopper...?*

The van carried the small group of soldiers watching over Andrew down an uneven road. There was no sign of the police-looking man.

"We've lost contact with the Command Tower," he heard one of the soldiers say, assuming Andrew was still knocked out cold. "It's been five days since we've last heard from the facility."

"That's 'cause everyone inside's dead."

"*Everyone?*"

"Those are the rumours. Why? Was there someone special in there you're worried about? You know we can't have anything nice, right? It's rule number one."

"Yeah, whatever."

The van came to a sudden halt, and the soldiers climbed out one by one. Keeping his eyes closed, Andrew felt they lifted the gurney he was laying on. He tried to take a sneak peek by half-opening his eye but shut it just as quickly when he saw the uniform walk towards him and the men carrying him.

"Bring him to the nurse's office. I'll be there shortly."

The soldiers grunted a sound that sounded like they were acknowledging their order, and Andrew felt he was moving again. It didn't take long until they opened a door and closed it, hoisting him on top of a metal-sounding table.

"That's good enough. Once I'm done examining him you can take him to his room," a friendly female voice spoke.

He felt someone tucking at his trousers and opened his eyes by accident.

"Hey there, take it easy. You're in good hands," she said.

As he lay his eyes upon her, he thought she was the most beautiful woman he had ever seen. She looked aloof and untouchable, yet so gorgeous that it took his breath away.

"This might hurt," she said, before attempting to put his bone back in place.

He let out a sharp cry of pain when a single tear rolled down his cheek.

*Bloody hell... She couldn't have given me something to bite down on?*

He squeezed his eyes shut as she began binding his leg with a slat to keep it straight. He knew he looked rather morose and defeated yet could care less as all he wanted was to get rid of this pain.

"Here, take this. It'll work better than the painkillers they've given you before."

He crushed a bottleful of it into a glass of water before drinking it all in one big gulp. Deep down inside, he was screaming in pain, and terror.

"So, what's your name?" she asked, casting his leg.

"Andrew."

A smile played on her lips. "My brother's name was Andrew too. And your resemblance… it's uncanny. You have the same honey-blond hair he had. And your eyes… just as blue as his."

"*Was*? Is he… did he die?"

She mused sadly as she finished casting his leg, looking out the window for a split second. "He went missing when he was playing outside in the backyard. I as his big sister was supposed to watch him, and I failed the only job I was ordered to do." She grinned and looked ponderous, which didn't last long when her smile widened. "How old are you?"

*My age? I don't even know my own age. I must be between fifteen and twenty…*

"Honestly, I dunno. I've been spending most of my life in a research facility which I escaped only a couple hours ago."

Without asking for permission, she lifted his shirt, looking at his nipple. Her jaw tightened as the sadness in her eyes turned to outright steely anger. He had never seen anyone that angry before.

"What's wrong?"

Hopeful yet angry tears burned in her eyes. She shook her head as her shoulders sag for a moment. "I can't believe it's *you*."

He watched her fixing him with a soft gaze, before she flung her arms around his neck. She tried to pull him as close to her as she possibly could, almost choking him. He awkwardly patted her back, unsure of what to say or do otherwise.

*If she truly is my sister, then why don't I remember her?*

She slowly let go, a soft teary-eyed smile curved her lips. "It's me, Amelia. Your big sister."

Then it hit him like a ton of bricks. "Minnie?"

Her slow nod made him hug her once more, tightening his hold on her.

"*You were the part of me I couldn't let go,*" she whispered, "*I never stopped looking for you. Never.*"

He loosened his grip on her, looking her up and down. "How old was I when I disappeared?"

"About three. One minute you were playing with your action figures in the yard, and the next you were gone. All that was left was your baseball cap."

"And mum and dad?"

She shook her head sadly. "They left to search for you, and never returned. The neighbours took me in."

He wracked his brain for a possible memory of his abduction when the wisp of a different memory returned to him. "What about our baby brother?"

"He died two days after you disappeared. The neighbours said it was polio."

His skull felt like a gasket ready to blow. He shook his head as though he could cast the traitorous memories from his mind.

"How did you end up here? Where even is here?"

She pointed at the files on her desk stacked precisely on top of one another. He noticed the gleaming surgical tools arranged according to size right next to it. "Normally I retrieve bullets from criminals but today I get to play nurse for my baby brother."

"You studied to become a nurse?"

"Not really studied for it, it kinda happened. When the war broke out... I was forced to remove a bullet from my neighbour's abdomen. I saved his life and told myself this was what I wanted to devote my life to. *Saving people.*"

"Which war?"

"Right, you dunno about that." She gave him a quick heads up on the war that reigned between the ALIENS and humans. "They broke the Dome, and we all live in peace now. Well, as far as peace exists within humanity."

"And this Sam... can he help us destroy the facility I was being held in?"

"Maybe. It's kinda hard to reach him nowadays but that doesn't mean we can't try."

He nodded, then looked around the room. It was so neat and tidy, it almost hurt his eyes. She chuckled seeing the glaze in his eyes.

"I trained myself to be as organised as I could possibly be. A dirty lab would be negligent, right?"

He let out a hearty chuckle, and for the first time since he had woken up there, he felt satisfied and safe. A brisk knock on the door made both look up.

"George wants to talk to the boy."

She nodded to the soldier, walking over to a smaller door on the other side of the room. She wheeled out a wheelchair and helped him sit in it. As she wheeled him over to the door, a large hand stopped her in her tracks.

"He wants to talk to him alone."

Her body language showed her vehement disagreement but all she could do was nod. The soldier took the handles from her and wheeled Andrew away. As he looked behind him, he watched her wave at him and mouth, *"I'll see you soon,"* before he turned the corner.

# CHAPTER FOUR

The soldier led him down a maze of corridors, each lined with all kinds of doors. Metal ones, wooden ones, heavily fortified ones. Even some made of material he couldn't recognise.

*This isn't your normal-looking police station, if I even knew what a normal one is supposed to look like. Is this what they're supposed to look like?*

He passed through a locked heavy double door, excess possible only via a key card hanging from the soldier's belt. For some odd reason, he recognised the system but wasn't given enough time to think further about it when the uniform smiled at him from behind his desk.

"Kid, it's good to see you awake. How are you feeling?"

The soldier wheeled him in front of the desk opposite the uniform and stood in front of the door like a guard.

"I uh... feel much better, thanks," he said, eyeing the guard suspiciously.

"Oi, don't worry about him, it's just routine. We live in a strange world in which protection isn't more than an overlooked luxury."

*Right... luxury isn't the word I'd use. Rather morose and sinister, honestly. Suspicious, even.*

The office wasn't a much pleasanter place than the offices he had been in at the earlier facility, let alone the medical centre he had just left. He wasn't imagining a sun-filled haven but expected something less dark. To him, it felt like one of those rather small, dark offices you stumble upon on the ground floor of any old apartment building. Then again, he had only seen those in certain documentaries he was forced to watch.

In addition to his desk and the two chairs, there was a Ficus tree and some oddly named dreary books in his bookcase. The walls were a pale yellow, a failed attempt to lighten up the room. Though the thing that stood out the most to him were the obnoxious folkloric-looking woven talismans.

Taking a glance around the office, he was deterred by how commonplace and expected it seemed. The window behind the uniform had a view of the roof of an adjoining building, something he couldn't quite recognise.

"Well, let us ease ourselves into a possible conversation, yeah?" the uniform said, extending his hand. "I'm George."

With faint uncertainty, Andrew shook his hand and stated his name.

"You mind if I call you Andy?" George asked, getting up from his desk.

"Only my mother called me that," he said, then gasped. *How the bloody hell do I know that my mother nicknamed me Andy? I... I don't remember her.*

Unable to shake the vague unease, he fixed a pile of papers on George's desk.

As he organised them, George grabbed a mirror and walked over to him. "Tell me, what do you see?"

Andrew looked at himself in the mirror, then back up at George. "That my greaser hairstyle could use a haircut."

George laughed boisterously, a laugh that made his ears ring. He leaned closer to Andrew. *"Mutatio,"* he whispered.

"Mu what?"

George shook his head, taking a tiny cameo yellowing portrait out of his pocket, its edges curled with age. He showed Andrew the photograph and repeated the word.

For a second, nothing happened. Andrew thought nothing of it and thought the man was crazy, until he felt a tingling sensation throughout his body. His hands were shaking. Pressing a hand over the other to prevent it from quaking, he hit the floor.

His stomach felt like lead as he seized on the floor, his skin began to shed. Closing his eyes, he jerked and screamed, until he stopped.

He slowly opened his eyes and looked up at George presenting him the mirror. Seeing an old man through his own eyes, he moved backwards until his back hit the guard's legs, who cracked a crooked smile.

"You're able to perfectly copy a person from their fingerprints to their teeth," George said, crouching in front of him. "You, my dear boy, are what scientists call a shapeshifter."

Andrew shook his head, looking at his wrinkled hands. "No, this... what did you do to me?"

"I didn't do anything, kid. I just helped you see what you are."

He showed him the old man's portrait again, along with a T-Rooper. Andrew once more began seizing uncontrollably, until he watched his arm changing into a cast iron arm, constructed from the base up to his wrist.

"You can even shapeshift into hybrid combinations. Both human and robotic, in which you copy the essential ingredients that make robots machines. Sensors, actuators, programs, the whole likes of it."

"No... no stop... stop it..." he begged, tears filling his eyes. As his tears fell onto the floor, a sob shook his body. "Make it stop... please..."

There was a hurried knock on the door. "George, there's a P-40 going on in sector three."

George sighed, looking at the guard. "Stay here with the kid, I'll be right back." He purposefully strode out of the room.

Andrew remained on the floor, until he heard the door reopen, and a faint loud thud. He turned around and looked upon his sister holding a baseball bat. She breathed heavily but not out of terror seeing Andrew's inhuman shape. Rather out of adrenaline.

She fell to her knees next to him, clutching him close. "I knew he was gonna do this and I should've stopped him."

"What?" he asked, grunting in pain.

"I'll explain everything later, okay? We gotta get you outta here." She put a hand on his forehead. *"Contrarium,"* she whispered, and watched as her brother shifted painlessly back to himself.

She helped him to his feet and pushed him into the wheelchair. Fighting against the sluggishness, she pushed forward through the hallway.

"I promise I'll explain everything later. Right now, we gotta find a way out."

They stopped in front of an imposing door leading outside, secured with a sleek-looking electronic lock.

Seeing the worried look in his eyes, she chuckled. "Don't worry, nothing sophisticated like that can keep me out."

She took out a device with two small antennas and held it against the lock. Watching in awe, he saw the tiny sparks crackle about the antennas.

"Are you... hacking the system?"

"Look at you and your brains still intact! That's good news."

He wanted to admonish her for her sarcasm but knew she meant well. The click he heard made him smile.

*All those skills... wish I had 'em. Wait, am I jealous? No, I'm not. I'm proud. Right?*

She wheeled him into the back office and closed the door behind them, just in time when the heavy footsteps of the soldiers ran past the door. She leaned against it, breathing heavily. "That was close. Better take what we need and leave."

She walked over to one of the file cabinets and started digging through it. For some odd reason the office was quite homey, which was something he didn't expect with how fortified the room was.

The aged leather chair, wood-panelled space and overflowing file cabinets and bookshelves added mystery as well as cosiness.

"I swear they filed the paperwork..." she muttered to herself, throwing documents all over the place. "Guess George really thought it was posturing..."

"What are we looking for, exactly?"

She turned around for a second to give him a glance over, then resumed her search. "We used to have these... preliminary meetings in which we discussed all kinds of things. Now, I'm perfectly capable of reacquainting myself with what was said, but I'll need proof for the higher-ups."

"Proof of what?"

She pulled out a file and smiled. "That you're a victim of this man's malfeasance." She opened it on the table and pointed at his profile. "See how boisterous he is about your ability? He has known about you for quite some time now and told me he wanted to arrange a rescue mission." She turned the page. "Once he'd retrieved you, he would've let me examine you. I specifically asked him to let it be me 'cause I just had this feeling it was you. But to be sure, I had to see you in person and ensure it was you; you know?"

He nodded slowly, his gaze lingering forlornly on the open file before him. "Wait... that's you." He pointed at her name. "You're listed under my family lineage... I thought you said you *weren't* sure?"

"I wasn't. I've never seen that before."

She sat behind the nearby computer, stumbling upon a locked map. Typing away, she cracked the password in only a matter of seconds. "Bloody hell..."

Andrew wheeled himself closer to her to see what shocked her, though he couldn't make out any of the encrypted codes appearing in front of him.

"What... am I looking at, exactly?"

"This map contains secrets and other files that are highly sensitive in nature..."

"Wait, but you were able to get in with just a simple password. Shouldn't that be, I dunno, better protected?"

She smiled at him, nodding. "You're a lot smarter than you give yourself credit for," she said, though he couldn't make sense of what she meant by that. "But you're right, normally there should be an authorisation code that's required to log in... it's almost too easy to 'bypass' that step."

"Attention. Unauthorised access to confidential files pertaining to Mister X. Attention. Unauthori—"

"Mister X? Who the bloody hell's that?"

She shrugged, typing furiously. "Should've known, why else would top-secret data be on a server with outside access to a local network..." She pulled up a three-dimensional map, pointing at a red line.  That's our way outta here but they locked the whole building down."

"That's... due to the alert being repeated every second or so?"

"You catch on quick." She chuckled, walking over to the vent in the back of the room. "Now that we've compromised their server, which for whatever reason can be accessed internally as well as externally..." She took a small screwdriver out of her pocket and began loosening the first screw, "this is our only way out."

"I can't fit through there with a broken leg."

She unscrewed the second screw, nodding. "I know, but I'll find a way to drag you with me. I'm not leaving you in here."

He looked back at the computer before shifting his attention back to her unscrewing the third screw. "So, the computer finished an analysis based on your... hacking?"

"Yeah, it's a built-in security bot that normally gets notified when classified documents are accessed by a third-party. But what's buggering me is that one of 'em contained intel on bioresearch. And it's located in the facility I had flagged for surveillance."

"Surveillance?"

"Yeah, the one you were being kept in. I... I pointed 'em to you, and I should've known better. I endangered you while I tried to protect you."

"You didn't know this was gonna happen. I don't blame you."

A smile curved her lips as she continued staring stonily at the vent's grilles, until she managed to unscrew the last screw. She took the grilles off and used her flashlight to scan the inside. "Aside from a few cobwebs, I think it's doable."

As she extended her hand to grab his, a sharp spike of pain made his eyes flit to someone standing behind them. A dart punctured his skin.

Icy dread filled his veins as his muscles began to weaken and failed to keep him upright in his wheelchair, falling to the floor.

He watched in horror as his sister awaited the same fate, falling next to him. Dimly, he could make out a shape walking closer to them, yet his thoughts were too murky and slow to give the shape a name.

"I'm sorry, Andy..."

Realising it wasn't his mother, but his sister who called him Andy, he closed his eyes and sank into darkness.

Bright lights whirled in his vision as he regained consciousness, sparking agonising pain behind his eyes. Unable to orient himself, he tried to sit up, only to find himself strapped down to a gurney. He heard grunting coming from all directions and blinked until his vision slowly focused.

Next to him, and in front of him, were five more people strapped to gurneys. They lay unconscious, hooked up to machines providing all kinds of information. He rubbed his eyes and noticed the brain-switching-looking machine attached to the boy next to him. Sniffing, a wave of revolting chemical odour swamped his nostrils, making him sneeze. He recoiled further back on the gurney to try and escape the stench of harsh chemical pollution, but to no avail.

Looking back at the screen of the machine to his right, he picked up an onslaught of information.

*Brain activity... EEG... fMRI... MEG... what the bloody hell? They measure everything...*

He only knew so much due to the fact that the scientists who kept him captive told him all about the experiments and tests they did on him, including those.

*I... I'm not back with the same people as before... am I? No... the room is different, and I dunno any of these boys. Wait, they're all boys? Where's my sister? Where's Minnie?*

Hearing a door open, he closed his eyes. Pretending to still be unconscious seemed like the wisest thing to do. Heavy footsteps came closer, and he had to stop himself from peeking through his eyelashes.

"Don't worry, you'll have the same fate as them. Now, this'll hurt only a lit—well, a lot."

Hearing George's voice, he opened his eyes and watched as he plunged a needle filled with reddish-orange liquid into his neck.

It took at least five seconds before he let out a scream of shock, feeling a sense of burning to death on the inside. The pain spread to every inch of his body. George's piercing smile made him shiver, though that was also caused by his bones doing stuff he couldn't explain. All he knew was that it was the most painful thing he had ever felt in his life.

Thinking he saw his entire body being enveloped by fire, he finally passed out as blackness overtook him once again.

# CHAPTER FIVE

A tuck at his feet startled him awake, and he found himself dangling face-down. His feet were tied to a wooden pole, just a few feet above a canopy of leaves. Surrounding him were large, hollow trees, and an eerie silence. Rain fell lightly, yet there was no cloud to be seen. Feeling another tuck at his feet, he looked up, noticing the rope was close to snapping.

*Well, swinging back and forth would be a profound dumb thing to do...*

He used his jelly-feeling arms to feel around his pockets, silently hoping he was in the odd luck of having a knife or other sharp object on him.

*Nothing, as expected.*

Trying to pull himself up with his upper body, he tried to reach the rope close to his feet. Grabbing hold of the rope, he began to haul himself up, straining with the sleepiness his arms were experiencing.

Having almost reeled himself back up to safety, the rope gave way, and he tumbled a few feet into the canopy, slamming into the ground with a thud.

*Ow... son of a... Guess I'm still too heavy with my malnourished body...*

Looking at his leg, he let out a deep sigh. *I'm not getting anywhere with a leg like this. I gotta find a way to make myself some crutches... or a walker.*

A rustle in the bushes put him on alert. Having no weapon nearby to potentially defend himself with, his hand caught hold of a branch. Though it had no sharp end, it was better than nothing.

Hiding behind the thickest trunk, he heard footsteps approaching him. Aiming the branch above his head, he readied himself to give someone, or *something*, a blow on their head. Then, to his surprise, an additional set of feet scuttled past him before the earlier heard footsteps disappeared deeper into what he assumed were the woods.

His relief was short-lived, covering his face in a thin sheen of sweat as a hand clasped his mouth.

Being shushed by the low but commanding voice, he nodded slowly, thinking to himself this person wasn't going to harm him. His voice had this undercurrent of calm fury that made him less anxious.

The hand slowly moved away from his mouth, and Andrew looked up into kind grey eyes.

"Don't worry mate, I'm not here to hurt you." Andrew nodded slowly, and watched as the young boy examined his leg. "Welcome to the world of previously sustained injuries," he said, pointing at his arm located in a sling. "Broke my arm two days ago."

"You've been here for two days?"

"Yeah, came down the exact same pole you did, tied up by my feet, blood rushing to my brain in the worst way possible." He extended his free hand. "Theodore, friends call me Theo."

"Andrew."

"No nickname? No Andy or something? Most lads I've come across have a nickname."

"My sister called me Andy, but only she gets to call me that."

"Right, noted. I'll go for Drew then."

Before Andrew could reply, he heard a scream coming from behind them. "The bloody hell was that?"

"One of the many animals that this uninhabited island habits."

"Wait, what? That's not—"

"A logical sentence? I know, lad, I know. More like... uninhabited by humans, teeming with wildlife. You know?"

His eyes grew wide. "Island? We're... we're on an island?"

Theo nodded. "And there's no way of escaping. There's no boat anywhere, and making a raft is useless as the current's way too rough to sail. Someone tried to escape this island before us, and we found his body on the shore."

"*We?*"

Theo nodded again, pointing in the direction Andrew had heard the footsteps earlier. "His name's Philip, or rather Phil. Was one of the Laeries I helped saving."

"The who of the what now?"

"Mate, you been living under a rock or what? The ALIENS? Doesn't ring a bell?"

He nodded slowly, though there was also a part of him that wasn't entirely sure they were talking about the same thing.

"Look, it's not safe to stay here. Phil is out there hunting something to provide us with food for the night, but you're defenceless without a weapon."

"I can't walk."

"I'm *not* stupid, lad. I know you can't." He sighed. "Just use that branch you picked up and lean on me. We'll make you something better back at camp."

He helped Andrew to his feet and provided him support on the way.

Upon arriving at the provisional camp, he set Andrew down near the remains of a campfire. Andrew looked around and noticed there were two makeshift tents built from branches to provide as walls, and a roof made of leaves.

A flock of birds scattered above their heads, and Andrew watched Theo stump on a thick branch to break it in half. Taking out a saw, he gave it to Andrew. "Here, you can do the sawing with your two working hands. All you gotta do is make two holes in which you can stick your hands through to give yourself support."

"I know what crutches look like."

"Good that, then go ahead and show me." He sat down across from him, looking up at the sky. "As soon as the rain stops, I'll make myself useful and make us a fire. But it'd be useless now anyway. Fire won't stay on for longer than a minute."

Andrew carefully sawed a hole in the branch, nodding slowly. "You seem to know a lot about survival. But you've only been here for two days, right?"

"I was a REBEL, but I bet you've also not heard of us if you haven't heard about the Laeries." He carved a few sticks into points to make spears. "We were rebelling against ex-President Ashwell and his regime and worked closely together with the Troopers. That say anything to you?"

Andrew carefully shook his head, sawing a grip in the branch. "I was abducted my whole life, kidnapped when I was young. I didn't know where I was until I escaped last night and met my sister whom I had lost ever since I was taken. And now when I just got her back… I lost her just as quickly."

Theo finally softened a bit, looking over at Andrew. "Oh, sorry I was… such an arsehole."

They heard footsteps and both looked up simultaneously when a man missing the pinky finger of his left hand walked over to them. "Good that, making us new spears for fishing after you broke the last ones?" he asked, patting Theo a little too hard on his broken arm.

He laughed in pain, wincing. "Yeah, well, what can I say. You kinda forced me to make one as you said that—"

"Not all men are annoying. Some are dead. Or will be when they screw up."

Both laughed, though Andrew didn't quite seem to get their sarcastic jokes.

"A newbie? Well, seems like it's just my lucky day. I got another one to bully the crap out of." He extended his hand. "Sup newbie, name's Phil."

"He's Drew," Theo replied for him, smiling, "I baptised him as Drew."

Phil laughed. "He nicknamed you, huh? Must be liking you already. Took him a whole day to nickname me."

Andrew stared at his missing pinky. Before he could ask what had happened to it, Phil snapped his fingers.

"My eyes are up here, sunshine." He laughed, throwing him some rope to use on his makeshift crutch. "Just kidding. Bet you wanna know how I lost this bad boy, eh?"

Theo shook his head. "You just had to stare at it, didn't you? He's the doctor outta us three, so he's gonna tell you in all its glory how he lost it. I swear when I first met him, he was a totally different guy."

"What can I say? Being turned back into a human… it changes a man," Phil said, making eye contact with Andrew. "I was one of the Laeries, Khax was my name. But now I'm me again." Theo leaned close, whispering something into his ear. "Oh, he doesn't…? Interesting." He noticed Andrew yawning, chuckling good-heartedly. "You know what, you look like you've been hit by a T-Rooper. I can tell you the story tomorrow. Just get some food in you and get some rest. We'll wake you when dinner's ready."

Andrew looked at the banana being offered to him and took it. He watched as Phil took the spear from Theo and walked over to the wide, shallow pool teeming with fish connected to the ocean.

As he stripped his clothes, Andrew couldn't help but stare at the muscles of his back ripple beneath his shirt before taking it off.

"Careful now, you might catch flies if you keep your mouth open like that."

Andrew quickly turned away; a blush covered his cheeks. "I wasn't… I swear I wasn't staring."

Theo laughed, walking over to the about-to-be lit campfire. "Don't worry, your secret's safe with me."

He began making a small tepee of wood, tinder, dry leaves and twigs. As Theo grabbed a length of soft wood with a small groove in it, he heard Phil thrust his spear into the water.

"Son of a—"

"Did you scare 'em away with your ugly face?" Theo asked dryly.

"Ha. Ha. Very funny. If you're not careful you're the next to scatter about."

He laughed, looking at Andrew. "Okay, I'm gonna need your help here." He gave Andrew a hardwood stick, pointing at the groove with tree bark serving as tinder. "Rub the stick up and down as quickly as you can to create friction."

After a few tries, the tinder began to ignite. Theo clapped his back before placing the tinder in the kindling tepee. He added larger pieces of wood to the fire.

"We got ourselves some food lads!" they heard behind them. Phil triumphally held a fish in front of their faces.

Andrew tried to not look at his abs, swallowing as Phil sat down next to him. He focused on Phil scaling the fish.

"Shouldn't we have more than one?" Andrew asked. "I mean, we're with three people."

"Go on ahead and try to catch another. Our helpless lad over here can't use his arm, so I gotta scale it for him. After that I was planning on going back, but you go give it a try." He offered him the bloodied spear. "Don't get your cast wet."

Andrew nodded and used his makeshift crutch to hop over to the pool, careful to keep his injured leg away from the water. Watching with hawk eyes, he noticed a demersal fish heading straight towards him. Fully focused, he stabbed his spear at it yet missed as it connected with the sand at the bottom. The fish flitted away.

He heard laughter coming from his left. He turned his head, looking straight into Phil's green eyes staring at him from a nearby perch.

The distraction caused him to drop the spear, the sharp end hitting his foot. Phil saw it happen and got up hastily, his jokey demeanour displaced by his medical background.

He kneeled and held the wound together by pinching the sides, looking up at him. "We haven't cleaned the tip yet so we gotta disinfect this." He ran to their camp and came back with a bottle filled with clear, presumably distilled water. Soaking a cloth in it, he ripped another piece of fabric in two sheets to serve as a bandage. "Now you'll have two sea legs," he said half-jokingly, gently dabbing the wound once it had soaked enough.

Andrew didn't even flinch. He was distracted enough by the tension in Phil's taut muscles to really care about the pain he should be experiencing.

"You're a tough one, eh? Must have a high pain threshold." He bandaged his foot, cleaning his hands with the remaining water. "There, that ought to do it." He looked up at Andrew who quickly looked back at the water. "Why don't you head back to Theo? I'll take it over from here."

"No, I..." Determined to catch at least one fish, he grabbed the spear off the ground. "I won't give up so easily."

Phil nodded, smiling cockily. "All right then, let me show you the ropes." He guided Andrew closer to the shallow water, twirling the spear deftly between the fingers of his right hand. "After I've taught you how to spear fish, I'll teach you how to whittle."

Andrew nodded, gulping as Phil stepped behind him, positioning his body like they were two equals. A few fish bounced beneath the surface.

"You've to aim right below your target, like this." He demonstrated with his spear, catching some tuna. "Now the reason why you wanna do that? One word: refraction."

Andrew nodded; his sight set on a large tuna heading straight for him. Holding back patiently for the tuna to come closer, he waited for the perfect moment before aiming the tip of his spear just under its belly, jabbing the fish right through the side.

He gasped in surprise, holding the spear with the dead fish in the air. "I caught one!"

Phil cheered him on, and Andrew felt his heart flutter. "Way to go, Drew!"

He shuffled back to deposit the fish into a manmade woven basket and went back to Phil to catch one more.

Both then lunged in sync, piercing the same fish easily. Phil smiled. "Once your leg's all healed up, I'll show you a different place to catch our food. It's a place where there's more than enough fish for us to last a lifetime."

Andrew nodded eagerly, then smiled ashamedly. A smile played on Phil's lips, lustful and amused at the same time. Having enough for the three of them, they moved away from the water, until Phil let out a gasp. He stopped moving.

"What's wrong?" Andrew asked, his heart thumping in this throat.

"Thought I fell a fish with quills swimming past me," Phil said, shaking his head. "Must be my imagination." He left the water unscathed.

They examined their catch, and Phil proudly clapped Andrew on his back. "You did good *rookie*. You've got a few clean catches right there."

Andrew smiled, taking the fish off the spear. "I had a good teacher."

"Oh please, I hardly taught you anything. Nah, this one's all you, Drew."

"Andy," he said, looking at Phil raising an eyebrow at him. "You can call me Andy."

Phil nodded, smiling meekly. He watched Andrew yawn. "I'll do the preparation myself and teach you how to whittle some other time. Get some sleep and I'll wake you when they're done. You can take my tent for now; we'll make you your own after dinner."

Andrew nodded in return and carried his fish to the camp before lying down on the pretty unexpected soft bed Phil had made from leaves. Watching with one eye open for a few seconds, he watched as Phil scaled the other two fish while Theo began cooking the first. Then, he fell into a deep slumber.

Phil cleaned and gutted the fish they caught, skewering them with ease. Giving the ones ready for consummation to Theo, he watched as Theo pierced them through, holding them above the campfire to cook.

"You do realise you were flirting with him, right?"

Phil looked up. "Yeah, so?"

"I dunno, it's not fair to him to lead him on like that."

"Who says I'm not bisexual?" He sighed. "Look, he's... I think he's adorable. He's got this kinda innocence over him that makes my heart skip a beat. And I mean, yeah, I thought I was straight being a Laerie and all, but I dunno. There's just something about him that gives me the good kind... of goosebumps."

Theo rotated the skewered fish, sighing. "Just, keep me outta this threesome, okay? I'm not playing for your team."

"Bob's your uncle, noted."

Theo rolled his eyes at him, then both looked up hearing Andrew scream. Phil set off running towards the tent.

# CHAPTER SIX

"Andy! Calm down!" Phil yelled, holding Andrew in his arms who kept screaming.

"Andy? Since when does he allow you to call him Andy? He didn't want me to call him that."

Ignoring him, Phil tried to wake Andrew up, who was clearly not waking up. "It's me, Phil. Wake up, lad!" He gently tapped his cheek a couple of times before Andrew gasped awake, looking at both staring down at him. "You're okay, calm down," Phil said, rubbing his back soothingly. "You're safe."

Andrew looked back and forth between both, breathing heavily. His throat felt dry, yet he didn't dare to ask for a sip of water.

"What happened?" Phil asked, his eyes gentle and concerned.

"I... I saw a man standing in front of me. His... his whole face was covered in... in shadows..." He knew how absurd that must sound, but he couldn't lie. He took a deep breath. "It... it was hard to make out if he had a real face or not. There was this darkness surrounding us, like a dark fog, almost like smog. But when he lifted that axe... it *wasn't* covered in shadows. It was plain to see." He put a hand on his heart, unconsciously thinking that it would calm his heartbeat. "There was blood on the axe, and it glistened in that light like a... like a star or something."

"It's the *Island Murderer*," Theo said, a serious look on his face. "That blood you saw belonged to his *last victim*."

"Last... *last victim*?"

"Yeah, he murdered the boys who were here before us."

Andrew's panicky face made Theo crack up, slamming his knee. "Oh, you should see your face, lad! It's *priceless*!"

Phil gave him the deadliest stare he had ever given him, shaking his head disappointedly. "Go on," he said, turning back to Andrew. "And *don't* listen to a word that comes outta this *numbskull's* mouth. He's screwing with you."

Andrew swallowed, nodding slowly. "Okay, well, he... he grinned madly at me, and the shadows on his face seemed... *alive*. They were kinda distorting the few features he had."

"Which features?"

"Well, he... he missed an eye, and he had a massive scar across his cheek."

Before Theo could make another misplaced joke, Phil nudged him in the balls. Theo groaned loudly, bending over. "Continue."

"He stood before me, and it was impossible for me to focus on him. It felt like I stood in some kinda... blind spot, you know? The shadows on his face began bleeding like ink does underwater when a squid excretes it, or like when a shark leaves this cloud of blood behind after he has bitten someone or something."

Theo stood straight again, staying quiet.

"I willed it to stop coming any closer, but he just kept going. It was like a scene from a nightmare... a horrific nightmare... but I was awake the whole time."

"Awake? You had your eyes closed," Phil said, "you were asleep."

Andrew didn't know what it meant that he felt awake through the whole ordeal but decided to shake it off for now. He knew it wouldn't do him any good to stay stuck in whatever feverish nightmare he just had.

Phil offered his hand to help him stand. "Why don't you sit with us until all fish are done cooking, eh? There's one left to cook."

"Crap!" Theo yelled, running to the fire. "Scratch that last one, mate. It's burned."

"We got plenty left. We can miss one. But next time, don't use flint atop of tinder. That'll enlarge the flame and burn food faster."

"Aye, *boss*," Theo replied sarcastically, rolling his eyes at him behind his back.

Andrew and Phil joined him by the fire, and all ate their fish in complete silence.

That didn't last long when Andrew looked towards the horizon, noticing a streak of thick fog heading their way. "Do you see that?" he asked them, pointing at it.

Both Theo and Phil looked up. Before any of them could fathom what was about to happen, the fog consumed them entirely, the campfire now nothing but smoke.

"Phil? Theo?" Andrew asked, looking around. "Lads!"

The smoke caused blisters to occur on his arms, itching like crazy. It didn't take long before they showed up all over his body, growing and growing. Desperate to get rid of the itch, he kept scratching until they had burst open, seeing his own muscles and bone appear.

Panicking, he kept tearing at the blisters with his nails, blood dripping all over. He scratched so vividly; it was only a matter of time before he began to peel and rip his skin into tatters.

*Make it stop... please, make it stop!*

He began to shiver, realising he had a fever on top of this monstrous condition. Shivering uncontrollably, he knew his temperature kept getting higher.

*Bloody hell, this hurts even more than your typical bad sunburn... At least, I think it would. How do I even know that?*

Whatever was causing the blisters was damaging his outer epidermis at a rapid rate, colouring all grey.

A tuck on his arm made him look to his right. Seeing his sister, he wondered how she had gotten there but decided not to question it as he was just happy to see her alive.

She pulled him along to a dark and dreary cave where the only sound he heard was the dripping of water. The air was thick with humidity, difficult to breathe due to the mouldy substances stuck to the damp walls. Yet it was ten times better than the fog he was breathing in.

The darkness surrounding him made it impossible to see more than a few feet in front of him. The smell filling his nostrils was something he could only describe as dry. Feeling his way through the cave, the rocks felt rough.

"Let's wait here until the fog has lifted," she said, sitting him down.

"Where's here?" he asked, groaning, "I can't see a bloody thing."

"I know, hang on," she said, fumbling around in the dark. "Wait, this feels like a piece of wood I can use..."

"That's my crutch."

"Your crotch? Bloody hell... I'm sorry, I... I didn't mean to—"

"No, don't worry, you weren't even near there. I said my crutch, as in crutches."

She chuckled softly. "Right, of course. The echo in here makes words sound all funky."

He looked down at his feet, one busted up by the spear he had dropped on it, the other casted due to a broken leg. He knew he was a liability to everyone present on the island. *Everyone...* "Have you seen two other lads who were with me?"

She shook her head. "No, you were all alone. That fog makes you hallucinate."

*Hallucinate? No, they... they weren't fake. When Phil stopped the bleeding on my foot... his touch felt as clear as day, as real as it could've felt. I can't be making this up.*

"You believe me, don't you? Your one and only sister?" She went on all fours, walking over to him. "Tell me you believe your own sister!"

Her loud yell made his entire body shiver. Her yell sounded almost like a growl, and not the good kind. The one that's ingressive, coming from the inside. It was almost as if she was experiencing a massive psychotic episode. Her wide glazy eyes looked disconnected from reality. It scared the living hell out of him.

"Minnie... you're scaring me," he said, his voice faltering.

She smiled a creepy smile that made the hair on the back of his neck stand up.

She began to scream, a sound that seemed filled with unbearable pain. She screamed until she had no voice left, panting as if she had run a marathon. She looked up at him, tears glistening in her eyes.

"Get... away..." she said, grunting. "I don't wanna... hurt you..."

"Hurt me? You're not gonna hurt me, I know you won't."

She let out a ferocious growl low in her chest, shaking her head. "No... please... don't..."

He put his hands on her shoulders. "Are you shapeshifting?" he asked her, wondering if she may have the same genes as he did.

She shook her head, growling menacingly. "No, they... they injected... me..."

"*They*? Who's *they*? And with what?"

She shook her head, continuing to growl. "Listen I... I can't hold it in much longer... this voice in my head keeps telling me what to do... tells me to kill you..."

"Voice? Whose voice?"

"A male... please, leave the cave and don't look back..."

He gripped her shoulder. "I'm not gonna leave you. You're my sister and I just got you back. I'm not losing you again. Not a second time. Not like *this*."

"Please... I'm... begging you..."

"No, I'm here, and I'm not going anywhere. Whatever's going on with you, we'll get you fixed."

She smiled, and for a moment, it seemed she had withstood whatever was building up inside her—until a gurgling snarl tore from her throat. Gripping his arm with startling strength, she hurled him to the ground.

He saw the black-coloured, vine-like veins protruding from her neck, the ulcers and blisters erupting across her skin. Her eyes were bloodshot, and where her teeth should have been, fangs gleamed.

She climbed on top of him, slamming her knee into his stomach with an immense force. The pain made him curl inward; swore he was tasting blood. While stunned, she wrapped her hands around his neck, using her full weight and insane humanoid strength to crush his windpipe as she squeezed.

Gasping for air, he clawed at her hands, leaving a few scratches behind. It wasn't enough for her grip to falter. Glaring down at Andrew, her kind and caring eyes had been replaced by a murderous glaze.

"M... Minnie..." he managed to say, tears streaming down his cheeks.

Distantly, he heard someone screaming his name, though he couldn't tell who it was. His ears were ringing, the edges of his vision blurred.

"Please... stop..." he begged, his lungs burning with the need for fresh air. Darkness began to close in around him. *Please don't let me leave this world having this look on her face engraved into my mind... this isn't my sister. This isn't her.*

He tried to reach her face one more time, even as the strength left his arm. Trying to claw past her grip, he attempted to dig his fingers into her eyes yet failed to do so.

"Andy!" He heard Phil's voice but couldn't determine which direction it came from.

He felt her being yanked off him, and gasped in a breath, scrambling backwards. Putting distance between himself and his sister, the world seemed to spin as he watched Phil and his sister wrestle over some kind of weapon. Trying to pry it from the other, Andrew's heartbeat thumped in his ears, adrenaline surging as he saw how Phil shoved at her face.

Tearing his fingernails across her cheeks, Andrew wanted to try and save her. Despite her efforts to kill him, she was still blood. She was still *family*.

She didn't relent, forcing Phil's grip to slip. With a sudden show of force, Phil managed to grab the weapon with both hands, yanking it from her hands. It was the same spear they had used before to catch fish with.

The sound he heard next was one he couldn't put into words. All he knew was that it sounded wet.

Daring himself to look up, he saw both of their hands on the spear, splattered with blood. He noticed his sister's clothes rapidly turning red, and for a moment, time seemed to slow.

"No..." Coughing from the strangulation, he dragged himself towards her as she sank to her knees, spear still stuck in her chest in a circular wound.

Blood poured across the tip of the spear, down the wooden handle to the cave's ground. She stared at Andrew, blood coming out of her mouth.

Her eyes were filled with fear once he had reached her, gripping her by her shirt. "It's not that bad, Minnie, really, it's not. If we don't remove it, you're gonna be just fine. We're... we're gonna patch you up and you'll be as good as new in no time." He wiped one of her fallen tears away. "Amelia," he said, his voice shivering, "look at me, okay?" He placed his hand near her wound, his entire palm covered in her blood. "I'll be the one to take care of you now, isn't that a plot twist?" he said jokingly, trying to distract her. "I've got you, Amelia, I've got you right here." He touched her face, tears continuously rolling down his cheeks.

His stomach churned as she drew a final shuddering breath, slumping forward into his arms, her eyes sliding shut. Holding her, he felt the weight of her lifeless body, the weight of his sister who saved him and went to such lengths to risk her own life for his.

"Who's gonna take care of me now, huh? Who's... who's gonna watch out for me?" He buried his face in her neck, sobbing raggedly.

"Andy, I... I'm so sorry," Phil said, putting a hand on Andrew's shoulder, who brushed him off. "It was either her or me, and she was already too far gone."

Over the hills behind them, he heard a crash of thunder. The first drops of rain started to spatter down on the dry earth of the island. The storm clouds churning across the sky mirrored Andrew's internal strife.

"What do you mean *far gone*?" he hissed, anger lacing his voice. "Far gone from what?"

He sighed softly. "They injected her with Serum C, and it's a serum created to turn people's loved ones into murderous abominations, set out to kill those they love, or be killed by those they love."

"How the bloody hell do you know that?" he asked, his eyes blazing with anger as he finally looked Phil in the eyes. "How do you know?" he yelled, demanding an answer.

"I killed one of my best friends, a fellow Laerie, right before you and Theo showed up. He had the same black veins as your sister did. I knocked him out cold and tied him up until he came to. When he did, he had one bright moment of clarity, begged me to kill him. I asked him what the bloody hell had gotten into him, and he said a cop named George had injected him with something called Serum C."

"George... he... he injected me with something too, right before I passed out." His eyes were feigning fear. "Was that... did they give that to me too?"

He shook his head. "No, I dunno what it was, but if it had been Serum C, we would've turned into 'em by now."

"Is there a cure? Can we reverse it?"

He shrugged. "I dunno. All I know is the name, and that they turn our loved ones against us. I can't tell you why or how."

He swallowed the knot in his throat, cradling her face. "I just had her back..."

"I know, and I can't tell you how sorry I am, Andy. I... I wish—" They heard the thundering crack of a massive tree falling nearby. "Look, we should go. I don't think it's a good idea to stay here with... her."

"Why?" he asked with a hard, almost angry expression lowering his brow. "She's dead, isn't she? What harm could she still cause?"

"No, I meant... I don't want you staring at her body for the remainder of the foggy storm. That's all."

"Oh." He looked at her black veins, having this fervent, desperate hope that they had killed something inside of her. But they hadn't disappeared. "I wanna bury her."

"Not right now. We'll come back once the storm is done raging. It's too dangerous to be out there digging a grave with you being injured."

"I don't care, Phil. I'm gonna bury her and that's that. If you don't wanna help me then don't."

He grabbed her feet and tried dragging her corpse through the cave. For a moment, it seemed as if he had no broken leg. His steadfast determination to give her a proper burial and resting place forespoke the ability to fight for love.

He fell to the ground, holding his head as he grimaced, yelling in pain. Phil kneeled next to him; worry edged all over his face.

"Andy? What's wrong?"

"My head… my head hurts…"

Phil held onto him, trying to help, even though he had no idea what was going on. Andrew's head felt like it was being stabbed on the inside of his brain, a sharp pain that felt like he was dying. He grabbed Phil's shirt with both hands.

Phil looked plain scared at Andrew's aching facial expressions.

"I see… I see someone…"

"*Someone*? Who?"

"No, not someone… *something*…"

"Andy, what are you going on about?"

He looked and sounded awful, making Phil worried he was sick. The headache got more intense and painful by the minute. Andrew desperately begged Phil to make it stop, wanting him to make it all right, feeling terrified.

"I feel outta control…"

"You'll be fine, okay? We'll figure this out, together." He steeled himself after his voice cracked a little, not wanting to scare Andrew even further. Truth was, this freaked Phil out just as much as it did Andrew.

Andrew, in a hasty moment, grabbed the spear and put the tip to his chest.

"Andy, stop, no," Phil said calmly, turning into protection mode. "Don't do anything you can't take back, please. I can't even begin to imagine how painful this must be, but this isn't the solution. Okay? Please." He put his hand on top of Andrew's, gently forcing him to lower the spear.

He clutched his head again once the spear was back on the ground, groaning. Phil put his arm around him, helping him over to the nearest wall to have some kind of leverage to lean against.

Andrew gasped, screaming "no!" repeatedly, his head aching like someone drilling right into his skull.

Phil touched his back protectively, both to try and comfort him, and to use touch to ground him. Phil's worry increased in that moment, though he still didn't let on. It wouldn't do Andrew any good if he were to freak out too.

Phil grabbed him, holding him protectively in his arms. "Listen to my heartbeat, Andy. Focus your breathing on my heartbeat."

Andrew listened to the calm and steady heartbeat, and finally, his headache faded away. He looked up at Phil, his eyes red, his cheeks wet from crying.

"I saw… I saw what she's gonna become, Phil. My sister, I… she's gonna turn into something much worse. And she's… she's gonna be cut into pieces by someone and she'll die a second time and…"

"Calm down, Andy. She's not gonna come back, okay? That's inhumanly impossible. And what do you mean you saw—"

"Like a vision, you know? Like… like a premonition. Maybe I'm not just an ordinary shapeshifter…"

"A shape what now? Andy, come on, you—"

"What if it's precognition? Can a shapeshifter have that 'cause they can shift into different people? Am I—"

"Andy!" Andrew looked over at him, surprised by the loudness of Phil's voice. Phil sighed. "Please, you're clearly exhausted. Whatever it was what you just endured, it tired you out," he said, trying to reassure Andrew that it was all going to be okay.

"No, I… I won't leave without burying her. I… I've to make sure no one can temper with her." He scrambled to try and get up but couldn't find the strength to do so.

Phil helped a shaken but determined Andrew to his feet. He tumbled outside to get some fresh air while Phil gently lifted Amelia in his arms.

Tapping the earth to flatten it, Phil looked over at Andrew who had found a few flowers still intact from what should've been a demolishing fog. He put them on top of the flattened earth. A single tear rolled down his cheek, falling unto one of the flowers' leaves.

Phil proceeded to carve out a cross, though Andrew shook his head. "No, don't. We never believed in any holy spirit or being. And this just shows. If there truly was something out there, whatever the bloody hell it might be, He or It doesn't give a crap about any of us. Why else would he let her be turned into whatever she was?" He noticed Phil wanted to open his mouth, stopping him from speaking up. "I know what you're gonna say. That what I just said is like an affront to whatever that higher being is, right? Well, guess what. Seeing as we're already in hell, might as well offend his ways."

Phil simply shook his head, then sighed. "Let's go find Theo. He must be around here somewhere." He helped Andrew up but was shoved away just as easily. He rolled his eyes, following Andrew, leaving her grave be.

# CHAPTER SEVEN

"Sam!" Tim yelled, knocking incessantly on his door. "Sam, wake up!"

The pattern of rapid knocking on the front door made little Zack wake up. He wobbled downstairs, smiling as he pulled the door open. "Uncle Tim!" the two-year-old yelled, lunging at Tim, grabbing his leg.

"Oi, kid, good to see you," Tim said hurriedly, rubbing the boy's head. "Where's your daddy?"

Zack pointed at the bedroom door opening slowly. Sam rubbed his eyes as he appeared. "Tim? What the bloody hell are you doing here at..." He checked the clock, "three in the morning?" His eyes widened. "Zack, go back to sleep," he told the boy, who nodded.

"Okay, daddy!"

He gave Zack a quick peck, then watched as the young boy closed his door.

He turned his attention towards Tim. "You wouldn't come here at this hour unless there was something serious going on. So, tell me."

Tim sat down at the kitchen table as Sam grabbed two bottles of beer, sitting down across from him. Tim took a map out of his bag, spreading it out in front of Sam. There were six tiny islands crossed out, surrounded by nothing but sea.

"An associate of mine told me Mister X's back. He's started a new project, and they called it Serum C."

"Serum C?"

Tim nodded, taking out an envelope, extracting documents from it. It didn't take long until the kitchen table was piled high with official research papers.

"Most of these are standard fares that my associate managed to copy," he said, taking a few away from the pile, "you know, like lots of finger-pointing and blame to President Ashwell's inability to see this through." He made three piles of documents, pointing at the smallest one. "These aren't fixated on personal responsibility. In other words, unusable for the point I'm about to make." He pointed to the second stack. "These involve data of Serum A and B, the serums they've used to make Serum C," he said, then tapped the final stack. "And these, well, these are what I came here to talk to you about."

Sam wanted to stop him as he was continuously brabbling words, but Tim was too keen on getting his point across. Or rather, make sure Sam was notified of the latest updates and developments.

"Remember I went to Sergeant Lawrence's place to extract all possible evidence after his case got reopened two months ago?" He showed Sam an USB-stick. "It's a security token. Once I was able to extract the WEP key from this dongle here, I was able to breach his network, and thus the network of the on-board computer of President Ashwell's kite."

Despite Sam being friends with Tim for over two years now, he still wasn't used to the whole 'nerd talk' Tim could sometimes get stuck in. Even when he lifted a finger to try and interrupt him, Tim wouldn't let him.

"I thought his alarm had been deactivated 'cause well, you know, he's been dead for two years and all," he said, taking out his laptop, "but when I broke in, the alarm went off. So, I beelined for the computer in what I think was a high-tech security research booth." He fished in his bag for a journal. "When I sat down, I opened his drawers to try and find hints for his password, which I know I should be able to hack as a hacker." He gave him the journal. "But then I found this and when I read through it, well, read it for yourself."

Sam took the journal from him, opening it up on the first page. There were all kinds of numbers and runic letters on the page, something he could under no circumstances decipher.

"So, once I had found his journal and figured out his password, which was such a dumb one. Who the bloody hell uses their birthday nowadays?" Tim typed something on his laptop. "Anyway, I inserted the dongle key into the USB-port and on the screen popped the expected 'account authentication required.' So, when I tried, and the screen said it was authenticating the account, I skimmed through the pages to try and see if there was any other useful information in there." He pulled the journal out of Sam's hand, stopping on a certain page, then gave it back. "When I saw this, I heard the beep of the laptop saying it had failed to authenticate. I didn't understand why at first, until I read this." He pointed at a weird-looking symbol on the page. "Apparently, that authentication was needed to open this huge armoury door which couldn't be seen with the naked eye. It was locked from the outside but would crack open if authenticated correctly."

Sam tried his best to keep up with all the terms Tim threw at him, even more so the enormous speed in which Tim presented it. No matter how hard he tried to interrupt Tim, he was an unstoppable force of information dumping.

"Apparently his computer had this pretty strong firewall protecting his accounting control service. So, when I hacked it, it said I was in violation of the *imperial protocol*, which doesn't make sense considering I used the man's own account to log in." He took the journal back once more, flipping to a new page. "I had to void his previous password and let the account generate a new one. I was in a way acting as if I had lost my password 'cause that's apparently what happens to some people. Not to me though, of course. Heh, not to me." He pointed at a copy he had printed out from the old sergeant's account. "See this? His salary got docked by this program he was enlisted in. A program, or rather *project*, named Serum C. And get this, he—"

Sam slammed Tim's laptop shut. Tim stared at him, his eyes wide and confused. "For the love of... just, stop talking for a second, okay? Please."

Tim leaned back in the chair, taking the bottle without saying another word. He took a huge sip.

"Just tell me calmly what you've discovered, okay? And none of that technical jargon crap, please. Just, normal English."

Tim nodded. His breathing slowed gradually as his tensed hands relaxed.

"Remember when we combined Serum A with Serum B to try and save Mike, which Zach injected himself with and died of?"

Sam hissed slowly as he spoke. "Yes. I remember."

"And then we mixed the bending agent, also known as Serum A, with your blood instead of with Jonathan's. The reason why that worked, and not Jonathan's, is 'cause it needed to be immune blood from someone still living, *you.* But what they've done is mixing Serum A with Serum B, the serum they used to give us injections with. Then they mixed it with both of your bloods. And what they've created now is called Serum C," he said, without taking a breath.

"And what *are* they doing with Serum C? Are they creating a new army?"

"Not exactly." Tim pointed at the map. "So, I dunno *everything,* but what I do know is that they kidnapped the REBELS and Laeries."

"They what?"

Sam grabbed the wicker chair he had been sitting on, tearing it apart, throwing it against the wall along with whatever else he could get his hands on.

"Woah, Sam! Calm down!" Tim yelled, trying to shield his head.

Sam stopped, holding his beer bottle in his hand. He put it down. "Sorry."

Tim removed his hands, looking at the big mess Sam had made.

They heard footsteps as Maddie entered the room, rubbing her eyes. "What's all the ruckus about?" she asked, gasping at the state of the room. "What the bloody hell happened here?"

Sam slammed his fist into the wall, his knuckles bleeding immediately.

"*Samuel!*" she yelled, crossing her arms. "Stop this—" They heard crying coming from Zack's room. Sam wanted to apologise to her, but she shushed him before he could say anything, leaving for Zack's room to calm him down.

Sam ran a hand through his hair, sighing. His expression turned from downright anger to maudlin. "I don't get it... how did they find 'em? And why did they take 'em, and not us?"

Tim shrugged, tapping on the second stack of papers he had brought. "I collected all the data I could find on our missing friends. They haven't been injected with anything, as far as I know."

Sam browsed through the data, shaking his head. "Then why kidnap 'em? What plans do they have *this time*?"

When Tim shrugged again, Sam chucked his beer bottle. Tim wanted to take it away from him, but it was already empty by the time he had reached Sam's hand. "Don't indulge yourself in alcohol, Sam, it's not gonna solve anything. And we need you sober."

"For what? Rescuing them? Go to those islands and try to take 'em back? I've got a family, Tim, I can't abandon 'em like that. What if I die? I can't let Maddie raise Zack all on her own. That's not what a father does."

Tim sighed, getting up. "I knew you were gonna say something like that." He left the information he had gathered on Sam's table, claiming he had his own copies. He walked over to the door, turning around. "I'll see you around, Sam." Tim left, closing the door behind him.

Sam sank into Tim's still intact chair, grabbing Tim's unemptied bottle, chucking it.

He lost count by the time Maddie had managed to calm Zack down, appearing in the doorway. She leaned against the doorpost. "Sam."

He turned around and got up. Taking a step towards her, he stumbled, and she barely caught him. The smell of alcohol was thick on his breath as he slumped in her arms.

"You're so... *beautiful!*" he said, his voice slurred.

She sighed, shaking her head. "I thought we were past this, Sam. You were sober since Zack's birth..." She forced him back into the chair, walking over to the sink to fill a glass with water. "What did Tim say that forced you back into drinking?" she asked, walking over to him.

"Oh, vodka!" he said, taking it eagerly. Taking a sip, he spit it back into the glass. "This isn't vodka!"

"No, but it's gonna help sober you up," she said, kneeling in front of him. "Let's get you to bed and talk about this in the morning, okay?"

She supported the wavering Sam as he got up, helping him limp over to their bedroom. Once she managed to get him to lie down, he was sound asleep. She covered him with the blanket and sighed, looking behind her at the stack of papers spread on the table. Walking back, she sat down, and began reading through them.

Sam woke up with a pounding headache, feeling extremely nauseous. He ran to the toilet, ridding himself of the nasty alcoholic acid that had been boiling in his stomach all night long.

Hearing the puking sounds, Maddie looked around the corner of the bedroom door. "How are you feeling?" she asked genuinely concerned.

"Aren't you supposed to be mad at me?" he asked, spitting. "I broke our promise."

She walked over to him, rubbing his back. "Yeah, you did, but I understand why." She kneeled next to him, flushing the toilet for him.

"Don't be so kind to me. I don't deserve it."

"Maybe not, but yelling at you with a headache won't do much good either, now will it?"

He grimaced, weakly shoving her away. "Just... give me a few minutes, okay? I don't want you to see all this."

"When we get married someday, I'll be there for you through the good *and* the bad. Might as well practice already."

"You sure this isn't something nullifying that?"

She chuckled, shaking her head. "No." She pointed at the English oak drawing hanging above their bed. "That symbol right there shows our strength of love. And with our names carved into an actual one right outside our house, I show you none of your flaws can make me run away. And you don't even have many flaws to run away from."

He looked over at her, staring deeply into her eyes. His exuberant joy mixed with a quiet, tender love expression, lighted up his whole face. "I hate how much I love you."

She gasped, slapping his shoulder. "Oh, such a meanie, aren't you?" She chuckled, offering her hand to help him to his feet. Staggering a little, she put a comforting arm around his waist, walking him to the kitchen. "I made you some hangover remedies. Or well, the ones I read about in a book a couple of decades old."

"You mean that old recipe book you found in that old lady's house?"

"Mildred had a fascinating arsenal of recipes, thank you very much. And you wouldn't like my cooking otherwise, would you?" She playfully kissed his ear, giving him the plate with toast and eggs, along with a smoothie she had prepared. "Just eat it. And thank me later."

He ate his breakfast in silence, smiling as he chewed. His hangover was slowly over-ridden by his love for her. "I think that your amazing cooking skills aren't the cure for my hangover," he said, watching as she raised her eyebrow in confusion. "I think it's your unconditional love, which you so happily applied to this delicious meal."

"Such a sappy romantic, aren't you?" she said, chuckling. Then her soft eyes looked worried. "I read the files."

Sam absently continued chewing, not making eye contact with her.

"I'm sorry, Sam. I know how hard you fought to keep 'em safe."

He put his cutlery down. "President Goldlib... Henry, promised me they'd be safe and couldn't be found by only those who knew about their location. And only the eight of us knew their location. There's no way Stan, Tim, Seb, Josh or Alex is the mole, neither are us two. It's gotta be Henry."

"What if it was one of the others?"

He looked up at her. "You mean... one of the Laeries or REBELS gave their hideout away? Why the bloody hell would they do that?"

"For money? For fame?"

He shook his head. "No, the Laeries wouldn't do such a thing. I can't say the same for the REBELS, but… no, they wouldn't be that stupid. We made an oath."

"An oath in which way? Verbally, black on white?"

He shook his head, showing her a scar on his palm. "Blood oath."

She sat down across from him. "I'll talk to Henry."

"No, this is on *me*, not you."

She gently rubbed his cheek, shaking her head. "It's on *us*. I'm gonna be your wife one day, Sam, please let me help you out with this. Let me help you carry a bit of the burden too."

"Following a lady's lead isn't really my style…" he said teasingly, grunting as she hit him on the chest.

"Anti-feminism, huh? My oh my, let me recall your law…" She cleared her throat, pretending to hold a book in her hands. "According to ZC-12, no man or woman should withhold women's rights or treat them any different than those of the opposite gender. Those defying these laws shall have to answer for their crimes."

"Crimes? I don't remember that word being in there."

He wanted to take the imaginary book from her with a playful smile crossing his lips, yet she turned away from him. "Those who break or refuse to abide this law will be punished in accordance with their crimes—"

She chuckled as she felt a tickle in her thighs. His nimble fingers worked their way up from her thighs to her stomach to start a tickle attack. Before he could launch the attack, she turned back to face him.

"You're treading on thin ice there, mister."

"Am I now? And what are you planning to do about it?"

She mock-pouted at him. "Beg you for mercy?"

Both looked over at the door as a polite yet incessant knock caught their attention.

"We sure are famous, aren't we?" he said awkwardly.

"Whoever it is, I'm here. I'm not gonna leave you."

He nodded and walked over to the door, opening it to reveal Henry. "Speak of the devil."

# CHAPTER EIGHT

Returning to their camp, they found Theo waiting for them, crouched down by something other-worldly.

"What the bloody hell's that?" Phil asked, his face grimacing.

"Beats me. It tried to attack me. But bloody hell does it have strong bones."

Andrew poked at it with his crutch. "Why does it have no face?"

"Ask it yourself," Theo said, "or well, you could've, if you had been here when it attacked me."

"I was attacked by my own sister," Andrew spat back, tears immediately welling up in his eyes, "and I had to bury her 'cause this son of a bloody arsehole right here killed her!"

Phil sighed. "I thought we had gone over this. It was either *you*, or her. What choice did I have?"

Theo shushed Andrew before he could reply, pointing at a huge blob on the creature's stomach. "There's something in there."

All three stared at something red moving around in the blob.

"Is that a... baby?" Theo asked, taking a step back. "I hate children."

Phil rolled his eyes at him, taking a knife-like shard of rock, he had found earlier that morning. "There's only one way to find out what *it* is. Andy, care to lend me a hand?"

Andrew nodded, kneeling next to Phil who began to cut open the blob. Peeling back the outer skin, Andrew stared in disbelief at the organs that were held in place with surgical forceps.

"Are those scissors?" Theo asked, watching from the sidelines.

"Yeesh, not the sharpest tool in the shed, eh?" Phil said, shaking his head. "It's more like a... metal clamp. To keep certain things in place inside a body."

"Gross..."

Ignoring Theo's comment, he used a flat piece of wood as a tongue depressor, parting the skin-lips protecting the blob. "I've never seen anything like it... this isn't natural. A human body doesn't look like this from the inside."

"Duh, that's 'cause it's an alien," Theo said. "Who's the dumb tool in the shed now?"

Seeing Phil's angry eyes flashing at him, he held his hands up in an apologetic way.

Once Phil had gotten through the skin-lips, he used his hands to gently pull the stomach downward, splitting it in half. Looking at the exposed blob, Phil noticed the seams bisecting a cord.

"Whatever it was, it's no longer being fed. The cord has been cut by its own body."

"Then how is it still moving?" Andrew asked, looking at the gaping maw of the creature, "when the host is dead?"

"Probably due to these," he said, pointing at a few tiny lumps. "The pheromone glands."

"So, it's a female?"

"Sure looks like it, though I don't see any genitals." He sniffed. "There's no strange smell either. There's no smell *at all.*"

"You're saying there should be?"

"Maybe, I dunno. What I do know, is that I want a sample of whatever those pheromones and seams secrete."

The blob split open, spilling out bile-coloured liquid with an overwhelming stench.

Theo covered his nose with his shirt, gagging. "Mate, you full on jinxed us!"

The tiny red egg was now exposed, no longer moving. Phil cut it loose, holding it in his hand. Theo gagged loudly behind him, running away to relieve his stomach in the bushes.

"What does it feel like?" Andrew asked.

Phil thoughtfully observed the blob, spinning it around to examine all its edges. "It feels… it's not as squishy as I thought it'd be." Then, it began to grow.

Andrew drew back, staring at it in disbelief. "How did it…"

Before he could finish his sentence, the blob continued growing at a rapid speed.

"Put it down! It's gonna blow!" Theo yelled, hiding behind their self-made tent. "Get to cover!"

The blob split open, foul greenish-black gore oozed from the inside like an explosion, ending up on both Andrew's and Phil's faces. Theo, watching from behind the tent, saw the gore covering their skin. His eyes rolled back in his sockets, hitting the ground only two seconds later.

"Did he seriously…?"

"Yeah, he did."

Andrew stifled a laugh, shaking his head. "Guess we know who the clean freak is outta the three of us."

Phil ignored his comment, using his finger to wipe some of the ooze off his face. Examining it closer by smelling it, Andrew raised an eyebrow at him. "You sure that's... safe? What if it hibernates again?"

Phil looked over at him, chuckling. "This isn't hibernation. Hibernation is something completely different." Andrew's fallen face made him gently pat his shoulder. "I know where your head's at though, but I can't think of any scientific name that'd logically explain what we just witnessed."

Andrew turned his head to Theo instead, bursting into a crystalline humourful laugh. Phil looked from Andrew to Theo, having a faint but distinct youthful twinkle in his eyes as he knew what Andrew was thinking.

"Do it."

Andrew nodded and took some of the greenish-black goo, crawling over to where Theo was still unconscious. Smearing it over his face, he heard Phil call out to him.

Wiping the remainder of the goo on a nearby leaf, he crawled back to Phil who pointed at where the eye sockets would be. "See this? Its eyes are there, but they're simply hidden by this skin growth here."

"So... they're not reliant on sight..."

"But on *smell*." Phil exchanged a quick look with Andrew. "That black ooze... it's..."

Its thin arm threw Phil across the camp like a rag dol, hitting a nearby rock hard. Andrew watched in horror as Phil's leg was bend the wrong way, knowing all too well what a broken leg felt like. Turning his gaze back to the awakened creature, he swallowed.

"Oi, look," he said, raising his hands in the air, "we mean you no harm. We uh... we're sorry about your... stomach. That wasn't kind of us." The creature grew a set of talons covered in the same greenish-black goo that had just come out of the blob, yet it was a lighter green mixed with the black.

"Poison..."

Phil wasn't in that much pain until he tried to move, feeling his broken rib stabbing him on the inside, not feeling the pain in his leg just yet. Howling softly from the pain he felt, and the fear creeping up inside of him, he looked over at Andrew who backed away from the creature.

"Look, I kinda don't wanna die so sudden and so, lonely, you know?" Andrew said pleadingly, covering his nose as the air was heavy with an awful odour, an odour that smelled like a rotten corpse had crawled up from its grave. Hearing Phil cough, he looked to his left, watching as blood dripped down from the sides of his mouth. His eyes drawn to the twisted shape of Phil's broken leg; he stopped trying to crawl away.

"Andy...?" Phil said weakly, witnessing Andrew had stopped moving. "What are you..." His eyes were wild with fear and terror, whining softly.

Andrew smiled weakly at him, nodding reassuringly. "It's gonna be okay." He turned his head back to the creature, whose attack on Phil had been vicious, not scaring Andrew as easily as he had thought it would.

A sudden surge of bravery hit him. Getting up on his good leg, he swayed, clutching himself onto his crutch. Behind his back, he held the knife-like shard of rock sturdy in his hand, watching the creature's every move.

The creature launched at him, and it went black.

Coming to, Andrew gasped for air, noticing it was completely dark around him.

"Drew?" he heard vaguely, trying to figure out where it came from. "Drew, can you hear me?"

Mumbling, he tried to make himself known, tried to tell whoever was calling out to him that he was alive. He felt the weight shift off him, and a couple seconds later, he was breathing fresh air. Gasping loudly, his breathing sounded aspirated, wheezing almost.

Looking over at Theo's surprised yet relieved face, he turned his attention to the creature, its skull cracked open and split around its thick tines. The sharp tip had easily stabbed through the rancid bone of its skull, nothing but pure black ooze dried out.

"I dunno how you did it, but blimey that thing collapsed in a tangled heap right on top of you," he explained, patting his back soothingly. "You okay?"

Andrew nodded softly, looking over at Phil squirming in pain.

"Phil..." He crawled over to Phil, examining his leg. "Bloody hell, it looks worse than my leg did."

"Thanks, captain obvious," he said, grunting as Andrew touched it slightly.

Theo walked over, kneeling next to Andrew. "I had to rescue you first."

"I know." He looked over at Theo. "Thank you."

Theo nodded, offering Phil some water, who refused. "Look, I probably have several broken ribs, and a couple of significant contusions on top of my broken leg." He coughed up more blood, grunting softly. "And probably on my inside too." Touching his head, he showed them the blood stained on his hand, "not to mention the possible hairline fracture somewhere on my skull and a likely concussion." Tears began to roll down his cheeks, breathing shakily. "Leave me; I'll only slow you down."

"Oi, mate," Theo said, shaking his head, "first, we're not leaving *anyone* behind. And second, we've set up camp here, haven't we?"

Phil shook his head. "You don't understand. Those things? They know where we are now. It's only a matter of time before their whole pack finds us."

"*Pack?*"

Phil turned his head to Andrew. "I know what they are, and I can assure you they're bad news."

Andrew moved away from Phil, shaking his head. "No, you... how do you know what they are?"

Phil grunted loudly, coughing. "I... 'cause I studied 'em before I woke up on this island. Not this... evolved form of it, but the second I realised they were blind; I knew what species they belong to."

"Have you... experimented on 'em?" Theo asked.

"No, I didn't. Someone else must've. Everything you see here, it's all new, everything except for the blindness." He turned his head to Andrew. "I swear I didn't do this, and I swear I had no idea they lived here. I was only asked to examine 'em as my leader—my *previous* leader, found one of 'em dead on his doorstep. He still lived in isolated exile, which was his own choice, and knew the area he lived in was now no longer protected."

"Meaning anything unholy or inhumane can walk there," Theo finished his sentence.

Phil nodded, not moving his eyes away from Andrew. "I didn't know they'd attack like that. I didn't even know they attacked *at all*. The creature I observed had no talons, nor any poisonous substance in its body. Whatever they did to this thing, it wasn't natural. It was *deliberate.*"

Andrew finally made eye contact with Phil, whose cheeks were wet from crying.

"I know what this must look like, I know what you must think. I didn't do anything to your sister, I swear. But it's likely that they wanted to turn her into one of those things. Perhaps this one..." He grunted, "perhaps this one was already in its final experimental stage, and perhaps she was becoming this too one day."

Andrew shook his head, covering his ears with his hands. "Stop, please. Stop."

Phil's tears ebbed, holding Andrew's hand. "I'm sorry, Andy. I'm sorry for not warning you of my knowledge. I should've. If I had, maybe I wouldn't be dying right now."

Andrew turned his head sharply, shaking it. "You're not dying," he said, "you don't get to die, you hear me? You don't get to die before any of us."

The gravity of Andrew's tone caught Phil off guard, though it wasn't reproachful. It was rather vulnerable.

Andrew took Phil's hand in his. "Either we die *together*, or I kill you myself."

Phil chuckled softly, grimacing in pain shortly after. "You clearly know how to kill it, so I know you'll do whatever you can to survive, to protect Theo." He put a tiny flash drive in Andrew's hand. "Find a way outta here, find someone you trust to give this to. It's the truth."

His hand began to slip from Andrew's grasp, though Andrew held onto his hand firmly. He tilted Phil's chin, kissing him tenderly. Phil's mouth curled up into a smile, then he breathed his last breath during the kiss.

# CHAPTER NINE

Sam hesitantly stepped aside to let Henry pass the threshold, watching him like a hawk as he headed over to Maddie. "Madeline, it's so good to see you again."

She gave him a kind smile, looking over at her boyfriend fuming. "Can I get you anything? Coffee? Tea?"

Henry shook his head, sitting down. "I won't stay long," he said, pointing at the two chairs in front of him. "Come, sit. We need to talk."

Maddie headed over to Sam, taking his hand in hers. Squeezing it softly, she guided him towards the chairs.

Sitting down, he gave Henry a deadly stare. "Why are you here, Henry? To coerce us? To feed more lies to me like you do to the others?"

Henry sighed softly. "Look, I know what this looks like, but…"

"No, let me guess. Someone contacted you while you were in exile, and they offered you a chance at revenge against your…. let's call 'em usurpers, eh?"

"If you'd just let me tell my story—"

"So that you can what, spew more lies?"

"Babe," Maddie said, putting her hand on top of his, "he deserves some leniency."

"From whom? Me? I didn't become his vice-president to be held in the dark like this. I thought *we* were a team, Henry," he said, turning his gaze back to him, "I thought that we had agreed on something, that we'd never betray one another." His jaw was clenched, and his fists flexed. It looked like he was about to pounce on Henry.

"I haven't betrayed you, nor anyone else. If you'd just shut up and let me talk—"

"Talk to us so you can lure us someplace under false pretences? We don't *need* to talk to you, and we *don't* wanna talk to you." He leapt to his feet, pointing an accusatory finger at him. "You claim you wanna talk to us both, but the truth is, you wanna assure her you won't do any harm to me before you force me to come with you and do exactly the opposite of what you'd make her believe." His whole face was now contorted with fury.

Henry stared at him in disbelief, looking at the empty bottles of alcohol scattered around the kitchen. Then it occurred to him. "Sam... really?"

Sam looked at the bottles, then at Maddie, slowly sitting back down. "I'm still under the influence, am I not?"

Maddie nodded softly, patting his leg. "You know Henry means no harm, to no one. Whatever silly scenario you've got cooking up in that nogging of yours, it's not true. And whatever Tim might've implied, whatever proprietary information he had written down in those documents about Henry's work, he's wrong." Sam looked over at her with a dazed, confused look. "I've... secretly been working with Henry to try and find the missing people."

Sam's eyes grew wide, staring at both in disbelief. "So, you're saying that... you knew about this? You knew about 'em missing and didn't tell me?"

"I know it was wrong of me to lie, but this, your drinking habit, it was exactly the fear I had. I was afraid you'd drink yourself to death if you knew." He stared at the table, his chest going up and down slowly. "I know me lying to you is inexcusable, but I did it outta love, I did it outta protection. Please, Sam, don't be mad at me."

He shook his head, though didn't look her in the eye. He knew he couldn't be mad at the love of his life, even though it still stung that she had kept him out of this. Then again, he knew she was right. He likely would've grabbed the bottle like he had done now.

"So, will you hash things out with us?"

He finally met her gaze, staring into her pleading eyes. Nodding slowly, Henry pulled a folder from beneath his coat, the word *CONFIDENTIAL* stamped across the front, and handed it to Sam.

He reluctantly opened the first page, leafing through. It didn't take long before he found himself engrossed in the provided data.

*"BRAL (Base Rebels and Laeries) was utilised since those enlisted to be protected were restricted to the camp. The only personnel that resided downtown were Joshua and his team, Coyote One, as appointed by President Henry Goldlib to protect Operation Bronze Pool. It was vital to the success of the mission that only the President and Coyote One knew of their whereabouts. The tactical difficulty of operating in an anti-access-area-denial environment has proven to be grounds for treachery. Even though the city needs*

*protection, it can no longer be Coyote One's top priority. All soldiers are under prosecution. The outcome of the operation has proven to have failed on the tactical level of classification. Working towards the right development of a solution on an operational level linked to a desired strategic end state, has been ceased until further notice."*

Wheedling over the numbers in the folder linked to the class action didn't feel like the right call to Sam. Dropping the folder onto the table, he stood up, pacing around the room.

*We're knowingly letting those traitors go free... the REBELS, the Laeries they... they were our clients, basically. That's not right, that's wrong.*

Sam turned around sharply, looking Henry dead in the eye. "I wanna talk to Josh. *In private."*

"Sam, you can't—"

"I know he's a suspect. But I know Josh. And I need to speak with him. You owe me that."

Henry sighed, nodding. "Okay, give me an hour." He got up and walked over to the door, then stopped in his tracks. "I'm sorry, Sam. And I'm even sorrier that our good intentions made everything worse. If anything, this is on *me. I'm* the murderer here." With that, he opened the door and left.

Sam sat silently at the table, staring at his sandwich as Maddie helped feeding Zack. "Here comes the aeroplane!" Making a zooming sound, she proceeded to give Zack his fruit, smiling as he clapped his hands enthusiastically.

Looking over at her boyfriend, he looked as though he would love nothing more than to run away, probably to the tree they had planted for Zack. It had become Sam's safe spot, a place of comfort and homeliness.

Noticing she was staring at him, he got a handle on himself with customary control, giving her a weak reassuring nod. Giving Zack the spoon so he could try to eat himself, she patted Sam's hand indulgently.

"I know you feel envy for my easy confidence in Henry back then and now, but I—"

Sam stopped her by putting a finger onto her mouth, shaking his head. "Please, stop apologising. I'm not mad at *you."*

"But you can't forgive me," she said, sadly.

"I'm just... trying to reconcile the loyalty I've got for Henry with this... callous disregard for how weak I've been acting."

"Stop," she said, planting a kiss on his lips. "Your soul is the most beautiful thing I've ever had the privilege of knowing and falling in love with." She kissed his hand. "Whether you fell back into an old habit or not, that love hasn't changed one bit for me."

"But you know it could've. That's why you decided to keep me outta the situation."

"No, I did it 'cause I didn't want your quick-witted, full of verve character to be suppressed by alcohol again. The last few months that you've been sober showed me that the sunshine in my appalling grey weather that I fell in love with, was still in there somewhere." She pointed at his heart. "Even after everything he had been through, he was still so lovely, romantic, caring, daring, and suave. You ticked, and still tick, all those boxes, Sam." A single tear rolled down his cheek, and she wiped it away. "You were an ambitious, handsome young man who poised for my love, as if fate willed it, even after losing the love of a brother. I know you don't see it, blaming yourself for what happened to Zach, but you're so good at cultivating love in the lives of your friends and family. You exude warmth and comfort to everyone you talk to, Sammy." Hearing her say the nickname she only used during emotional talks, he knew she was being sincere and comforting. "You're a brilliant man, Sam, and you deserve the best of what the world has to offer." She kissed him again. "Including a vivacious woman by your side."

He chuckled, shaking his head. "If you don't stop right now, you won't have any compliments and sweet speeches left for the future."

"Don't worry, I've got plenty more stocked up in here," she said, pointing at her head. Then she smiled warmly. "*I love you, Sam.*"

Holding her firmly in his embrace, he kissed her neck. "*I love you too.*"

An obligatory knock on the door made both look up. He gave her one final kiss, kissed his son on the head, gathered his things, and left his home.

Following the Trooper, Sam felt an uneasy pit in his stomach. He was the co-founder of a newly improved prison, yet it felt wrong walking there. Lost in his own thoughts, he didn't realise the Trooper had stopped moving and crashed right into him.

Shaking his head from the impact, he looked up. "Sorry."

The Trooper didn't say a thing but simply urged him inside a room with a computer. "We need your fingerprint scanned so you've access to the cellblock."

"Access? You mean the technology has been upped since the last time I was here?"

"Basically." The Trooper sat down behind the computer, clicking on *security*, opening a new window. Staring at the screen to identify the system they were using, he watched as he typed in the *security password* and the *user ID*. Enabling the security function, he began to set up a fingerprint recognition tool, registering it under the folder named *security data*.

"Which user ID would you like?" he asked, not looking up to Sam.

"Oh, I uhm…" He thought long and hard, thinking about Zach.

*Is there something I could use that sounds like something only Zach would know for the ultimate security? I mean… no, that's barbaric, I can't do that.*

He sighed. "How about… Bráthair."

"I'm sorry, what?" The Trooper looked up. "How do you… spell that?"

As Sam spelled it out for him, the Trooper didn't bother to question Sam's choice, let alone ask the story behind it. After a quick run-through by the password generator, he pointed at a tiny device which surface was a clear, thin glass.

"Put either your index finger or middle finger on the surface."

Sam did as he was told, placing his index finger on the glass, watching as a luminous blue sensor went from top to bottom, and back. He heard the slight buzzing as it moved up and down, and swore he felt the electromagnetic field gently kissing his skin.

"All done, you can remove your finger from the console."

As the computer scanned the fingerprint, Sam read the set of security levels that were displayed. All this technology was new to him, and he wondered why Henry went through the trouble to install something else than they had initially discussed, and why he didn't mention that to Sam.

The head-up display had flashing data on either side of the screen. *I wish Tim was here. He'd be able to explain this to me. Wait a minute… did he… make this?*

At the bottom of the screen, he noticed a number, *50. Tim's Trooper number.*

Saving the registered fingerprint, he got back up from the chair. "Follow me."

Heading over to a heavy steel door, the Trooper pointed to a scanner sensor on the right side of the door. Noticing Sam's raised eyebrow, he rolled his eyes. "It's already fully registered, lad. You've got your own biometric passport now."

Placing his finger on the scanner, an automated female voice sounded from the tiny, embedded speaker.

"Scanning fingerprint... Samuel, Trooper 33... Access granted."

A beep sounded, colouring the display screen green. The Trooper headed over to the door, pushing against it. The metal scraped over the floor until it hit the wall. Clicking it shut so they could go through, he motioned for Sam to enter first. Once Sam was through, he followed him, and the metal door shut a few seconds after he had entered. Gulping softly, it somehow felt as if Sam was taken somewhere he didn't want to be, somewhere he wasn't supposed to go.

A part of him was still weary of Henry's supposed intentions but if his girlfriend trusted him, then Sam did too. He trusted Maddie with his life, and she had an eye for the true nature of people.

Entering a cellblock, Sam tried to observe who was locked inside. He recognised a few of the inmates as the Troopers trained by Josh, yet a few seemed older, if not elder.

"You've got a visitor," the Trooper said, clanking his weapon against the cell bar.

Sam saw a shadowy figure sitting in the dark, slumped down like a ragdoll. If that was Josh, he didn't look like the Josh he knew. Whatever they had done to him, it couldn't be anything good.

"*I said I wanted to be left alone.*"

His voice sounded hoarse, as if he hadn't had water in days. Sam began to wonder if Henry knew about the circumstances these prisoners lived in. If he did, why would he let this happen? Sam had told Henry explicitly that whoever was going to be imprisoned here, no matter their offence, would be treated humanely.

*I'll have a thorough talk with him about this later. And if he doesn't know, then we ought to do something about this.*

"It's a friend of yours, Joshua. You better be nice to the very few friends you still have."

Sam noticed the shadowy figure's head lifting slowly, then turning his head towards him.

"Sam?" Getting up, Josh slowly walked over to the light. *"Is that... you?"* His voice sounded so hoarse; he was forced to whisper.

Appearing in front of him, Sam had to hold in a gasp. He looked impaired, beaten by someone who used full strength on him.

His black eye was so thick, it was clear Josh had trouble seeing with it, and the cut above his eye looked infected.

"*What have they done to you...?*" Sam whispered, making sure the Trooper couldn't hear it. Josh didn't answer. "Can you let me inside the cell?"

The Trooper looked over at Sam. "No, that goes against policy."

Sam made eye contact with the Trooper, using his pleading puppy eyes. The Trooper sighed, moving to a padlock on the left side. Unable to see which code he was entering, Sam looked back at Josh, who still hadn't said a thing after getting closer.

The cell door opened, and the Trooper urged Sam inside, closing the door right behind him. "You get ten minutes." He walked away, heading outside.

As the metal door clanked shut, Sam turned to Josh, hugging him soothingly. "It's okay, Josh, I'm here." Rubbing his back softly, making sure he wasn't wounding him, he noticed Josh sobbing softly into Sam's shoulder.

*Bloody hell... they really did a number on him. Josh and crying are... well, it's not a good sign.*

"Please... get me outta here..." Josh begged him, snickering softly. "I'll do anything."

Sam continued rubbing his back, shaking his head. "Trust me, I wasn't planning on letting you rot in here. Whatever happened, I know it wasn't your fault. You don't belong here, Josh, none of you do."

Josh moved slowly away from Sam's embrace, staggering. Sam caught him, sitting him down on the bed. "Oi, sit down. Are you okay?"

He shook his head. "*They... they tortured me for answers. They never stopped. Not until I gave up all the names of my team.*" He looked down, sniffling. "*I betrayed my men... and for what? To stop the relentless beating? Who knows what those bastards did to some of 'em 'cause of me...*"

Sam put a hand on Josh's knee. Normally, Josh would've swatted the hand away, would've made a remark about him being gay. But not this time. This time, he was a broken soul who wanted to be comforted, to be rescued from hell.

"But I don't get it," Sam said, scratching his arm, "they don't have a specific suspect. All they do is pit their so-called circumstantial evidence against you, and they know bloody well that it leaves way too much room for juridical errors."

"The public likely thinks we're guilty too... and our alibi is... flimsy at best. Probably damaging."

"Why'd you say that?"

Josh sighed. *"We were out drinking instead of doing our job, but we stayed in the near vicinity of the REBELS and former Laeries so we could still respond immediately when necessary."* He coughed softly. *"They even claimed we're actively impeding our own case every step of the way 'cause we're not as cooperative as we could be."*

"They wanna blame you... they want you to be guilty..."

Josh nodded slowly, sighing deeply. *"I'm screwed, Sam, I'm never getting outta here. Not alive anyway."*

Sam shook his head. "Hey now, don't talk like that. The rules that Ashwell made are long gone, Josh. Henry and I, we wrote new laws. None of those say you'll be executed for something like this."

*"Well, then at least one jury member will reach the conclusion that we're innocent,"* he said, coughing weakly, *"but this case? It's more holistically examined than any other."* Josh looked down at Sam's belt, then up at him. *"Do you... have a weapon on you?"*

"No, they searched me thoroughly, why?"

Josh shook his head. *"Let me paint the picture the way I see it."* He pointed at the cell door. *"I'm not walking outta here, not ever. I'm either sentenced for life, or someone of my team will murder me when they get the chance."* A single tear rolled down his cheek. *"I want you to kill me, Sam. I want it to be you, and no one else."*

Sam made sure no one could hear them as he leaned closer. *"Nobody's gonna kill you. I won't let that happen, and I won't do it either, Josh. I'm gonna get you outta here, even if it's the last thing I do."*

Josh wanted to reply, beg him for mercy, but all he could do was collapse face first onto the floor after his eyes rolled back in his head.

"Josh?" Sam kneeled next to him, placing two fingers in Josh's neck to make sure he was still breathing. "Josh, wake up," he said, patting his cheek lightly. *"Josh, I don't wanna call the Trooper over... I don't trust 'em with looking after you, and not in your current condition. Just open your eyes for me, lad."*

Noticing he had a weak pulse; Sam drew the conclusion that he had passed out from lack of oxygen. That suspicion seemed to be correct once he lifted Josh's shirt, seeing the bruises covering his whole chest, and neck. Those on his neck seemed fresh, as if he had been choked minutes before Sam had walked in.

Taking out his phone, he rang Henry's cell.

*"This is the voicemail of the President. The President's not—"*

Sam sighed, ending the call. Looking back at Josh, he shuddered at the sight of Josh's emaciated figure as his shirt was still lifted. He was incredibly thin, and his ribs were clearly visible. Leaning a little closer, he saw a few tiny entry points at the back of his neck. *"They've sedated you..."*

Looking out of the cell, he noticed a young boy lying shrivelled in a drugged stupor. He too was an obvious victim of the torture and starvation going around Josh's team.

The ten minutes were over, and he heard the footsteps getting closer. He lifted Josh gently, lay him down on his bed, and covered him with the dishevelled blanket, turning around once the Trooper showed his face.

"You done?"

Sam nodded. "Yeah, he was tired and fell asleep, so I just waited until you came back."

The Trooper opened the door, letting Sam out. Closing the door behind Sam, he put a tiny pin between the door so it wouldn't close off completely yet would close far enough to not notice the small opening.

Being led back outside, the Trooper stopped Sam from leaving by tapping his shoulder. "Turn around."

Sam did as he was told, letting the Trooper search and scan him to make sure Josh hadn't given him something that could potentially lead to his escape. Deeming Sam allowed to leave, he opened the electronic door with a special code, numerals that Sam could see from the corner of his eye.

Storing it in his memory, he thanked the Trooper and went home.

# CHAPTER TEN

Sitting up straight, Andrew let out a gasp, breathing heavily. He wiped the perspiration from his forehead, tried to calm his racing heart rate and racing thoughts. He felt nauseous, not to mention disoriented and disassociated with time and place. Hearing the cackling of the fire, he turned his head sharply, finding Theo poking with a stick at the wood.

"Oi, Drew, take it easy," Theo said, hearing Andrew's ragged breathing. He walked over to him and offered him some water. "Here, drink."

Andrew gulped it in one go, looking at Theo with bloodshot eyes. "He's... he's dead. Phil's dead..."

Theo raised an eyebrow at him, shaking his head. "What the bloody hell you going on about? Phil's fine." He pointed at the improvised makeshift tent he had conjured up earlier that evening. "Sure, he's been outta it ever since he got injured, but he's *not* dead."

Andrew shook his head, having trouble swallowing. "No, he... he died in my arms and he... he coughed up blood and had internal bleeding and..."

"Drew, *breathe*," Theo said.

The panic in Andrew's chest was so tight that he could barely breathe, but he tried it anyway with Theo's help. *In and out. Deep and even.*

Closing his eyes, he tried to corral his thoughts into a semblance of order.

"So... you're saying I had a nightmare?"

Theo nodded. "That's what it looks like to me, yeah."

"It was all... fake?"

"Not everything, no." Theo gestured towards the blood. "We did pull you out from beneath whatever the bloody hell that was after you killed it, and Phil *did* know about it. But no, he didn't die. He's *very much* alive, I can promise you that."

"And his injuries... what's true of that? And how did you pull me out with a broken arm?"

Theo threw new wood onto the fire. "To answer your first question, he does have broken ribs and a broken leg, but nothing severe and not as bad as your nightmare pictured." He watched as Andrew's gaze moved over to Phil's tent. "He probably has a concussion too, but there are no bad complications whatsoever. All he did was faint, after which you did too from exhaustion." He offered Andrew some more water. "After you two collapsed, I dragged Phil to the tent, or what was left of it, and built him a new, temporary one. He woke up a couple of times when you were out but fell back asleep almost immediately." He watched as Andrew sipped some of the water. "And to answer your second question, I just did. When the adrenaline kicks in, you just *do*."

Andrew took a few more sips before nodding, then the memory about him kissing Phil came to the surface. He swallowed.

"Theo..."

"Yeah?"

Theo turned back to Andrew after he had turned the other way seconds before.

"What did I... do, when Phil fainted?"

"You just kept shaking him and screaming that he had to wake up, but that's about it."

*So, I didn't kiss him... Why did I dream about it, though? Is it... was I scared of losing him? Why can't I admit that to Theo if it were true? And what does it mean? Is it... am I desiring... no, no I can't be... I can't do that, I don't dare... I don't... I...*

"Why are you asking?"

Andrew got pulled out of his chaotic thoughts, staring blankly at Theo. "What?"

Theo shook his head. "Nothing, not important. Are you hungry?" He gave Andrew a well-cooked fish, and the memories came flooding back about how happy Andrew felt when he was fishing with Phil yesterday.

Theo noticed the absent stare, but knew it was a happy one, and let Andrew be for a minute.

After eating the fish, Andrew sighed as he leaned back on his hands, staring at the starry sky. Theo sat down next to him, gazing up at the sky.

"What do you think is out there?" Andrew asked.

Theo chuckled. "Far away galaxies that we know nothing about."

Andrew poked him playfully, biting his lip to suppress a laugh. Stealing another glance at Phil, he sighed.

Theo heard the sigh, and his grey eyes sparkled tantalisingly with humour. "Hey, Drew."

"Hm? Yeah," he said, once again being pulled back to reality. "What's up?"

"What do you call a galaxy that's allergic to milk?"

Andrew quirked an eyebrow at him, not knowing an answer to that question.

"Galactose intolerant."

He gave a lopsided smile before bursting out laughing, tears rolling down his cheeks as he shook his head. "That's such a bad one, and yet it's so bloody good."

Theo laughed alongside Andrew, smiling as he knew he had made Andrew forget about the pain for just a little bit.

"Thank you," Andrew said softly, nodding to himself. "And for... you know, listening to me wallow in self-pity."

"You didn't—" The sideway glance he received from Andrew said enough. "But that's what you're about to do." He sighed. "Go, before I change my mind."

Andrew chuckled lightly, though the sorrow was clearly etched across his features. "So... what my sister was... or *did*, do you too think she couldn't be saved?"

"Honestly? I dunno. I've not come across it myself before. This is *completely* new to me. I think I would've reacted the way you did if it had been my family. But the truth is, I don't have family. Okay, my fellow REBELS are kinda my family, but it's not the real deal." He threw more wood onto the fire. "I've never really felt at home with 'em. I always felt like the odd one outta the bunch, you know? Like a freak, or a loser. Kinda like they got sick of talking to the *perching weirdo*. Became more like a routine to bully me than to consider me one of the team." He sighed. "Well, would you look at that. You were gonna endow yourself in sorrow and I took the reins. Sorry about that."

"It's okay," Andrew said, chuckling softly. "We all gotta let it out at some point."

Phil woke up, hearing voices outside his tent, wondering where he was and who those voices belonged to. Trying to move, he grunted, realising he was too injured to move on his own.

"How's your leg doing?" Theo asked, offering Andrew a few berries.

"Honestly, probably a lot better than Phil's. Mine wasn't as badly broken as his. I swear, the state of his bone..." The thought made him shiver. "I just hope we won't have to run 'cause there's no way in hell you can help two disabled people."

Theo shook his head, sighing. "Probably not, no." He looked at the tent. "We need to make him a crutch too." He took a long stick off the ground and began creating a crosspiece at the top. "Let's see if my skills can step up to the plate."

Andrew heard rustling coming from inside the tent, gently swatting Theo's arm. Theo heard it too, putting a finger to his mouth.

Phil didn't hear the voices anymore and thought whoever was out there had left. He managed to reach the far end of the tent, lifting whatever kind of canopy served as its roof.

Peeking through the leaves, he noticed two boys staring at him and sighed of relief. "How about you two come help me out here, eh?"

Theo and Andrew exchanged quick looks before Theo headed over to the tent, giving the stick and handmade knife to Andrew, who continued crafting the crutch.

"Here," Theo said, offering him a hand. "Think you can get up?"

Phil shook his head. "Nah, not happening. I dunno what the bloody hell happened, but it sure hurts a bloody lot."

"You don't...? What's the last thing you remember?"

"Killing..." He sighed. "Saving Andy from his ferocious sister."

Theo nodded and slid his hands beneath Phil's body. Phil looked at him, confused. "Don't worry, I don't play for your team," Theo reassured him, lifting him up. "Besides, I know who you've set your eye on." Ignoring Phil's deadly stare, he carried him over to where Andrew was.

Setting him down gently, Andrew immediately wrapped his arms around Phil, practically crushing him.

"Oi, take it easy with the merchandise, huh?" he said jokingly, patting his back. "I still killed your sister. If everything, you should be pissed at me."

Andrew backed away slowly, looking at Theo who shrugged. "Says all he remembers is killing her, nothing else after that."

He nodded, sighing a little. "Well, I've already forgiven you for that. Haven't forgotten about it but have moved on. I can't dwell on it too long, won't do anyone any good."

Phil nodded proudly. "That's the spirit, Andy." He looked at the crutch in the making. "I see we're gonna be twins. Care to explain how I ended up breaking my bone if it wasn't you getting back at me for murdering your sister?"

He eyed Theo, who nodded. "Well..."

"You're kidding."

Andrew shook his head. "Nope, and you told us you had dealt with one before. The research you were a part of?"

"Right, yeah, I remember those. Huh, interesting. Did I tell you what we learned?"

"Not... really? I mean, all you explained was that you had come across 'em and whatever had happened to 'em now wasn't your fault."

"Right, yeah, that sounds about right." He cleared his throat. "Guess I didn't tell you the whole deal then, huh?"

"The whole...? No, I suppose you didn't."

Phil nodded, looking over his shoulder as if he wanted to make sure no one else could hear what he was about to say.

*He's acting strange... and it can't be the concussion. There's something off about him. Am I sure this isn't just a dream? What if he's truly dead and my mind's playing tricks on me?*

"So, if someone, or *something*, attacks you and they look injured despite not showing any physical damage, don't fight 'em."

"Are you talking about... Minnie?"

He nodded solemnly, sighing. "Those injected... or rather *infected*, have that weird illness looking thing that transforms 'em. It's like what you saw with your sister."

*The premonition... is this another? Is this me telling myself what Phil was supposed to tell me before he died?*

"If they get to the new stage, the *final* stage, there will be black liquid coming outta their eyes, ears, and nose. Imagine the black plague if it was merged with cancer, that's what this is. They inject 'em with a biologically living virus which is a form of black plague imbued with cancerous cells."

"Why? Why the bloody hell would they do that?" Theo asked, arms crossed. "What would they gain from that?"

"With that, they can destroy planets and galaxies if not taken care of properly. It's all connected to the different elements the universe has to offer us, and it's not stoppable. It's a hybrid of a fungal infection that's not even close to being related to an actual fungus. With the virus they've created, it has found a new way to mutate itself—"

"In human beings..." Theo finished his sentence, putting one and one together.

"Bingo."

Andrew grew more sceptical by the minute. *If Phil knew all this, then why's he here? With us?*

"How do we stop it? Is there a cure?" Theo asked, bringing Andrew back to the present.

"No, but a very important step to take to slow down the mutation process is—"

Gasping awake, Andrew looked around the dark camp, noticing the fire he was sleeping next to was fully extinguished. Rubbing his eyes, he looked over at Theo sleeping across from him, seeing his silhouette in the dark. Looking over his shoulder, he stared at the tent, finding it empty. He sighed deeply.

*So, it's true... he's dead. Phil's dead.*

Falling backwards on the makeshift pillow, he stared at the pinpricks of stars littering the sky above him.

*So, what? Did his spirit visit me in my dreams? Did he try to warn me?*

He slid his hands beneath his head, blinking slowly.

"Couldn't sleep either?"

Hearing Phil's voice, he shot up, backing away instantly.

"Oi, calm down," Phil said, raising his hands calmly, noticing how desperately Andrew wanted to flee but too terrified to move. "You look like you've just seen a ghost."

He pointed his crutch at him, threatening to hit him with it. "You were injured!" he yelled, "you died in my arms!"

Phil got up, gingerly balancing on his injured leg, then showing Andrew how his good one barely bared the weight. Shifting his body to show he had bruises on his stomach, he winched as a flash of pain shot up his leg from the motion.

Andrew's brows knitted in concern, though he hadn't lowered his crutch an inch. "What do you remember?" he asked him, "and don't leave out any details."

"Well, when I woke up an hour or two ago, the pain in my body had all but disappeared, and—"

"Before that," Andrew commanded, beginning to have doubts about what was real, and what wasn't.

*What if I shapeshifted into him? What if this is a delusion from my own unnatural abilities?*

"Andy," Phil said, shaking his head, "what the bloody hell's gotten into you? You asked me that same question *literally* two hours ago."

Andrew slowly lowered his crutch, eyeing him suspiciously. "So... you do have a concussion, and you don't remember what happened after killing my sister?"

"Andy, did you hit your head?" He came a little closer, which made Andrew back away from him even further. "I didn't hit my head. The thing threw me against the rock, yes, but I landed on my leg after my ribs were the first to meet the rock. I assure you I never had a concussion to begin with."

Andrew trailed off, looking questioningly at him. *Did I... suffocate? How much oxygen did I lose when that thing was on top of me?*

"Andy?" Phil looked concerned at him, then down at Andrew's feet. The suspicious greenish-black stain on his well-worn shoes and torn trousers were all that was left of the evidence that Andrew had been crushed by the thing. "Look, we buried the body, or carcass, corpse, or whatever the bloody hell it was, 'cause that dark, bloody ichor that dripped from all the entries and exits of its body stank like rotten flesh. But yes, that *really* happened."

Andrew's head began to spin. Rubbing his temples, he took a deep breath. "Maybe I'm just... hallucinating a bunch. I—" He held his hand to his forehead, getting up, ignoring the pain flaring in his leg. "I keep seeing things that aren't real and now I'm not sure what's *real* and what's *not*."

"What's going on with you?" Phil asked, "you're scaring me."

Andrew began to make anguished noises, sinking down to crouch on the ground. "It's... it's my head, it's..."

Screaming in pain, Phil hopscotched over to him, grabbing his arms. "Andy!" He gently shook him, watching as he slowly came to from whatever headache he was having. "Andy?"

Andrew slowly looked up at him with watery, fearful eyes. "They're getting worse...'"

"What... you're not referring to your so-called *shapeshift abilities* again, right?"

Andrew made eye contact, having a sincere look on his face. "Phil, I'm a shapeshifter whether you like that or not. I'm not lying to you." He sighed. "I think... I think my shapeshifting abilities have awakened psychic abilities 'cause now I keep having these headaches and vivid dreams and I can't separate what's true from what the future's trying to tell me or what the past should've looked like but has been changed somehow due to choices I've made and—"

"Andy!" Andrew looked up at him in shock. "Please, take a breath. You're talking non-stop and I really think you should lie down. You might have an actual concussion or oxygen deficiency and I just—"

"You don't get it!" Andrew yelled, crying softly. "I'm now having those attacks when I'm awake and those visions, or whatever they are, they're getting more intense and more painful and… and from everything that I've experienced I dunno what's true and what's not. You *died* in my arms, Phil. I sobbed over your lifeless body and the next minute you're awake but have this concussion and no memory whatsoever. Before that, before all the bloody crap went down, you told us about knowing what that thing was and how you originally came into contact with it and then when I thought you were dead you told us some very sinister plans with those things and now you're—"

Phil met him with a sensuous kiss, stopping him from continuously rambling on without taking a much-needed breath. Even though Andrew wanted to think about his nightmare and the goodbye kiss he had given Phil, he couldn't think about anything but the smokey taste that mingled in his mouth.

Before it would get out of hand and their tongues would accidentally get pressed together, Andrew moved away from the kiss, staring at Phil in utter disbelief.

"What? I had to think of something to get you to stop straining your vocal cords," Phil said, gently pulling Andrew into his arms, comforting him.

The nearness, the presence of being in Phil's arms made his skin penetrate, speeding his pulse, but the caressing head rub washed the desire away. Replaced by a gentle calmness, he finally relaxed.

"Phil, what's true?" he asked him, his voice uncharacteristically hesitant. "I… I've completely lost the ability to think straight and separate reality from… from fiction."

Phil looked up at Theo sleeping soundly, sighing softly. Even though he tried to deny it, their heightened bond awakened his ability to feel Andrew's confusion.

"Please, just… give me the truth. I don't want any sugar-coated answers."

Phil sighed, nodding slowly. "When you were trapped beneath that… *thing*, the wind got knocked outta me. I couldn't move. I saw Theo rushing over to you, trying to pull you out from under the dead weight. He lay on his stomach and offered you his hand—the only thing visible from where you were." He pointed at the huge pile of ooze on the ground. "That... *snot* dangled over his head, and it was the same kinda snot *you* were covered in."

"I was... *covered in it?*"

"Yeah, you uh..." He swallowed. "I shouldn't get ahead of myself, otherwise it's not coherent enough to understand." He cleared his throat. "Anyway, he reached with his hand and grabbed your wrist, though you didn't grab his in return. Waiting before he started to pull, we both thought you were... that you were a goner. I've never seen a face get so red as his did as he tried to pull you out, inch by inch."

"So, he... *he's* the reason I got out? *Theo* saved me?"

"Not entirely, no."

He was afraid of where this was going, his suspicion grew by the second.

"As soon as you were close enough to be pulled free, I crawled closer and grabbed your other hand, pulling you the rest of the way out."

"But it wasn't me that came out, right?"

Phil shook his head awkwardly, nodding. "You were *one of 'em.*"

# CHAPTER ELEVEN

"They did *what*?" Maddie circled the room, her arms crossed. "I can't believe they'd do that to him…"

Sam sighed softly, sipping his coffee. "I need something stronger than this."

Giving him an unsatisfied side eye, he apologised for making that remark.

"So… what do we do now? How do we get him and the others out?"

He looked up at her, a surprised look shown on his face. "I thought you didn't want anything to do with this. That you didn't wanna do anything dangerous that could possibly take our son away from us."

She whisked a paper away from the table, stowing it in a map. Having her back turned to him, he just stared at her, examining her non-verbal communication. When she turned her attention back to him, she had a knowing, determined glint in her eye.

"I don't like that look. I don't like that look one bloody bit."

"You taught me that we rescue our friends, no matter the consequences. Well, I believe Josh needs saving."

"What do you wanna do? Go in there guns blazing? Whoever's in charge of that prison, it *isn't* Henry. I think he's being played."

"Like a mole? Someone on the inside?"

He nodded. "I swear the air in the presidential setting became more and more stifling when those new people came in. I remember Henry had no idea who they were as he hadn't hired 'em. But I'll never forget this smirk on that one lady."

"Did it look like a betraying smirk?"

He chuckled softly. "How the bloody hell would I know what that looks like?"

"You know, like a malicious, unpleasant smirk. Kinda like someone's mocking you, or it could even be an intimidating half-smile."

Thinking back to the preliminary meeting in which Henry had laid out his plan for the city, he was too worked up to realise the way the personal assistant Olivia had looked at Henry. His eyes widened as the implication of her words began to sink in, looking pensive. "I think… I think *Olivia* might be the traitor."

"Hold up, Olivia as in Olivia who acted as my midwife when I went into labour? No, it can't be her. That's impossible."

She wanted to walk past him, but he put his hand on her shoulder, holding her back. "I don't want her to be the culprit any more than you do, but maybe she's part of something bigger. She doesn't have to be *the* mastermind behind it all, but we can't exclude her either as a possible pawn. Everyone we don't trust is a suspect."

She sighed, nodding slowly. "You're gonna have to kill her if she is, right?"

"I'm... afraid so, yeah." Her hands balled into fists, her heart stammering unsteadily. He took her fists in his hands. "I know she's your friend, and I hope it doesn't have to come to this. But if it does..."

"I won't blame you." Her eyes were rimmed with tears, her voice sounded iron. "Just... do it."

He gently rested his forehead against hers. "I'm sorry."

"Just... go, please. Get the job done and come back home in one piece." Running her fingers through his hair, she planted her pillowy, smooth, almost velvety lips on Sam's. Inhaling together, he felt her breath tickling his nose softly. "Don't you dare not come home."

He nodded slowly. "I wouldn't dream of it." Pulling away, he planted a soft kiss on her forehead.

Heading over to the basement, he looked over his shoulder as the tears rolled down her cheeks, then headed down the stairs.

Packing up his pocketknife, tranquiliser gun and small handgun, and a few other items, he sighed deeply.

*And here I thought I had finally managed to leave my Trooper life behind me. Guess I jinxed myself.*

Hearing the doorbell, he swung his bag over his shoulder, heading downstairs. Sam smiled as he looked at Seb strolling inside after Maddie opened the door for him.

"If it isn't Sam the man," Seb said, walking over to Sam. Embracing him tightly, Sam chuckled.

"How did you know where I was?"

"Oh, please, I sensed you were standing right here. As a matter of fact, I'm tuned in to your presence, and you are to me. And you can't deny that."

Sam let go of him, shaking his head. "No, you're right, I can't. But mate, you've got no idea how much I've missed you."

Seb nodded, walking over to Maddie to hug her next. "I was about to say, you don't turn to face me and forget I exist?"

He laughed loudly. "Ouch. I thought I was the one making such remarks and not the gentle lady of the boss."

She patted his chest playfully. "Well, it's good to know I've been keeping company with a mob boss and the like. Kinda caters to the whole exotic and erotic needs."

Seb's raucous laughter echoed through the room, shaking his head. "Bloody hell, you would've been a perfect fit for me with remarks like that."

"I don't think it would've worked, 'cause dots on my nipples serving as braille? I bet they'd read something very narcissistic and sexist."

"Bloody hell, you're on fire today," Seb said, unable to see Sam's mouth which had fallen open. "Uh, Sam, I think your hole stands open. I can hear you breathe differently."

Sam closed his mouth, turning red like a tomato. Even though he knew these were her nerves taking over, it was still quite shocking to hear those words leave her mostly purified mouth. Even though she had just been joking, she knew how grave the situation was. He felt her heady fear pulsing across their unified bond, sighing solemnly.

"I'll see you soon, both of you," he said, looking over at Zack playing in the backroom. "I love you."

"I love you too."

He dropped his mouth to hers for a searing kiss, his heart giving a leaden thump once she pulled away. Touching her cheek gently, she nodded. He wiped away her tear and walked over to his son who was playing with a toy soldier.

"Daddy!" he said enthusiastically, holding out his tiny arms to Sam, indicating he wanted to be picked up.

Sam bended over and lifted his son in his arms, smiling as he watched his son showing him the toy soldier in front of his eyes. He took it from him, trying his best not to get emotional or show how much fear he had creeping up inside of him. "This is a soldier, and what are soldiers?"

"*Heroes!*" Zack answered, giggling cutely.

He nodded, smiling proudly. "Exactly, *heroes*. And right now, your daddy's gotta be a hero," he said, swallowing the lump building up in his throat away. "What that means is that I must leave to do a very important job—a critically important job for the protection of our tiny city, to keep you safe."

Zack nodded slowly, throwing his tiny arms around Sam's neck, which made Sam tear up. "Back soon?" he asked hopeful.

*I can't make promises I can't keep... I can't... I dunno when I'll be back. Once we've rescued Josh, we gotta find the others and... crap, it might take more than a few months to get all this done. I can't lie to him, but I also can't tell the truth...*

"Daddy?" Zack stopped hugging him, awaiting an answer to his question.

Sam cleared his throat, taking a deep breath. "Don't worry, kid, daddy will be home in a few months." *No! I said... ugh, forget what I said.* "No matter what, I love you, and I'm gonna do everything I can to keep you and mummy safe."

Zack seemed to understand the brevity of the message, showering Sam with extra hugs and kisses, which made saying goodbye ten times harder. He tried to speak, but the first word that came out of his mouth was barely audible as his voice cracked.

Maddie walked over to them, putting a hand on both her son and boyfriend. "Don't worry, Zack, daddy will call us every day to let us know that he's doing okay. And you'll see his face each time he calls thanks to Uncle Tim."

Zack nodded slowly, giving Sam one last hug before he continued playing, going back into his fantasy world. Maddie took Sam out of the room as a car approached their house. Looking out of the window, they watched as Stan and Alex jumped out of the car, Tim following closely behind them in his own car.

As the door opened, they watched Seb hugging the three of them.

*I had hoped our reunion wouldn't have been under such... dire circumstances. Why can't it just be sunshine and happiness? Just for once...*

They didn't seem to notice Sam was there, and as he raised his voice slightly, everyone slowly turned to look at him. The room was silent, save the inaudible brabbling of Zack coming from the next room. Taking a deep breath, Sam stepped forward to address the room.

"I know we all left the life behind us, but we must be the source of hope for Josh, for the citizens who still seek freedom from the terrorising past that haunts 'em. They deserve, well, salvation, if you wanna name it that way. And whoever these new people are, whatever they're doing to Josh, we can't allow 'em to interfere with the city we've rebuild, the homes and lives we've changed. A lot of the citizens are new, immigrated here on behalf of the presidential campaign, wanting to discover more about the city, live in it.

They're pursuing what many of us take and should've taken for granted, and the opposing side had to overcome the hardships to walk this new path. Outta every one of us, *Josh* has been there to guide 'em. So, for him, for his and our new friends, for our future and of their future children, we shall do everything in our power to save Josh, to recreate peace and even prosperity for those who were taken along with Josh. And those ruled by greed, threatening the peace, those *won't* be welcome here and must be eliminated. We'll stand at the forefront of saving the peace and stability in our city, and so we shall lighten the path to freedom, for Josh, his fellow men, the people stuck on those islands, and for *ourselves*."

      They put their thumb against their middle finger, their index and ring finger on top of their middle finger, holding their hand backwards, their knuckles aiming at the floor. Raising their hand high in the air, they did their Trooper sign. The sign of *never-ending victory*.

# CHAPTER TWELVE

Andrew looked at his arms, the blisters still present. When his sister touched him, still in the preliminary stage of whatever kind of disease she was carrying, she infected him, which had been worsened by the creature crushing him.

"What happens now? With me, I mean? What did you do to... *cure* me?"

"Nothing." Phil looked over at him. "Whatever... anatomy you've got going on, it *protected* you. At least from the infection spreading significantly further."

Looking over at Theo, Andrew sighed. "And mister afraid-of-germs over there, doesn't he wanna exterminate me?"

Phil laughed a little harder than he wanted to, shaking his head. "Nah, he's fine. You can't infect us. We've both touched you while you were under."

Andrew ducked his head; a light blush heated his cheeks. *Bloody hell, what have they done while I was out? Did they... wash me?*

"Mate, you should see your face right about now, it's as red as a tomato."

Andrew gave a chagrined little half-laugh, but his pride was assuaged by the sparkle in Phil's eyes.

"Get off me!" they heard before they saw what was going on. Andrew's sister was on top of Theo, snarling at him. She had regressed into an even more animalistic state, her eyes bloodshot, her veins still as black as before.

Andrew froze in his tracks as if her ferocious instinct had seized him by the heart. Standing face to face with his sister, who he had buried only a few hours earlier, was now squeezing the life out of Theo in a murderous rage.

Phil took the spear they used for fishing, running up to Theo. Her arm hit him in the stomach, sending him flying backwards like a ragdoll.

Her bloodshot eyes lowed eerily in the low light of the fire, churning his stomach just as much as the first time he saw her like this, moments before she tried to kill him in the same fit.

"Andy! Call her by her name!" Phil yelled, groaning.

But Andrew didn't hear Phil. He stared at her, awestruck. Her gaze remained locked on his; her eyes burning into him.

"Minnie..." He finally looked at Theo, who was only seconds away from succumbing to her sociopathic behaviour. "Take *me* instead."

She didn't stop choking Theo, her eyes fixated on his. "You carry the virus... I don't attack my own people."

"She's not your sister anymore!" Phil tried frantically. "She just admitted it! Andy, please, do something!"

Looking at the spear Phil had tried to attack her with, Andrew looked back at her as she sank her teeth into his jugular, ripping through his tendons.

"No!"

Both Phil's and Theo's screams died in their throats. Andrew grabbed the spear, watching in pure fear as she gnawed on a piece of Theo's flesh. His blood formed a pool beneath his head.

He started to back away, hand halfway to the spear. She slowly stopped chewing, spitting out the last remaining skin. Turning around to face Andrew, her arms hung by her sides, making no move to strike. Her mouth was covered in blood.

"How are you alive?" he asked her, tears welling up in his eyes. "What happened to you?"

"I fed off the earth I was buried under. Dead insects, dead plants, everything that's dead is food to still my hunger, to satiate the virus."

"What kinda virus is it? How does it spread?"

She licked her lips, removing a piece of skin from her teeth. "It's aerosolised."

"To spread infection throughout a population more expediently..."

Nodding softly, she growled lowly. "When my hunger is stilled... you have nothing to worry about. I won't hurt you."

The first tears rolled down his cheeks, shaking his head. "Who did this to you? Who gave you this virus?"

"Whenever someone wants you to do something they consider wrong, they claim it's simply reality, but—"

Feeling the spear slip from his hand, he watched as Phil stabbed the needle-sharp spear point through her brain, out of the top of her skull. The fluid resembling blood that fell from the spear point was a tinged, slightly green. Jerking the weapon free, she toppled onto the grass.

Staring at her lifeless body a second time made Andrew let out a howling cry, sinking to his knees as he stared at both his sister's body and Theo's. He felt Phil's arms around him, holding him on the ground, crying until he couldn't see the path for the tears.

Having packed their stuff in a hurry, they had no time to bury Theo. Afraid his sister would come back a third time made Phil command Andrew to simply leave it all behind and pack necessities. Pooling together the last of their resources, he looked at both bodies one final time before following Phil up the mountain the cave was located in.

"I'm sorry."

Phil stopped in his tracks ascending the rocky path, looking behind him at Andrew who struggled to keep walking with his injured leg. "You can be sorry once we reach safety. Come on, we're almost there."

Phil ignored his own injury, climbing as quickly as he could to lose their scent. He knew they needed soap containing enzymes to fully hide their body odour, but moving as fast as possible was the only kind of enzyme they had at their disposal.

Having broken the spear, Phil held the makeshift knife in his left hand, looking over his shoulder at Andrew using the one remaining intact spear as a means of moving forward.

"We're almost there," Phil said reassuringly.

"Is it a good idea to head back to the place she first attacked me? Isn't my scent, and yours, all over that place?"

"It's the only place I know on this side of the island where we're dry and high. It's a risk I'm afraid we're gonna take."

"You really think she's... *not* dead?"

"I dunno what to think. Whatever the bloody hell that virus is she was talking about, it's not just aerosolised. It's airborne, it's blood-borne, it's infectious in every way possible. It's the worst kind I've ever come across."

"But if it's airborne, you're not infected. And neither was Theo."

"Airborne diseases can only be spread by small respiratory droplets. Like saliva, sweat, snot, that sorta thing. It's not necessarily an air thing." Reaching the top of the mountain, Phil used a makeshift torch to shine around the cave, looking over his shoulder at Andrew. "It seems safe. We should set up camp for tonight and move on at dawn."

"To where?"

"A safer place. There's gotta be more on this island than meets the eye. Even Theo and I never got around to scoping out the whole—"

Someone, or *something*, attacked Phil from the left, hitting the ground hard. The knife he was holding slid towards the edge, teetering on the steep drop-off. Watching as Amelia now tried to kill Phil, he tiptoed backwards towards the knife. Almost reaching it, it began to wobble and tipped over the edge.

Diving towards the falling knife, he slid on his stomach over the edge, his injured leg making it impossible to hold any kind of grip. Securing the knife in his hands, his body dangled off the edge.

Feeling someone hugging his feet, keeping him from falling, he turned around to watch Amelia holding onto him for dear life. Phil gasped for air behind her, clutching his throat.

"You saved me…" He secured the knife to his person, looking over his shoulder at her.

Amelia's bloodshot eyes turned human for a second, a tear rolling down her cheek. "You're still my little brother. I'll never let anything bad happen to you."

Staring in her amber eyes, he smiled softly. "Minnie, I forgive you. For *everything*."

She remained quiet, closing her eyes to fight her instincts flaring up.

Panic began to overtake his body as his legs were aching. To his terrified mind, every tiny slip was an inch closer to the shadow of death, the crouching monster awaiting him down below.

He watched as the glint of light shone in her eyes; the gusts of wind blew her hair like beautiful angelic wings.

"Come back to me," he pleaded, "I can't lose *you* too."

She looked over at Phil who stared at both, then back at Andrew with a soft smile. "I'll always be here," she said, pointing at her heart, "and I'll never leave you." She gave Phil a nod towards Andrew's legs.

As she began to loosen her grip, Phil dove towards Andrew, gripping them tightly. Both watched as she moved closer to the edge, her heels tiptoeing at the very end.

"Minnie, no!"

She spread her arms with an almost serene look on her face. A low scream escaped her throat, feeling her body tensing less, enough to be able to think more clearly with a tranquil mind, no longer controlled by emotions.

"It's better this way," she said, locking eyes with Andrew who tried desperately to move back to stop her. "*I love you.*"

His voice echoed across the whole island as he screamed her name, feeling a concussive shock reverberating through his body. Phil clasped his hands as tightly as he possibly could around his legs, feeling he was slipping as he tried to reach out to Amelia.

Her body became smaller and smaller, until there was nothing left to see.

He took a deep, shuddering breath. All the adrenaline and pain fell away as something else began to take its place; the terrorising realisation that *no one*, not even a mutated infected, would survive a fall like that.

Phil tucked at his legs with all his might, until he managed to get Andrew to safety. He scrambled to the edge of the abyss, poking his head over to double-check if she was truly gone. There was no sign of her in the emptiness that stretched below him.

Andrew took a step backwards, only for his knees to buckle. His last ounce of strength disappeared. Phil caught him, wrapping a sturdy arm around his waist, helping him down to the ground.

Curled into a ball on the ground, burying his head in Phil's chest, the tears finally came, no shred of self-control left in him as he sobbed and thrashed, dissolving into hysterics.

# CHAPTER THIRTEEN

In the middle of the forest stood a cement bunker, surrounded by a barbed wire fence. Hiding in the nearby bushes, Tim worked on deactivating the numerous security cameras hanging around the area.

"How are we looking?" Sam asked, looking through his binoculars.

"I'm almost done."

Sam raised his hand in the air. The others emerged, trotting under cover towards them. He pointed up to a sign, high up on the fence.

**Security notice. Building is property of RALPH.**

Beneath it, a smaller, faded, and filthy sign remained, still legible despite the grime.

**Authorised personnel only. Keep out.**

Protruding from one of the walls of the prison, visible through the barbed wire fence, were machinery that weren't authorised by Sam nor Henry. It almost looked like a giant logging spider of an industrial drill.

"We gotta look out for those. If they spot us and run us over... there's no coming back from that," Tim said, deactivating the last camera.

"No shite, sherlock," Stan replied, rolling his eyes.

Looking at the machine beyond the fence, Sam searched for any obvious big red buttons or anything that would potentially dismantle it, but there was nothing.

"Your ID works, correct?" Tim asked, searching the nearest open entrance via the 3D blueprints in front of him. "If it does, we can enter that door with your clearance." Pointing at the one most south, Sam nodded. "Once we're close, and inside, we gotta find the locker room, dress up to blend in while Sam gets us through all the doors."

"Seb, you stay here with Tim, communicate with us everything that's happening outside *and* inside," Sam told him.

"Got it."

"Alex and Stan, you're with me. Once we're inside, we take an immediate right turn, then the second door on our left to get you two dressed. We won't have much time. Once I'm logging in, they can see where we logged in from."

"Understood."

Sneaking towards the fence, Sam scrabbled for a handhold, ripping and tearing at the metal post and the surrounding chain link. Creating a gap big enough for them to squeeze through, the fence creaked, revealing a hidden wire behind the bars. Looking over his shoulder, Tim nodded, deactivating the electrified wire.

*"All magnetic waves are disabled."*

"Now," Sam said, holding the fence up to let Alex go through first. Stan followed suit, holding the fence for Sam.

"Bird."

Looking up, they saw a silent-motored helicopter circling the area. Sam quickly climbed through, staying low as they sneaked over to the backdoor. Following the search light's movements, they gave a thumbs up to Tim that they were safely positioned.

Sam got up, planting his finger on the scanner.

*"Welcome, Bráthair."*

Receiving confused glances from both Alex and Stan, Sam shrugged, indicating this wasn't the time to explain. Heading inside, Sam crushed himself against the wall, looking past the corner into the hallway.

"Clear."

Walking at a quick pace, they stopped in front of the locker room. Sam planted a tiny device on the door, activating it once it was secured in place.

*"Scanning for movement. Stay clear."*

They took a step back as Tim worked on his laptop, typing in code.

*"Clear. Proceed."*

Sam removed the device, opening the door. Alex and Stan took two guard outfits, getting dressed in a matter of seconds. Nodding at Sam, they put their masks and helmets on, taking their rifle gun out of their bag.

Sam's eye fell on a little black book. Walking over to it, he skimmed through the pages. "I see names, meeting dates, even IRC logs."

"IR-what?" Alex asked, receiving an annoyed eyeroll from Sam.

"Stands for Internet Relay Chat. Basically, enabling chats and collaborations, a network of internet servers that some groups use as protocol."

"Thank you, Tim," Sam said, sighing. "I recognise a disconcerting number of these names. Most are dead, but some belong to those who're over the hill."

"Tommy incoming."

"Copy that."

They all went silent, mulling over how best to proceed. Hearing the footsteps walking past the locker room, Sam opened the door slightly, peeking through the tiny opening. Moving his hand to indicate they should move, they quickly walked towards the sealed-off door.

Putting his finger on the glass, they heard heavy footsteps behind them.

"Brace yourselves. Dead incoming."

"Sam? What brings you here?"

Hearing Henry's voice, Sam slowly turned around. "Paying a visit to... *our project*."

Henry gave him a confused look, though Sam's eyes darted back and forth between him and the two *disguised* guards next to him.

"I see. Well, we still have that appointment scheduled afterwards, don't we?"

"Yes, sir. I'll be there."

Henry gave him a nod, then patted his shoulder. Leaning closer, he whispered in his ear. *"Get proof, whatever it is you're after."*

Sam nodded, then patted Henry on his back. Watching as Henry left them be, followed closely by two guards, Sam turned around to retry opening the heavily fortified electronic door.

Finding themselves at the bottom of a long stairwell, Sam closed the door behind them, destroying the electronic keypad from their side after unscrewing the panel where Tim said the wires would be.

Cutting the green one, then the red one, he got the clear the system was deactivated.

Hurrying down the stairs quick and quiet, they heard the door slam open below them as soon as they had descended the second flight. Footsteps pounded up the first flight of stairs at the bottom.

Having nowhere to hide, they continued their descent, meeting the two guards running up the stairs.

"You two, we have a security breach. We need you on stag downstairs."

"Yes, sir," Stan said as confidently as possible. The two guards nodded, leaving the three be. He let out a deep breath, shaking his head. "That was *way* too close."

Sam nodded to Stan's reply, pointing at the bottom. "Just three more flights and we're there."

"Isn't it weird that it's all going so easy?" Alex asked sceptically, holding his rifle with sweaty hands. "It's like they don't even care we're down here."

"Don't jinx us," Stan replied, holding his boyfriend's hand. "Getting *in* is easy. Getting *out* is a whole different story."

Alex's nerves increased, but neither of them had time to talk that down when they heard a prisoner scream.

"Help! I need help!"

Rushing down the last flights of stairs, they burst in through the door. Alex and Stan gasped at the sight of the emaciated prisoners. Some were hooked up to machines, others to tubes, and it wasn't something Sam could recall when he was here only a day ago.

Struggling to put it together, Stan rushed over to Josh's holding cell, watching as Josh was seizing on the floor, the tube he was hooked to protruding from his right arm.

"Are they giving 'em something or trying to take something from 'em?" Alex asked softly, watching as Stan desperately tried to open the cell.

"They're next," Sam said, almost in a whisper.

"Next for what?"

"To be send away. To go *missing*."

Sam finally found the strength to rush to Stan's aid, throwing his shoulder into the cell's door.

"Why's everything in this bloody hell hole activated by technology, but not these bloody doors?" Stan asked, grunting with effort.

"Guess if there's a security breach like the one we caused, at least the prisoners can't escape."

Falling into a crouch as a shotgun blasted through the air, so close Sam could smell the burning gunpowder, he turned around to look at Seb.

"What? Figured you lads could use a little help."

"How the... you know what, never mind." Sam had every right to be mad at Seb for almost blowing their heads off, but at least he got the job done. Rushing to Josh's side, Sam removed the tube from his arm, then took off his jacket. Folding it up, he placed it beneath Josh's head.

"What if we're already too late? What if the stuff they've given him has already begun to change him like it did two years ago?"

Sam eyed Stan for a second, shaking his head. "Let's not think that far ahead. Maybe we're on time. Maybe this is his body responding to whatever the bloody hell that liquid is. We'll take it back so Tim can sample it."

Stan nodded, turning Josh gently to one side to help him breathe, knowing no other touches were allowed until he would come back to his senses.

"Josh, can you hear me?" Sam tried calmly, timing how long the seizure had been going on since the second someone screamed help. "Go help Alex and Seb free the others, I've got him."

Stan nodded, joining Alex and Seb who had been blasting the other doors to get them open.

"Josh, it's me, it's Sam," he said, gently touching his forehead. "We're here to save you. But to do that, you gotta fight whatever you've got running through your veins right now. I need you to open your bloody eyes and be okay. We've lost too many friends in the past two years, and I won't let you become one of 'em. So, open those bloody eyes of yours or so help me."

*"We got someone injured?"* Tim asked, having listened in.

"Yeah, it's Josh, he's seizing. It's been going on for two minutes already."

Loosening Josh's prison outfit, he looked over at Alex and Stan guiding the other prisoners upstairs.

Seb joined Sam. "Nothing in his mouth?"

"No, not that I can see."

Seb nodded, gently feeling his throat. "There's nothing stuck down there, not that I can feel."

"Come on Josh, come back to us," Sam pleaded, watching as he kept seizing.

The door got thrown open and two guards in full gear stepped inside. One guard hauled Sam onto his feet, gripping his shoulder hard enough to bruise as he shoved him forward.

"It was a big mistake coming back here without official clearance." Sam watched as they marched Seb up the stairs out into the hallway.

One of the guards wasn't wearing a helmet but was still wearing his mask to hide his identity. Seeing the glasses he was wearing, Sam slammed a punch right into his face, the bridge of his glasses snapping as his knuckles connected with his nose.

The other guard sprang into action, dragging Sam back. The skin below the guard's eye was already turning a deep shade of purple.

"Why are you Troopers always so *reliant* on violence?" he asked, wiping the trail of blood from his nose with the back of his hand, his furious scowl deepening as he smeared it beneath his nose and across his upper lip. Stalking up to Sam, he seized his chin, forcing him to look up as he tightened his grip. "You and your *accomplices* may have managed to free the others, but the three of you'll *never* see daylight again. *That*, I promise." He patted Sam's cheek condescendingly before kicking his legs out from under him, sending him crashing to his knees.

The other moved to flank him as he stepped forward, drawing his gun, keeping it trained on Sam. Raising the gun to his temple, he pressed the cold barrel against his skin.

Sam's heart hammered in his chest. His hand moved down to his pocket, but the guard caught him doing so. "Oi! Hands where I can see 'em!"

Sam slowly moved his hands above his head, hearing more footsteps coming from above. Two more guards entered the cellblock, gathering under the watchful eye of the one aiming his gun at Sam, holding machine guns to shoot him to bits if he would try anything funny.

Looking past the two guards who had just entered the room, he spotted Seb at the back in the doorway. As soon as he realised who the two guards were, they made a rush forward, attacking the guard holding Sam at gunpoint.

Sam surged to his feet and grabbed the knife from his belt, swinging it at the side of the guard's head. Even though the guard caught his arm, the blade teared across his face from his temple to his jaw. Crashing to the floor, Sam took another swing, stabbing the blade right into his shoulder. Before ripping it out, he lodged it deep into his flesh, tossing it to the side.

Watching as Stan and Alex struggled to take the gun from the guard without having to shoot him, Sam fired a shot in the air, ceasing the fighting. Everyone turned to see the guard's body on the floor. The guard still standing bolted for the door, where Seb stood ready to stop him.

Aiming his gun at him, the guard raised his hands above his head, and was guided into one of the now empty, still operational cells, along with the guard clutching his shoulder.

Closing the door and locking it tightly, Alex and Stan lifted Josh, who had finally stopped seizing.

"Careful with him," Sam said, watching as they took Josh away. Looking at Seb, he patted his shoulder. "The guard who took you away, what happened to him?"

"Sleeping soundly."

He chuckled, shaking his head. "At least none of us got hurt for a change. I call that a *win*."

Seb nodded, putting an arm around Sam. "I'll drink to that."

Guiding Seb out of the prison, they headed back to the surface to reunite with the others.

# CHAPTER FOURTEEN

Stumbling along the overgrown path, Andrew trailed Phil, who led the way to the river's edge. Watching the burbling water flow downstream, Phil turned around to look at Andrew. "We're making progress. If we follow the stream, it should lead us to the other side of the island, where we can set up a new camp."

Andrew didn't say anything, looking battered and exhausted.

Phil paused just ahead, carefully observing the forked trail. Andrew didn't realise he had stopped walking as he proceeded through the underbrush, his mind wandering, thinking over the events of the last two hours. His foot caught on an exposed root, stumbling forward.

Phil wanted to catch him in case he would fall, but Andrew shoved him away. He sat on one of the large boulders at the water's edge, his shoulders slumped in defeat.

Phil kneeled in front of him. "I can't even begin to understand the feeling of losing someone like that, but she'd want you to move on, Andy." His voice was steady, unwavering. Looking over his shoulder at the sunset, he sighed.

"No, you can't!" Andrew yelled, spatting in his face, "nobody can!"

Phil whirled to face Andrew, confused to find rage etched into his features.

The rage and anguish overcame him, staring Phil dead in the face. "This... how am I supposed to sleep at night knowing I'm irreparably damaged 'cause I've lost the one last person I truly loved in my life?"

"Andy..."

"No! No! I'll die alone due to my inability to accept loss and find new ways of loving someone 'cause I've got feelings for you, but I can't 'cause I've just lost my sister, and it wouldn't be fair to just find a replacement for the love I've *just* lost!"

It felt like a punch to the gullet, almost, but just as quickly as his hair-rigger rage flared up without warning, it visibly deflated, his anger washing away as if it had never existed.

Even though Andrew had threateningly waded into Phil, he didn't blame him.

"Come," Phil said, giving Andrew his hand to grab. "we'll set up camp here for the night so you can rest. We've done enough trekking for today."

"We've only been walking for two bloody hours," Andrew spat, watching as Phil collected some fresh water from the river.

"Right, let me rephrase that. We've had enough *excitement* for one day." He looked at the sun, sighing softly. "One problem though. With the sun that low, our best bet is a friction fire." Receiving a lifted eyebrow from Andrew, he chuckled. "Unless you've got flint on you."

He shook his head, observing Phil wrapping a frayed piece of rope around a small stick he had found. Understanding what he was doing, Andrew came a little closer, watching as he sandwiched the roped stick between two quickly carved out pieces of wood.

Phil pulled, and Andrew gave slack, doing the opposite when Phil gave slack. The wood started to smoke. Both leaned down to blow on the faint spark, their foreheads nearly touching as the kindling ignited.

Realising how close they were, Andrew moved away. Phil looked disappointed, but tried to hide it, stoking the fire into a small inferno.

"Andy," he said, looking over at him. "If you're afraid of losing me 'cause you've lost those close to you, that's not gonna happen. I won't *ever* leave you. I promise."

Andrew scoffed, shaking his head. "Don't promise something like that. That always ends bad."

"I know, but a promise sounds a hell of a lot more worth fighting for."

Andrew met his eyes. Phil's hand landed on his knee, making Andrew's gasp sound like a soft mewl. Coaxing his mouth open in doing so, Phil claimed it in a hard, penetrating kiss.

Rising to meet his kiss with equal ardour, Andrew gave in, not wanting a scrap of fabric or breath of air serving as a separation boundary. Pulling Phil flush with his own body, he lavished him with kisses in his neck.

Clothes were thrown all around the area, their shadows cast onto the nearest tree by the crackling fire.

Looking at the smoke billowing from the dying fire, Andrew slowly moved Phil's arm away from his waist. Walking over to his clothes, he dressed himself to collect more wood.

The smoke rose high in the sky above the tall peak of the tree. A part of him wished a ship would sail past and see the smoke, thinking it was a distress signal. Of course, no ship would sail here. From where they were before, in their first camp, he could see the choppy water and heavy mist surrounding the island, hiding sharp, jagged rocks for people out on the sea.

He imagined a boat bucking over the water, crashing into a rock, sinking before they could even reach them. The boat veered away from a series of grey spikes, sails whipping savagely.

Despite the helmsman's masterful manoeuvres around the obstacles, moving steadily forward, a gust of wind forcefully rammed into the ship, threatening to capsize it. Looking towards the horizon, which seemed strange to Andrew in the middle of the night, he saw the thick fog shift, revealing a massive rock directly in front of the ship's path.

Gasping, Andrew looked straight into the fire, his forehead covered in sweat.

*That felt real. That felt way too bloody real.*

Thinking back to Phil's death, which turned out to be a nightmare, he began to wonder if this was one too. If he was simply sleeping still. Pinching his own skin, he moaned softly. *That was real. Very bloody real. Was that a... premonition? No, no that doesn't exist. That's a fable, that's...*

A cloud passed overhead in the dark sky, weirdly enough too bright to be ignored. Trying not to think of it as a shadow of precognition, he focused on his breathing. Struggling to retain his calm, he took a huge gulp of the water Phil had collected only hours earlier.

Hearing frantic fumbling, Andrew turned sharply, looking over his right shoulder to Phil who was soundly asleep. Hearing it again, his breathing turned into a panicky, heavy heave, clenching his jaw to stop any potential sounds from escaping his mouth.

There was a grunt, a harsh and brutal sound that didn't sound human, followed by a click. Then *silence.*

Sitting in terse silence, he brushed aside the leaves of a frond to scan the area, taking in all the visceral details.

A primal shadow darted past. Before Andrew could see *who* or *what* it was, he struggled beneath a much stronger force, thrashing violently. Tearing a tiny chunk from his arm, he let out an agonising scream.

Phil shot up in an instant, racing towards his target. With a swift strike, he took down Andrew's attacker. They left Andrew bleeding in the dirt.

Looking over at Phil grappling with his attacker, he recognised her. "Minnie?"

For the third time in less than forty-eight hours, she had come back from the dead.

Without thinking twice, he grabbed one of his crutches and swung it, striking her in the head. Yanking Phil out from beneath her, both scrambled to their feet before taking off.

"How the bloody hell's this possible?" Phil shouted over his shoulder, trying to create as much distance between them as he possibly could.

"I dunno, but this isn't scientifically possible!"

As his feet brushed past scorched leaves, he felt a sudden jolt of electricity surging through him. It felt like a searing, breath-stealing burn that had his whole body in its grip.

"Andy!"

His presence felt distant as he lay on the ground, dazed. His skin and muscles were still buzzing with electricity. Phil tried to reach him but found himself being stopped by an invisible field that wasn't there minutes ago.

"What the..." He put his hands against it, unaffected by whatever kind of energetic force had electrocuted Andrew right in front of him. "How the bloody hell's that—"

He watched in horror as Minnie staggered over to Andrew, a fresh gash on her forehead. Staring down at her brother, she saw his angry red-purple burns, both chemical and electrical, and the chunk of his arm that was missing.

"Bloody hell..." She crouched beside him, having her humanity take over her animalistic tendencies once more.

Andrew tried to stay conscious as he observed her. Her skin had a frightening grey pallor, her bloodshot eyes and black veins unchanged.

"Lay still," she commanded, removing the contaminated clothing surrounding his wounds with her claws. She looked behind her for a second to examine the trail of blood he had left behind, then back at him. "Bloody hell... I did that..." She shook her head. "No, focus. Focus, Amelia. *Focus*." She breathed heavily, ignoring Phil's frantic cries to reach Andrew. "This is gonna hurt like bloody hell." She took the water bottle he had stuffed in his back pocket, flooding the affected area as best she could. "Tell me when the burning sensation stops," she said, her nurse-brain taking over her animalistic brain fully. For a second, it seemed as if she was *just* Amelia.

Phil fell through the invisible field, landing on the ground. He scrambled up, took a branch from the ground, and ran towards her.

"Don't," she said, holding her bloodied hand up to stop him, "you've got every right to kill me. *Again*. But let me help him. I'm *me*." She sighed. "I dunno for how long, so every second counts."

Phil wanted to believe her, but every bone in his body told him to strike her. But he *didn't*. He slowly lowered the branch, his face vacant and eyes full of tears. He fell to his knees beside Andrew, his hands clenched into fists leaning on his knees.

"Refill this," she commanded him, "we need a lot more."

Phil did as he was told, running back towards the river.

"I need you to hold on for me," she said, her voice harsh and raspy. "Please."

He could hardly choke out any words, his gut roiling with nausea as he looked her in the eyes. The wound on her head was bright against her papery skin, the blackened edges of the wound remnants of whatever kind of virus was pumping through her veins.

His eyelashes fluttered, his chest rose and fell shallowly with each breath he took.

"Don't you close your eyes on me," she said, tapping his cheek, "and don't you dare let one of those breaths be the last one to leave your lungs."

Phil returned with the water, giving it to her. She continued to flush the burns with water while Phil took Andrew's hand in his. He was clearly struggling against the unnatural, suffocating worry that gripped him like a cocoon. A tremor of unease rippled through him as he watched her douse him in water.

The world spun around Andrew in a nauseating blur. It took every scrap of willpower to focus on his breathing, and not on the wounds he had suffered.

Then it hit him.

"No... sensation..."

She took it as the sign to stop, quickly covering the visible burns loosely with a dry, clean pad she carried on her in her tiny medical fanny pack.

Trying to speak again, but not able to quite form words, he nodded with all the energy he had left in him. A nod that he was okay.

He was far from okay. Dizzily, he looked at Phil, then back at her. As the world blurred, he tried to focus on the situation, grasping feebly at whatever kind of reality he had left. Slipping through his fingers, it sent him adrift.

# CHAPTER FIFTEEN

Hooked to the ECG, Josh lay soundly asleep in the infirmary of the bunker, Tim standing next to him to observe his vitals.

Sam knocked on the door leading to the infirmary, hopeful for any signs of improvement, then walked inside.

"How's he doing?"

Tim didn't look up from the chart he held in his hands. "Well, the HUD motions his graphic features quite nicely," he said, pointing at the screen without looking up. "His heart rate and physiological responses have improved. Whatever they've done to him, it seems to be wearing off."

Yet, he looked worse than Sam anticipated. There was a touch of jaundice shown around his eyes, his skin ashen coloured. He walked over to the screen, observing the animated data relating to a human's anatomy. He didn't have much knowledge about the DNA shown on the screen, but did see his lungs and heart were improving, so was his brain.

"I still can't fathom the fact that you've built all this," he said, watching the full skeleton shown on the screen. "It's still fascinating, even after all these years."

"Yeah well," Tim said, finally putting the chart down," what can I say? I'll never say no to someone basking me in glory."

Sam rolled his eyes at him, then chuckled. "Don't let it get to your head, okay, Doctor *know-it-all*." He saw a blackish spot on the screen, pointing at it. "Is that...?"

"A chip designed to record his vitals as well as any potential feral data? I'm afraid so. They embedded it in his body only a few days ago, it's fairly new." He lifted his shirt. "See? The scar is fresh."

"Can we... take it back out?"

"Not yet, he needs his strength back first."

"And is there...?"

"A potential for him to hulk out on us and go feral? No. They didn't get to that stage yet." He pointed at the double helix. "He's clean. On the *inside*, at least."

Sam knew he was referring to his sickly skin colour, nodding slowly. "How far along are we with the plans to liberate our other kidnapped friends?"

Tim looked over at Sam, shaking his head. "Not far. We were so focused on rescuing Josh that we needed all the manpower for that operation."

Sam sighed. "Okay, so, we know that they've made a new serum, *Serum C*, and that they took both the Laeries and the REBELS to six islands spread out over an ocean we didn't even know the existence of." He was hoping Tim would add any kind of new information to that, but no words left the boy's mouth. "That's all we have?"

Tim nodded. "Afraid so."

"That's not entirely true," Seb said, walking inside. "Alex and Stan raided a few documents back at the prison." He gave them to Tim. Sam peeked over his shoulder.

"How the bloody hell does he plan to contain these chemical runoffs? He literally turned 'em into an airborne virus." He hasted towards his laptop, typing frantically.

"What does that mean? And please, English."

Tim gave Sam a side-eye, then sighed. "He has basically contaminated our entire ecosystem. What these are? They're weaponised viruses. *Way* worse than ours was."

"You mean that when he turned us into soldiers, that was mild in comparison with this?"

"Precisely." He shook his head. "That bright green runoff I saw close to the prison? A by-product of Serum C."

"Bright green—what?" *He never mentioned anything bright green... Did he?*

Tim sighed again, eyeing him. "Look, I can't spell out *everything* for you, okay? But what I can't even spell out for myself is how he's containing this so-called *control group* with an airborne virus like this. Why use syringes when it's gaseous?"

Finally, a lightbulb went off in Sam's mind. "The islands. It's literally nothing but nature. That's how he does it. Remember the fake weather they created in the Dome?"

"They're using the same kinda technique…" He typed something else. "So, those syringes they used on us were part of their initial tests… and now, they've devised a gassy type of it to reach an even bigger population."

"They're guinea pigs, and they're sitting ducks on those islands," Seb said, sitting down. "Whatever that virus is gonna do to 'em, we gotta reach 'em before it gets outta hand, find an antidote and destroy it all before he can infect the world."

Sam nodded, then looked over at Josh. "But we won't leave without him. We've almost lost him once. I won't let that happen a second time."

"Time is of the essence, right?" Seb said, getting back up. "We'll take him with us. Can we do that?" he asked, addressing Tim.

"Sure, yeah, I just need some help getting him set up in the Kite, but it's doable."

"Then let's get to work."

After transporting Josh to the Kite, Sam secured his belt in the room next to the landing platform, sighing to himself. He heard a knock on the door. Turning around, he saw Henry standing there. Before Henry could say a word, Sam handed him a letter.

"If anything happens to me, you make sure this reaches my family. No more lies and secrecy. You owe me this."

Henry sighed. "I didn't know what they were doing in the prison, Sam, you gotta believe me. I'll find out who's behind this, I promise you. You've got my word."

Sam shook his head. "Don't endanger yourself. The last thing we need is for you to die and our hierarchy destroyed, back to square one. Just lay low, stay outta sight, and we'll deal with it once we've brought our boys home safe and sound."

"Don't be a stranger, Sam, and don't end up becoming a martyr. Promise me."

Even though Sam was mad at him, he couldn't help but hug him, holding onto him for as long as he could.

"Be careful, please," Henry said. "You come back; you hear me?"

"I promise." He sniffled softly, and the small hatred he felt ebbed away like it had never been there in the first place. Henry had taken care of him like an adopted son, and Sam was thankful for that, more than he could ever possibly explain in words.

"Sam, we gotta go," he heard Tim say on the other side of the door, letting go of Henry.

Henry put his hand in Sam's neck, squeezing it for a second before nodding. Sam nodded back. He opened the door to join the others, taking a deep breath. *One last time. I'll be a hero one last time.*

Dusting off a locked case filled with flare guns, Sam looked over at Stan opening a can of baked beans. *I didn't miss the soldiers' rations. Still tastes as terrible as it did the first time.*

He put the case back next to the barrel of crowbars, his smile widening as he realised what this looked like. A typical scene in any type of action film where the hero must gear up and arm themselves to the teeth to win whatever kind of war—whether it's a battle for survival, justice, or revenge—against an enemy that's more dangerous than they could ever imagine.

*And here we are, throwing ourselves into the fray once more, right in the line of fire. I really must have some kinda death wish to do this again.*

"Weapons ready?" he heard Seb ask, joining him.

"Locked and loaded."

Seb said down next to him, sighing softly. "You know, the more I think about this, the more I believe we're expendable."

"You're joking, right?" Sam turned to face him. "We're not, Seb. *You're* not. Don't you think for one second that your blindness makes you a liability. You've adjusted beyond our expectations. Don't sell yourself short or I'll kill you dead."

Seb chuckled. "Meaning I can haunt your arse for eternity."

"Maybe you get your eyesight back as a ghost."

"Ouch. Low blow."

Both now chuckled. Sam shook his head. "I mean it, Seb. We *still* need you. And we'll *always* need you. We can't do any of this without you."

He blew a raspberry, shaking his head. "I swear feelings and friendships are convoluted."

"All right mister *doomsday*, go get some sleep."

"Only if you're coming to bed too, *hun*."

Sam punched his shoulder. "I think I threw up in my mouth, thanks."

"What can I say, someone's gotta keep the flirting alive."

"Yeah, yeah, all right. I swear you and Zach are alike sometimes."

He looked away, hoping Seb didn't hear the tremble in his voice. When he glanced back, Seb's face was uncharacteristically grave. He swore he saw a hint of sadness flash across Seb's face, but it vanished as quickly as it appeared.

"Just remember that even when times are difficult, our unity and perseverance will get us through the heartaches, just like it did back then," Seb said.

*Philosophical much? Who is this and what has he done to the Seb I know?*

"If Sergeant Lawrence was still here, or President Goldlib, I bet they'd have said something along the lines of," Sam cleared his throat, "*the sacrifices we've made and will continue to make will allow us to rise above the threats and brutality plaguing our people.*"

Seb barked a laugh, shaking his head. "Bob's your uncle, you're a bloody idiot."

Sam patted his back, then watched as he found his way to the sleeping quarters. Sam sighed, looking down at the wolf tattoo on his arm. To commemorate Zach, he chose the wolf as a symbol of Zach's bravery and fearlessness, as well as his loyalty. Rubbing over it, he closed his eyes.

*I miss you so much, Zach. So much.*

A tear rolled down his cheek, which he wiped away.

*If I could just see you one last time or hear your voice…*

He buried his head in his hands, trying to focus on his breathing.

"Sam?"

Sam shot up, looking around the Kite with eyes so big, they almost bulged out of his eye sockets. It felt like a vice crushed his heart shut, making it hard to breathe. He knew that voice unlike no other.

"Zach?"

Making sure no one heard him say Zach's name out loud, he got up, turning in circles to try and determine where the voice was coming from.

*"In those two years, you never called for me. Is something wrong? Are Zack and Maddie all right?"*

"Zack and Mad— How do you know I've got a son?"

He could swear he heard Zach chuckle. *"I promised you I'd never leave you, didn't I? I told you I'd be right here."*

Sam felt a hand on his heart, and he staggered back, breathing heavily. "How on bloody earth is this possible? This isn't happening… this is just my mind playing tricks on me…"

*"No, it's not. You can communicate with the dead, Sam. With me."*

"Stop! Stop it!" Sam yelled, covering his ears with his hands. "This isn't real… it's not real…"

"Sam, what's wrong?" Stan asked, walking over to Sam who was hunched over. "Oi, Sam, breathe. *Breathe.*"

He placed a hand on the exact same spot as where Sam felt an invisible hand, which made Sam push Stan away. "Get away from me!"

"Oi, Sam!" Stan moved back, pushing Sam against the wall with his hand. "It's me! It's Stan!"

*"Sam, don't be afraid of me."*

"Sam!" Stan shook him. "Sam!"

Sam came to, blood slowly poured out of his ears.

"Okay, sit down lad, sit down," Stan said, getting Sam to sit back down, taking a cloth out of his back pocket to clean his ears.

"What the bloody hell's going on? Why's blood coming outta your ears?"

Sam didn't notice a thing, didn't feel *anything*. He slowly shook his head. "I dunno… I… I dunno…"

Stan sighed, making sure he wouldn't accidentally push the blood into his left eardrum as he tried to clean it. Sam's heartbeat thumped loudly in his ears as Alex stalked over to them.

"What's going on?"

"Nothing, babe, go back to bed," Stan told him, hiding the blood. "He had a nightmare, fell asleep in his seat. No biggie."

Alex was too tired to ask further and nodded. He kissed Stan before returning to bed. Stan let out a relieved sigh, looking back at Sam. "Look, sublimation won't get you anywhere, all right? I need you to talk to me."

Sam couldn't possibly explain that he heard Zach's voice. *I'm not even sure if it's in my head or if it's real.*

"Sam!" Stan said, getting a little impatient. "How's it possible that there's blood literally pouring outta your eardrums?"

Sam looked like he was about to pass out, and Stan had to catch him as he fell forward.

## CHAPTER SIXTEEN

Huddled on a bed of leaves, Andrew awakened from his stupor, wide-eyed and drained. He looked wearily to his left, where his sister was tightly bound to the trunk of a tree. He only then noticed how gaunt she truly looked.

Her back-to-inhuman dead eyes were fixed upon him, growling lowly. Andrew watched in horror as she tried to break free, her immense strength causing the wood to creak and splinter.

Her clothes were dirty and dishevelled, as if she had been fighting. Her hair was tangled with leaves, but she didn't have a scratch on her. At least not that he could tell.

*Phil... where's Phil?*

He looked around him, worry etched across his face. He knew Phil had to be the one who had bound her, but he couldn't help his concern. After all, Phil could've died from his injuries sometime after, if he had sustained any.

"Phil?" A tiny voice came out of his throat, sounding almost miserable. He coughed. His throat was so dry, he could barely swallow. He tried to move, but just as he put his hands firmly on the ground, they gave away, and he hit the ground chin first.

His eyes fluttered open and saw the flicker of firelight coming from his right. He blinked, his vision resolving to show Phil cutting a tiny piece of wood into even smaller parts.

"Phil?" His voice sounded even coarser than it did before.

"Oh, thank heavens," Phil said, pouring Andrew a coup of water from a rough-looking bottle. *Is that the same bottle he so randomly found near our escape site from the first camp to here? It looks way worse than I remember.*

He gave the bottle to Andrew, who drank thirstily.

"Easy, don't drink too much at once. You're severely dehydrated and that means you gotta take it slow. Or so *she* said before she went all feral again."

Andrew looked over at his sister's hatred-filled eyes, listened to her screeches and snarls filled with rage.

"I think she's truly gone this time, Andy."

He felt his brain break as he tried to imagine his sister as a renegade, which made him shiver. *No, she's not. It's not her fault. She didn't... she didn't choose this.*

He tried to fight the urge to blame her, focusing his anger on the ones who truly did it, but he couldn't. He didn't even know who *they* were.

"We can't kill her, Andy," Phil continued, sighing mournfully, "but we gotta make sure she can't come after us anymore."

*Can't come after... us... No...*

He shook his head so quickly; it was a miracle it was still attached to his body. "No, we're not gonna cut her legs off!"

"What other choice do we have?" he asked, sighing again. "Look, I hate the thought too, but she keeps finding us. At least if her legs are gone, we have the upper hand. We'll be a step ahead of her."

"No!" Andrew yelled loudly, "Minnie's *my* sister! She's *still* my sister!"

"I *know* she is, Andy! But we gotta do this if we wanna survive!"

"Then I don't wanna survive!" He shuffled away from Phil. "You won't touch her, you hear me? You won't!"

"Andy, please... be reasonable."

"*Reasonable?*" he scoffed. "You want *me* to be *reasonable?*" He shook with rage. "To bloody hell with that!"

"Andy, stop yelling, your throat, it's..."

"I don't care! I don't bloody care! I don't—"

They heard rumbling in the distance. Thinking it was thunder, Andrew turned to look at his sister. Opening his mouth, he was stopped by a violent spew of lava erupting out of nowhere. *That's... there's no bloody volcano here!*

His eyes found Phil's, who seemed just as terrified as Andrew. Both looked up at the sky as a heavy layer of smoke covered it completely.

"Holy..."

Fireballs began to rain down, and Phil hurled Andrew to his feet. "Run!"

As they sprinted away from Amelia, they heard the fireballs hitting the ground where they just were, echoing across the woods. The trees surrounding them seemed to rise like pillars, streaking up to the sky blanketed in grey smoke.

Sprinting as quickly as they possibly could, they heard a hissing noise from above. Looking up, they saw a giant fireball hurling right at them. "Get down!" Phil yelled, throwing his body to the left.

Andrew noticed the fireball curving to the right and did the same as Phil, landing with a soft thud. He felt the heat of the fire caressing his cheek as it crashed into the sand only a few feet away from them.

Looking for Phil, he saw no sign of him. The haze and smoke were too thick to see anything close to reality. A streak of red sliced through the trees surrounding him, crackling the branches and leaves with fire. What was once a luscious patch of trees, was now slowly burning down to the ground. A river of fire burned a path towards them, consuming the jungle completely, toppling every tree in its wake.

Fuelled by adrenaline, Andrew pushed himself to his feet, then hauled Phil up with him. The fire continued its unrelenting path, swallowing Andrew's crutch without a change of saving it.

"Come on!" Phil yelled, forcing Andrew along with him.

The fire hurled through the treeline, boxing them in. Both felt their nerves hardening as even the water of the nearby river couldn't stop the fire from spreading, erupting into a wave of flames.

"There goes our idea of quenching it!"

Andrew felt the heat of the fire reaching his face. Before he could comprehend how dangerously close it was, he was awakened from his *shocked slumber* by Phil's excruciatingly laced-with-pain scream.

Looking to his left, he watched as Phil's leg was on fire, slowly burning his flesh away. He took off his shirt, tried to stop the fire from spreading further, but it was already too late.

A part of him hoped this was another premonition, but it wasn't. Squeezing himself, he knew it wasn't. *This is real. This is bloody real.*

He felt like he was stuck in a dream, one where you're trying to run away from something but feel utterly helpless.

He *felt* helpless.

He *was* helpless.

He knew any burns longer than twenty seconds would cause permanent damage. And from the look of it, his leg was beyond saving.

*The fire likely killed his nerve endings... he has stopped screaming.*

Andrew thought he had died, and his eyes had failed to close. Panic rose up in him as he moved two fingers to his neck, feeling a faint heartbeat. Letting out a sigh of relief, he watched as the fire never stopped creeping closer, threatening to burn Phil's legs a second time.

He began to pull Phil away from the fire as fast as he could but couldn't move quickly enough with his still busted up leg. The whirring of blades made him look up, looking at an aircraft he had never seen before.

The backdoor opened, and Sam looked down at the two people in distress. "I found Phil!" he yelled, readying a rope to throw down at them.

Andrew had no idea who they were, but they seemed to know Phil. Catching the rope, he forced it around Phil's body, securing it with a tight knot.

"Stand by and wait for my order," Sam commanded Alex and Stan, waiting to pull the rope up, "I've got a visual on 'em." Sam wasn't passed out for long, and with what they witnessed flying above the island, he ignored Stan's initial worry and interrogation.

"The wind is fifty at fourteen knots," Tim said, "coordinates are seven-six Echo Whiskey Sierra, niner—"

"Tim! For the love of bloody hell, shut up!" Sam yelled, watching as Andrew held his thumb up. "Pull!"

As Alex and Stan began to pull with all their might, Andrew knew he couldn't wait for them to lower the rope a second time, darting away from the ever-getting-closer fire.

"Hurry up!" Sam yelled, looking over his shoulder at their pilot. "Follow him to the west! There's a hill over there! If we can get close enough to it, he might make the jump."

"That's very risky," Tim said, "the wind's knots are..."

"Shut your bloody mouth and do what I say! We're not losing any people that were ours to protect in the first place!"

Tim knew Sam didn't mean to yell at him, but it still hurt all the same to hear him talk so condescending.

Alex and Stan hauled the unconscious Phil into the aircraft while Sam kept an eye on Andrew, who was limping across the clearing. With his entire focus on Andrew, Sam coordinated with their pilot to ensure he wouldn't lose sight of him. Out of nowhere, a girl—or what seemed to be one—attacked Andrew, knocking him to the ground and scratching his upper body and face.

Andrew stopped when he heard the footsteps, seeing the movement from the corner of his eye. "Minnie!" Andrew yelled as the woman-shaped shadow lunged at him from the bushes. He threw up his hand, and his world exploded.

He heard her heavy panting above him as he tried to cover his eyes, her black limbs reached him with clawed hands, scratching his skin and catching at his clothes and hair, slowing him down completely.

His pain was a constant, thought-sapping pulse, echoing back and forth through his willpower to stay conscious. "Minnie... stop... Please..." Trembling, he looked up at her, no longer covering his eyes. He was writhing in pain as blood seeped from deep slashes across his chest. "It's... me... Minnie..."

She dragged herself off him, looking at his face so bloodied that he was barely recognisable. They were surrounded by nothing but ash and lava, the once lush foliage now burning away slowly, being consumed from whence it came.

She looked her brother dead in the eye, nothing of humanity left. Not even a tiny spark. A nearby tree was sturdy, but the impact of a fireball soaring directly towards it turned it into splinters.

At the last instant, Andrew changed direction and rolled away from the splinters, while his sister got hit by them. His lungs burned, was too exhausted to move any further. He knew this was his only chance to flee, but he couldn't get himself to get up and run. He tensed as he waited for the killing blow, either by the fire or by his sister. *But it never came.*

He raised his head. Nothing moved in the darkness beyond, not even the orange light he had been consumed in. A pool of bright light covered him like a mother covering her child ready for bed, and as he bathed in the cold light, he didn't know if he was *safe*, or *not*.

# CHAPTER SEVENTEEN

He was back in the yard where he disappeared all those years ago. He heard giggles and turned around to see where they came from, looking at a three-year-old version of himself playing with his action figures, wearing his red and blue baseball cap. Holding his *Techno Tiger* figurine up in the air, half-man, half-tiger, he ran through the yard.

*That's me... and then that's...*

"Andy! It's time to eat dinner! You can play after you've eaten your veggies!"

Completely ignoring his sister, the young Andrew kept on running around. Andrew walked towards the backdoor, heading inside the kitchen. He watched his sister wearing a white apron carrying a huge pot with vegetable stew towards the table.

He had never seen his sister like this. Her hair was securely tied into a knot, humming the song their mother sung for them every night before they would go to bed. He looked at the set table, the two plates that were on it instead of four. This was the day his parents had gone out on a date.

*Their wedding anniversary.*

His chest began to ache as he relived this memory, looking over at his sister who was still unaware of his presence.

*I had to leave her behind once already. I wasn't given a choice back then, but I'm given one now.*

He walked over to her, and tapped her on her shoulder. "Minnie?" She didn't turn around. "Minnie, it's me."

Screams came from the yard. Minnie dropped the glass she was holding, shattering into a thousand pieces. Running outside, she watched in horror as her little brother was nowhere to be found.

"Andy!" Searching frantically wherever she could, tears rolled down her cheeks. "Andy! Where are you?" She fell to her knees, burying her head in her hands. She sobbed, curling into a ball.

Andrew walked over to her, getting emotional himself.

*This has gotta be her worst memory. So, why am I seeing this?*

Before he knew it, he heard himself giggle once more, watching as his younger self ran around the yard with *Techno Tiger*.

"Andy! It's time to eat dinner! You can play after you've eaten your veggies!"

*What the...?*

His younger self ignored her call once more and kept on running around. Andrew got up, rushing inside the kitchen.

"Minnie?" He watched her turn around with the pot in her hands, bringing it over to the set table. "Minnie, it's me, Andy. It's your baby brother."

Again, no response. He waved his hands in front of her face, then he heard screams coming from the yard. Minnie dropped the glass she was holding, once more shattering it into a thousand pieces. He watched her run outside, frantically searching for him, but to no avail.

"Minnie, listen to me," Andrew said, walking over to her once more, "I'm right here. I know he's gone, but *I'm* not. I just need you to see me."

She was curled into a ball, sobbing.

Then, he heard himself giggle, and saw his younger self run the same pattern as he did twice before.

*What the bloody hell's going on here? Is she stuck in a... loop?*

He didn't even wait until she called for him to eat dinner. He immediately went over to her, putting both of his hands on her shoulders. "Minnie! Look at me! I'm right here!"

"Andy! It's time to eat dinner! You can play after you've eaten your veggies!" she yelled in front of his face, turning around as if she couldn't feel Andrew's touch.

*How the bloody hell am I able to touch her, but she can't feel that?*

He quickly rushed after her as she made her way to the stove to carry the pot towards the table.

*I gotta find a way to remove all that makes this horror possible... including myself. It's gotta be the only way to banish this... this dark memory that's been unleashed on her. I gotta free her.*

He watched as she put the pot down on the table, then moved closer to her. Cupping her face in his hands, he made her face move up to his eyes. She looked at him through the eyes of a dead person, unrecognisable in both ways.

"Minnie, listen to me, you're stuck in a loophole. You're... you're no longer in existence on Earth, okay? You're... stuck in this horrific war inside your mind while you're an animal on the outside. You've attacked me more times than I can count. But I need you to wake up, Minnie. I need you to see me, and fight. I need you to *fight*."

He felt a languid warmth seeping into his limbs like he was sinking into a bath. All his muscles loosened, his eyes drifting out of focus. Through the warm, soothing haze, his mind grasped at the distant realisation that she was calling his name.

A slight frown creased her face as his focus shifted back. He struggled to focus on her words, sounding strangely muffled.

A sudden bright light made both fall backwards.

Having hit his head against the counter, he looked over at Minnie who had hit hers on the stove, looking warily at Andrew.

"Andy? How… you're…"

"I know, this must be super confusing," he said, crawling over to her, "but I can assure you I'm *very* real."

She slowly moved her hand up to touch his face. Once her palm touched his cheek, he put his hand on top of hers, leaning into the touch of her hand. Their eyes locked.

"It's really you," she said, tears forming in her eyes, "but how? How are you—"

"A grown-up? That's… it's a long and complicated story, and we don't have that much time." He crossed his legs to sit more comfortably as she moved her hand away from his face. He pulled back his own.

"Look, Minnie, I…"

"I *remember*."

"What?"

She looked over at him, more tears forming, the first began to roll down her cheeks. "I remember." She looked down at her hands. "I've got claws… I've hurt you with 'em…"

"Minnie…"

"I've hurt your friend. I've tried to choke you to death."

"Minnie, that…"

"*I almost killed you*."

"Minnie, stop." He put a finger on her lips, shushing her. "Just stop, okay? None of that's your fault. You…" He sighed. "I dunno *who* or *what* did this to you, but they transformed you and locked you up inside your own mind. I think the few times you were…" He paused. "You managed to find the exit yourself, and you came back to me. And I need you to do that again."

"How do you expect me to *just* do that? And after everything I've done? How can you even look me in the eyes and forgive me? I know I couldn't. In fact, I *can't*."

"You must," he said, sternly, "I think that's the only way you get out."

"Out where?"

"Outta this prison loophole. I can't have you whither to nothing like this, Minnie. You're living in an all-too-realistic hell. It's worse than war."

"No." She shook her head. "No, I... At least I can't hurt anyone in here."

"Yes, you're hurting someone in here," he said, grabbing both of her hands, "you're hurting *yourself*."

He knew her mind was reeling as she tried to figure out what was going on.

"Even if you can't remember how and why you got outta here the first time, it's what I need you to do, Minnie. I *need* you to remember."

She shook her head. "No, I... I've hurt you..."

"No, you didn't. *They* did. Whoever *they* may be, *they're* responsible for everything that's happening to you. Not you."

He realised they were no longer in their kitchen, instead completely surrounded by blackness. Then something caught his eye.

Looking into the darkness, he spotted a glowing pair of amber eyes. As they moved closer, it revealed a humanoid figure with spikes growing out of its head and shoulders and its flesh that was hardened into plates.

"What the—"

The figure loomed over both. Somehow, Andrew could sense its surge of possessive energy, its powerful resentment towards Andrew. He could feel the coil of its humanoid muscles ready to pounce on him.

*"You shall not take her."*

"I don't take orders from *anyone*," Andrew said, grabbing her by her arms. "And neither does she. Whatever the bloody hell you might be, we're leaving. And you won't be able to stop us."

The profound sense of confidence that tried to overshadow the figure's overpowering energy, found its way to Andrew's core. It didn't last long.

Its powerful anger roiled within, a dangerous foreboding which made Andrew step in front of his sister, who was frozen in place. He knew whatever this figure was, it had made his sister fitful in this dark place that seemed like its home and prison.

*It's hungry. And in pain.*

The pain stemmed from the nights of glory the figure had dreamed of and the horrors it had called from the depths of his sister's memory, giving it a brief, terrible taste of power and freedom.

*I've stirred her from the deep sleep he has sunk her into.*

The figure took a step closer and looked wrong somehow. It had teeth and showed these to create a smile, tracing a finger down its own cheek in full approximation.

Andrew felt as if he were falling asleep as the figure's whisper curled around him, ice-cold and dark. Yet his knees didn't buckle. Touched by its essence, he drifted into a dreamscape where everything was black and grey.

Something scalding poured over his head, yanking him from the figure's grasp. He jerked back, his breath sharp, and looked down—his skin, or what little remained, bathed in molten agony. It burned like lava, eating through flesh.

A raw scream tore from his throat, his body as mangled as his thoughts. Tears spilled over, streaking down his face. A touch—firm yet careful—wrapped around his injured hand, pressing cloth against the wound. Blinking through the haze of pain and tears, he saw her. His sister.

"Minnie..." he said weakly.

She shushed him, elevating his arm above the level of his heart. "I don't have much time, he's looking for me," she said.

"Who's... who's he?"

"Trike. He's... I dunno what he's supposed to be. I just know it's a... *he*, not a *what* or *who*."

"What does he... want with you?"

"All you gotta know, is that you can't save me. But you've given me the chance to escape long enough so *you* can be saved." She pointed at the Kite hovering above them, keeping a close eye on Andrew. She stood up and looked at her little brother. "I love you so much, my baby brother."

Using her claws, she managed to slice a tree trunk clean from its roots, watching as it tumbled down into the fiery substance. She lifted Andrew up, forcing him to sit down on the tree's trunk, then spun him ninety degrees.

Before he could tell her to join him, she let go, and he sailed onto the fire away from her, further and further, until all he saw was her being consumed completely. His agonising scream faded away in the loudness of the angry tumult surrounding him. He could no longer tell where the stream was as the fire had devoured its banks entirely. All around him were swollen trees clotted with some kind of fiery residue and debris.

The chaos made up and down impossible to recognise as trees tumbled all around him. He was pelted by debris, shielding himself as best as he could with some of the tree's bark.

The hill the Kite hovered above came closer, and Andrew saw a rope being lowered down with a guy swinging at the bottom of it. Waving at Andrew to jump off the tree and make a run for it, he just stared at his potential rescuer with no intention of listening.

*I'm tired... I'm just so incredibly tired...*

He thought back to his sister, how she had given her life for him. Surely, burning alive would've made her return impossible, and he knew it was *definite* this time. There was no coming back from that.

"Run!" he heard the guy screaming at him. Retrieving some sense of the current situation he was in; he came back to full realisation. Looking over at the dangling guy, he found a new form of strength in himself he hadn't felt before.

Dragging himself off the tree, he set foot on the hill, feeling his foot sink away in its muddy surface.

*Don't give up.*

Shadows stirred around him and in front of him, the wind picked up as he ran. He felt the fire turn its gaze towards Andrew, as if it had a life of its own, as if it was *human*. The Kite was blotted out by dark shadows that raced violently across the sky, moving too swiftly to be natural. Andrew noticed the darkness that gathered around it. He was certain no natural path had brought him there.

*They're watching us. They're watching all of us.*

He tried to shake that thought out of his head, tried to refocus on the task at hand. He could feel the fire reaching his heels, and knew he was running out of time. Having almost reached the top of the hill; he knew he wasn't going to make it. He had to jump.

*It's the only way. It's literally the only way. This is the day I die.*

He limped as fast as he could towards the outstretched hand, and as he felt himself tripping, he took the risk to jump instead, flying mid-air for what felt like eternity.

*Just let me die. Just let it end.*

Closing his eyes, bracing himself for the heat that would eat him alive, he felt a hand grasping his firmly, and blacked out.

## CHAPTER EIGHTEEN

"How's he?" Sam asked Bramley, the Scottish medic from Josh's team who hadn't been tortured enough to be kept in the medical bay back at the bunker.

"He's stable, fer now. But teh injuries he has sustained, both o' 'em really, it's gonna take 'em weeks to recover. Phil's lucky he won' lose his leg."

"And Josh?"

"Still no improvement. He's still out o' it."

"Call me as soon as any of 'em wake up."

"Aye."

Sam nodded at him, a confirmation nod that was typical for soldiers to understand their order. He walked over to Tim who was looking down at the obliviated island, marking it on the map as *non-existent*. He then walked over to the cockpit, adding the new coordinates to the navigation system, giving the pilot a head's up they would take a break after they were nearing the island and had deemed it safe enough to wait with any rescues. Unless, of course, things proved to be as dire as the first island they visited.

"Once they wake up, I need you to interrogate 'em," Sam told Stan, who had joined him near the coffee machine.

"Ask 'em if anyone else was on that island?"

"Exactly. According to Tim's data, there should've been three people. We're missing a REBEL. Phil is… *was*, a Laerie before he became human again. And the boy," he said thoughtfully, looking over at Andrew, "we've no idea who he's supposed to be. Or *what*." He took a sip of his freshly brewed coffee. "But it's clear that he must be special. Tim thinks he was injected with something, but he couldn't decipher what kind. It must be, and I quote, '*a new concoction that they cleverly developed.*' He's hoping to have answers before the boy wakes up."

"And if he won't?"

"He will. He *must*." He took a deep breath. "We need answers."

"Alex's guarding 'em both. If anything changes, he'll let us know."

For the dozenth time, Sam's hands dropped to his sides, making sure both his gun and knife were still there.

Stan noticed, patting Sam's shoulder. "I know you're afraid for their safety."

Sam looked over at him, wondering what gave it away that he wasn't worried about his own. Then again, they had known each other for twelve years already.

"We assigned all the new additions to the patrols and gave 'em all jobs to fulfil while we're gone," Stan continued. "You tested 'em all, Sam, figured out what they were good at, and what not. You personally selected Percy to protect your family."

"Yeah, I know I did. But there's this... thought... what if she cheats on—"

"No, mate, I'm gonna stop you right there." He took Sam's coffee. "She's as loyal as they come, and you know it. You've never doubted her before when any of us were alone in a room with her."

"But I've—"

"You've known Percy for two years, Sam. Yes, you've known us longer, but I know you trust him. So, whatever lie is creeping into that foul head of yours, don't let it." He put the mug down. "Look, Maddie is a shrewd woman, she knows who to trust and who not. She trusts *you*, she trusts *us*, and she *knows* she can't trust everyone in the city as far as she could throw 'em. So, whatever the bloody hell makes you think otherwise, you better get that outta your head, 'cause it's soiling her as an individual. Even more so, as your future wife."

It felt as if he had a short circuit in his brain, as if someone, or *something*, tried to convince him otherwise.

*It can't be Zach, right? No, he'd never do that.*

"Sam?"

Sam had zoned out, blinking a few times as he looked over at Stan. He then nodded and laughed. "I'll never forget what she said to me the first day we decided to move in together."

Stan gave him a suspicious look, but even if the laugh had been faked to mask any true emotions lurking beneath, he wasn't about to call Sam out on it.

"You mean the day you assigned that patrol to your neighbourhood?"

Sam nodded again, smiling. "She was so mad at me. *'Are you seriously expecting those sultry sacks of toxic masculinity to keep us safe?'* I swear she would've been a great politician."

"Well, she kinda already is, with you being the vice-president and all."

"Yeah, 'cause that worked out so great for everyone."

Before Stan could reply, Seb walked over to them. "We're nearing the next island. And it's not looking good."

Sam walked over to the window and gazed out at a hundred square miles of land scarred with dark, gaping craters. He stood in shock, staring at the sprawling contours of what remained of the island as it receded into the heat haze that surrounded it on all sides. Most trees had fallen, crushing whatever lay beneath them.

"There's no way any of 'em survived that," Stan said, looking grim. "There's just no way."

"What the bloody hell's going on here? Who's killing 'em? This can't be Mother Nature's doing."

"Oh no," Tim said, joining them, "surely not. Mother Nature doesn't have wires coming from all directions through majestic waterpipes leading from the islands to an unknown destination."

"Well, we clearly haven't hit the motherlode." They all turned their heads towards Seb, who sensed they were staring at him. "What? Too soon?"

No one replied.

"Can they watch 'em? The people on the island?" Sam asked.

"Well, he's got his utilities running through there. I mean, he's got hydraulics, electrics—"

"English, please."

Tim sighed. "Basically, my scanner picked up lines that denote a liquid that moves in a confined space by means of the waterpipes, under pressure of course."

"Okay, and that pressure would then..."

"Cause floods that aren't formed by the sea, or make a volcano erupt while there's none."

"Hold up," Stan said, "you're saying that the whole island was a... a *fake*?"

Tim shook his head. "No, it's like he has control over Mother Nature. Remember how they made weather appear in the Dome?"

Sam took a step back, bumping into the wall. "It can't be... they both died." He looked visibly upset.

"It's gotta be somebody else stepping up. Perhaps a third complicit. Whoever they might be, they must have video feeds of some kind, maybe even a recording deck. If we can find out that location..."

"We can put an end to all this," Seb finished his sentence. "We can stop it *once and for all*."

Sam punched a nearby mirror, then slammed a lamp off the table. Before he could wreck the Kite any further, Stan's arms came around Sam's waist. As Sam yelled, Stan just held him, not letting him go. As Sam sank to the floor, Stan followed suit, allowing Sam to weep in his arms.

Tim sat behind his laptop, talking to Seb seated next to him. "We need to find the nerve centre, his director's suite."

"And how are we gonna do that? I don't assume you can track the lines to his exact whereabouts. It'd be too easy, right?"

Tim hummed softly. "Yeah... something's not right. Why would he leave it out in the open like that? Why did he want us to find—" He got up, walking towards the map pinned on the wall. "Unless... this island was a test subject."

"I don't see how," Seb said.

"No, you don't see anything anyway."

"Oi!"

Tim realised he had said that out loud, looking apologetic at Seb. "Sorry, I... I didn't mean it like that."

Seb scoffed at him. "You know, those kinds of words make me return to my old cantankerous self."

"I said I was..." Tim stopped himself, then laughed. "Cantankerous? Bloody hell, where did you learn a word like that?"

Seb's boisterous laugh echoed through the Kite, shaking his head. "I dunno. Guess my vocabulary expanded. It happens when you lose your sight."

Tim nodded slowly, sighing. "Okay, so what I meant by test subject's that maybe the maker, creator, or whatever the bloody hell we should call 'em had to figure out how to get everything working beneath the dangers of the ocean. Yes, technology has come far in terms of being water-resistant, but it's still *not fully developed*, and there are still snags."

"So, you're saying that he simply *forgot* to get rid of the evidence?"

"I mean, think about it," Tim said, sitting back down behind his laptop, "I don't think we were supposed to find out. My associate began to do undercover research as he had suspicions about possible descendants or accomplices that were left alive." He skimmed through a deck of papers. "They likely infiltrated under Henry's command so they could imprison Josh's army." He gasped. "They couldn't erase the evidence on time, so their next step was to get rid of the last remaining eyewitnesses..."

"*Us.*"

"Only so they could then continue their experiments. Experiments whose true purpose I haven't figured out yet. Phil seems fine, but the boy... they gave him something even my scientific knowledge can't decipher. I must be missing something else... if this was already on the nose, and whoever's behind this is truly this sloppy... there's gotta be more clues they recklessly left behind."

As Tim began to frantically search through his papers, sending them flying throughout the room, Seb left unnoticed, wanting to check up on Sam.

Opening the door, Seb accidentally hit Sam's shotgun standing next to the wall. As it fell with a loud sound, Sam remembered Zach's death, the way his body dropped to the floor. He began to breathe heavily, teleporting in his consciousness to the past.

But this past was *different*.

He walked along a long, almost endless corridor. He could hear Zach's cries for Sam from afar, glued in panic. He tried to open the door at the end of the corridor, but the door wouldn't budge.

"Sam! Help me!"
"Zach! I'm here, I'm right here!"
"Don't leave me here to die, Sam! Don't leave me!"

Sam sat in the corner, screaming. His eyes were going wide with almost newfound anxiety. Seb managed to reach him, touching his shoulder. "Sam? Sam, look at me," he said, of course not having the faintest clue if Sam would be looking at him or not. "It's okay, you're safe. You're safe, Sam. *Breathe*. I need you to breathe."

"I can't..."

The long corridor was no longer in front of him. All he saw now were images of what had happened. He felt the same sensation in his body the day Zach died. He felt the pain and pressure, even when there wasn't anything hurting him. Not mentally, not physically.

His heart rate increased; his breathing had now turned into a full-on panic attack. He heard a guttural cry for help in the distance, sending a chill up his back. He wheeled around, panic building as he tried to find out who was screaming. But *no one* was.

His body tensed and quivered as he felt panic wave after panic wave surging through him.

"Sam, I need you to focus on your breathing. Slow and steady, okay?"

Seb knew Maddie hugged him to calm Sam down. Seeing no other way to do so, Seb embraced Sam, who basked in his warm hug.

He took a deep, trembling breath, slowly coming back to his senses. A preternatural calm settled in as he sucked in a breath.

"You went through quite a rough attack just now, Sam. It's very important that you stay calm, okay? I don't want you to have another episode."

Amidst the chaos of it all, he schooled his face into a mask of calm once Seb rubbed his back, conveying the sincerity of Seb's words. Two years ago, Seb was the complete opposite, could've cared less about Sam's welfare. But now, after everything they had been through, he was there for Sam no matter what.

*No, he could never replace Zach. He isn't even trying to. But he's the closest thing to a brother I've got right now.*

"Look, I dunno what kinda deals you made with some of the boys," Seb said, "but they've made me promises too, you know."

Sam, being able to finally speak again, moved away from Seb's embrace, looking him directly in the eyes. "I dunno what—"

"If you were to die, and I... if you'd sacrifice yourself for me, I'd have no one left, no one who cares enough about me to keep protecting me. And you know it's different for you, right?" He took two photographs out of Sam's pocket. "These two need you, Sam. Your *family* needs you. That means that no matter what happens, *you* gotta be the one to live. Not me." He put the photographs in Sam's hands. "For your son and girlfriend, you *must* live."

Sam shook his head, mumbling under his breath. *"No."*

"Nobody needs a cripple like me."

Sam looked him in the eyes, shaking his head once more. "That's not true, Seb. *I* need you."

"I'm nothing like Zach. I can't be his replacement."

"You're not." A single tear rolled down Sam's cheek. "Seb, you've been there for me since the moment he died. You've never left my side. You've helped me with my drinking addiction, with my PTSD, *everything*. If it weren't for you, I wouldn't have had a son. I would've been long dead before I ever got the chance to meet him."

Seb took a deep breath, putting his hand on Sam's shoulder. "Then you gotta break the boys' promise."

"The—?"

"The one in which they save *me* over *you*."

"Seb..."

"No, Sam, I mean it. We're not gonna be martyrs for one another, okay? We deal with anything that gets thrown our way together. And if we die, then we'll do that together too. Understood?"

Before Sam could reply, Bramley walked in. "He's awake."

# CHAPTER NINETEEN

"How's he doing?" Sam asked as he followed Bramley to the sickbay.

"He's talkin' all right. Keeps askin' 'bout tha boy he was with. He ain' awake yet." Sam nodded, stopping in his tracks as Bramley put his arm out, blocking Sam from entering. "Be gentle with him, 'kay? Fer yer own sake." He patted Sam's shoulder, then left.

Sam took a deep breath, slowly opening the door. The second Andrew saw the door open, he tried to get as far away from Sam as he possibly could, though the only thing he could do was push himself against the wall. His hand was chained to the bedpost.

"What do you want from me? Who are you?" he asked, fighting against the trembling that seemed to have overtaken his entire body. "Are you bringing me back?"

"Back where?"

Andrew looked around the room he was in, then to his cuffed hand. "You're gonna inject me, aren't you? You're one of 'em."

"No, I'm not," Sam said, moving a little closer towards his bed.

"Stay back!" Andrew yelled, throwing his f hand in the air to use as a shield.

Sam knew he wouldn't get the chance to undo whatever harm was done to him, but as he moved his hand to his pocket, he retrieved a set of keys, showing them to Andrew. "I'm gonna take that off, yeah?" Sam moved slowly towards him. "I'm gonna destroy the shackles that they've placed on you. I mean you no harm."

Andrew looked at Sam, scoffing at him. "You're lying."

Sam took the handcuff off, putting the keys back in his pocket as he took a step back. "We've got a wheelchair for you so we can take you to your friend."

Andrew raised his eyebrow, a sceptical look etched on his face. "So, you can *interrogate* us? I heard you earlier."

*Flicking his eyes open, Andrew could look through them half-lidded.*

*"Once they wake up, I need you to interrogate 'em," Sam told Stan.*

*"Ask 'em if anyone else was on that island?"*

"Exactly. According to Tim's data, there should've been three people. We're missing a REBEL. Phil is... was, a Laerie before he became human again."

Andrew folded his arms. "What's a Laerie? What exactly *is* Phil?"

Sam sat down on his bed, though he kept his distance. He sighed softly and began to explain everything he possibly could.

Suspicion crept inside of Andrew, begetting his scepticism even more. "Is there any physical proof of that? You say you were experimented on, that... that Phil wasn't human before this. Either show me or kill me."

Sam shook his head. "We're not gonna kill you. We just wanna understand what—"

"What they've done to me? Why I'm different? Yeah, I heard *that* too."

Sam sighed softly, looking over at the door. "Look, I didn't... I didn't ask for any of this, okay? I didn't *want* any of this." He stood up, walking towards the other end of the room. "All this? You know where it got me? It got my best friend killed, I lost almost all my friends, I'm scarred for life, and as the vice-president, I doubt my own president whom I believed was good for a change." He walked over to a lamp on the table, slamming it off, watching it hit the floor. "They killed almost everyone I called family," he spluttered, turning back to look at Andrew, who seemed even more frightened by Sam's sudden outburst. "I got famous 'cause a sick psycho decided experimenting on young kids to create an army and keep 'em as slaves was *just*, and he murdered basically everyone I grew up with but couldn't kill *me*. And I wish he had! Who the bloody hell wants to be famous for escaping manslaughter?"

His voice grew louder and angrier with each word that escaped his mouth, forcing Andrew to make himself even smaller.

"I may have been renowned as a lifesaver, but the truth is kid, you're likely gonna die if you stay near me. 'Cause they all die. They *always* do." He walked towards the door, then stopped to turn around one last time. "So, ask yourself, are you *truly* saved?" With that, he left Andrew alone.

Stan stood around the corner, his arms crossed, receiving an eyeroll from Sam as he passed him.

"Mate, what the bloody hell? You've scared the poor lad!"

"Shut your mouth!" Sam yelled, overtaken by anger. "He questions *us*? Well, good for him, he has every right to. Maybe *we* should become bad. Perhaps *they* actually have a shot at ending this thing once and for all! Maybe *they* can bloody end it all!"

He brushed past Alex, who had heard the commotion, coming to see what was going on. Stan shook his head as Alex wanted to open his mouth, watching as Sam walked away from them.

A soft knock on the door made Andrew sit up straight in his bed, afraid that Sam had returned to continue his yelling. Seb opened the door and walked in with a tray filled with food. He made his way to Andrew's bed without spilling anything, smiling to himself as he whispered under his breath, *"I'm finally getting the hang of this."* He held the tray in front of Andrew, who looked at him.

"No, thanks. I'm not hungry."

Seb put his finger in the mashed potatoes, then licked it off with his tongue. "It's not poisoned. You need your strength back. I highly doubt you've eaten anything fancy besides fish and berries."

Andrew hesitated for a second longer, then took the tray from Seb, looking at the carrot soup, salad, and chops alongside the mashed potatoes. "You could feed so many people with this. There's no way I can—"

"Yeah, you can," Seb said, "I've heard you're very skinny. You're gonna need every bit of nutrition you can get. Especially with what's to come."

"Gonna visit the islands to rescue the others, you mean? Those like Phil, like Theo, like me?"

"*Theo?*" He sat down on the bedside. "Theo was also on the island?"

Andrew nodded aggrieved, taking a bite of the pork. "My... *something* killed him. Part human, part animalistic."

"Did that *something* hurt you and Phil too? There's no way all your injuries are caused by anything but humans." He knew Phil was probably staring at him as he said that. "Tim and Stan told me."

Andrew hummed good-naturedly before taking another bite. "We went through a lot. That's all you gotta know."

"Fair enough." Seb took a strange-smelling herbal brew out of his pocket, giving it to Andrew. "It's to help detoxicate your body. If you want me to take a sip, I will."

Andrew shook his head, then nodded meekly, taking the concoction.

Before he could take a sip, Bramley came in, smiling as he looked at Andrew. "Yer lover is awake."

Andrew's cheeks turned red as Bramley bluntly spat out the true nature of their feelings, but decided he only cared about seeing him again. "Take me to him, please."

Bramley nodded, helping Andrew into the wheelchair. He wheeled him to Phil's room, who smiled weakly upon seeing Andrew.

Andrew ignored the pain in his body, getting up from the wheelchair to embrace Phil, who grunted softly upon the impact. "I thought I'd lost you."

Phil chuckled, patting Andrew's back. "Not a chance. You don't get rid of me that easily."

Bramley walked over to Seb leaning against the doorpost. "Are the results in yet?"

Bramley put a paper in Seb's hand. "There's somethin' odd 'bout 'im. Show it to Sam, report back to me. I won' do anythin' without Sam's permission."

Seb nodded, patting Bramley's shoulder briefly. "Keep an eye on those two, see if you can eavesdrop on 'em. Sam will wanna know *anything* weird or suspicious, or useful."

"Yeh got it," he said as Seb left the room.

Sam rubbed his knuckles, sighing. Hearing a knock on the door, he sat up straight. "Yeah?"

Seb opened the door, chuckling softly. "Don't be so official with me, mate. It's just me. Did Stan give you a beating or something?"

"I wish. Maybe that would've helped me set some of my anger management issues aside."

Seb headed over to him, handing him the paper. "Bramley said some test results came back for the boy."

"Still nameless, eh?"

Seb rubbed the back of his head. "Huh. Guess I forgot to ask." He sat down next to Sam, relaying the few things Andrew had said to him. Sam's face fell hearing Theo hadn't made it.

He looked at the piece of paper in his hand, reading it out loud so Seb could hear its contents too.

*"In the boy's blood and saliva, we found a serum that's unknown to us. The serum is of a calibre we haven't seen before, one that has remnants of a microscopic parasite. The parasite has entered healthy cells yet hasn't burst any of the cells counting as its host. Whatever this serum does, it hasn't released any new parasites into the bloodstream. Nothing has spread to the major organs; the brain is*

*completely intact. We did, however, find something else. Even though the parasite might not have done anything, we found an oral concentration of a spiked protein with extracted generic material from the boy's own DNA. The orders of magnitude are higher than those of the parasite, which suggests that the parasite isn't a reliable means of transmitting anything. The parasite is relatively fragile and has been dead for a while, seemingly unable to survive the kind of nature it was exposed to. The inability to study any live samples, however, severely limited the ability to test further. For now, it's thus unclear as to why a part of the injection survived, and a part perished, considering the creator of this serum must've known the boy would be exposed to unnatural circumstances. Under normal circumstances, the boy would've likely had a decreased survival rate, not even a chance with the use of certain medications. However, the data we've collected thus far is still complicated and incomplete, as the parasite residing in the boy's body should've fatally attacked him. The wounds he has sustained, too, should've been fatal. Whatever kind of enhancement the serum has given him; it's beyond the normal biology of the human body. One thing we did notice after a full examination of his DNA is that his DNA shows severe decay. His DNA was likely non-functional before he was transmitted to the island. It's unclear how he stayed alive and motile when his DNA was rotting away. In this short period of time since injection, his body has undergone numerous drastic changes. This adaptation likely facilitates the transmission of the proteins and general material. While I normally have answers for any type of observation or report, I can't conclude my findings in this case. What doesn't make sense to me is why his DNA decays. If this parasite hasn't affected him, not even likely in an ideal environment, then why would his DNA be destroyed instead, when the parasite hasn't done anything harmful? One would think such deterioration of the DNA would make it impossible for the boy to survive as well. If that were the case, then how come he's alive? I'm talking myself in circles, I realise that, but there must be some answers or details that I'm missing. So, maybe you, or anyone reading this report, can see it.*

Sam set the paper down in front of him, clenching his fists beneath his chin with a sigh.

"What are you thinking?" Seb asked him.

"I'm thinking we talk to the boy. Maybe he can shed some light on this."

Seb nodded and got up, following Sam to Phil's room.

## CHAPTER TWENTY

"Dr. Cretin is his name, the man who injected me," Andrew said, holding Phil's hand. "He took all kinds of samples from me; from things I didn't even know one could take samples from. He said he gave me a *scientific addition* to awaken something in me, and to carry out the plan they had in store for me."

"What kinda addition? What plan?"

"I dunno what plan it was, but the addition I *do* know." He took a deep breath, turning himself into a plant, then turning himself into Phil.

Everyone present gasped, even Phil, who realised Andrew's cries about him being a shapeshifter were in fact true.

He turned himself back, looking into Phil's terrified eyes. "I can turn into someone, or *something*, by either touching 'em or concentrating hard on their features. But that's not all." He looked away from Phil, addressing Sam directly. "I could see the future; I could see what the future *could* look like. Premonitions, if you will."

"Did they come true?" Seb asked.

"No, not all, but some did." Andrew sighed. "Phil died in one of 'em, which thank heavens didn't come true. But the other… about my sister…" He took a deep breath, feeling Phil's hand slipping into his, squeezing it. "What I saw about her fate was true."

Bramley knocked on the door, looking at Phil. "It's time."

Phil nodded, looking at Andrew. "Don't worry too much about me, okay? It's just a simple procedure. And whatever the bloody hell you're gonna do while I'm under, you're not gonna risk your life for me."

"How did you—"

"Know you're gonna do something stupid after that premonition of yours? 'Cause you think you can stop the premonition from happening. You've done that already, and you're gonna try to keep doing that until you can't. And I'm not gonna let you."

Andrew touched Phil's cheek. "You'd do it for me, *wouldn't you?*"

Phil didn't answer Andrew. Instead, he planted a kiss on Andrew's lips, which made Sam smile. *At least love still exists in this macabre world.*

As Phil moved away from Andrew, he squeezed his hand. "Now there's no way I'm letting you go to that surgery."

Phil chuckled softly. "I'll be okay. They're gonna save me. You know they will."

"Can we even trust 'em?"

Phil nodded. *"They saved my life once. I'm sure they'll do it again. I trust my life with 'em."*

Andrew kissed him one last time before Bramley ushered everyone outside. He and Tim closed the door to make sure no one could disturb them.

Standing over the map Tim had drawn, Sam, Stan, Alex, and Seb devised a plan. Approaching the next island, they went over the plan one more time.

"We're gonna hover over the island to try and find the three castaways. *No one* sets foot on that island. I want you to be near your posts. Stan, Seb, I want you near the rope in case someone needs to be hauled up. Alex, you're on telescope duty. I'll keep giving the pilot directions."

The others nodded in response.

"And what can I do?"

They all turned around to look at Andrew, his arms crossed. "I'm *not* gonna sit back. I've seen things on that island that I can't describe. The least I can do is help to get others outta their misery." Sam wanted to open his mouth, but Andrew stopped him. "I know I'm a gimp, but I can still shoot a gun. I can shoot at anything chasing 'em down."

"Even if it's their family? Like yours was?" Seb asked him.

"If it saves lives, then yes. I'll take that responsibility."

Sam nodded. "All right, I'll get you settled then."

The others went to their assigned posts. Andrew followed Sam to his in his wheelchair.

Sam pushed a button on the wall nearest to the hatch. Andrew watched in awe as he saw the minigun mounted atop a moveable steel-plated platform. Whistling, he situated himself behind it, peeking through its iron sight.

"It has a capacity of two-thousand rounds. I'll stay close-by so I can reload for you when it's necessary."

Andrew nodded, looking at Sam. "I don't think I've properly thanked you. For saving us."

"Thank me *when* we're safe."

Andrew gave him a firm nod, then positioned himself behind the gun. He took a deep breath, steadying himself and his aim.

As they approached the island, Alex looked through the telescope for any signs of movement as the Kite turned off its engines, hovering in silence to avoid detection.

Alex observed a broken palm frond, following the what-used-to-be a treeline. It seemed mowed down, as if something big had stomped over it. He raised his hand up, his palm facing forward over his head.

Sam nodded, commanding their pilot to keep the Kite steady.

Maddie carried Zack to his crib, smiling as she hummed a song to him. An urgent knock on her door made her stop. She gently put him down in his crib before hurrying towards the door. She opened it and found Percy waiting on the other side.

"*Percy*? What's *wrong*?"

He pushed a bag in her hands, quickly locking the door behind him, securing it tightly with a wooden chair.

"We've lived in prosperity for about two years," he said, mumbling under his breath, "we did normal things like sowing gardens, building houses, taking our children to school." He put a new magazine in his handgun, aiming it directly at the door. "We had finally found a peace unlike anything we had known during our days trapped in the Dome."

"What's going—"

"Our numbers grew as more and more people outside the original borders of the Dome became disillusioned with the capitalistic President Ashwell and his followers." He looked over at her. "We need to find shelter. *They're* coming."

"Who's—"

She heard the tires, the bellowing engines finding their way towards her house. She rushed to get her son, stuffing some clothes and toys in the bag, then quickly made her way to the kitchen to get some provisions.

"The root cellar," she said, "Sam and I kept it well stocked in case we had to stay cloistered for whatever *plague* would torment us."

"Go."

She nodded, taking the key from the cupboard, opening the hatch to the cellar which couldn't be seen by the naked eye. Only those who knew of its exact location knew where it was. She opened the lock, descending down the tiny stairs into the darkness of the cellar. Percy followed suit, closing the door behind him just in time as the front door was rammed open.

*"Our lives aren't ours,"* he whispered, *"neither will our deaths be."*

Her breath trembled as she heard the footsteps above her, praying silently to herself that Sam would barge in and save them. Percy grabbed her hand, Zack cooed softly.

*"We don't have a real life that belongs to us. Whatever happens next, we didn't have a choice."*

He showed her the three pills Sam had given him in case of an emergency. She shook her head, tears streaming down her face. Percy unlocked her closed hand, putting the two pills in her palm, then closed her hand.

*"Who are they?"* she managed to ask, her body heaving.

*"Mister X's soldiers. They know."*

She cried softly, thinking about Sam. In her mind, she could hear his voice. *"Stay with me,"* he would say, *"no matter what."* And she would reply, *"always. Until the end."*

# CHAPTER TWENTY-ONE

After having scoured the general acreage of the island, Alex shook his head.

"I see nothing y'all. Either they're all dead, or the island hasn't been touched yet."

"My money is on the latter," Stan said, sighing deeply. "We must go down there. It's the only way."

Andrew shook his head, panic flared up in his eyes. "No, you can't. It's dangerous. *Very* dangerous. Whatever they do to you down there, it was worse than just a scuffle at a random rally."

Alex hastily geared up; Sam quickly walked over to stop him. "There's no way I'm losing anyone else from our Squad. *No one.* You hear me?" He looked at Stan, then at Seb, "you hear me?" he yelled.

"That's not for ya to decide, is it?" Alex said nonchalantly, attaching his holster around his waist. "Ya taught us to *never* leave behind a soul. Well, from where I'm standing, those people down there are souls in need of saving, eh?"

In that moment, Sam hated himself for ever having said those words. He shook his head, gripping the edges of his scalp with his hands, breathing rapidly. "I can't lose *anyone* else. I can't." He bumped against the wall with his back, his blood pounded in his ears. He felt his heart thudding in his chest.

"Sam," Seb said, slowly making his way over to him. He grabbed Sam's shaking hands. "I know you're scared, but you know we were never truly safe. We knew there were people out there who could still hurt us. And when no one came to our rescue, we had to do it ourselves. We can't let 'em suffer the same fate. We *lost* Theo. You said it yourself; we can't lose *anyone* else. That includes those not initially in our Squad, but those who are our allies."

He clutched Seb's shoulder before finding his way to the ground, Seb following suit. Seb coached his breathing and pointed at his water bottle on the floor. When Stan walked over, Seb took the bottle from him.

Sam took a few gulps, still breathing with great trouble. "You're not suffocating, Sam, and you know that. You've been through this numerous times before." Noticing Sam was shivering, Seb took off his jacket, wrapping it around his shoulders.

Alex kneeled next to them both, rubbing his back soothingly. Then, as Seb went in for a long hug, Alex joined. As the three of them sat there in pure silence, Sam slowly calmed down, his breathing more even.

Andrew couldn't even comprehend what he had just witnessed. It was clear Sam had been through way more trauma than he had, and it almost pained him that he couldn't join them. *At least I can assist from up here. I can keep 'em safe.*

As Alex and Seb let Sam go, Tim appeared behind them, clearing his throat.

"I know this isn't the right timing, perhaps, but I came to tell you that the surgery was a success. If you wanna—"

Before he could finish his sentence, Andrew had wheeled off. Tim chuckled softly, then regained his stern look. He took a silver case from behind the pilot's chair, walking towards the map table. Upon opening it, everyone else gathered around the table.

They all looked down at the metallic green blaster with seemingly decently efficient coils. The coils around it were less green, and bluer, but still metallic all the same. Tim picked it up, spinning it around in his hand. "This gun uses intense magnetic waves to quite literally disassemble someone." He pointed at the barrel. "It has two separate triggers for each barrel. The one in the back doesn't just disassemble a body, but it also puts every molecule together and reprograms it. Basically, all you need is one trigger pull, and you can basically kill any living thing no matter *what* they've got living inside of 'em."

"That's so—"

"Cool?" Tim finished Alex's sentence. "Sure, it seems that way, and sure it seems badass, but that bloody shite was way harder to make than you might think. I've been secretly working on this ever since we *won* from Ashwell. It took me a million minutes to make this."

"A million minutes? Why can't you just say two years like a normal human being," Stan scoffed.

Tim ignored him, looking back at Sam who was slowly coming back to his full senses. "I also have some alcohol solution I've been working on." He gave a bottle to Sam. "It helps healthy cells duplicate and eventually replaces the dying or dead ones. You've to dilute it with water so it doesn't hurt as much, and you might need a bite gag. When I used it on myself it almost shattered my jawbone."

"And why the bloody hell should we use it then?" Stan continued questioning Tim's scientific abilities.

"Like I said, it replaces dying or dead cells with living ones, but duplicates living cells and speeds up red and white blood cell production."

Sam understood what he was trying to say, nodding slowly. "He's saying it can basically cure *any* type of infection or wound. It's the ultimate medicine."

Before Stan could open his mouth a third time, Alex took him apart to silently lecture him. Boyfriend or not, he still had a lot to learn about being one of the team.

Sam looked at the blaster, pointing at the front trigger. "And this one?"

"Non-lethal, mostly. The back, as lethal as they come. The front, not so much. If you just wanna stun someone, you can use the taser. It's still using magnetic waves, but it won't kill anyone."

With much hesitation, Sam took it from him, feeling how light-weighted it was. It almost surprised him. He took a deep breath, then turned around to look at Alex and Stan. "You're right." They stopped their bickering, looking at Sam expectantly. "We need to help those who can't help themselves. So, grab whatever gear you can carry, and lower the rope."

Stan nodded, going back to his previous station to get the rope positioned.

Sam turned to face Seb, putting a hand on his shoulder. "How's your aim?"

"I shoot as if I was never blind."

Both chuckled lightly, then Sam shook his head. "Bloody straight."

"Command, this is unit Wildcat AK-1. We're currently eighty miles northwest of the base. Our altitude is at a steady fifteen hundred feet. Requesting clearance for Operation Snow."

*"Wildcat, this is Command. Are you preparing to engage?"*

"The militia is ready to converge with the ones in need of rescue. I'm requesting clearance for the operation."

*"Negative. Your task is to stand by. Don't engage."*

"I can't tell 'em to stand down, Command," the pilot said, nodding at Sam, Stan, Alex, and Seb who prepared themselves to leave the Kite. "They've already left their formation. You could say... *hostiles inbound.*"

He winked at Sam, then watched as they left the Kite one by one.

Setting foot on the hot, moist biome, Sam looked up at the Kite hovering silently in the sky, sighing deeply to himself.

Surrounded by dense canopies of vegetation forming three layers, he moved his hand behind his head, his palm up. Sweeping his hand overhead to the left, the others followed him.

"Is it me, or has it just rained?" Seb asked, his feet sinking away in the mud below him, sighing deeply. "I just had these cleaned."

Taking out a flashlight, Sam shined forward towards the dark and humid shade caused by the canopy's leaves. "Stay close. No one falls behind."

They fell in line behind Sam, moving seamlessly together like they were part of a single entity. Perfectly coordinated, there was no need for spoken language. With expert manoeuvring, they made their way through the lush foliage.

Sam's eyes adjusted to his surroundings, picking up the smallest signs of movement in the darkness of the trees, most belonging to innocent birds. Coming upon a spring, Sam felt anguish building up inside of him, gasping softly at the spring's state.

Peering into the oily slick, he looked over his shoulder at the others. "They've poisoned it beyond cleansing. There's no way there's anyone near here if this was their primary source of water. They might've moved on."

Outraged, he kicked against a tiny rock. *We were supposed to just get down here, find 'em, and leave. And they were supposed to be near water. This was the only spring we could see from above.*

"Bloody hell!" he yelled in full dismay.

The others cringed at his outburst.

Seb stepped forward, touching Sam's shoulder, who brushed him off. "We shouldn't have come down here. We gotta go back." He looked over his shoulders. "We're retreating."

"But—" Alex started.

"No buts. If the spring is poisoned, there's no telling what's next."

Before anyone could protest, a greenish-looking fog came creeping through the trees from behind them. Stan patted Alex on his shoulder. Alex turned around, watching as it came close enough for him to touch. Upon doing so, he collapsed to the ground, unable to move or talk. His veins turned dark red, seemingly ready to burst. His skin blistered, gasping for air.

"It's paralytic poison!" Stan yelled, dragging Alex away from the fog as quickly as he could.

"We gotta move," Sam said, looking at Seb. "Grab my hand and stay close!"

Seb nodded, doing as he was told. Stan went on his knees, forcing Alex onto his back with all his might.

Strange veins of glowing, pulsing green ran through the trees on all sides, as if it was guiding them towards a certain point. Stan felt small pustule-like growths forming on Alex's hands, clinging to him like a leech.

The path ahead grew thinner as they ran, then Sam lost his footing.

He rolled down a steep hill with trees all around, hitting trunks almost every inch of the way as he rapidly descended. Seb rolled down right behind him, somehow managing to reach the bottom first.

Sam came to a halt, peering ahead of him to see if there was more of the poisonous fog, but it seemed safe. Spotting a rushing stream on his side, he looked back at the hill, watching as Stan and Alex toppled over one another, landing sideways.

Sam quickly crawled over to Alex, who was still paralysed. Checking up on Stan, he noticed he had the same dark-red veins. *The fog must've reached him just before he rolled down. Shite. This is bad.*

He looked over at Seb who scrambled to his feet. "How are we looking?"

"It's bad. They're both paralysed. There's no way we can get 'em back. The fog leads all the way to the Kite. We gotta contact Tim to fly to the other side of the island. It's the only way."

Seb nodded. "I can carry one of 'em."

"You can't, you're—"

"Blind? Disabled? A cripple? Believe me, *I know.*"

Sam took a few seconds to himself before he responded. "Seb, you know I wasn't gonna say that. You *know* that."

"Yeah, sorry, I…" He sighed. "I'll carry one of 'em, no big deal."

"All right." Sam helped Stan on Seb's back, then took care of Alex. As both were secured as tightly as they could possibly be, they continued their trek down the island.

# CHAPTER TWENTY-TWO

After finding a clearing, Sam set Alex down and helped Seb lower Stan. Taking out his walkie-talkie, Sam contacted Tim.

"While you make your way to the other side, can you tell me how to tell me how to cure paralytic poison?"

"Like a venom-induced poison?"

"I wish. It was caused by a fog."

"A fog? What kinda colour was it?"

"Very green, almost vibrant. Almost *too* green. Not natural."

"I got some neostigmine up here. I'll come down."

"Don't. I can't risk having someone else down here. Just see if you can drop it somewhere near us. I'll send up a flare."

"Copy that."

He took a flare out of his bag, firing it into the air, watching as it arced up into the sky.

"What do we do now?" Seb asked.

Sam shushed him. His paranoia triggered, but it felt oddly mellow, as if something he couldn't stop was going to happen. And all he could do was accept it. He unzipped his bag, taking the blaster out of his bag. Pushing the button, he slid the mechanism towards him, aiming it directly at where he believed someone was watching them. He pulled the trigger, which made all the coils heat up. It disbursed a magnet wave, in which the beam flew at a ninety-degree angle. It completely obliterated whoever was coming towards them, leaving only blood and flesh bits behind.

Seb had heard the shot but couldn't see what had happened. "Sam?" he called out cautiously.

Sam walked over to the thing he killed, examining it. "It was a *human.*" He stared at the young girl in disbelief. "But she also wasn't." He kneeled next to what was left of the body, noticing the black-coloured vine-like veins protruding from the tiny bits of flesh that were left. Touching one of the blisters, he moved backwards with a grunt. "That's nasty-looking. Not to mention the smell that comes off it."

"If she's... *wasn't* human, then *what* was she?"

"I dunno. But she fit Andrew's description, and with what happened to his sister... I might've murdered someone's family."

"Sam, we're above you. I'm dropping the antidote."

Sam looked up at the Kite hovering silently above them. He watched as the container came down with a tiny parachute, catching it mid-air. He kneeled next to Alex, opening it. Looking at the thick, tar-like ointment, he dug his fingers in, then lubricated it onto the blisters. Within seconds, scabs appeared.

"I think it's working." He quickly gave Alex the injection found in the same container, then moved on to Stan to treat him.

"Did it work?"

He took the walkie-talkie out of his pocket. "I think so, yeah. Is it a one-time-thing only?"

"Considering the especially resilient strain of the island's radioactive readings I'm receiving now; I'd say it requires frequent applications. And perhaps some puss draining every now and then."

"Got it. Prepare for immediate extraction."

"What... say... Sam... hello...?"

"Shite." Sam threw the walkie-talkie onto the ground. "They're blocking our signal." He looked over at Seb, sucking in a deep breath. "Stay with 'em. I'm gonna see if I can find wood for a campfire. I've got a feeling we'll be stuck here tonight."

He left Seb with the others, walking over to a row of orderly and pruned trees. Taking the axe out of his bag, he began to chop away.

Returning to the others with his arms full of wood, he smiled seeing Alex and Stan sitting upright. "Good to see you two responsive and aware." He dropped the wood. "The way your eyes stayed open... it was a terrifying sight."

Stan nodded softly. "Thanks for... your adequate handling. It saved us."

"*You*? Thanking *me*? What else was in that fog? Someone, pinch me, please."

Stan threw a rock at his chest. "Not funny."

Sam chuckled, giving Stan a wink. "Ah come on, it was a *little* funny."

As Sam worked on the campfire, Seb walked over to the stream to fetch some water, filtering it the way he had been taught. He could feel the paved path beneath his feet, which didn't make much sense given their current environment. Stretching his arms out in front of him, he sensed the overgrown bushes beside him— hardly the reason the path existed in the first place.

Without realising what was going on, the path he took was darkly shaded by a thick canopy that closed in on him, thorny vines surrounding him. The path he was on led him deeper into the woods.

"Shouldn't Seb be back by now?" Alex asked, "the stream wasn't that far away from us, eh?"

Sam got up, nodding. "Knowing him and his insane abilities to manoeuvre around the world without sight, you're right." He took the blaster out of his bag. "Be right back."

Looking down at the muddy ground, Sam followed Seb's footsteps, until they stopped. *What the... it's as if he vanished. That can't be.*

"Seb?" he whispered, not sure what was out there. Looking up at the trees above him, he was afraid Seb had perhaps been caught in a self-sprung trap. Hearing one splash after the other, he hurried towards where the sound came from.

Pelted by debris in the muddy water, Seb fought to find the surface, bleeding from his head. Trying to preserve his oxygen as best as he could, he moved through the water with combined arm and leg motions. Despite the consistent propulsion of his body, which to him felt like he was going upwards, he never reached anything remotely close to the surface.

His lungs felt like they were bursting, his muscles slowly failing one by one. Despite being blind, he could tell his vision was darkening.

He gasped mouthfuls of air as Sam wrestled him to safety on the far side of the stream. Unable to do much more than keep Seb's head above water, he quickly swam backwards towards the stream's edge. He made sure Seb could stand before pushing himself up on the muddy ground, getting out of the water.

He dragged Seb out, smoothing his damp clothes against his skin as he settled to his haunches beside him. Despite Sam being wet himself, he embraced Seb once he felt him shivering. Somewhat warmed by Sam's touch, Seb's shivering gradually eased.

"Come on, let's get you warmed up by the fire."

He pulled Seb to his feet, guiding him back towards the others.

"Someone *pushed* you in?" Stan asked, eating one of the ration packs they had packed.

"It's the strangest thing, really," Seb said, holding his hands above the fire. "First the path was almost like I was back in the city, reconstituted outta thin air, if you will."

"And then you hit the water?"

"Yeah, I guess. I honestly don't remember much after realising the path didn't belong there."

"And the push? What did it feel like?" Alex asked.

Seb frowned, shaking his head. "What else is a push supposed to feel like? It was a *push*."

"Ya, but y'know, was it like a hard *'I'm gonna kill ya' kinda push*, or *just* a push?"

"Just a push!"

"Okay, chill, mate, chill."

Seb leaned against the trunk of the tree he was seated against, closing his eyes. Alex shrugged as he saw Stan's impenetrating look, then closed his own eyes. Sam looked at Stan, nodding to take the first watch. Stan returned the nod, settling in for the night.

"Calm down! You're *safe*!" Tim yelled, shielding himself with a tray, he dodged as Phil hurled object after object at him.

"They're gonna release *more* pain!" he screamed, his forehead beading with sweat. "They're gonna bring so much more sorrow and danger! You just had to go and *ruin* it!"

"Ruin it? What the bloody hell—"A needle flew straight past his ear, missing him narrowly. His breath shuddered, looking past the tray. "Who do you mean by *they*?"

"*They*! The ones who put us there! *They* warned me! They're in my head!" He put his hands to his head, wincing, his breathing laboured. "You weren't supposed to rescue two people! There was supposed to be just *one* survivor!"

"*One* survivor?" Tim put the tray down. "Was it part of a... a game?"

"I dunno!" He exhaled slowly, looking over at Tim. "All I know, is that only one, the *victor*, could go home. And you've *ruined* their desired plan. And they're *mad*." He shook his head. "In fact, they're *so* mad, they said they'd make us feel *how* mad."

Tim slowly got up; worry etched on his face. "Phil..."

"He says... he says that history is replete with killers."

"Who's *he*, Phil?"

He shook his head again. "I dunno."

Tim walked over to him; his hands raised in the air. "Where do you *hear* this voice?"

A tear rolled down Phil's cheek. "*Everywhere*." He looked away from Tim. "And it's scaring the bloody hell outta me."

Tim wanted to ask more, but for the time being, he decided not to.

Sam's lungs felt like they were burning. The thoughts swirling in his mind grew sluggish from the lack of air he was experiencing. As he sank into the darkness, his fingers closed on the rough fabric of his jacket.

He gasped awake, covered in sweat. Realising he had fallen asleep, sunk into one of his night terrors, he looked over at the others, still soundly asleep.

He paced around, his mind still churning.

*I should've come up with a contingency plan. We can't reach Tim, or anyone, and I haven't seen the Kite in hours. We're screwed. We're so screwed.*

Lighting and thunder filled his hearing, obscuring his vision. Looking up at the sky, he noticed a dark storm cloud going right over their heads.

Scanning his surroundings, he noticed a figure veiled in shadow, standing on the opposite side of the path. His back was turned to Sam. Lifting his axe, his heart thundered, somehow even heavier sounding than the actual thunder.

Walking over to the figure, he braced himself, his hands clasped firmly around the axe's handle. The figure turned around, simply watching as Sam came closer, its head cocked slightly to the left. His eyes were shadowed behind a fall of unkempt hair, its fringes still visible.

Sam moved towards his belt to grab his flashlight. The thunder was right above their heads, but neither of them moved.

Turning it on, Sam shined directly into the figure's brown eyes.

"Jed?"

He smiled upon seeing the black-haired ex-Laerie, his broad chest and big arms hadn't diminished an inch since the last time he saw him.

Jed smiled back, laughing. "Look who Mother Nature coughed up."

Sam turned off his flashlight, bracing himself to hug Jed as a jet of lightning streaked through the air, right into Jed's face. He let out a wail as he flailed about, trying to escape the electromagnetic radiation surging through him.

Sam watched in horror as he crumpled to the ground in an ashy puddle, watching as the electrostatic discharge sputtered out, hearing nothing but a brief sizzling noise.

"Sam?" he heard behind him, Seb's voice laced with worry.

Stan and Alex followed suit. They had all heard the vibrating particles caused by the lightning strike. Upon reaching Sam, Stan and Alex looked down at the burnt body.

"Why does it smell like someone roasted chicken?" Seb asked.

All eyes were on Seb, who took the deafening silence as a sign he shouldn't have said anything.

"Who was that?" Alex dared to ask.

"Jed."

"No... Baxal?"

"Yeah."

"Why was he all alone out here? Where are the other two he's supposed to be with?" Stan asked.

"They must've gotten separated," Sam said, almost whispering. Another thunderclap sounded above them. "We gotta go. It's not safe to be out here."

They moved back to their makeshift camp, gathering their belongings.

"Be honest," Seb started, zipping his bag closed, "is this thunder *natural*?"

Sam looked up at the sky, shaking his head. "No, it can't be. Normal lightning wouldn't cremate someone alive. Sure, it may leave burns, but no. This was *unnatural*. And I've got a bad feeling that someone's watching *all of us*."

# CHAPTER TWENTY-THREE

Tim waited with Andrew in front of Phil's room. Andrew hadn't been in the room during Phil's outburst as he had been stationed to mount the minigun. Jittery nerves coursed through Andrew, trying his best to not let them take over.

*What's taking him so long? I swear the anticipation is killing me. I can literally feel it tingling inside of me.*

He wheeled around the tiny hallway in his wheelchair, not caring if it would drive Tim nuts.

The door finally opened. Bramley walked out with a clipboard in his hands.

"And?" Andrew asked, praying silently that he hadn't discovered anything, and Phil was simply traumatised.

"Well, there's a tracker inside of 'im, but it's not fer trackin' his location or anythin' like tha'. It's probably fer keepin' tabs on him, keepin' track o' his vital signs an' all tha'. Oh, an' this." He gave the clipboard to Tim. "It's a two-way transmitter kind o' *thing*. Whoever's on teh other side o' it can hear us, an' only Phil can hear 'em in return."

"But it's not a device, per se?"

"No, he was injected with somethin' tha' nullified teh immunity yeh've given 'im. Like a virus."

"So, he's back to being non-immune?"

"Looks like it. Or perhaps they weren' fully immune to begin with. Perhaps only yeh an' teh other Troopers were after taking teh mixed serums."

Tim's mental gears were working overtime, trying to make sense of the possibility that the REBELS had never been immune after receiving the cure. Andrew had no idea what they were talking about, vaguely recalling that he, too, had been injected with something. But for the time being, he decided it was unimportant.

Tim walked over to his laptop. "Can we see where the source of this *transmitter* is coming from?"

Bramley shrugged. "I'm 'ere fer teh medical stuff, yeh're teh nerd."

"Blimey, thanks." Tim let out a sigh, pulling up the map with the islands. Typing the transmitter's code into the respective section, he pointed at a red dot. "There, it seems to be coming from the centre of it all. Like it's an epicentre."

"Isn' tha' a mountain?" Bramley asked, pointing at the screen.

"It does seem to be someplace high up, but that could also be an illusion. It might very well be a simple tower or maybe even a funky-looking skyscraper. Honestly, at this point, I don't see why such things couldn't be popping outta thin air." He looked over at Andrew. "Do you mind if we perform some tests on you too? Just for precaution."

Worry was written on Andrew's face; afraid he might have something lurking inside of him without his knowledge. He took a deep breath, shuddering slightly. "Do what you must do. You've got my permission."

Tim nodded, giving Bramley a look. Bramley sighed, wheeling Andrew away. Tim took the walkie-talkie off the table, closing his eyes as he pressed it against his chest. "Sam?" He hit the table as no one replied, shaking his head. "You better be okay out there. *All of you.*"

Examining Jed's body, Sam touched the ashes that were left, smelling it.

"That's disgusting," Stan replied, "and very disrespectful. Who the bloody hell would smell someone's remains?"

"Shut up." Sam closed his eyes as he smelled it again. "I thought I smelled the tiniest hint of petrol, which wouldn't make sense given the circumstances, but," he looked over at Alex, "I'm sure *you* recognise it too."

Alex hesitated at first, then kneeled next to Sam, taking a sniff. "That's chemical accelerant."

"Exactly." Sam spread the ashes back onto the ground.

"What's a chemical accelerant?" Stan asked.

"It's a quick burn," Seb replied, "it's mostly used to set something on fire without spreading it to places it shouldn't spread to. Like when you don't wanna set the whole woods on fire, but still wanna set one."

"So, what, *someone* hit him with electricity while covering him in that stuff to burn just him?"

Sam nodded, getting back up. "There's something systematic about it."

Stan scoffed. "Duh, it's *clearly* systematic. It's all part of a plan, isn't it?"

"I don't mean it like that," Sam said, turning around to face Stan. "It's like a methodical game of chess. Whoever's doing this, is taking out the weakest links first."

"Like they did with *us*... They're looking for the strongest people just like Ashwell and Lawrence wanted. It's happening *all over again*."

"How's that even possible, eh? Both are dead, y'all!" Alex exclaimed. "There's gotta be a rational explanation for this y'know?"

Sam looked at Alex, who had a glum look on his face. "I think we ruined their plan. That's why Jed combusted the way he did. We rescued both Phil and Andrew, and only *one* was supposed to live, right? And from all those islands, if what we believe is true, only six will remain..."

"We're with six too," Alex concluded. "Mate..."

Sam nodded, a sense of execrable worry finding its way towards his brain. *I never should've left home. That's exactly what they wanted. They wanted us gone.*

"Attention all personnel. An intruder has been spotted. Terminate all activities immediately. Evacuate the premises until safe conditions are re-established and verified by USO. Attention all..."

"What's going on?" Henry asked Callum, his head of security.

"There's been a breach, sir. We must get you down to the central lift to evacuate to the bottom level. The train will be waiting on the platform."

Henry nodded, hitting the button Tim had installed in the Kite to warn them. He rushed after Callum,

*"Attention all personnel. All personnel must evacuate the facility. All crews must evacuate the facility."*

A barrage of bullets ripped through the roof and glass walls of the floor they were on. Crouching behind some furniture, Henry covered his ears and closed his eyes. Focusing on his breathing, he told himself it was going to be okay. That Callum was going to make this right.

A looming shadow appeared in front of him. Opening his eyes slowly, he looked straight into the barrel of a handgun, a hooded figure on the other end of it. Pulling the trigger, he shot a bullet straight at Henry's chest cladded with a bulletproof vest.

The bullet ricocheted, and a single shot rang out from behind him. Between the hooded figure's eyes, a bullet wound appeared, and his body dropped to the floor.

Henry looked over the piece of furniture at Callum, who made his way over to Henry. "Come quick, sir, this way."

Heading straight for the lift, Callum and two other members of USO joined Henry, pressing the button to head down to the lowest level.

"Status report," Callum asked the red-haired guard.

Before he could reply, bullets teared into the lift from above, showering shards of glass onto all four men. The bullets bounced off the metal as the three guards shielded Henry as best as they could, firing up without a fixed aim.

"We're almost there!" Callum shouted. "Come on!"

The lift dinged, and the three men quickly escorted Henry towards the train waiting for them.

Three shots called out. The three guards dropped dead instantly.

Henry looked around him at the three bodies, his face laced with shock. Looking up at the smoking barrel of a gun, another masked figure stared down at him. Taking out a sword, the blade sliced clean through his bulletproof vest, sending him sprawling.

He tried to crawl away from the masked figure, scrambling backwards as fast as he could. "No, please," he said, "please, don't do this. The people are finally living in peace. I'll give you whatever you want, any sum of money you desire. Just name your price."

The figure sliced his chest again; fresh blood begun to soak Henry's clothes.

"What I want," the figure said, holding the sword straight above Henry's heart, "is *your life*." He plunged the blade straight through Henry's abdomen, watching as Henry squirmed and screamed. "But first, I'm gonna make you suffer 'cause no death should be swift."

He sliced Henry's chest a third time while Henry cried out for help.

Moving through the muddy landscape, the four boys tried to free their feet with each step they took, sinking deeper into the merciless gobbling of the mud. Dawn had begun to rise, signalling the start of the morning twilight.

Having survived the night, Sam knew they couldn't linger a second longer. Sinking deep into the mud, he grunted, pulling his leg free with more effort than the last.

Rain pelted down on them, making the mud even more slippery. Seb held onto Sam's backpack for safety, Alex following closely behind him, Stan closing the line.

"I think I see the last remnants of a campfire up ahead!" Sam yelled over his shoulder, pointing at the smoke, "that must be where—"

He slipped, scrambling for something to hold on to. The mudslide took him down yet another tiny mountainside of the island, wrapping him in its slippery embrace, Seb following suit.

Pulling them down the steep hill at an alarming speed, Sam dug his fingers into the wet sludge to try and slow their rapid descent. Glancing at a tree coming dangerously close, he fought against the grasp of the mud. "Hold on!"

Preparing to fling both himself and Seb at the tree's trunk, he noticed how Alex and Stan moved from tree to tree along the side to keep up. They swept from one still-standing tree to the next as the ones behind them rushed forward with rapid speed.

With a burst of adrenaline, Sam lunged towards the tree, pulling Seb along by the hand. Both of their arms wrapped around the sturdy trunk, holding themselves upright.

Clinging tight to the coarse bark, the mud kept flooding down, trying desperately to pull Sam and Seb along.

"Hold on!" an unfamiliar voice sounded from behind them.

Stan and Alex were nowhere to be found. *No, please don't let 'em have fallen in...*

For once, Sam wasn't worried about the unknown voice he was hearing, though he knew he should be. Hearing the creaking sound of a tree, he looked to his left, looking at a golden bronze boy with a nose so round, it could easily be used to secure a ship to the quay, pushing hard against a tree.

If Sam hadn't seen it with his own two eyes, he wouldn't have believed it.

The boy stared intensely at the tree, then at his own feet, launching himself towards Sam and Seb. Wrapping his muscular arms around both, he pushed off, pulling them to safety.

Laying on their backs on the ground, Sam and Seb rested their aching legs, catching their breath.

Stan and Alex hovered over them; worry written on their faces.

"Ya good?" Alex asked them.

Sam nodded slowly, breathing heavily. Looking over at the boy, he noticed just how thin his lips were. They were barely noticeable.

"I'm not gonna disappear or anythin' if you stop starin' at me like that. I'm not a hoax." He came a little closer. "Name's Val.

Short for Valentine, but I despise that name. So, if anyone dares to call me that, I'll hurt you without even touchin' you."

"Is that how you reached us?" Sam asked, sitting up, "I saw what you did. No *normal* human could've done that. What the bloody hell *are you*?"

Val scoffed, crossing his arms. "I can control things with my mind. And before you freak out, no, I'm *not* a psychic or a freak. I just possess some kinda superpower that *saved* your life." He looked at Seb, cocking his head to the right. "He blind?"

"Yeah, what's it to you?" Seb asked, "afraid I've got laser vision?"

Val shrugged. "One can never be too sure." He looked at all four of them, then stopped his eyes at Sam. "You're thin. Been stuck here longer than the others?"

"No, it's just the way I'm built."

Val nodded thoughtfully, pointing over his shoulder. "I've set up camp not far from here, on the beach near the shore. You can come with me if you want."

As everyone scrambled to follow Val, Seb pulled Sam's arm. "Can I talk to you?"

Sam spotted the others skirting around the mudslide using the fallen trees as a path, giving Seb a quick pat on his shoulder. "We'll talk later, okay?"

As Sam walked away, Seb whispered, *"if there will be a later."* He followed Sam without saying another word.

# CHAPTER TWENTY-FOUR

"Is it just you out here?" Seb asked, warming his hands above the campfire.

"I dunno, I guess. There were two other lads here, Jim and Jed, but I kinda lost sight of 'em after the earthquake."

"Earthquake? Is that why most trees are no longer standing upright?" Stan asked.

"Mate, do I look like a nature scientist to you?"

Alex snorted, then grunted as Stan slapped him across the back.

"Jed is dead," Sam said, looking over at Val. "When did you see Jim last?"

Val idly whittled a small piece of wood with a makeshift knife, shrugging. "Dunno, but you sure act as if you knew him. *And* Jed." He looked up at Sam. "I never pointed out what they looked like, so you *must've* known 'em."

Resting with his back against a still-standing tree, Seb threw a small booklet towards Val, which landed a few feet away from him. Taking it from the ground, Val glanced briefly at Sam, then opened it.

Skimming through it, he let out a sarcastic grunt. "Guess I should've known this was all a test. Just some *sick* game they've put us in." He threw it back at Seb, landing straight in his lap. He returned to carving off chunks from the piece of wood he was holding.

"We don't have all the answers ourselves yet, but that's what we know so far. And we keep adding notes as we go," Stan said, folding his arms. "But what kinda game do *you* think this is?"

Val dropped the carved wooden figure into the fire, watching as it burnt. "I know that they experimented on me, and five other boys my age. We've all got... *superpowers*, if you will. Each one of us is unique." He took a new piece of wood, carving it up. "I remember hearin' somebody talkin' about wantin' us to fight to the death, and we, *the experiments*, were supposed to win no matter what. They injected us with somethin' far greater and far more potent than the other two *categories*."

"What did they inject the other two with?" Alex asked.

"All I know is that it had to restrengthen the basic impulses of humans. Startin' wars, fightin' until there's one man left standin'. The *ultimate* weapon."

"For?" Stan asked.

"You really think I'd know? They made me fall asleep and then I woke up here."

He looked over at Seb holding the booklet in his hands. "Want me to write that down for you? Doubt you can make the letters stay onto the paper."

Seb gave him a crooked grin, hurling a tiny rock his way, which hit him straight in his face. Even blind, Seb knew how to hit the bull's eye.

"Mate, what the bloody hell's wrong with you? Could've taken my eye out with that!"

"Huh, guess you would've joined me. Or well, *half* of you would've."

Val aimed his hand at Seb, but Sam stopped him. "We came here to *rescue* you; not have you kill one of us."

"Tell *him* that." Val sat back down, moving his finger past his cheek, finding it covered in blood. Stan offered him a cloth to wipe away the blood, but Val slapped his hand away. "I don't need rescuin' anyway. So, go back where you came from and leave me be."

"We can't do that." Sam looked at him. "We already ruined *their* plan by saving two people from an island close-by. They're hitting the other islands way harder than they did the first."

Val scoffed at him, shaking his head. "Of course, you bunch of plonkers had to come and make it worse. Well, congrats, hope you're *proud* of yourself."

Sam watched as the ground heaved, breaking apart the tree Seb was leaning against as if it was made of thin twigs.

"Bloody hell. Not again." Val got up. "You better find somethin' to hold onto!"

The ground shook beneath them, the surrounding trees toppling into the ocean, swallowed by violent waves. Before Sam could ask what exactly Val meant with *again,* he looked down. He saw the ground crumbling below him, barely holding himself onto the edge with one arm as the ground gave way.

"Hold on!" Alex yelled, throwing a rope towards Sam which he had taken from his backpack.

"Everyone else, towards the cliffs!" Val yelled, giving himself a head start.

"Go! Take Seb!" Sam yelled at Stan, who tried to help Alex pull Sam up. "That's an order!"

Stan, hesitant to listen, nodded, giving Alex a quick kiss before dragging Seb away from Sam. The seismic activity was almost overwhelming, making Sam nauseous as he hung above nothing but blackness.

Sam, having lost a lot of his strength over the past few days, felt himself slipping with each try he took to climb up, swearing under his breath.

"Come on! Climb!" Alex yelled, his hands burning from holding the rope, "I can't hold on much longer!"

Sam wanted to tell him to let go, to drop him— but he heard Zach's voice in the back of his mind. *"You're stronger than you think, Sam. Remember that you always must keep fighting. No matter what. I'm here to carry half of your burdens if you'll let me. But I can only carry 'em when you do."*

Sam screamed as he put his feet against the rock that had formed, taking one step at a time to reach the top. Once Sam's hands appeared, Alex let go of the rope, grabbing Sam's hands instead. Pulling him to safety, the ground behind them tore up, creating a similar hole Sam had just climbed out of.

Looking for a way to cross it as Sam caught his breath, Alex heard the tree next to them give way, watching it land perfectly over the gap. Making eye contact with Sam, they nodded at one another.

Sam scrambled behind Alex down the larger branch stretched out over the gap, clinging onto it as it shook wildly. The gap extended on both sides at a rapid speed, forcing Alex to jump ahead of Sam. Sam watched as he landed on the other side of the formed cliff, swallowing the heavy lump in his throat.

"Come on! Jump!" Alex yelled, extending his hand. "I'll catch ya!"

*I know, that's not what I'm afraid of.* Sam sighed, looking up at the sky. Feeling the tree shaking more violently, he leaped off, landing just over the edge of the cliff as the tree gave way, Alex's arms wrapped around his stomach.

Looking behind them, they could only go one way. Holding their legs together with toes pointed, straight like a pencil, they took the jump into the ocean.

"No!" was the last thing both heard.

Hitting the water, both slid in smoothly, almost like torpedoes. They tried to grab hold of each other, but the waves pushed them apart.

Sam had no idea what was up, or down, as he rolled around in the water. He looked around in the murky water, seeing nothing but complete darkness. Once the waves gave him a moment of rest, he resurfaced, gasping for breath. Letting the fresh air rush into his lungs, he looked around.

"Alex?"

He looked behind him, realising he hadn't drifted far from the cliff and shore. All kinds of debris cascaded from the still-crumbling island.

"Seb? Stan?"

He was forced to swim further out into the ocean to avoid getting hit by branches and boulders that were no longer just pebbles. Battling the newly growing waves, he fought the current trying to pull him back towards the island.

"Anybody?"

He turned around, seeing the destruction the earthquake had left in its wake. Most of it now resided in the ocean, some earthly pieces making it seem as if the ocean was simply shallow.

*They must've all jumped. There's no doubt about that.*

He dove beneath the surface, looking for any sign of life, but to no avail. Squinting, he saw only a tree trunk that had sunk to the bottom of the ocean, jutting upwards as though forming a ladder.

He went back up to catch his breath, wanting to cry, but unable to. He feared the worst, his heart pounding in his chest.

*I dunno what eruption this bloody arsehole thinks he's creating... Creating being the operative word here... but this is a timeline I don't wanna be a part of. If I could just go back in time to prevent all this from happening...*

He felt powerless, the cold water permeating his limbs one by one. He heard Zach's words echo in his mind, but he didn't care anymore. *He just wanted to sleep.*

Just then, a hand grabbed his foot, pulling him under the water. He screamed, his voice diminishing once he was under the surface. The fallen tree seemed to shuffle in the darkness of the water, *and then he saw it.*

Quickly parting the branches, he freed someone who was stuck. Both swam up to the surface in a hurry.

Panting heavily, Sam looked to see who he had freed, sighing in relief once he saw who emerged. "Seb!" He hugged him tightly, the worry instantly disappearing from his face.

A relieved grin replaced Seb's pout. "Never thought you'd ever be this happy to see me." He paused. "Wait, you *can* see me, right?"

Before Sam could reply, they heard voices not too far behind them. "Sam! Seb! Over here!"

Looking over at Alex and Stan waving their arms on a not-so-distant-shore, Sam began swimming towards them, with Seb following close behind. Once they had swum a safe distance away from the destroyed island, Sam halted so he could guide Seb with his voice. Nearing the rocky bluff, Sam saw something in the water. Swimming towards it, he gasped.

"Jim…"

He looked at the vascular marbling of his body, the dark discolouration of his skin. He had been dead for more than a day at least.

*Val was rather vague about Jim's disappearance… could he have…*

The thought certainly crept into his mind, that Val wasn't as *innocent* as he looked. *Perhaps he's done it to survive, to follow their plan. He can't be trusted.*

"I'm sorry, Jim. You deserved better."

He swam back to Seb, guiding him towards the shore.

Alex and Stan helped them onto the dry land, hugging them both.

"I don't wanna interrupt anything important or anything lads but," he pointed at a cave in the distance, "we can lie low in there for a few days," Val said.

Sam broke free from the hug, advancing with such aggressive speed that Val was forced to take a step back.

"We're not going *anywhere* with you. You know who I just found out there? *Drowned*? Jim!" He pushed Val back. "*You* killed him!"

Val threw his hands up in defence, shaking his head. "Mate, I killed nobody. I'm *not* a murderer. I know my telekinesis might've set us off on the wrong foot but come on, do I look like a cold-blooded killer to you?"

"Could've pushed him in, could've let him float away along the waves without lifting a finger to help him back out. We know *nothing* about you, but it sure as bloody hell looks advantageous enough to you!"

His heartbeat pounded in his ears; the adrenaline of confronting Val released all the pent-up anger that had been simmering inside of him since he left home. He closed his eyes, forced himself to take a few deep breaths. *I'm gonna attack him if I don't calm down. I'm gonna kill him if I don't calm down.*

Taking a few more breaths, he hoped that the influx of fresh oxygen would help settle his anger, at least enough to stop him from violently assaulting Val. He slammed his fist into the nearest rock, his whole body coiling up tight. Whatever he felt churning in his stomach, whether it was confusion or fear, it all turned to anger.

He felt Seb's hand on his shoulder, trying to calm him down without success. Sam stormed off, heading towards the cave. He just wanted to be left alone.

Seb wanted to go after him, but Stan stopped him. "Let him be. We'll get a fire going so you can dry up. He'll join us when he wants to."

"Maybe we can even make a signal fire," Alex suggested, "maybe they can see it."

Stan nodded, and as Alex set out to try and find anything useful to serve as kindling or firewood, he escorted Seb away from the shore. Val was left behind, watching as the waves crashed onto the rocks, sighing loudly. He then followed them, having nowhere else to go.

## CHAPTER TWENTY-FIVE

Josh sucked in a huge breath as he awoke, gasping loudly. "No! Let me go! Stop!"

He looked around the room, panting for air. His eyes landed on the IV bag hanging from the IV pole. He felt for the cord, pulling the soft, flexible tube out of his vein. He tried to sit up, but a sharp jolt of pain shooting through his body made him lie back down. His head was throbbing.

"Pain... is just weakness... leaving the body," he told himself, retrying to sit up. He repeated those words more times than he could count. It was all he had heard during his time in imprisonment. A horrifying pain flared through him, forcing him to give up.

"Josh?"

Hearing his name being spoken, he screamed and shivered. He looked over at Tim, who had the biggest smile on his face, ignorant to Josh's bellow.

He ran over to Josh, hugging him as tightly and as carefully as he possibly could. "We thought we lost you, mate. Don't you *ever* scare us like that again."

Josh hated hugs. He despised them. But hearing Tim sniffle softly, despite his clear attempts to hide that from him, he gave in, patting his back. "It takes a lot more than some... beatings and *experiments* to end me."

Tim let him go, quickly wiping his tears away. Once more, he ignored what Josh said, or simply refused to listen. Something Josh *knew*.

Clearing his throat, Tim squeezed Josh's shoulder. "Well, you still need to take it easy. You've been out cold for at least three days. You were kinda stuck in bardo, which is this state in which you're floating between life and death, and I know that doesn't sound like much but—"

Josh stopped him by putting his hand up in the air. "I know you're one of the reasons I'm still alive, *and Sam too*. And I normally don't say this, but..." He sighed. *"Thank you*, for saving my life. For... for taking care of me." He looked over at Tim, expecting an *'I knew you were a softy!'* But nothing came.

Tim just nodded. "That's what families are for. We take care of our own."

His bashful grin made Josh smile, chuckling softly as he shook his head. "Yeah, about that. I need to tell my... *family*, something. But then again, I dunno if I can ever really... talk about it, I—"

"Tim!"

Tim looked over at the door, finding Andrew in his wheelchair with big eyes.

"Who's—"

"What's wrong?" Tim asked, interrupting Josh's likely burning question.

"The island. It... it's gone."

Tim hurried past Andrew, who could barely wheel out of the way in time. Josh gave him a suspicious look, then watched as Andrew wheeled after Tim, leaving Josh alone.

*A distraction... A welcome distraction. I don't have to think about what happened to me in there. I can focus on something else. I can focus on... whatever this is.*

Forcing his legs over the side of the bed, he took a deep breath. Setting both of his feet down, getting up off the bed, he hit the floor with a loud thud, grunting.

"Oh, come on!" It was only then that he realised he wasn't in the Sicknic back in the city. He had to find out what was going on, practically dragging himself across the floor to find Tim and Andrew.

"It was like... like annihilating cosmic forces came into play. I've never seen anything like it," Andrew explained, looking out of the window at the now open sea. "It was like a bomb had gone off, like that island was but a player on a board. There's no way *they*, or *anyone* really, could've absorbed the impact."

Tim paced around the deck, shaking his head. "No, I *know* those lads, they found a way off the island before... *before* it vanished. They're alive, I can feel it."

"Tim, with all due respect, but—"

"You dunno 'em like I do! Don't you dare soil your mouth with saying they're *dead!*"

Andrew, in a reflex, wheeled backwards until he hit the wall.

"Sorry, I... I didn't mean to yell at you like that. I..." He collapsed against the wall, burying his head in his hands. "I don't wanna be alone again."

Andrew wheeled towards him at a steady pace. "What do you mean, *again*?"

Tears rolled down Tim's cheeks. He spoke with a shaky voice. "Two years ago, I was but a puppet, bullied by most of my fellow Troopers for having privileges. They used me for the IT stuff and that sorta thing, and I couldn't say no 'cause they always threatened to hurt one of 'em. And despite 'em treating me badly, I..." He fidgeted with his hands, more tears rolling down his cheeks. "I couldn't let 'em get hurt. They were still *my* family. But I felt so alone, and I swore to myself I'd never feel that way again. I don't ever wanna feel like a *nobody* ever again."

Breaking down in tears, Andrew was starting to be unsure as to how to calm Tim down, especially considering he had known him for just a little over a day.

Josh, who had finally reached the deck's door, watched as Tim sat on the floor, crying uncontrollably. *I cried like that... No, forget it. Need to forget it. All of it.* Something inside of Josh found its way to his legs, a wave of giddy energy washed over him. "You're *not* a nobody, Tim," he said with sincere earnestness, falling to his knees in front of him, "you're a *somebody*. You're *our* somebody."

Tim looked up at him with a cocked head, snorting in his own way of expressing bashfulness. "How did we get so jaded?"

Josh chuckled softly, shrugging, pretending he was fine. "Mate, I've no idea."

As Tim's sadness subsided, he stared pensively at the window, getting up once his eye caught something. Rushing over, he practically bounced with excitement, bursting into the cockpit. "They're over there! Get over there!"

The pilot nodded, flying the Kite towards the tiny cloud of smoke rising up to the sky.

Building the fire pit, Sam modelled it after the one Zach taught him, looking over at Alex who returned from his search in the woods, his arms laden with kindling and logs. Sam nodded at him, taking the piece of flint from his backpack. Its flat façade was only a couple of inches wide, but it had always done the trick in the past.

"I dunno if relyin' on a friction fire with this dampness is gonna work," Val replied, his arms crossed. "Seems rather *stupid*."

Sam ignored him, arranging some of the kindling in the fire pit. He took his pocketknife out of his back pocket, striking at the hunk of flint with the steel blade.

A couple of minutes passed; no sparks emerged. Staring at the setup in puzzlement, he looked at the wet logs, sighing deeply. "Wish I hadn't lost my lighter."

"You need some pointers?" Val asked, leaning against the rocks. "You need dryer tinder for starters, like husks."

"As if I've got access to that now," Sam scoffed.

Stan rubbed Seb's arms, trying to get him warmed up. It was the second time in a row he had gotten wet, and he had been complaining about a headache and a dry cough. "We gotta start that fire," Stan said, "I don't want him developing pneumonia."

"I don't want that either, Captain Obvious!" Sam snarled, shaking his head.

Alex pointed at the wood. "Can't we use some of the inside of the wood? I mean, sure the exterior is soaked, y'know, but I suspect that there's gotta be some dry spots beneath the bark, eh?"

"Now see, *he's* smart." Val squatted to peel back the wet bark from one of the retrieved logs. Shaving off the smaller, dry fibres, he added the dry material to the top of the pile, smiling sheepishly. "Try again."

Sam scoffed, not wanting to give in to the fact that he clearly stole Alex's idea. Striking the flint again, nothing happened.

"Ouch, no luck? That's 'cause you got bad technique. You've gotta hit the sharp bit at the slight angle, like so," he demonstrated with his hands, "not parallel, not perpendicular, if you know what I'm sayin'."

"I know how to bloody light a fire!" Sam spat. "Shut your bloody piehole!"

Val threw his hands up in defeat, taking a step back. "Sorry geezer, just tryin' to help."

Sam ignored him, gritting his teeth. A couple minutes later, little embers began to glow from within the pile. Before it died out, he leaned towards it, blowing on the tiny embers with Alex following his example. Smoking more and more, the tinder burned brighter, and the first flame came to life.

Sam sat back for a second, smiling to himself. *I never doubted myself for a second. I knew I could do it. And no thanks to him.*

Alex fuelled the fire with some twigs, building the flames taller. It didn't take long for the embers to turn into a raging bonfire.

Stan quickly moved Seb closer, who rubbed his hands together to warm them.

Alex patted his shoulder, giving him a proud nod. *"Good job, lad."*

Sam smiled, looking over at Val who rolled his eyes at them. He sat down, far away from them, but close enough to be warmed by the fire.

"I just hope they can see us," Stan said, still rubbing Seb's arms, "he needs dry clothes. You *both* do."

"I'm fine," Sam replied.

"No, you're *not*, I can see your lower lip trembling, and your lips are turning blue. We need to get off this... whatever the bloody hell this rock is."

The air turned bitingly cold as the wind reached them, leaving Sam shivering in his thin clothes. *Of all the days, of course I had to wear my summer Trooper uniform.*

Even the weighted gear didn't do him any good. Stan waved Alex over to take over Stan's place in warming Seb up. He went over to Sam, offering to do the same, but Sam pushed him away. "I said I was fine!"

"No, you're not fine, Sam. Stop acting like you're fine." Stan raised his head, ready to slap some sense into Sam, then halted. He slowly lowered his hand. "I know you see yourself as a great fighter of our generation... no, of our Squad, and that you think you can take care of things on your own, but you *can't*. When are you gonna learn that we're stronger in numbers? Have you not learnt *a single thing* from Zach?"

"Don't you bloody dare get his name involved in this equation! You don't have the *right* to use him as an example! You *never* bloody cared about him! You don't care about anybody but yourself and maybe, just *maybe*, about Alex!" His eyes spit fire as he spoke, barely blinking. "And maybe, *maybe* this is my punishment for not saving him! For leaving him to *die*!"

Stan huffed, growing irritated at Sam's irrational outburst. "Don't you say that to me. Not to me," he told him in a reprimanding tone. "I miss him just as much as you do, but this... self-persecuting tone of yours..." It irritated him greatly, and he had even lost his appetite over this nonsensical talk about Sam believing he was being punished. Still, since the others hadn't eaten much either since their landing, there was no reason to linger.

He moved away from Sam and began to unpack the tiny amount of provisions they had packed, hearing Val scoff nearby. Ignoring it, he began to divide the food, skipping Val. After all, they had only packed enough for themselves.

The approaching storm consumed the last light the horizon had to offer, darkening the sky in a matter of seconds. In the distance, Tim saw the massive waves violently crashing against the tiny rock his friends were stranded on. It almost seemed like the waves rocked the piece of hardened earth.

Broken branches and toppled trees were left near what was the previous island, ravaged by the earthquake he didn't even know about.

The storm followed a choreography that seemed laid out in a manuscript, growing stronger and stronger. It moved from one scene of destruction to the next.

"We gotta be quick!" the pilot yelled, "I don't like the look of that."

"I know, it's gonna be tight," Tim replied, typing something on his laptop. "If we can reach 'em within ten minutes, we can leave before the tropical cyclone hits us."

"That's a very tight spot to work with, mate."

"That means time's of the essence then."

"Lower the ladder!"

Tim nodded, hurrying over to the door. Opening it, he had forgotten to tell Andrew and Josh to hold onto something, both finding out in the heat of the moment that the air pressure was slowly making them its victims. Neither was capable of any kind of arm muscle use, and so Andrew tipped over in his wheelchair, landing on top of Josh who screamed in pain.

The storm raged on in the distance as Tim walked unsteadily away from the door to untangle the rope ladder, not paying any attention to what was going on. His mind set to the rescue mission at hand.

Val, having been excluded from the others, noticed the depths of the dark sky that rapidly approached them. "Uh, lads?" He did a few steps back, accidentally kicking over the last bit of water they had left in their canteen, extinguishing the campfire.

"You bloody arsehole!" Sam yelled, getting up so quickly, Val had no time to react in defence. He pushed him against the tree, his arm against his throat. "What the bloody hell's your problem?"

Val, having trouble breathing and speaking, pointed at the sky. "Dark... ness... behind..."

"Shut the bloody hell up! Shut up!" Sam yelled, his eyes blazing with fire. "I swear, I should just kill you right here and now! I—what?" he yelled towards Stan, who tapped him on the shoulder.

"Mother Nature isn't done with us."

It took every ounce of willpower within Sam to turn away from his bloodlust, looking at the storm that was coming for them. At that same moment, a bright light almost blinded them. Looking up, it was the Kite's searchlight.

"That's our cue! Go!" Stan yelled, rushing over to Alex to help Seb to his feet. Sam slowly moved his arm away from Val, who coughed and gasped for air.

As the ladder was lowered, Stan and Alex carried Seb over. "Can ya climb?" Alex asked him.

"Yeah," Seb said, nodding. "Yeah, I think I can."

Alex went first so he could guide and help Seb whenever necessary, Stan following right behind them. As they climbed the rope ladder, Sam looked over at Val who was still coughing. Giving him nothing more than a second's glance, Sam began climbing, hoping he was quick enough to leave Val behind.

The ladder moved violently beneath him. Looking down, he watched as Val had gotten ahold of it, slowly making his way up. As Sam began to calculate how many metres he had left, he heard Val scream in agony.

What he saw was something he could barely describe.

A young boy, about eleven years old, had sunk his teeth in Val's leg, his veins completely black, his eyes bloodshot. His skin was so pale, he looked like a ghost.

"Help me!" Val yelled, though Sam climbed extra fast. He didn't even think about helping Val, he just needed to reach safety.

Val kicked the boy in the head, continuing his ascend with a bloody leg. Sam was meanwhile pulled up by Tim, while Stan rushed to aid Andrew and Josh, and Alex held Seb in his arms.

Sam looked down at Val climbing up as the boy advanced.

"Help me!" Val yelled again, looking at the reflection of a shiny object that caught his attention. Sam held a knife in his hand, holding it close to the left rope.

Val's eyes showed pure disbelief, pure *fear* that Sam hadn't seen in a long time. He was truly scared.

Sam moved the knife back and forth as if on autopilot, oblivious to the fact that he was commencing murder.

*"Sam, no. Don't become someone I can't recognise."* Hearing Zach's voice in his head, a tear rolled down Sam's cheek. He closed his eyes, took a deep breath, and began to loosen the knife. "Catch!"

Val watched as the knife began to fall. Holding onto the ladder with one hand, he stretched to catch the knife, catching the sharp end first. Ignoring the blood slowly oozing down his hand, he began to cut the rope below him while the boy hastily climbed up.

The boy's finger touched Val's leg, but then the rope gave way just in time. The boy slowly fell into the waves as Val watched. "I'm so sorry, *Patty*." He continued to climb until Tim pulled him to safety.

# CHAPTER TWENTY-SIX

The storm was petering out as Tim closed the door. He looked over at the damaged state his friends were in and took a deep breath.

"Okay, Alex, get Seb some dry clothes and make sure he takes a hot shower. Oh, and give him some medicine. Stan, take Josh back to his bed, we'll deal with his awakening and everything else later. Andrew, I need you to get me a first-aid kit."

As everyone did as they were told, Tim looked over at Sam who stared at the knife Val had slid back towards him. "Sam, if you can walk, do the same thing I told Alex. Get dressed, take a shower, take medicine. Got it?" He then turned to Val. "Your trousers need to be cut," he explained, then examined his hand. "Hope they weren't trousers you were attached to." Val slowly shook his head.

Andrew came back with the kit, giving it to Tim who took out the scissors. "Go and clean his arm if you can." Andrew nodded, doing as he was told.

Sam didn't move. His brain was shut down. At least, it felt that way.

"Sam! Bloody hell, get yourself sorted out!" Tim yelled. "Sam!"

"Who was he?" Sam asked in a barely audible voice. "I heard you said *Patty*. Who was he?"

Val slowly moved his head towards Sam, tears streaming down his cheeks. "My nephew... Patrick. He was my everythin'. I've been protectin' him my whole life. My uncle he... he was abusive. He... sexually assaulted Patty when he was six years old. He's been livin' with us ever since the trial and... when I was taken I... I thought I'd never see him again but *this*... this isn't how I wanted to see him."

Stuttering, Val couldn't contain his tears, one after the other rolled down his cheeks. Sam wanted to ask what that thing was, or what Patty had turned into, but he couldn't get himself to say those words.

"We can talk about everything in the morning. Get up, go to your room, and take care of yourself for once!" Tim yelled again. "I'm not screwing around; Sam. Get the bloody hell up!"

Sam nodded slowly. His head hung; embarrassment filled every fibre of his being. He finally left Tim and Andrew alone and headed to his room to take a much-needed shower.

Sitting down on his bed after getting dressed in a fresh set of clothes, he clicked his cassette player for what felt like the last time. Leaning back against his pillow, he played the same song he always listened to when everyone he knew died, or when he was ashamed of himself. The song served multiple purposes.

He saw many memories flash before his eyes as he zoned out. Some made him feel as if he was there, reliving those moments. Others felt unreachable and untouchable. He could still imagine Zach sauntering through his door to talk to him about the situation with Val. *The whole situation, really.* The deaths they had witnessed, Mother Nature acting contrary to her nature, something they always talked about with each other. If only to make sure it wouldn't become a bottled-up thing that would overwhelm them in the long run.

"You ever have a fork-in-the-road moment where you... shake up *fate*?" Sam asked, as if talking to Zach. "I lost you the first time, you know, 'cause I couldn't save you. And now... with what you said to me... I know you left me. If that's it, if I lose you again I... I think you're trying to force me to re-examine that fork. Aren't you?" He took a breath, closing his eyes for a second. "I'm trying to defer to you, mate. I'm sorry I didn't sooner, but I'm doing it now." He opened his eyes, looking around his room. "Please, Zach, don't leave me. *Not again.* I'm sorry for letting you down today. I'm sorry for acting contrary to who I... *am*." He paused. "I'm sorry for everything. *I'm sorry!*"

He heard a knock on his door but chose to ignore it. Having locked it from the inside via the keypad, whoever was on the other side of the door couldn't get in, not without the personal clearance code they each had made.

Footsteps walked away from the door, and he leaned his head back against the wall.

*"Ignoring your trauma doesn't make you healthy, babe,"* he heard Maddie's voice say, smiling softly to himself. *"Yes, it does."* He thought back to the day she said those words to him, a year after Zach's death. *"You're shouldering this... burden, Sam, and I don't like you doing that alone."* He could feel her hand leaning against his cheek, comfortingly rubbing his cheekbone. *"It may not be ours, the trauma you've got, but it shouldn't be yours alone. I can carry you, even when I can't carry it for you."*

It felt like she was using those words against him. As if that memory was working hard to catch him off guard, to *manipulate* him. *Deceive* him.

He had it so ingrained in his head, that he couldn't think about anything else. To him, he was alone in the world, with *no one* left to care about him.

Andrew wheeled himself into the tiny infirmary on the Kite, heading straight for Val as Alex and Stan talked to Josh, relieved he was awake and well.

Val heard the squeaking noise of the wheels, sighing deeply. "Well, if it isn't mister shapeshifter."

Andrew stopped right next to his bedside, pulling the brakes. *"Houdini."*

Val laughed, shaking his head. "Guess your nickname for me did always work better." He eyed Andrew. "Care to explain who these people are and what you're doin' with 'em?"

"They rescued me, same way they rescued you."

Val scoffed. "They didn't *exactly* rescue me. It was more outta… pity. And *duty*. I know they're Troopers."

"Look, they're nice blokes, I *swear*," Andrew said, "they saved two people of our island. Me and some other guy they knew."

Val crossed his arms. "They also seemed to know the lads who were stuck with me. The Asian lad blamed me for their deaths, said I was a murderer."

"But you're not. *Right?*"

"Seriously?" He scoffed. "If you're gonna be sittin' there blamin' me for somethin' I didn't do, you can leave the way you came."

"That's not what I—"

"Right… I know I'm the telekinesis freak, but that doesn't make me a bloody killer."

Andrew raised his hands up in defeat. "Look, the guy who was with me, he said to the others only *one* of us was supposed to leave the island alive. I think we cheated whatever kinda sick game they're playing with us."

"*They?* Those lads who experimented on us? So, what? Me bein' the only survivor was their plan, but they still had to go through great lengths to *eliminate* me near the end?"

"I don't think that was targeted towards *you*."

"Well, I'll be damned. It's like I'm readin' a book about some… *cult,* the one that sacrifices books as if it's a real page-burner." Andrew had to admit he didn't quite get that punchline, but he wasn't about to open his mouth on the matter. Val laughed rather exuberantly, shaking his head. "Oh, I swear this is bringin' back recollections that I had buried in the back of my mind many years ago."

"*Recollections*? What do you mean?"

"I dunno, like everythin' I went through today was somethin' I experienced way back. I always thought it was just a recurrin' nightmare, but maybe it was my telekinesis tryin' to warn me."

Andrew fidgeted his fingers, unable to ask the question that was practically begging to leave his tongue.

Val noticed the look in his eyes. "What? Did I say somethin' wrong?"

Andrew shook his head slowly, sighing deeply. "If what you're saying *really* happened to you, feeling like some kinda déjà vu, you might be having visions too."

"I'm not more of a freak than I already am. It didn't exactly play out the way I saw back then. Some details were changed. Look, whatever happened to you, *and* me, it's got nothin' in common, 'kay? We're just a bunch of weirdoes tryin' to scrape by."

Andrew gave it a rest for now, wheeling himself away. Passing Josh, Alex, and Stan, he heard them vaguely talking about something he probably shouldn't get involved in and chose to ignore it. He wheeled himself back to Phil's bed, holding his hand as if he had never left to go talk with Val.

Tim sat behind his laptop, scanning the map for the next island they had to reach. He knew he had to likely go down there. With Seb and Sam unable to join, Stan and Alex would never be able to scour the island with just the two of them.

It almost scared Tim to go back out there. Ever since the last fight with Ashwell, he hadn't touched a weapon and had relied solely on his technology. He swore to himself to never hurt another living soul *ever again*, not even out of defence.

But watching Sam become someone he wasn't, scared him even more. He had never been the same since Zach's death, but this ambition that fuelled him, the competition that almost drove him mad, Tim knew whatever kind of power Sam was wielding had its price.

"Collateral damage..." he murmured. "*That's* what we're becoming."

Pinging the next coordinates to the pilot, he pulled up the ID of the one survivor of the island. In doing so, something caught his attention.

"*An audio file...?*" he whispered under his breath. Clicking on it, he heard Val's voice loud and clear.

"*Command, or whoever's out there, I dunno if my telekinesis works on such a great distance, but I need evac. And I need it fast. The island... it's come to life. It's tryin' to kill us. Whatever experiment this is, I don't wanna be a part of it no more. Code thirteen has been activated; code eight dismantled. Listen to me, I'm stuck here with two other lads and we need—*"

A whole bunch of static made Tim turn it off. The screeching noises of the corrupted sound data caused a headache.

Coming back to his senses, he interpolated the data, then extrapolated it, though nothing out of the ordinary came out of the scan. He sighed.

Hearing loud heaving sounds, he left his laptop unattended. Hurrying over to where the sounds came from, he stopped in Seb's room, who projectile vomited onto his floor.

"Oh bloody hell..." Tim said, rushing inside to get Seb's bin, holding it in front of his mouth. *Every* muscle and *every* tendon in his body wanted to make him walk away. But knowing no one else was available or even remotely nearby, Tim took it upon himself to overcome his greatest fear: emetophobia. "There... there..." he said, patting Seb's shoulder. The sounds Seb was making made Tim gag.

Once Seb had it all out of his system, he apologised profoundly, though Tim dismissed it as he cleaned the bin, even cleaning the floor to make sure Seb couldn't slip and fall and make matters even worse. Touching the vomit, albeit by using a cloth, barely kept Tim from gagging a second time.

Tim looked over at Seb, who looked like he might be more than just sick. Tim forced Seb to lie down, covering him with the quilt Henry had gifted them. It was the only tangible thing they had left of Zach's childhood.

"Remember how Henry told us he used to let Zach sleep with it? How his mother made it for Zach as he got sick so often?"

Seb nodded slowly, not resisting an inch. Tim covered Seb and watched him doze off almost immediately.

As Tim walked past the bin on his way out, it was only then that he noticed the mixture of completely black liquid combined with a similar look of blood. Tim rushed back over to Seb, scared he was suffering from internal bleeding. The fact Seb was knocked out so quickly, didn't sit right with Tim.

*If he already felt his conscience slipping away, fading into the dark... There's no telling how much time I've got to—* Seb gasped awake, coughing in a fit. More black liquid and blood came out, and Tim knew this wasn't an ordinary cold.

He knew he had to trigger an adrenaline rush. Maybe it could help save him. He rushed through the first-aid kit with quick succession and got what seemed to be a hazard marked epinephrine autoinjector. He stabbed it into Seb's leg and hit the button, raising Seb's heart rate as the production of adrenaline was increased. It helped for only what seemed to be ten seconds before Seb was back to throwing up.

"That water... it was *poisonous*." He looked at the door. "Then how come Sam isn't affected?"

He checked Seb again, but there was no external or internal bleeding. Still, the poison affected Seb's respiratory system. Then it hit him.

"Radiation poisoning. But *how*? Unless... those creators made the water radiated somehow. I mean, he's got severe nausea and vomiting... he lost consciousness for a bit, and his skin feels hot. *All signs point to it.*"

He rushed out of the room to find Stan and Alex.

As they were gathered around Seb's bed, they looked at him sleeping soundly.

"We know there's no cure, right? So, what can we do?" Alex asked, biting his fingernails.

"Well, we already removed all the clothing he was wearing, so we decontaminated him before we were even aware of this. That's at least a good start," Stan replied.

Tim took his laptop out of his bag, typing as fast as he could. "Okay, we've got three options. We can try potassium iodide, Prussian blue, or DTPA."

"Okay, can you pretend we're English, please?" Stan asked.

"The first is something he needs to take within a day of exposure, so we're technically too late with that anyway. The other two are still doable. We just need to find the materials." He got up to search the *special* medicinal cabinet.

"And if we *don't* have it on board?" Alex asked.

"Then Seb's screwed. We're too far away from home to go back, and we're out in the open near the ocean. There's no way we'll find any of that stuff anywhere near here."

Stan sat down behind Tim's laptop. "Can't we just check inventory?"

"I doubt it's mentioned anywhere. Why would we—"

"Found it."

"Oh, you found it. *Great.*" Tim cleared his throat as he rushed over, looking over Stan's shoulder at the screen. "Okay, we've only got DTPA, so that'll have to suffice." Tim memorised the compartment it was in, then went to get it.

Alex looked at the screen too. "So, it's supposed to shorten the time it takes for the poison to leave his body?"

"That's what it claims. It only mentions three radioactive materials though, so I'm not one hundred per cent certain that we're dealing with the right one. It'd be a little too easy considering everything we know about these people, right?"

"Yah, right that."

They looked at Seb's skin, which was abysmally blistered and red. "Lest we forget," Stan said softly, almost whispering it under his breath.

Alex looked at him, perplexed. "Did ya just give up on him?"

"It's untenable, you and I *both* know that."

Seb woke up, expectorating a great deal as his terrible cough returned.

"Can't you see he's debilitated?"

Alex wanted to speak up, but Tim rushed in with a syringe, injecting the medicine directly into Seb's vein. He took a step back. "I found some potassium iodide too, and I know what the internet said, but I'm not taking it on its word."

"Think it's *safe* enough to mix the two?" Alex asked.

Tim shook his head. "Not in the slightest. But I'll take the leap."

"What about Sam? How's he?"

Tim looked over at Sam's closed door, sighing. "I assume he's fine. I haven't heard any heaving sounds coming from his direction."

Alex walked over to the door to listen as Stan nudged Tim. "You're an indefatigable defender of our well-being, and I'm *proud* of you for it."

Tim slowly turned his head towards him as his jaw dropped. "Did you just—?"

"Don't get used to it."

Alex returned, shaking his head. "He opened the door for me for a split sec, he seemed fine. I told him about Seb and he's on his way here."

Alex had barely spoken the last word as Sam rushed in, immediately kneeling next to Seb who had gone back to sleeping. He held his hand. "You're saying the water he fell in was *poisoned*? Then *why* am I fine?"

Tim shrugged. "I dunno. You must be... *immune*."

"No, I'm *not*." He shook his head. "I refuse to be. *I* wanna be in that bed, *I* wanna take Seb's place. It should be *me*, not him."

A part of Stan wanted to say Sam was right, and that it indeed should be him lying there, but he knew that would be unfair towards Sam. Seb falling into the water wasn't his fault. Alex put a hand on Sam's shoulder, squeezing it. A token of affection that for Sam said more than a single word.

Sam sighed deeply. "Why can't we just stop with all these medical atrocities? Why's our life *always* surrounded by sickness and death? Why can't we just go back to the relative peace we found back home?" He sounded wistful for a second, but it didn't last long as Seb seized.

# CHAPTER TWENTY-SEVEN

"Where do you want her body?" a masked man asked his fellow comrade, dragging Maddie's lifeless body across the floor as the other held a lifeless Zack in his arms.

"Just throw her in a separate room, next to the guy's body."

"What did they take anyway?"

"I dunno, but they *knew* we were coming. Someone must've tipped 'em off." They threw Maddie in a room next to Percy, locking the door. "We'll examine the kid first, see if that gives any results. Perhaps we can revive him. We need some kinda living leverage after all."

The other nodded as they moved down the hallway, leaving Maddie alone on the cold floor.

As the masked men entered the laboratory, their leader awaited them, his back turned towards them. "You didn't think to run any of this by *me*?" he asked, his voice harsh and cold.

"Sorry, sir, we—"

"This is *precisely* why I didn't trust you two knuckleheads with another secret. You've proven how careless both of you nitwits are with these kinds of matters."

"Sir, permission to speak?"

"Granted. You've got *one* minute."

"We weren't informed of a mole on the inside, sir. They *knew* we were coming. By the time we found 'em hidden, they had already taken whatever they took. We're here with the kid to have him examined first so we can determine *what* they took."

They both stared at their leader, waiting for his response. But before they could perceive his thoughts, a snide voice accosted them from behind. "If anyone can fool the 'head honchos' without taking blame for the betrayal, you thought wrong."

The leader took his gun from his holster, shooting both masked men straight between their eyes, watching as the man caught Zack before he could hit the floor. He gave an affirmative nod to the leader.

"Have him examined."

"Yes, sir."

The man gave the leader a firm nod before leaving the room.

Maddie gasped awake, coughing loudly as she sucked oxygen into her lungs. Groaning, she looked around the room. "Zack…?" she asked, coughing and spitting at the same time. "Zack? Baby?" She kept her arms in front of her to search the dark room, feeling nothing but walls and the floor made of rough stone. Next to her she heard Percy cough. "Percy, *where's* my baby?" she yelled.

"They must've taken him."

"To where? If we woke up… bloody hell, what are they gonna do to him? We need to get outta here and find him!" She pounded on the walls, ignoring the fact that she might be bleeding upon the impact.

"He… he won't wake up. Not anytime soon, anyway."

"What?"

"I… gave him the highest dosage I had on me."

"You did *what*?" she screamed, to which he shushed her.

"Don't raise your voice like that! We can't have 'em know we're awake!"

"You expect me to believe you're on *our* side? For all I know, you betrayed me *and* killed my son!"

"I didn't, Maddie. *You know me*. Deep down *you know* I'm not capable of such a thing."

She stared ahead into the darkness, a part of her confused, the other part knew he was right. Dread seized her in icy claws. "Does he need an antidote? Do we even have that?" Terror filled her heart as she feared the answer.

"We've got about twenty-four hours, I'd say. I set an alarm on my watch, and it'll go off every hour. Once the screen lights up, I can see how many hours we've got left."

"And if you had to make a guess? With our unconsciousness added?"

"Probably twenty."

She sucked in a deep, shaky breath. She thought back to the day she got kidnapped as a child, remembering every single word the guy spoke who took her away from her parents. *"You wanna know what terror is? It starts with something called fear. Your little head might not understand what that means, yet, but it's something we're gonna cultivate so we can watch it spread. That's when you've got terror."*

Hearing footsteps, she couldn't play dead in time. She scooted back against the wall as the big, masked guy walked towards her. "Good that, you're awake. Boss knew y'all were fakin' your deaths. But that little boy of yours…" He put handcuffs around her wrists, lifting her arms far above her head as he secured her to a beam.

He turned away from her, moving towards the doorway. He grabbed a bucket filled with water, and as he walked back to her, she shook her head heavily. Somehow, she knew what he was about to do.

"No, please, don't. *Please*."

He threw the ice-cold water over her head, making sure *every* piece of her body was wet. She spurted some water that had entered her mouth, coughing. She noticed the taser in his hands, trying to move away from him on her tiptoes.

She felt an overwhelming muscle contraction once the taser contacted her wet body, screaming excruciatingly.

"Leave her alone!" The plea from next door was ignored as the masked man tased her again.

Her screams ran in the stillness of the hallway, crying as each taser discharge felt like an eternity.

"Take *me*! *I'm* the one you want!" Percy continued pleading, to no avail. "She's *pregnant*!"

The masked guy stopped shocking her, watching as her head hung, having difficulty breathing. He chuckled as he looked her over. "I'm assumin' her boyfriend doesn't know that, but *you* do... Ouch." He finally walked over to Percy's cell, leaving her be. "Don't tell me you *cheated* on your boss?"

"No, of course not. It's *his*."

"Well, in that case." He took a knife from his sheath. "I'll just have to cut the little bugger outta her. Can't have Samuel have *anything* nice now, can we?" Returning, he noticed the blood on the floor, then he looked at where it came from. "Interesting... Guess there's no need for that no more."

She cried softly, her tears falling and mixing with the blood on the floor. *I'm so sorry, little one.*

She woke up chained to a bed, looking directly at a bright light that made her headache and nausea even worse. She looked around the room, noticing the medical equipment surrounding her. In a jar next to her head, she saw what her unborn baby must've been.

She heard footsteps and as she looked up, she saw a woman approaching her with a wet rag. She tried to move away; afraid she would be wetted again and tasered. But the woman shushed her, sitting next to her on the edge of her bed, putting the wet rag on her forehead.

"I begged 'em to take you here," she began, wringing the wet rag to wet it again in the tiny jug she brought along. "I didn't want you to bleed to death. You *still* got a son to live for."

Maddie shook her head, turning her head away from the woman. "He'll be dead soon. There's no saving him. I know they've killed Percy, and he's the *only one* who knew the antidote."

The woman shook her head. "They tortured it outta him. Your son's awake and alive. They'll use him as bait for your boyfriend to come home. To *ambush* him."

Maddie looked at her, tilting her head ever so slightly. "*Why* are you telling me this? Who are you?"

The woman finally looked Maddie in the eye, and she noticed her. "*Abby?*"

Abigail, one of the women she was captured with two years ago, sat in front of her, alive and well.

"Look, we don't have much time. Can you stand?" Maddie nodded slowly as Abby began to undo her restraints. "I need you to stay close to me as we go and save your friend, okay? Then we go and save your son, and we get the bloody hell outta here."

"If you plan to escape *now*, why didn't you do so before?"

Abby looked at her as Maddie slowly moved her legs over the bedside once she was free. She gave a faint smile. "Let's just say *you* being here sparked hope in me."

As Maddie got her footing on the floor, she staggered, her legs frail. Abby barely caught her before she could make any noise. She put Maddie's arm around her neck, escorting her out of the room.

Abby led her through deserted hallways. The creaks of the floorboards set Maddie on edge as they headed down the hall to a set of rickety stairs. Taking the stairs down, Maddie knew they were heading to where Percy was.

The hallway was lined with cell doors, only one of which was wide open. It *had* to be hers. They stopped in front of the one to the right of the open cell.

Abby carefully leaned Maddie against the wall. She kneeled in front of the lock, looking behind her to ensure the guard she had knocked out earlier was still in the corner, out of Maddie's eyesight. She moved to grab a bobby pin from her hair, moving it in the lock to open it.

Once the lock clicked open, the door swung open but was stopped by something blocking it. Maddie sank to the floor in horror as she saw the bloodied body of Percy as the cause. His breathing was scarce as she rushed to his side in her weakened state. She dropped to her knees, pulling his mangled body into her lap.

"Maddie..." he said weakly, to which she shushed him.

"Keep your strength, *don't* speak," she said, holding back her tears.

"No... they managed to lower... my defence walls," he said weakly, "I'm sorry, Maddie... I'm sorry I told 'em..." His eyes were glazed over as they met hers.

"Shh," she said, shaking her head, "*don't.*"

"Every time they dropped... a wall, they... begun again. They managed to drop all my walls... they managed to... to get full access... I had no defences left... I was completely... completely passive. My train ride is over..." He looked at her. "I'm... sorry about the baby..." He put his hand on her belly, her hand grabbed his, squeezing it. "I'm sorry about... Zack..." A single tear rolled down his cheek as he let out a final, shuddering breath.

Her breathing became erratic from the mix of adrenaline, sorrow, and physical pain. She tried to take deep breaths as she cradled Percy, checking out his injuries with a side eye. Before she could determine the cause of death, she felt a sharp pain in her head. Then *darkness*.

A sharp jolt of pain shot through her wrists. Glancing up, cold metal handcuffs tethered her to what appeared to be a stone slab. Looking to her left, she noticed a knife on a surgery tray.

*There's no way they've left that unattended like that.*

She heard someone scream in the room next to hers, pounding on what sounded like a pane. Clearly, no one else but Maddie heard that person.

"*Abby*? Is that you?"

She scanned the room, looking for anything that seemed inconspicuous. Or suspicious. Preferably, both.

Something stabbed her in the back, *deep*. It weakened her knees as she let out a cry, her vision reddening. Blood slowly made its way up to her lungs and mouth, coughing it up.

Footsteps from behind slowly passed her, moving towards the knife on the tray. He put the knife he just stabbed her with next to the unattended one. With his back turned towards her, he let out a mirthless chuckle.

"By hurting a loved one... *killing* him... I think we've reached the point where the only leverage we've got left, is *your son*." The figure slowly turned, his face unrecognisable, a mixture of robotic engineering and human skin. "We can hurt him, until you give us what we wanna know."

"*Which is?*" she managed to ask, blood coming out of her mouth with rapid speed.

"How we can *disable* the Kite your boyfriend's flying in. It needs to be destroyed. With its protections and invisibility shield, we can't track it *nor* attack it. We can't have 'em jeopardise our… *plans.*"

Her stomach was in knots as she took in the scene laid out in front of her. She *knew* they would kill her no matter what, and her son *too.* The masked men snapped his fingers, and the bucket of ice-cold water returned, dumping it over her head. Muscle spasms took over as she screamed in agony, blood pouring out even faster. She began to shiver.

"You won't talk?" He walked over to the surgery tray, his hand hovering over the knife. Then he shook his head. "No, that doesn't work." He crossed the room, opening a drawer, revealing a blow torch.

Maddie's breathing accelerated, though each deep, anxiety-ridden breath she took hurt her blood-filled lungs even more. The man lit the blow torch, squatting down. He brought the blow torch towards her left foot. Trying to move her foot away, she begged him not to do it. The man burned her foot as she screamed.

She groaned weakly, her head hanging, blood still dripping from her mouth.

"*No one* can take *that* much pain, Madeline. *No one* can and *not* break. *No one.*"

"Yeah well," she said, spitting blood, "I gave birth to a child. There's *nothing* more painful than that."

He walked around her, touching her neck. "You've got a needle puncture here; did you know that? That must be from the drugs you used to kill yourself. *Temporarily.*" He grabbed the bloodied knife and scraped it along her neck. "Torture isn't really my strong suit, you see." He sniffed her neck, grinning. "But you could say that I'm a quick study." He plunged the knife in her upper leg, a devilish smile played on his lips as she screamed.

Soaked and bloodied, she looked up at him, breathing heavily. "Screw… you!"

He chuckled, grabbing an ice pick-like device from the surgery tray behind her. "Did you know there are parts of the body that can't withstand intense pain? The most sensitive parts?" He seized her face. "There's the decaying tooth… or your ear drum…

and then there's my favourite part, *right* here... *right* under your eyelid." He moved the tip beneath her eye, making her shiver even more. "I don't have to tell you that it's possible to die from pain, hm? I mean, your chum *Percival's* a prime example of that possibility."

Her voice and hand quivered, though no coherent words came out of her mouth.

"What's that? I can't hear you properly," he said, leaning closer to try and make sense of what she was babbling.

She spit into his ear, which made him shoot backwards with blazing eyes, his large nostrils dilated. His face morphed into a scowl as he grabbed her ponytail, moving her head back with violence. She grunted loudly as he did so.

"Listen, *missy*, I can make sure we reach your pain threshold much slower than your friend over here. I'll get my answers, just you wait. I *always* get what I want."

# CHAPTER TWENTY-EIGHT

Thirty minutes after Seb's seizure, Sam crossed the hallway to check on him and headed up the tiny stairs towards the infirmary. Sam sat by his bedside, holding his hand as Seb lay asleep. Anxiety churned his stomach as he thought about the consequences Seb's condition had already brought and might bring. He shook his head, trying to get those thoughts out of his head.

He nuzzled up to Seb's shoulder as he sat on the floor, putting his nose to Seb's ear. "You showed me what it felt like to live again after—" He burst into tears. "After Zach died, you were there for me, you *and* Maddie. And now I'm standing… sitting, here, and I gotta watch someone I care deeply about… die? *Again*? How can I?" He moved his head away from Seb's ear. "You changed me, Seb, you showed me that losing Zach wasn't the end of the world. And what? Now I'm supposed to lose you too?"

He stood sullenly as he looked at Seb who, of course, returned no answer.

"My nightmares are usually about Zach, about losing him. But every time I wake up, I'm okay. 'Know why? 'Cause I realise you're right there next to me. You *and* Maddie."

He sat back down on the chair next to his bed, shaking his head.

"It's unfair, you know? You get to lie down all day and *we* gotta risk our lives." He chuckled through his tears, sniffling. "So, you better haul your ass outta bed to join us." He watched Seb's unmoving eyes, watching as his chest rose and fell slowly.

"Sometimes suffering is just that. *Suffering.*" He turned to find Andrew wheeling himself inside, stopping in front of Seb's feet at the footboard of his bed. "It won't make us stronger; it won't build our character. *It just hurts*. And it's okay that it just hurts, you know? It's part of being human. It's part of the fact that *not* being okay *is* okay."

Sam wanted to shout at him that he had to shut up, that none of those words mattered. That he was talking *nonsense*. But he had to admit that he really needed to hear those words.

"I'll watch over him. You've got my word." Sam looked over at him, nodding slowly. "Both you, and your heart, need a rest."

Sam wanted to ask how Phil was doing, but he had no energy left to speak. He gave Andrew a pat on the shoulder before heading to his bedroom.

He stared at the ceiling. *"I wish you knew how I feel,"* he whispered aloud before drifting off to sleep.

Lightning flashed across the sky; a clap of thunder sounded like an exploding firework. Sam gasped awake, hearing the alarm of the Kite blaring. As if the world had been drained of all colours, he knew what that sound meant. *Collision alert.*

He rushed to the cockpit, looking at the screen. *Status: autopilot.*

He sat behind the throttle, but it wouldn't budge. He threw a glance over his shoulder as something whizzed past his ear, slamming into the forehead of a ghostly pilot sitting in the co-pilot chair. *A crossbow bolt?*

Not recognising the bolt, he knew there was an intruder on board. Whoever it was had steered them the wrong way, away from the next island they were approaching. Looking at the cliffs they were flying towards, Sam diverted the power to the main shield to initiate the impact protocol.

"How the bloody hell's no one else awake?" he yelled, the alarm still blaring in his ears. "Unless… The intruder got to 'em." Sam looked back and forth between the autopilot system, the nearing cliffs, and his friends who might be in danger. "Bloody hell!" he yelled as he left the throttle behind, rushing to Tim's room.

He skidded to a halt as he saw the shadowy figure holding a club in his hands, staring Sam down. "I was wondering when you'd show up. I've drugged all your friends so only *you* and *I* would remain."

"And who the bloody hell might you be? How did you know where I was?"

"Oh, a little *birdie* told me. She's got a port-wine stain in her neck."

"*Maddie*? What the bloody hell did you do to her?"

He chuckled, finally stepping out of the shadows. Sam gasped upon seeing the man's face, horror struck his whole body. He couldn't move, he couldn't speak. He could hardly breathe.

"You look like you've seen a *ghost,* Sammy."

Sam stumbled backwards against the wall, totally stunned, left breathless with fear. *"J… Jonathan…"* he managed to mumble under his breath.

There he stood, alive and in the flesh. *Jonathan*, Zach's non-blood brother, his mentor, *their* mentor. They had read his file two years ago; he was assassinated. But, seeing his face, Sam knew someone from Tim's calibre had nursed him back to health, had saved him from death. Like an android, he seemed devoid of humanness.

"But to answer your question, your girlfriend is *fine*. I *didn't* lay a finger on her." He walked towards Sam, still holding the club. "I'm sorry Zach died. He wasn't my target. *You* were. And well, seeing as he died, I'm holding *you* accountable for it."

Before Sam could ask him anything, Jonathan swung the club, nearly hitting Sam's head. He ducked out of the way just in time, crawling over the floor towards the door. He had to get Jonathan away from Tim.

Getting back to his feet, he rushed down the hall towards the cargo hold, turning around to find Jonathan in close pursuit.

*Crap! I left my gun in my room!*

Looking frantically around for anything that could serve as a weapon, Jonathan closed in on him. *All right, fistfight. I got this.*

He twisted the large club out of Jonathan's hands. Gripping the club tightly, he used it to create some distance between them. Then, out of nowhere, Andrew barrelled into Jonathan, knocking both to the floor with a thud. Sam's glance flickered to Andrew on top of Jonathan, who was straining for dominance as they grappled with each other.

Signalling his readiness to fight Jonathan, Sam didn't even care to think how Andrew had escaped the comatose state Jonathan had inflicted upon everyone else.

In perfect unison, they each lunged at Jonathan, keeping him pinned down to the floor. In that second of them exchanging looks, Jonathan managed to throw Andrew off, causing him to hit the wall. He was knocked unconscious immediately.

Jonathan darted towards Sam, reaching for his throat. Sam reacted almost instantly, recalling his training lessons, brandishing the club he was still holding. Slinging the club at Jonathan's centre of gravity, he tried to dodge but wasn't quick enough. Unable to avoid the heavy weapon coming at him, Sam nailed him right in the stomach, knocking the wind out of him. Jonathan crumpled to the floor, letting out a scream of pain. He tried to stand, clutching his stomach. Easily moving out of his reach as he doubled over again, Sam rushed over to Andrew, checking his pulse.

The cry of anguish he heard drew his attention away from Andrew. A look of concern was written on his face as he saw the screen Jonathan was holding in front of him. His son was crying uncontrollably.

"Zack! What the bloody hell did you do to him? *Where's* my son? *Where's* my girlfriend?"

Jonathan took advantage of this moment of distraction, kicking Sam in the stomach. Sam rolled away from Andrew who attempted to stand, but Jonathan swarmed him from behind, pinning him in his arms. Sam's eyes furrowed in anger, moving back and forth to try and loosen Jonathan's grip.

Feeling that moment of looseness, he seized his opportunity, driving his elbow hard into Jonathan's stomach. *Again.* As Jonathan toppled over, Sam slipped free from beneath his arms and pressed the forgotten club under his chin. In one fluid motion, he forced Jonathan to his knees, pulling the club tight against his windpipe. Jonathan struggled in his grip.

"You trying to be a hero, Sam? I'm merely here to seek revenge for my little brother. The one *you* killed."

"I didn't kill him! He killed himself! He *chose* to die!" Jonathan didn't speak. He just stared at Sam. "You'll never understand how stressful, no, how *awful* it has been for me to explain what's going on in my bloody head when I don't even understand it myself! Don't you think for one second that the scene doesn't play in my head repeatedly—'cause it does, almost every bloody day! Not a day goes by that I wish it was *me* who's dead instead! That's something I carry around with me for the rest of my life! It's not somewhere I just go to or am okay with!"

He felt a sharp shove from behind, throwing him to the floor. Looking up, he saw an unknown figure looming over him, scowling. Jonathan wiped some blood from his mouth as the unknown figure had murder in his eyes.

The unknown figure lunged at Sam, hoping to get the jump on him before he could react. Sam shifted his grip on the club, jabbing the hook end up as quickly as he could. It hit the figure straight in its jaw. Rearing back for a moment, Sam seized the opportunity to deliver a final kick, forcing the figure to fall backwards. Nudging the figure with his foot, it appeared to be unconscious.

Having dropped the club, Sam caught movement out of the corner of his eye. He ducked behind a crate and watched as Jonathan surged forward, ripping the club from Andrew's hands—who had just come to and had managed to get his hands on the club—and clipped his shoulder. Jonathan swung the club at Sam, slamming it into his ribcage as Sam lunged to protect Andrew from his hiding position.

Jonathan swung again, inches from connecting with Sam's face when Andrew barrelled into Jonathan a second time, slamming his head against the floor as they tumbled down. Sam clutched his injured ribs, rising to his feet. Leaving the club behind, Sam sprinted towards both, pinning Jonathan to the floor.

A devilish grin appeared on Jonathan's face as he glanced at Sam. "Let's fight this somewhere else, eh?" A bright light consumed Sam, and he closed his eyes to shield them.

Upon opening them, he was no longer in the Kite. Wherever he was, he didn't recognise the area. He gazed down the coast, seeing a large boat docked in the shallows. He couldn't make out the weathered name painted on the hull, but something else caught his attention; Maddie, tied to a tall mast on the boat. Her mouth was covered with tape, but she seemed uninjured.

He dashed towards the boat but came to an abrupt halt as Jonathan emerged. Turning around, the boat was now behind him. Whatever was going on, they were messing with his mind. He made his way through the haze, finding a double-outrigger secured to a small dock. A large plank extended from the edge of the dock, leading up to the boat's deck.

A creaking sound drew his attention to the boat's deck. Stepping out from the main cabin was Zach, hauling a large crate.

*What the bloody hell's going on here?*

Rage fuelling his movements, Sam sprinted past Jonathan across the dock to reach the ramp. Zach shoved the ramp away, detaching it from the boat.

All Sam could do was stare at the now widened gap between his footing on the dock, and the tall boat that held his girlfriend captive. Sam took a few steps back, getting a running start. Leaping off the dock, he slammed into the boat.

Clinging onto the side, his fingers dug into the wooden surface. As he struggled to climb up, he saw Maddie. Zach lunged at her, delivering a well-placed punch to her jaw. Sam screamed, but his scream died out as a hand yanked his clothes, forcing him down. He plunged into the shallow water.

Jonathan stood over him, forcing his head beneath the waves. Water rushed into Sam's nose and mouth, and as his limbs flailed about, he fought and struggled to breathe.

Sam gasped awake as Andrew had driven a needle filled with adrenaline in his chest, bringing Sam back to reality. Having him back, Jonathan lunged for both, but Andrew sidestepped his attack.

The two of them wrestled with each other, moving away from Sam into the hallway. A shriek caught his attention. Forcing himself to look up, he watched Jonathan's foot caught in what appeared to be a snare trap. His eyes widened at the encroaching doom. Andrew circled him to ensure he would stay put, signing to Sam. Sam followed the wire that had trapped Jonathan's foot, noticing the unknown figure working to undo the knot at the base. He tried to crawl towards the figure but wasn't quick enough.

The figure loosened the snare trap enough for Jonathan to escape, who scrambled to his feet. Jonathan sprinted as fast as possible towards the door, with the figure following closely behind. Jonathan stumbled on his injured foot as Sam leapt at him with all his strength.

The figure hurried further, looking over his shoulder at Jonathan still locked in battle with Sam. The two of them wrestled over a metallic object between them. As the Kite hit the cliffs with its empennage, it caused them to tip over one another. The object flew out of Jonathan's hands, skidding across the floor, landing at Andrew's feet. *A pistol.*

Andrew grabbed the pistol and pulled the trigger.

The figure slumped against Jonathan who rushed towards him, blood seeping through the fabric of his clothes. His words were strained as he spoke. Jonathan shushed him, telling him he had bravely defended the mission. It didn't take long before the figure went completely limp, *lifeless.* Jonathan pushed the dead body away as Andrew tossed the now empty gun aside.

Sam was pulled from this tiny moment of victory as the Kite hit another bit of the cliff, which caused both him and Andrew to slam into the wall.

Jonathan held onto the door's handle, looking over his shoulder at them both. "Well, if I can't kill you by my *own* hands, I'll let Mother Nature and technology do it *for* me. Farewell, *Sammy.* I'll see you in the afterlife."

Jonathan jumped out of the Kite. As Sam crawled towards the door, he watched as Jonathan's parachute disappeared into the clouds.

*Error. Fusion reactor malfunction. Directing power. Initiate repairs.*

Sam looked over at the cockpit, then at Andrew who crawled back towards his wheelchair. Sam knew they had to reach the escape pods *before* it was too late.

"You go to the cockpit and buy me as much time as you can muster. Can you do that?"

Andrew nodded once he had situated himself, wheeling as fast as he could towards the cockpit to try and keep the Kite in the air as long as possible. Sam rushed to the infirmary to get Seb out first, hauling him on his back as he kneeled in front of the bed, holding Seb's legs as he leaned forward to carry Seb's comatose weight.

He put him in one of the safety pods, securing him with the seatbelts before he rushed back to get Tim next.

Andrew realised that all the important things, the controls, the Kite's reactors, and engines were all behind firewalls. "That's not good."

*Diagnostic system failure.*

"That's even worse..."

He was hit by a vision, staring ahead through the Kite's window. Sam wouldn't be able to get to everyone in time, and he watched helplessly from his pod as the Kite crashed into the mountain, bursting into flames. *Josh was still inside.*

Andrew was brought back to reality, and knowing he had to keep the Kite afloat for as long as he could, he had to help Sam to avoid worse.

Sam heard the errors go off, and as he saw Andrew wheeling past him towards Phil, he *knew* they were running out of time. He hit the button to shoot the second pod after firing the first, with Seb and Tim inside, and this one containing Stan and Alex.

Phil, Josh, and Val were the only ones remaining that Sam had to get to as he knew the pilot was dead. As Andrew got Phil in the pod, he rushed to get Josh.

"You get Val and put him in his own pod. Then you leave with Phil."

"What about you?"

"I'm leaving with Josh. We'll find each other eventually. *Go!*" Andrew did as he was told, wheeling back to the bedrooms to get Val.

Sam went back to the cockpit to see how much time he had left. He looked at the screens. "Shite. The clock chip... it's burnt out. The whole bloody thing went haywire. Which means... which means every failure on board is a burnt-out processor..." *Guess I learned a thing or two from listening to Tim's nerd talk.*

*Warning. A mission-critical failure is imminent. Systems are failing. Life support will shut down.*

"The reactor vent failed... Okay, manual override required 'cause the containment is unstable... *What containment?*" He tried to remember Tim's manual for the Kite, but he realised he hadn't given it a thorough read. *Should've listened to Tim when he told us we all should know how to fly it.* "Okay, I'll have to bypass it."

He heard the next pod leave the Kite. Then the second. Only he and Josh were left.

He left the cockpit as the mountain got closer, and as he ran, he tripped. Scraping his knee, he ignored the blood, scrambling back to his feet. He swung Josh over his shoulder, rushed to the final pod left and got inside. Then he hit the button.

*Boom.*

# CHAPTER TWENTY-NINE

Andrew watched from his pod as the Kite crashed into the mountain, shattering in a fiery explosion, raining metal across the sky. The large explosion created a huge wave that rocked the pod further away from the mountain.

*No, this isn't right... My vision only showed Josh staying behind... Maybe the explosion launched them to safety. It had to.*

His train of thought derailed immediately as he saw what appeared to be a body go up in flames, falling from the Kite at such a speed, that it disappeared within a matter of seconds.

The pod activated its parachute, slowing the pod's descent to minimise the risk of injury. Andrew scanned the area to try and find the other parachutes, seeing only one still in the air. *The other two must've already landed somewhere.*

He cradled Phil in his arms, sobbing softly, mad at himself that his vision proved wrong. His intense, teary eyes analysed the whole landscape with fierce scrutiny: from the vast ocean to the distant islands.

All Andrew could hear was the roaring of the Kite's propeller, which grew louder and louder. Looking up, he noticed how it had detached itself during the impact and had found its course towards his pod.

Andrew knew the only way to descend quicker was to lose weight. He looked around the pod, but there was no window or tiny latch he could open. The door he had entered through would likely only open once it had landed safely.

He saw airwaves reaching the propellor, steering it upwards from below. Soaring directly overhead, Andrew followed its newly acquired course, crossing over the pod, and watched as it disappeared into the thick clouds on the far-right side.

Looking down from his pod, he saw the other pod way below. *Val...*

Val's mind control had prevented worse from happening, and knowing he was awake gave Andrew hope that the others who had been drugged would soon wake up too.

Once the pod reached the ground, the airlock door opened, and Andrew pushed it open. Looking around, he realised he had landed on one of the islands they had set course for. It was much bigger than the one he was previously on, and much bigger than the last one they had visited.

The first time he was on board with the others, looking at the map, he never cared to admit that he found it rather ominous that of the six islands, only one was as big as a country. For some reason, he had always thought that this island would be their last stop.

"*You're wounded,*" he heard a weak voice say next to him.

Looking over at Phil, Phil's eyes stared at him in a worried grogginess. Andrew threw his arms around Phil's neck; grateful he wouldn't have to talk to himself like a maniac.

"*What happened to you?*"

Andrew began to slowly explain all that happened as Phil took care of Andrew's bloodied shoulder.

"So, we're stuck on this island, having *no idea* if the others landed here too, and we've lost *three* people? I consider our odds great."

They intertwined their hands; their foreheads touched one another. They sat like that for a while, refusing to speak further on the matter. Any word that would be said was a depressed one and neither could muster the strength to deal with it.

That was, until Andrew noticed a pod landing not too far from them, and he pointed at it. "There! Someone's here!" He looked over at Phil, realising both were still injured and likely unable to walk without any help. Exchanging looks, they knew walking was still the only way to move forward.

They helped each other to their feet and began their hike through the island's dense vegetation.

The island was ominously silent. No birdsong, no wind, the leaves barely made a sound as Andrew and Phil made their way through the woods. Reaching a river, Phil noticed Andrew rubbed his shoulder.

"We should probably redress it. It's been a while since we left our landing spot. *Sit.* The clean water here should help us out."

Andrew sat down with Phil's help, then helped Phil in return. Shrugging out of his shirt, he pondered how to reach the gash. Phil fetched supplies from the tiny first-aid kit that the pod came equipped with. Andrew winched in pain as Phil poured disinfectant on the wound. Andrew drew in a sharp breath, closing his eyes.

Phil felt Andrew's muscles ripple beneath his touch, taking his merry time to pour more disinfectant on the wound. Even though it hurt, Andrew knew what he was doing. He opened his eyes and looked straight into Phil's, chuckling. Phil felt Andrew's deep chuckle reverberate through his fingers, still laced on Andrew's back. Phil pulled Andrew to him, dipping him back slightly before kissing him affectionately.

Every time Andrew got a little touch or kiss from Phil; it made his heart soar.

Phil moved slowly away from Andrew's lips, smiling at Andrew's loveable gaze, wrapping his injured arm in gauze.

Going in for a second kiss, they were surprised by a spray of bullets shredding the trees surrounding them. Andrew gasped as Phil tugged him to the ground, rolling both behind a rock for cover.

Once the firing had stopped, Phil slowly looked over the rock at the dead werecat that lay before them. Its teeth and claws looked like razor blades, sharp and deadly.

"If they *bite* you, or *claw* you, it's lethal enough to cause internal bleeding."

They looked up at a broad chested guy with big muscles. His grunge strawberry blond locks barely hit the edges of his squared face. His grey eyes were a lot kinder than his initial appearance.

"Yeah, I know, how come I've got a gun on an island while we're all stuck with the basics? I never leave anywhere without a spare gun up my—"

"Okay!" Phil yelled, stopping him before he could finish that sentence. "I know you, mate, so there's no need to explain yourself."

"*Know me*? How do you…" He paused. "You a Laerie too? Like Dom?"

"Dom's here?"

The big man nodded. "Yeah, left him and the new guy back at our camp. These werecats, or whatever the bloody hell they're supposed to be, keep coming at us. Normally we try different methods to spare bullets but, I wasn't given much choice in this matter." He extended his hand to help both up.

"Who's *he*?" Andrew asked Phil.

"We call him Cal. He was a rebel, like Theo was."

"*Was*? Don't tell me Theo's dead."

"Afraid so. So's Jim."

He turned away from them, barely keeping his bristling anger in check. Andrew felt his anger, and he had to admit he had never felt it before. It was a white-hot, almost murderous rage that didn't sit right with him. He could almost *smell* it. The air surrounding Cal was rife with a kind of homicidal rage, something akin to unadulterated fury. He knew this kind of anger shouldn't be underestimated.

"Are you okay?" he asked carefully. "You're angry and it, quite frankly, scares me."

Cal turned to face Andrew, then realised he must have superpowers. "Right, you're *not* a REBEL or a Laerie, so you're just like the new guy."

"The *new* guy? Is he... *special?*"

Cal scoffed. "You could say that. He's got this... *electrokinesis* kinda thing. There was thunder and lightning a few hours ago and mate, you should've seen what he did to our camp. We've forced him to rebuild it all by himself."

"*Ray*..." Andrew mumbled under his breath.

"Ah, yes, that's the lad's name. Raymond. And Dominic. Or, *Dom*, you said it was?" Phil nodded. "Well, let me take you to Ray and Dom then, skin this bloody bad boy here for some meat tonight."

Reaching the camp, they saw the shards of debris scattered around, and a dark-skinned broad-chested guy hauling some rocks around. His arms were even bigger than Cal's, which frightened Andrew. His black dreadlocks seamlessly moved around his shoulders.

Phil noticed his body covered in cuts and bruises and pointed at it, giving Cal a questionable look. "Oh, yeah, he uh, a bit of bark got him good. That's his own bloody fault though."

"Well, we should clean those up. He can't outrun anything if he has to deal with an infection." He grabbed the bottle of disinfectant he had used on Andrew earlier and limped over to Ray, who after a short conversation agreed to sit down on one of the rocks they used as seats.

Andrew watched as Phil poured some of it on Ray's leg, who winced at the sharp and sudden pain. Looking away from the *medical procedure,* Ray's eyes met Andrew's, and he smiled. "Oi, doc," he said to Phil, "don't suppose that bottle of rubbing alcohol you've got there is for consummation?"

Andrew chuckled, shaking his head. "Still an alcoholic, I see."

"You can take the alcohol outta me, but you can't take me outta the alcohol."

Andrew's brows lifted confusedly, but he just nodded and hit Ray's extended fist with his own. "So, you still have no control over your powers?"

"What can I say? Doesn't come with a manual." He got up once Phil was done, stretching his injured limb. "What brings you here, crippled and all?"

Phil and Andrew told their story, including the situation Ray and Cal found themselves in.

Cal sighed loudly. "Figures. I knew peace didn't exist. It's a *metaphor*. And a bad one at that." He got the fire going, skinning the werecat. Looking around, he finally realised Dom wasn't there. "Oi, Ray, where did Dom go?"

"Dunno, he went after you when he heard the gunshots, thought you were in trouble."

"Shite." Cal got up hastily, taking the makeshift axe along with him. "Y'all stay here, you got that? Whatever you *hear*, or *see*, or *smell*, you *don't* come after me. It's safer here."

Before anyone could object, he was gone.

Ray signalled for Andrew to sit down next to Phil, warm themselves up near the fire. The soft ocean breeze rustled through the leaves, the thunder from a few hours ago nowhere to be found. The canopy above their heads stirred slowly due to the calming wind.

"It's finally peaceful again," Ray said, holding the werecat meat above the fire with a makeshift stake. "I've always hated the sound of thunder. Ever since I found out I had powers, my fear for thunder and lightning grew even more."

"May I hazard a guess?" Phil asked. Receiving a nod, he continued. "As a child, you were struck by lightning, *survived*, and became energy-charged?"

Ray chuckled. "It sure seems like the easy explanation, eh?" He shook his head. "Afraid I can't tell you whether that's true or not. The things Drew and I went through, I think it's safe to say we weren't exactly *born* with our powers." He chuckled again. "Or maybe we were, and they activated it. I dunno what to believe. It—"

"Run!" they heard from behind.

All heads turned to Dom and Cal, running out of the woods, chased by a black-veined ferocious human. Andrew recognised the state all too well: it was a loved one who had gone mad, created to either kill, or *be* killed.

Ray started in disbelief at his little brother who caught Dom's ankle, biting him. Dom screamed as Ray's little brother teared off some of his skin like a dog. All stared in horror at the mangled bite mark that formed on Dom's leg.

"He's infected!" Cal yelled, tripping over his own feet as he landed in the mud.

"They're not infectious," Andrew replied, helping him up, "they're *hunters*. And *we're* the hunted."

Before anyone could step in to help Dom, rain pelted down on them in a horrendous stream. "Great, now we're—" Before Ray could finish his sentence, he crumpled to the ground, unable to move any of his limbs.

Soon after, Phil and Andrew dropped to the ground too, just as unable to move. Slowly but surely, Ray's little brother moved up to Dom's abdomen, and began to tear his intestines out as if he was being dissected.

His blood-curdling scream caused Andrew's eye to tear up as he knew it would only be a matter of time before he had reached Dom's heart or throat.

"They're trace amounts of digoxin!" they heard a familiar voice shout from behind them. Tim held a piece of the escape pod above his head to shield himself from the rain. "It's a pharmaceutical normally used for heart conditions, but they've increased the dosage and use it to paralyse people!"

Andrew managed to look over at Phil, who stared back at him in horror. Dom's scream of fear made Andrew's body go rigid. He could vividly see, and *feel*, the cold breath of death that was surrounding Dom. It wasn't just visions anymore. It was also channelling into people's energies and look into their future when it was only seconds away. It was something Andrew wished he could've passed up.

# CHAPTER THIRTY

As Dom's dying screams echoed away, Andrew realised it was only a matter of time before any of the others were next. Tim, still shielding himself from the rain, sneaked closer to them, though he knew there was nothing he could do as the rain pelted down.

"Is Seb somewhere safe?" Andrew asked him, knowing Sam had put the two together in one pod.

"Yeah, he's still inside. I secured the door." He looked over at Dom's body which barely had a bone left, watching as the young boy shoved chunks of Dom's torn flesh down his gullet. "Bloody hell, they're barbaric. He's picking that corpse cleaner than clean. It's *sickening*."

"Okay, Tim?"

Tim turned his head towards Andrew. "Yeah?"

"We've no time to talk about how stomach-churning this is, okay? We gotta get the bloody hell outta here."

But the young boy was done devouring Dom, and as he turned to find his next victim, he lay his eyes upon Tim. Before Andrew could warn him, the young boy surged forward, clamping his massive hands around Tim's ribcage. Tim felt its grip tighten; his bones creaked in protest.

"Wes," Ray tried, a lump in his throat clearly audible. "Wesley, look at me."

The young boy didn't listen. His ears turned into pincers, which spread wide towards Tim. The rain hit Tim's face, and he felt his limbs turn into stiff planks. As Wesley leaned closer, his rotten breath filled Tim's nostrils, swallowing the bile of acid that found its way up from his oesophagus.

Wesley opened his mouth, his tongue swiped across Tim's cheek, who shuddered in defeat. Tim squeezed his eyes shut as Wesley bellowed right into his face, dragging Tim closer to its jaw.

Andrew could see his razor-sharp teeth nearing Tim's skin, and knew that whatever they had given Wesley was an upgrade from what they had given his sister. He watched helplessly as Tim searched frantically for a way to escape Wesley's wrath.

"No!" Ray yelled, absorbing the campfire that was somehow unaffected by the rain, directing its fury towards Wesley. Andrew could feel the energy cackle as it hit Wesley straight in the stomach, setting him aflame.

*It's not just electrokinesis... it's pyrokinesis too.*

Watching as Wesley's whole body burned alive, he slowly reduced to a cinder, filled with a cosmic energy TNT that Andrew thought impossible. This was some Johnny Storm-level galactic genocide instilling fear in him.

As Wesley's body smouldered, the rain stopped. It took a few minutes after that before everyone could move their limbs again. Andrew immediately crawled over to Tim to check up on him.

"I think he *broke* my ribs..." he complained, grunting softly as he tried to sit up. Cal walked over to them both, offering to lift Tim so he wouldn't have to walk.

As Tim accepted, Andrew went over to Phil, who shook his limbs awake. "Bloody hell, it felt like fire in my veins." He sighed. "Add all this up, and it's not so innocuous anymore, is it?"

"Like it *ever* was."

Both chuckled briefly. "You know, when Minnie told me the truth, it was tough to hear it all hashed out that way. And I remember how people always told me that He gives his toughest battles to his strongest soldiers." He stopped for a second, letting out a tiny chuckle. "I mean, he has *grossly* miscalculated the amount of strength he believes *I* possess."

"When did *we* sign up for this war?"

"*Exactly.*"

Phil looked at Andrew, touching his chin. "At least I've amassed my own little army who believes in me."

Andrew gave him a playful nudge, glad to see he was at least on the mend to be joking around like that.

They followed Cal, who was carrying Tim, towards where Tim had left Seb, Ray followed closely behind, still partially paralysed after killing his little brother.

Phil signalled to Andrew that he should fall in line with Ray to check up on him. As Andrew rolled his eyes at Phil, he planted a quick kiss on Andrew's lips. *"For good luck,"* he whispered.

Andrew slowed his pace once he walked next to Ray. "I'm sorry for your loss. I know what it's like to lose your sibling to this... whatever *this* is. Minnie, my sister, she was just like your brother, and she tried to kill me. I'm still not over the fact that someone else had to kill her for *my* sake... but I've come to realise that they're no longer our siblings. They're... *mutated*. Transformed. Transitioned *beyond* recognition."

Ray looked over at him, nodding solemnly. "I'm just glad my parents aren't around to see any of this. They'd be so... disappointed and heartbroken."

"We're living vicariously through 'em," Andrew said, "both our parents *and* siblings."

"If only we could stop this... this *evil*, terrorist crime syndicate that's been tormenting us since the day they took us as little children."

Andrew couldn't help but chuckle as Ray spoke those words, which made Ray laugh too. "A bit of a stodgy description but, it'll do."

Once they reached the pod Tim and Seb had been in, they found Seb still unconscious but, for the most part, unharmed. Cal put Tim down, who slowly lifted his shirt. A big bruise had formed where his ribs are. As he inhaled, his face contorted in pain.

While Cal carefully removed Seb from the pod, Andrew kneeled in front of Tim. "Let me see that." He saw the swelling around the bruise. "Is there an ice pack in the pod?"

Tim nodded, pointing at the orange box. "It's in the trauma kit, I think. That's the orange box, not the usual white one."

Andrew moved past Cal to take the kit, then walked back to Tim to give him the instant ice pack, visibly relieved once the cold hit the bruise. He noticed how Tim looked over at Seb.

"I know you must be wracked with guilt, just like your friend, *Sam*. I heard him talk about how he made all these mistakes, how he let everyone down. Including *you*. But maybe... maybe all of us being apart from each other will give us perspective. A way to move *forward*."

Tim rubbed his hand over his face, but when his hand dropped, he made eye contact with Andrew. Looking at him imploringly, he exhaled sharply, pain written across his face. "You think Sam made it out?"

Andrew couldn't bring himself to tell Tim what he had seen, and that it was unlikely that Sam had survived the explosion. But he knew optimism was all they had right now to not succumb to the darkness.

"It's *Sam*. From what I've heard from all of you, he's a *cockroach* that can't be killed."

Tim laughed, then grimaced.

"I dunno about y'all, but I'm famished," Cal said. "We need to find food."

"If we're going full tilt," Ray answered him, "then I need sleep *more* than I need food."

"You can take the night off if you want," Cal replied, "govern yourself. I'll go and see what I can find. Anyone care to join me?" Looking around the group, he realised he was the only one, *besides Ray*, who was uninjured. He sighed. "I'll be back soon."

As he left, Andrew helped Phil to make a campfire while Tim and Ray went to sleep next to Seb.

"Anyone ever told you you're as astute as you're handsome?" Phil asked Andrew, who shook his head.

"Nice try, but flattery will get you nowhere," he quipped.

"You sure? What if I change it to... *astute as always*?"

"How about you go back to your selfless leader duties when we were trapped? You shouldn't abscond yourself with your handsome *boyfriend* over here in the middle of—" Saying the word *boyfriend* out loud made Andrew gasp. *I did not just say that. I've ruined it all. I've—*

"That's a hefty accusation," Phil replied, "one that I'd *happily* take on as a challenge, especially if I erroneously believe I've got an advantage over the fairer side of that title."

"Are you saying you're *better* than me?" Andrew replied teasingly.

Phil bristled, albeit pretending to, at Andrew's teasingly underlying aggression. Then he grinned smugly at the other's teasing. "How are you so incorrigibly romantic?"

Andrew laughed hoarsely, then shook his head. Phil gazed lovingly into his eyes. Andrew could hear the faintness of a song his sister used to play for him on the piano, one that she told him, *"would always sound wherever you might be to ensure I'm right there beside you. It's a token of love, in whatever shape or form that may come."* As the song slowly crescendoed, Andrew lifted his arm to twirl Phil, who was chuckling by the gesture.

*"Someone's* bright-eyed and bushy tailed."

"If you keep saying such sweet things to me, I think I might blow a fuse," Andrew replied. Though, he was loving the attention way too much to be serious about asking Phil to calm down the flirting.

Cal returned with a few fish he had caught and watched as Andrew and Phil moved away from each other, blushing heavily. He shook his head, then began to prepare dinner.

A few hours passed as they had eaten their meal. Ray had gone back to sleep, so had Tim. Phil was dozing against Andrew's side, while Andrew and Cal stayed awake taking the first shift of the evening.

"You two together?" Cal asked. "Not that I'm judging, I mean, *love is love*, but you don't mind that Phil was technically an *alien* two years ago?"

Andrew shook his head. "He was *human* before that. He still was when he was a Laerie. Honestly, I think *I'm* more of an alien here."

Cal looked over at him. "Just 'cause you're special or different from us doesn't mean you're an alien."

"Then why did you still use that term to describe Phil's past?"

"Touché." Cal chuckled nervously, poking the wood to make sure the fire stayed lit. "But in all seriousness, why do you think of yourself that way?"

"On more than one occasion, I tried to explain to myself how it felt to be afraid of that darkness inside of me. It's not just simply the absence of light, it's... much more *tangible* than that. It's something I can touch *and* feel. Honestly, worse than that, it's like my powers have a mind of their own. When I shapeshift, it feels like something malign. Something malicious and foreign that's not so innocent as it seems." He looked over at Phil. "I somehow love him with a frightening intensity, as if he's the only one who can keep me grounded. I haven't shapeshifted ever since I met him. I could've, but I *didn't*."

Cal offered him some water, chuckling softly. "You know, you're armed with a makeshift axe and saying things people normally get put in padded cells for." Andrew laughed, giving Cal his water back. "But I get it. Ever since I met Ray, I've to admit that it's both terrifying and astonishing what he can do. But I can't deny that he saved a guy's life. He might save *more* in the future. So, *maybe* that darkness you feel isn't so dark after all. This shadow you feel is just a transient phenomenon. Darkness will pass, and there will be another day in which that light will increase. Just, *don't* give up believing."

"But how can I *not* believe in danger and gloom? I don't wanna know how things end, 'cause I know a happy ending for any of us is impossible. How can the world return to its previous state after so much terror has occurred?"

"I know we shouldn't even be here, but there's no going back now. It's like the stories we've read; you know? The ones about the greater heroes who fought in the dark to find the light, the ones that remained in your memory. Those people had several opportunities to go back, but they chose not to as they were clinging to something."

"What do we still cling to?"

"That some positive things still exist in the world. Like the love that's blooming between you and Phil, that harmony's something worthwhile, *something to fight for*."

Andrew took a deep breath. "And what if you can see the future and know how it ends?"

Cal put a comforting hand on his shoulder. "Then you do *everything* in your power to prove that future wrong."

A chill wind rustled through the trees. Andrew thanked Cal who nodded, closing his eyes.

Andrew had dozed off, forgotten to wake Ray for the second shift, as he heard leaves rustling in the distance. He shot up straight, taking the axe firmly in his hand. He watched with bated breath as the bushes in front of him moved. Preparing himself to throw the axe, he narrowed his eyes to ensure he wouldn't miss.

Believing he had locked onto the target, he swung the axe towards the bush, narrowly hitting Alex who jumped out with a scream.

"Oi! It's us! It's Stan and Alex!"

By some miracle, the scream hadn't alerted anyone else. Andrew, limping, rushed over and embraced Alex, even though he hadn't known him that long. "It's so good to see familiar and friendly faces," he exclaimed.

"That makes two of us."

Andrew let go of Alex, waving somewhat awkwardly towards Stan, whose arms were crossed. "Sorry, didn't mean to—"

"*Whatever*." He brushed past Andrew once he saw Seb and Tim.

"How long have ya been out here?" Alex asked him.

"I lost track of time. But how did you find us?"

Alex pointed at the campfire. "Wasn't that hard, honestly." He looked around the campsite. "No sign of Josh or Sam?"

"No, no sign of Val either. They're the only ones missing."

"Well, if we all made it to this island, I'm sure *they* did too. It's hard not to land on here. It's *gigantic*." He noticed Andrew looking over at Stan with a hurt expression. He gave him a gentle tap on his shoulder. "He *never* takes kind to strangers. Don't take it too personal. It took him a long time to trust me and everyone else too. Give it some time." With that, he left Andrew alone with his thoughts and headed over to Stan.

Andrew caught a glimpse of the sky, streaking orange with the first blush of sunset, and smiled to himself.

# CHAPTER THIRTY-ONE

Sam woke to the steady lapping of the waves. The drumbeat of his pulse thudded in his head as he tried to put his left fist up but was unable to. An acrid and pungent smell reached his nostrils. He felt a neuropathic pain flare up combined with a burning sensation and pins and needles.

He slowly turned his head to the left, and seeing his dermis all shrunk and split open, he couldn't even open his mouth to scream. It hurt too much for him to speak. *I must've blacked out from the pain. It hurts like bloody hell.*

He clenched his teeth as he touched his severely burnt arm, his face twisted with pain. It looked infected. *Sepsis. I might have sepsis.*

He moved his head slowly towards Josh, who was no longer in the pod. Trying to breathe through the pain, Sam crawled out of the pod, convulsing with pain as the sand grazed over his burn.

"Sam, that you?" Looking up, he saw Val running over to him. "Bloody hell..." He kneeled next to Sam, whose breathing was so shallow, Val thought he was close to dying. "Okay, don't move. *Don't move!*" He stopped Sam from moving away from him, positioning him against the pod.

"Josh..." His voice was rough as he spoke. "Where..."

"I dunno, I've been scourin' this entire side of the island lookin' for any signs of life. I've not seen anyone but you. The silvery colour of the pod caught my attention." He noticed the fat leaking out of Sam's skin, then again, it could hardly be called skin. It was stiff, leathery, and so swollen that he could hardly make out Sam's original skin colour. "Look, I know you might think I'm crazy for suggestin' this, but we need to *amputate* your arm. If we don't, it'll *kill* you."

Sam, barely conscious, knew Val was right. He *hated* admitting it, but there was no other option. Yet, if he went through with it, he would lose the wolf tattoo he had gotten for Zach. *No... I... I can't... But I... have... to...* And beyond that—despite the times he had wanted to give up—now *wasn't* one of them. He had to find his family *and* his friends.

"Do... it..." he said weakly, barely staying conscious.

Val nodded and removed his belt, wrapping it around his arm just below the shoulder. He looked inside the pod's weapon crate, taking out an axe. Walking back to Sam, he stared at him. "Last chance to say no."

Sam said nothing, and Val was honestly not sure if Sam was conscious enough to realise the brevity of the situation, the thing Val was about to do to him. He sighed deeply as he hefted the axe above his head.

Josh had found Andrew and Phil's empty pod, but as he approached it, he found it empty. "Crap." He searched around the pod, but the first-aid kits were gone. "How the bloody hell am I gonna find something to help Sam? I gotta find something to help him. I gotta..." In the far distance, he saw one of the Troopers staring at him. *"No..."* he whispered, "no! No, leave me alone!"

He fell to the ground, crawling backwards as the figure approached him menacingly. He felt the branding iron scourge his skin, screaming. As the scar emerged, the Trooper forced a vitriol attack on him, and he found his hands bound together, high up so his arms would feel weak.

"Stop it!" he yelled. "Please, stop it! I'll do anything! *Anything* you want!"

His body burned, his back skin tissue not only branded, but also damaged by the hydrochloric acid.

*"Join us,"* the Trooper said, "join us in assassinating President Goldlib and vice-president Samuel. Join us in taking back what's *rightfully* ours."

"No, no, I can't... *I can't...*"

The Trooper took his cigarette out of his mouth, burning Josh's forearm with it.

"Stop!" he yelled, his voice tight with pain, robbed of his rational thought. "Go on then, kill me! I *won't* betray 'em!"

"Then we'll just have to keep you here."

"They'll start asking questions," he said, rigid with agony. *"Then what?"*

The Trooper snorted, spitting in Josh's face. "We'll make you seem guilty, so they'll forget all about you. And until then," he said, branding Josh again, right below his new scar, "I'll just keep on having *fun.*"

Val took a deep breath as he looked at Sam, who drifted further away from reality. "Shite. Big fat, bloody shite." He shook his head. *"Forgive me."* He took a swing, aiming just below the makeshift tourniquet. Blood spurted from the wound which soaked both of their clothes and coated the ground. The axe fell from his limp fingers as Sam let out a scream so high-pitched and shrill that it made the hairs on the back of Val's neck stand up. A sound of pure terror that neither would *ever* forget.

Hearing the terrorising scream, Josh looked over his shoulder to where he had left Sam behind.

"Sam! No! Leave him alone!" He looked at the Trooper who had vanished, though he was still stuck in the underground prison. Looking up at his hands no longer bound, he slowly moved his arms down.

Another scream made him break into a sprint, bursting through the woods. In his mind, he was still stuck in the hallways of the dark prison, but branches smacked and slashed his cheeks as he sprinted through the untamed landscape, converging on Sam's pained screams.

It was only a matter of time before he was covered in scrapes and bruises.

Val turned away from Sam as he tried to apply pressure to his wound. Knowing Sam needed his help, he put his hemophobia aside.

A prick in his arm made him stop in his tracks. "Who the bloody hell chunked that small pebble at me?" he asked. But as he looked down at his arm, he realised he had been *shot*. "Oh, shite!" He fell to the ground, clutching his upper arm. "What the bloody hell!" He looked at Josh whose gun was smoking, his face determined and angry. "Oi, mate, calm down, you're gonna seriously injure someone with that. *Put it down.*"

"Get away from my friend, you bloody bastard! I won't let you hurt *anyone* else!"

"Oi, I'm not hurtin' anyone! I *saved* him. Or well, he might *still* die if we don't cut off the blood flow!"

He tried crawling towards Sam but was hit with another bullet in his other arm, The shot that rang out made Josh dive to the ground, covering his ears with his hands. "Stop! No more shooting, please!"

Val, who was now trying to stop the bleeding in two places, looked over at him. "I'm not shootin' *nobody*! *You're* the one shootin' innocent people here!" Watching Josh curl into a ball, he realised he wasn't in his right mind. "Are you kiddin' me? The severely traumatised lad's the one I'm saddled with... Oh, this is just my lucky day!" He sucked in a sharp breath as he crawled back over to where Sam was; a sickly trail of blood dripped down both his arms.

He managed to make Sam lie down, elevating the site of his arm that was bleeding. He removed the tiny bit of sleeve that was left, applying steady pressure while his own arms were gushing blood.

The blood soaked straight through the makeshift cloth of Sam's other sleeve, to which he applied another piece, not lifting the first.

Sam's pupils dilated, his breathing became rapid and shallow. "No, please, mate, I need you to *not* do that right now." He looked over at Josh. "*You*! Get your shite together and help me! Your friend's life is on the line!"

Josh didn't snap out of it. He was so overcome with trauma that he heard nothing but the Trooper yelling at him and scolding him.

"Mate! Listen to me! Whatever you're experiencin', it's *not* real, okay? You're safe! Snap the bloody hell outta it!" He yelled, both in pain and from the effort as he kept applying pressure, doing everything he possibly could to prevent the wound from further injury and infection.

He noticed Sam's chest was no longer rising. Pure panic took over his body. Knowing the bleeding hadn't stopped, he wrapped the injured area with a piece of clothing he found in the pod, blessing whoever had put it there.

He quickly lay Sam on his back to open his airways. Feeling no pulse whatsoever, he put the lower palm of his hand over the centre of Sam's chest, placing his other hand on top. Keeping his elbows as straight as he could with a bullet in each arm, he positioned his shoulders directly above his hands and began the chest compressions.

Josh finally came to, and as he did, he witnessed Val with two bleeding arms performing CPR on one of his best friends. Reality slowly sank in when he saw Sam's severed burned arm.

He rushed to Sam's side and took hold of his bloody, crudely bandaged shoulder to apply further pressure. With every chest compression, more blood oozed out.

After every thirty chest compressions, Val performed two rescue breaths before resuming compressions.

"Come on!" Val worked with such a strained effort, that he trembled from the pain himself. He began to cry the more he strained himself. "I heard you've got a *son*! Don't you freakin' think about dyin' today!"

"Zack," Josh replied. "His name's Zack."

"Think about Zack, you hear me? Sam, *wake up!*" Out of frustration, Val began to smack Sam's chest harder and harder, until with the fourth blow, he noticed Sam's chest moving. He quickly checked his pulse which was *weak*, but *present*.

He moved backwards as relief washed over him, letting out an exaggerated sigh. He held himself back from smiling as he was surprised at feeling the joy that suffused him. Sam was bloody, but *alive*.

Sam opened his eyes and gasped loudly, sucking oxygen into his lungs. Perspiration covered his face. He looked from Josh to Val, coughing and groaning as they helped him to sit up.

"*Your heart stopped*," Josh said, his voice laced with anxiety and relief. "It stopped, Sam, your heart it—"

"It's working now," Sam reassured him, "it's ticking… just fine."

Josh chuckled softly, wiping away his tears. "You always were a petulant son of a gun." He carefully hugged Sam, who returned the gesture by patting Josh's back. "You could've saved yourself from this," Josh said, "you could've just left me and save your arm."

Sam shook his head, looking Josh straight in the eyes. "I… I wasn't planning on abandoning you… a second time. And I certainly wasn't planning… on betraying you. If I had, it… it wouldn't have been an arm worth saving." He looked over at Val next, extending his hand. "Thank you. I… I *owe* you."

Val took his hand, shaking his head. "You saved *me* first. I returned the favour. We're *even*." Val found Josh's eyes, who tried to avoid Val's gaze. "What was that back there?"

Sam gave Josh a questionable look, who dismissed him. "Nothing, just shock. I'm *fine*."

Before either of them could ask further questions, Josh turned his back towards them. His back was exposed by cracks in his shirt, and for the first time, Sam saw the branding scars and the scourging acid spots. He had seen Josh's severely bruised ribs, but he hadn't seen his back. He swore he even saw whip marks.

*How the bloody hell did no one see this? Why did nobody tell me it was this bad?*

Josh walked away from them both to search for food. Val kneeled next to Sam in the sand, sighing deeply. "You're bearin' a tremendous amount of weight. One that's clearly cripplin' you." Sam raised his eyebrow at him. "I've overheard some convos from the other lads when I was on the Kite. They're all worried about you,

you know? You're shoulderin' this by yourself while you *don't* have to." He took a tiny shell from the sand, throwing it towards the sea to try and skim it. "Look, I'll *never* understand what came before this, but I know that this *new* burden you've got predates that. You need to confront whatever past you've got goin' on, or you'll be held down by it. They *need* you." He put his hand on Sam's uninjured arm. "Don't conflate the things that are easy with those that are possible."

    The pain hit Sam again, which forced him to double over. Val rubbed his back, something Sam would've stopped him from doing had he not been in so much pain. He tried to regulate his breathing.

    "I was *angry* with you," Val explained, "and only 'cause I saw a genuine second of doubt in your eyes when I screamed for help." Sam grunted, breathing away the pain as best he could. "But I know that if I've got tears, words, *concern even*, there's *care*. And you got the same in you. You're a genuine good lad, Sam. I can learn *a lot* from you."

    Josh returned with a few bananas. Seeing Sam doubled over, he rushed to his side, worried Val had done something to him. After confirming he hadn't, he looked at Val's arms, and the realisation hit him.

    "*I did that...*" he whispered under his breath. He pressed both hands on the gushing wound on Val's left arm, trying to stop the bleeding.

    Val gave him a short nod of gratefulness. "I'm *lucky* you're such a good shot. Both bullets went clean through."

    Josh chuckled softly. "Years of training will get you there."

    Val jerked away as he heard something rumbling in the distance, which tore his wound open even further. Pain shot through his body as blood poured down his arm. Josh knew he had to tie it off tightly and worked as fast as he could to do so. Moving on to Val's other arm, Val touched him on the shoulder to get his attention.

    "We've got *bigger* problems."

    Josh ignored him and finished bandaging his right arm, then turned around to stare straight at the cataclysmic tornado approaching them at an alarming speed.

# CHAPTER THIRTY-TWO

The Kite flew as fast as it could to the last known location of Sam's Kite. Alfie, Percy's brother, sat behind the throttle, focusing on the task at hand. He sighed as he looked at a photograph of his brother, shaking his head. "Hang in there, mate. I'll come back for you." He turned on his comms. "Hawk to Eagle."

"Eagle, come in."

"I'm nearing the site of disappearance. I'm nearing bad weather."

"*Copy that. Try to suppress it while proceeding to point. No change to your mission.*"

Alfie hit a few buttons at the overhead panel. "Roger that. Preparing to drop on the nearest island."

"*Negative. Don't leave the aircraft unmanned.*"

Alfie sighed, shaking his head slightly. "Yes, sir." Nearing the island, he noticed the multiple-vortex tornado that was advancing fast. "Shite. That's not good." He reactivated the comms. "I'm encountering hostile weather, Eagle. I need to move in to engage."

"*Stay in your aircraft, Hawk, that's an order.*"

"Aye, sir." He closed the comms. "Stay put my arse. You can't pull that psyops crap on me, not after what happened to Percy. Classified bull crap." Nearing the island, he activated autopilot, leaving his seat. "Target ahead. Looks like I'm just in time to crash the party and ruin those bastards' plans. I know what they did to Josh and the others. Paramilitary trying to shut us down, silencing us, not if *I've* got a say in it. I won't let 'em erase *all* of us. I've done enough recon to say with certainty that I know of their plans." He chuckled. "Of course, I'm talking to myself. First sign of going crazy."

"*Hawk, come in.*"

Alfie sighed, walking back to the cockpit. "Hawk to Eagle."

"*After you rendezvous with any of the survivors, we'll proceed with the operation as planned. Do you copy?*"

"There's *no way* he's giving me the clear to go down there. There's *no way* he just changed his mind. Did someone brief him? One of 'em superpower lads, I'm sure. Bet they can read my mind or something." He shook his head. "Still talking to myself. Great. I'm *officially* insane."

"*Hawk, do you copy?*"

"Yes, I copy."

He grabbed his special tactics assault rifle, readying it for use with thirty rounds. Rounds that would blow someone's arm off by firing it just once, a perky update Percy had made for both.

He cocked the gun, looking over at the photograph of him, Percy, Jack, and Alec that hung next to the door. "Don't worry, I'll avenge *all* of you. We'll expose those arseholes and their ops."

*"Hawk, proceed with extreme caution."*

Alfie mockingly repeated the words without making an actual sound, then opened the door. A slight terror filled his heart as the wild wind rose about, menacing storm clouds loomed over him and the Kite. The air turned bitingly cold as a shiver ran over his back. He attached the tether to his belt, then proceeded to jump out of the Kite.

"We need to move," Val said, "we need to find a cave."

"Then what? The tornado will still hit us. Worst case scenario, it blocks us from getting out. Then we'll starve to death," Josh replied.

Val scoffed softly. "If you've got a better idea, genius, I'm *all* ears."

*"As if you're such a genius*," Josh whispered furtively. Instead of answering Val, he dashed over to a bush and scanned the horizon for danger. *"Someone's* here."

Val wanted to dart after him, but a cry of pain that echoed from behind him made him turn towards Sam. "Josh! As one would say, we can't wait for the grass to grow! Sam won't survive a tornado, *nor* a second cardiac arrest." Hoping he had prodded Josh, Val looked over towards the direction he had disappeared into. "Josh!" He sighed.

Someone shoved him from behind. Val fell to his knees, gasping from the impact.

"Get up and step away from Sam with your hands in the air. *Slowly.*"

Val did as he was told, feeling the barrel of the gun poking his back. He moved away from Sam, crying out in pain as the figure put his hands behind his back, cuffing him.

"That freakin' hurts, mate! I was shot, *twice!*"

"Not my concern." The figure kicked him against his knee pit, forcing Val on his knees once again.

"Kindness won't kill you; you know?" Val scoffed, "I'm no threat."

"I don't see anyone nearby who can vouch for you, *do you?*"

"*I can.*"

The figure heard Josh's voice, lowering his weapon astoundingly. "You're *alive?*"

Josh's hands were visibly shaking, clenching his fists. His nails dug into his skin. "No thanks to you, *Alfred.*"

"Yeah, about that. I wanted to apologise with how... *spotty*, I've been. I know I've been showing avoidant behaviour since the first day they took you in."

"And you didn't lift *a single finger* to try and get me out. If only Percy knew the truth about how you turned on us."

"I didn't turn it's... It's *complicated.*"

"Can the chatter," Val replied furiously, "we've got bigger fish to fry."

He moved his head to show the nearing tornado. The wind began to pick up to the point where Val moved back towards Sam to shield him.

"This pathetic empathy of yours is a terrible reason to wanna fight for us now," Josh scoffed. "But you, of all people, know just *how* fake empathy *really* is. If the truth can't help someone, you should lie. *Right?*"

"Josh, please..."

"You're all like *weed*, you know that? Pull one, and another grows back in its place to stab you in the back. Tell me, how long did you think you could keep your shady, dark side business a secret from the people you love? You *do* realise that those people have now stopped being the people—"

"Shut the bloody hell up!" Val yelled. "Shut up!" He yelled so loud; it made Sam gasp awake from his half-asleep, half-awake state. "He's clearly here with a way for us to leave this bloody island before it's too late," he said, having caught a glimpse of Alfie's tether. "We can get Sam up to safety if you *stop* your bickerin'."

Alfie nodded, then lowered his gun. "I can only take one person with me before I can come back for someone else."

Josh scoffed. "You'll leave us here. You *hate me*, and you *don't* even know Val."

"I don't hate..." He sighed. "If you'll let me, I can explain *everything*, all their plans. And how to stop 'em."

Josh barged over to Alfie until he stood face to face, breathing angrily. "Talk. *Now.*"

Alfie sighed, looking over his shoulder at the looming threat, then turned back to face Josh. *"Fine."* He put his gun down in the sand, typing something on the control panel on his arm.

"They've developed a new type of serum to create bio-organic weapons. For military use."

"Bioweapons?" Val chimed in, "so not *just* a serum. But a *virus*. A test-run."

Alfie nodded as he crouched. "Every time you think you've defeated your mutated loved one, they administer the drug when you're not looking to keep 'em in check. They're trying to find the right dose to make soldiers who *can't* die."

"Why?" Val asked.

"I know why," Sam replied weakly, "it's 'cause we... Josh and I, the first Troopers, the serum they gave us... it didn't have the desired effect... Not for *all* of us, anyway."

Alfie nodded. "As long as they're given regular doses of that inhibitor, they can fight much longer and harder than they could before that."

"So much for revolutionary," Josh scoffed.

"They claim they've been doing it for the sake of the nation's security. They said that two years ago, and they've been saying the exact same thing."

"Profitin' off the fruits of their labour, yeah why not," Val said, shaking his head. "And if it causes sacrifices, then who cares, *right?*"

"We do," Sam said, coughing, "that's why we defeated 'em... two years ago. And it's exactly why... we'll defeat 'em... *again*."

"Wait," Val said, "that means the experiments they've been doin' on people like me—those *superhero powers*—that's done by a pharmaceutical company then? What role do *we* play in all this?"

Alfie sighed. "On each island, one of you is put to eliminate the Laeries and REBELS and force 'em to create an even more advanced virus to make sure they're in fact *unkillable*."

"So, we're doin' their dirty work. *Great*." Val slammed his fist against the pod, which sent a pain flare up his arm. "So, the more the other lads on the islands fight against those things, the stronger they become until they can't be defeated no more and we *all* die. Yeah, I sure as bloody hell like those odds."

Alfie heard his comms roar to life, and he sighed. "I haven't told HQ about any of this. They dunno I've gone rogue on 'em, and I'd like to keep it that way. But they're requesting a damage estimate, and—"

"What made you change your mind?" Josh asked, his arms crossed. "Why help us *now* and have *me* tortured?"

Sam looked at Josh, noticing how his hand was trembling. He looked over at Val, who noticed it too. *"He had an episode* earlier," Val whispered to Sam. "He shot me 'cause he believed I was him. Alfie. I dunno what they did to him, but you gotta talk to him. He needs to process it, or he'll get people killed on accident."

Before Alfie could respond to Josh's question, they noticed a column of violently rotating air approaching them rapidly. Alfie pointed his arm with the control panel towards it, swearing under his breath.

"That's five-hundred miles *per hour*. I've never seen such a tornado before."

"It's not natural," Val replied, "nothin' has been on these bloody islands. It's not just us who are supposed to eliminate the threats. They know we're onto 'em, and like you said, they only need *us* freaks. If we don't kill each other off, they'll do it *for us*."

Alfie took his gun. "Okay, I'm taking Sam up first." Receiving a side-glance from Josh, he sighed. "I'm not gonna convince you to trust me, you'll just have to."

They got Sam to his feet, who grunted loudly. Josh assisted him by having Sam's uninjured arm around his shoulder so Sam could use Josh as a crutch. Val was behind Sam to provide support every time he stumbled backwards.

They walked towards the spot where Alfie initially landed, the tether a straight line down from the Kite. Alfie felt a few droplets of water hit the top of his head. He looked up. The encroaching clouds overhead looked too menacing for comfort. He took a harness out of his pack, having Val and Josh assist Sam in stepping through the leg holes, carefully lifting it over his hips.

Alfie adjusted his carabiner before gripping the tether, then hit a button on his arm's control panel before he and Sam were pulled up by the mechanistic pulley.

"What about the others?" Josh asked Val, "we *can't* leave 'em."

"Once we're in the Kite, we'll scout from above. I promise you we won't leave *any* of 'em behind. After what I've learned today, I now understand I was an arsehole. And *none of you* deserved that."

The howling wind made the pod creak ominously behind them, its eerie tune made them cover their ears. The wind itself was deafening, slowly drowning out all the other sounds. It was a chilling prelude that marked the approaching tornado.

Val forced himself to open his eyes as the sand flew everywhere, and he tapped Josh's shoulder. Both stared at the tornado that had awakened a hurricane.

"Oh, come on!" Josh yelled. "*Both?*" He sank to the ground. "We're doomed. This is how we die."

No one could blame Josh for his shift of mood considering how daunting the situation was. He sighed and socked the ground, burying his head in his hands. Val put a brotherly hand on Josh's shoulder. As they made eye contact, all animosity from their early challenges were evidently gone in the face of this much larger threat.

They stood stock-still for a long moment, feeling the weight of the responsibility heavy on their shoulders.

From above, they saw Alfie descending. "Come on!"

Josh gave Val the opportunity to go first considering the fact he was still bleeding. Josh looked at his feet, abashed, as Val and Alfie left him alone. He still felt guilty for shooting Val. He looked up as the last rays of sun dipped below the looming clouds.

"Back for more?" he heard behind him.

He turned around slowly to stare at the Trooper who he had seen earlier. He tried to run away, but the Trooper fired a shotgun point-black into Josh's shoulder. He fell to the ground, breathing hoarsely. He turned his head to look at the Trooper who had doused himself in Josh's blood in the process.

He retreated, clutching his bloody, mangled shoulder. The Trooper shot him again, in his back, which made Josh drop to the ground in an almost dead-like fashion. He snatched up his gun, rolled onto his injured back, and breathed shallowly. He looked at the grinning figure standing over him, smoke still rising from his sawed-off shotgun.

"I'm running low on ammo," he said, tossing the shotgun aside for a second. "Only got two rounds left." He grabbed his shotgun from the ground, popping open the barrel to show Josh the two rounds that were left before closing it again.

Josh tried to get up, falling into a crouch just in time as the shotgun blasted through the air a third time. The shot was so close that Josh could smell the burning gunpowder.

He turned around to shoot the Trooper with his own gun, who ducked as the bullet whizzed by his head.

The Trooper chuckled menacingly. "I'm surprised you're still alive. You sure you're not *one of 'em*?"

He rushed at Josh, plunging a syringe in his neck. Josh let out a wail of pain, thrashing as he shoved the Trooper back. The liquid in the syringe disappeared into his bloodstream. Josh looked down at his hands that were slowly transforming. His nails fell off, replaced by talons that made him gasp in horror. He watched his veins turn black, taking a few steps back as if it would slow down the process.

"No! No, not again! Please, *not again!*"

"You thought it hadn't worked, did you? It takes time for the virus to take hold of a person, especially someone who's recently been cured. But you can't escape your *destiny*, Josh. You're destined for *great things*."

The Trooper shot again, but Josh's talon caused the bullet to ricochet back towards the Trooper, who dodged it narrowly.

He grinned. *"There's* the Josh I know."

Out of ammo, the Trooper grabbed the stock of the gun, swinging it like a bat. He smashed the still-hot barrel into the side of Josh's head, who crumpled unconscious to the ground.

"Josh!"

Josh gasped awake, looking up at Alfie who had come back down from the Kite.

"What the bloody hell are you lying on the ground for? We gotta go!"

Josh looked behind him, then checked his unharmed shoulder. Unable to reminisce on what just happened, he let Alfie secure him into the harness before ascending to the Kite.

# CHAPTER THIRTY-THREE

Alfie closed the door behind him as Josh got himself out of the harness. He looked at Sam who was propped against the wall, barely conscious. Rushing to his side, he watched Val observing the radar system for electromagnetic waves, and the sonar system for transmitted acoustic waves.

"We've got five minutes to find 'em before they'll be stuck in a whirlwind. *Literally*."

Alfie hastened over to the cockpit, repositioning himself behind the throttle. "Navigate me!"

Alfie navigated the Kite through the deadly clouds, but it was moving much too slow due to it being sucked back each time Alfie tried to active the boosters. A sudden gust of wind forced Alfie to veer off course. He tried to counteract the downdraft to avoid being pulled into the raging storm.

"Hold onto something!" he yelled, diving sharply to get beneath the wind flow.

Josh tried to keep Sam seated, though Val wasn't fast enough. He slid backwards, crashing right on top of Josh and Sam.

"Navigator!" Alfie yelled.

Val crawled over to the sonar and radar panel, hoisting himself up as he grunted. "I see movement. A few green dots altogether."

"Directions!" Alfie yelled again, hitting the booster once more to try and reach them before it was too late.

"To the right!"

As they tried to reach the others, Josh knew they had to think of something to hoist all up at once. One by one would mean they would *all* die. He thought of lowering the biggest crate he could find and began to empty its contents, sending it flying everywhere across the Kite. He pulled the cables from the walls, attaching them to the pulley as fast as he could.

Val saw what he was doing and rushed to help him, knowing he would need someone else to drag them in. "Good thinking," he complimented Josh, who gave a quick smile.

"I'm on top of 'em, I can see 'em!" Alfie yelled. "Open the door and lower whatever the bloody hell you're working on!" Trying to keep the Kite steady, he grunted with effort, the throttle shook in his hands.

They lowered the crate as slowly yet quickly as they could, hoping the others below would understand what they were doing. They watched as Andrew looked up; his brow creased in confusion.

"Get in!" Josh yelled at the top of his lungs, hoping someone down there was able to hear him on top of the Kite's propellors and the violent raging storm.

"Who are *they*?" Cal asked, trying to shield his eyes from the sand and mud that was flying everywhere.

"I think it's the cavalry," Andrew replied jokingly. "I think it's Josh up there."

"That means Sam must be with him," Stan said, hopeful.

Long talon-like fingers clamped down on Stan's shoulder, whirled around in horror. He stared at the barely human-like boy that stood behind him, his razor-sharp teeth glinted in the low light of the campfire they had relighted.

"Bloody hell! I thought you killed him!" Cal yelled to Ray, who stood just as perplexed as everyone else.

Alex charged at the boy, tackling him to the ground. He kept the struggling boy pinned, stabbing his pocketknife deep into his leg, accidentally slicing through the boy's muscle and tendon. The boy dislodged the blade with ease.

"What the bloody hell's this thing?" he yelled, scrambling back as the boy viciously crawled towards Alex.

Cal took the axe from Andrew's hands, cutting off his foot. Screeching in pain, the boy thrashed about. He trailed dark blood as he retreated in a shuffling limp.

"Are ya hurt?" Alex asked Stan, whose shirt had holes in it. His shoulder had endured a few bloody claw marks, but he seemed fine otherwise. Returning the question, Alex assured him he was unharmed.

"Quick, get in here," Phil commanded. "The hurricane, tornado—*whatever* it's called—is coming way too close. And then there's those things," he said, pointing at the boy. "I vote we go. *Now*."

They lifted Seb into the crate after Andrew and Phil had gotten in first. Tim joined them, and they yelled to Val and Josh that they were ready to be pulled up. The remaining four watched as the crate slowly left the island, hovering in the air, swinging back and forth in a dangerous matter.

"I hope it won't break," Stan said.

Out of the shadows, he saw the young boy jerking in their direction. Before he could warn anyone, the boy had jumped on top of his brother Ray. Ray tried to hold the boy off as he viciously bit towards his skin.

Ray's eyes glowed as he used the fire to his advantage, setting his hand aflame as he pushed his hand into the boy's chest. The boy tightened his grip on Ray's arm, who didn't give in. He yelled as he sent the fire from his hand into the boy's chest, threatening to tear his own hand.

The boy bared his blood-caked teeth at Ray, whose eye dropped a single tear down his cheek. "Wes, it's me. It's *Ray*."

The boy loosened his grip on Ray, his chest burning. He cocked his head, staring at Ray in disbelief. "R...*a*...*y*..."

The crate lowered again, and Alex and Stan climbed inside. "Come on ya two!" Alex yelled, "leave him!"

Cal gripped the axe, ready to strike at any moment. Ray shook his head at him, silently telling him to lower it. He carefully slipped out from beneath the boy's body and touched his mangled cheek. "I'm so sorry about this. You didn't deserve *any* of this. I'm sorry I couldn't protect you." He removed his ring and placed it on the boy's finger. "When you find your way back, *find me*. Until then, *forgive me*." Before the boy could react, Ray snatched the axe from Cal and swung it, slicing across the back of the boy's knees. His tendons popped beneath the blade, and he crumpled to the ground with an angry screech.

Cal kicked him in the chest as he tried to rise. The boy toppled backward. He and Ray sprinted for the crate, slipping inside just in time before the boy could reach it. Slowly, they ascended toward the Kite, the hurricane closing in around them.

"Keep on pulling 'em up!" Alfie yelled, "and hold onto something!"

He could no longer wait as the hurricane and tornado were right on their heels. The shock wave caused by the approaching hurricane knocked the Kite off kilter. They were thrown about the Kite.

The crate with the four remaining boys swung wildly in the air. "Oi, I'm getting sick!" Cal yelled, tasting the vomit lacing his throat.

Ray, still slightly affected by the fire he absorbed earlier, caused an explosion that turned one of the approaching tornadoes into a firenado, burning through one of the cables holding the crate. Hanging by a thread of three cables, they moved towards the side that had both cables still intact to even their odds.

"What the bloody hell, mate?" Cal bleated. "You trying to kill us *for real*?"

"Sorry! I *can't* control it somehow!"

"That's 'cause there are *two* of you leaving that island," Stan said, looking at Alex. "Remember what we discovered? Andrew and Phil weren't supposed to be alive either, only *one* of 'em."

Ray realised what was happening. He looked over at Stan, who had a tiny bottle hanging from his belt. "Give me that." Upon receiving it, he dumped the contents of the bottle on himself.

"Oi!" Stan yelled annoyed.

"If I don't, the consequences will be dire," he said earnestly, looking over at Alex's bottle, who gave it to him.

Finally, they managed to haul the crate up, pulling all four of them to safety. Val closed the door as Stan and Alex hugged Josh, relieved to see him. They looked over at Tim kneeled next to Sam, and together with Josh, they joined him.

"Bloody hell…" Stan exclaimed; his face laced with pure shock. "His… his *arm*…"

"We could've saved his arm, boil some echinacea so we could've treated the burns," Tim said after briefly hearing from Josh what had happened.

"It wouldn't have mattered," Josh told him, "I dunno how he burnt his arm beyond saving, but I bet he did it saving *me*. That's just the kinda lad he's always been."

The Kite's alarm blared throughout the ship. Tim rushed towards the cockpit, ignoring the pain he felt in his ribs.

"We're not going fast enough! I've overheated the boosters!"

Tim hurried to the back of the Kite, opening one of the crates. He smiled to himself as he found what he was looking for. *"Thanks for not changing the cargo of our Kites, Mr. President."* He motioned to Alex and Stan to help him out. As they headed over to Tim, he showed them the copper wire. "I need enough of this to create a closed loop," he said, pointing at the control panel, "leading from this circuit right here to the booster hinge. It's gonna get a bit buggy for a second, but after that, we'll be outta harm's way." He gave a gallant bow, which both Alex and Stan ignored.

As Alex and Stan worked on that, Tim darted to the Kite's maintenance panel. He pulled a handful of wires free, then plugged them back in. He took the looped wire from Alex, constricting it tightly around the maintenance panel's transducer. "Ray! Need your help over here!"

As Ray walked over, he knew what Tim's plan was. Focusing on the electrical energy that was present in the Kite, he breathed in deeply, closing his eyes. His lips twitched as he directed the electrical surges towards the transducer, recharging the Kite's booster.

It was as if he contained the spark of the divine. Everyone stared at him in disbelief, the energy he was packing powerful to electrocute them all. To both create, *and* end life. If he were to let his mind wander off, or if they found a way to reach him, they would be done for.

Ray's vessel grew stronger and stronger with each surge of energy he absorbed and transmitted, knowing that all the experiments done on him had prepared him for this moment. *For the good of it*. With that in mind, he reclaimed his human soul as he began to start the elemental chain reaction he was looking for.

Fusing his soul and grace into a metaphysical almost supernova-like form, he felt his inner self collapse into a black hole for the divine energy he was directing towards the transducer.

Ray felt the energy consuming him, which exhilarated him, but there was a hint of fear too. As he opened his eyes, they lit up brightly, sending the last surge of power necessary to cause a turbocharged booster. The Kite skidded off, leaving the hurricane and tornadoes far behind.

# CHAPTER THIRTY-FOUR

A few hours later, after everyone had patched themselves up and had something to eat and drink, they went to bed to catch up on sleep.

Andrew lay on his back, staring at the ceiling, his hands resting beneath his head.

*I can't believe we're halfway. We've visited three of the six islands, and we thwarted 'em slightly today. I call that a win.*

He heard footsteps approaching. Looking over to the door, he saw Phil, who sauntered over to Andrew's bed. Andrew smiled at him as he watched Phil don a white tank top and shorts. He sat on Andrew's bed with a flourish.

"Grace and poise. I like it."

Phil lay down next to Andrew, wrapping his arms around him as Andrew folded against his chest.

Andrew felt tiny, sharp pains sting him. Looking up, he noticed tiny wood shards that peppered both him and Phil. Feeling Phil's fingers slip from his grasp, Andrew reached up without thinking, grabbing his wrist.

In perfect sync, he pulled Phil towards a dense thicket. Branches whipped at their faces as they crashed through the woods, clutching each other's hand. Andrew tried to avoid either of them stumbling on a trap in the looming darkness.

As they raced away from the spot of impact, Phil pointed to a tiny shape emerging from the nearby bushes. Andrew followed his finger as he pointed at the ground. A trap was concealed beneath the bush. At first, Andrew thought it was a snare trap, then he realised what it was attached to.

From behind, Josh came running at them, no longer human. Andrew tried to stop him, but as they ducked out of the way, Josh crashed straight into the bush, setting off the bomb.

"Andy!" Andrew snapped back to reality, breathing heavily. Phil leaned over Andrew, his hand touching Andrew's chest. "What happened? One of those *visions*?"

Andrew nodded softly, nestling further into Phil's embrace, holding on to the hope that both were safe in each other's arms.

Out of nowhere, Phil pushed Andrew back against the headboard. A spark raced through Andrew at the contact. Phil leaned closer, his lips hanging tantalizingly close. It wasn't near enough as they were just out of reach, and Andrew chuckled at Phil's distracting playfulness.

Both shared a laugh as Phil brushed his fingers against Andrew's cheek. Andrew's chest gave a strange lurch as Phil looked as sweetly intoxicating as he did back at the island. Andrew relished the feel of Phil's rough calluses—the ones nearly every single one of them had developed since being left on the island. As Phil's hands moved down Andrew's body, Andrew felt the fire flare up in him, drawing Phil closer to him.

He gripped Phil's hips, lifting him onto his lap. Switching the dominance over to himself, his fingers splayed out against Phil's lower back, who moaned softly.

"Make love to me, Andy," he whispered, *"make love like there's no tomorrow."*

In one swift motion, Phil tugged his shirt over his head. Andrew couldn't help but admire Phil's taut chest, chiselled abs—which honestly surprised him—and bulging arms.

*"How did I never notice your sexiness before?"* he whispered back.

He trailed both his hands up Phil's chest, enjoying the heat radiating off both. Smirking, Andrew skimmed a finger across Phil's pert nipple. Phil, in return, smirked as his featherlight touch ran up Andrew's leg, making Andrew shiver with delight.

*"I want you. Now."*

Phil's words made Andrew's breath hitch; heat rose in his cheeks. Andrew slid his fingers down the muscled planes of Phil's chest. As soon as Andrew took off his shirt, the air shifted. He unbuckled Phil's belt and helped him out of his trousers.

Stirring in his slumber, Phil slung his arm over Andrew's chest, who smiled to himself. He was finally no longer a virgin.

"Please, wake up. He can't lose you."
"I won't let him."

He felt his life almost ending, felt death at any minute, but he kept going.

Seb gasped, waking with a start as he choked on the tube in his throat. He pulled it out, sucking in a huge breath.

"Sorry, we had to tube you to make sure you got the right medication," he heard a familiar voice speak.

"Alfie? That you?"

Alfie walked over to Seb, sitting next to him. "Let's just say I knew which medication you needed. I packed everything normally not necessary before I left to rescue all your arses."

Seb sat up, feeling the IV tube that was still attached to him for hydration purposes. "What did you use?"

"Amorphophallus titanum."

"What now?"

"It's also referred to as the corpse flower, used in ancient times for all kinds of ailments."

He chuckled softly, shaking his head. "Well, if *that* happened, and you're *here*, then an awful lot must've happened. Care to fill me in? Unless you don't wanna be forthcoming?"

Alfie grinned, letting out a soft chuckle. "That was the impetus for that."

Sam stirred in his sleep, reaching unconsciously for something nearby as a wordless chant joined the rising chorus of distant voices echoing all around him.

He wandered the empty streets of Zacropolis, calling out for anyone. His girlfriend, his son, his friends, but *no one* answered. Every corner he turned, every building he entered, all were eerily empty. The deafening silence surrounding him weighed heavily on him.

He ran along the streets, shouting everyone's names, but no one heard him. He watched as the last streaks of sunlight faded into the distance, leaving nothing but complete darkness. An overwhelming sense of desolation engulfed him.

From above, he heard something snap loose. Looking up, he watched with horror as a billboard tumbled down, moving with an immense, undodgeable speed. He snapped his eyes shut.

Realising nothing had happened and still able to breathe, he opened his eyes, finding himself in the middle of a dense island woodland. Trees with twisted and broken branches loomed over him. The blood-turned moon shone on the branches, casting long and sinister shadows.

"Sam..." A chilling wind whispered his name. As he turned around, he saw all his dead friends, *all* he had lost in the past. They accusingly pointed at him, all their eyes seemed hollow, their voices dripped with blame.

"*Give in to the sweet release of death...*" he heard one voice speak clearly above the others. It wasn't accusatory, and as much as Sam wanted to steer his attention away from the voice, he couldn't. "*The gift we call death... to nevermore feel any pain... or fret... or worry... Isn't that freeing?"* Sam began to hum a song Maddie always hummed whenever he had dark thoughts, trying his hardest to drown out the voice. *"The hardest part of living... is taking the breaths to stay... those are your words, Sam... You're not good for anything... not good for anyone... after all these years of searching, you still haven't found it... No one's above death, Sam... take up the mantle, become one with peace ... forge your own path to freedom..."*

"Sam?"

Tim's voice forced Sam to wake up, who coughed upon waking. Tim offered him some water, but Sam refused. Tim sat down next to Sam's bed, who looked over at his arm. As he touched the residual limb, he closed his eyes, breathing in deeply.

"How am I *ever* gonna explain this to Maddie? To Zack?"

"By just telling 'em," Tim replied calmly. "I know this isn't... a palatable option, but I *know* Maddie. She loves you with every fibre of her being, Sam. She won't see you any differently. She loves you for *you*." Even though Tim raised the possibility to Sam, he wasn't receptive. "Perhaps I should tell you then that Seb woke up."

Sam's eyes widened in sheer astonishment and gasped, taken aback by this revelation. But even though he was visibly staggered, he shook his head. "No, you can't tell him. Don't you *dare* tell him about my arm."

"Sam..."

"No! He *never* fully accepted his blindness, and I can't have him go back to that dark hole that took him a long time to crawl out of. And I remember he told me that he was never sure he crawled out as much as I pulled him out. I can't have history repeat itself. I *can't* and I *won't*."

"So, you're apprising me of your decision, and you expect me to just go with it?"

"Yes. It's not like I'm asking you to kill someone in cold blood for me and hide the body. It's a *simple* request."

"*No.*" Sam stared at him, pressing his lips tight, his eyes focused inward. "You can't just be rationing such a truth. Besides, what if he accidentally touches you, eh? Blind or not, he still hugs you. And if you by some miracle, manage to hold him off... what if someone mentions it outta the blue? What then? It'd all hinge on a *lie* that you can't come back from." Sam avoided Tim's eyes, going stone-faced. "He's your *best friend*! The last thing you want is to break his trust. Or worse. You can't seriously be considering breaking the bond you two have? I'm honestly jealous of that bond. I wish... I wish *someone* would look at me the way you two do sometimes. That look of brotherly and familial love, the same look you and Zach gave each other. I was honestly relieved I would never have to look at that look again when he…"

He swallowed, afraid Sam would attack him, but nothing happened. He noticed Sam's eyes had teared up, tears slowly rolling down his cheeks.

"*I don't wanna break his heart,*" Sam said, his voice a tremulous whisper. Each word was punctuated by a stifled sob. "I *don't* wanna break him. I don't wanna… I *can't*… I…"

Tears streamed down his cheeks, coming in an unrestrained rhythm. The sheer intensity of his emotions was reflected in his usually bright eyes, now dulled by the weight of the sorrow he felt.

"I can't watch him try to end his life, *again*! I can't! He cuts himself! Did you know *that*? He cuts himself 'cause it's the only way he can cope!" His words struggled, fighting through the tightening of his throat. Each syllable he spoke was heavy with the burden of the pain he had been carrying unknowingly.

Tim didn't know this, and as he listened to Sam's intense cries, his own cheeks glistened with the wetness of a grief he hadn't felt before. He tried to maintain his composure, but Sam's broken sentences that were fragmented by his rhythmic cries made him break down too.

But Tim had to admit it all made sense. Ever since Seb's blindness, he had never been wearing T-shirts, not even during the summer. Tim never thought much of it, and now he began to blame himself for never questioning it, blaming everyone around them for not questioning it.

"How did *no one* notice when we took off his clothes? When he fell into the water?"

"Makeup. He's been using Maddie's makeup ever since we left. He wanted to keep it a secret for as long as he could." Sam's voice faltered as he spoke those words out loud. "I wasn't supposed to tell *anyone*. I was supposed to take it to the grave and keep it a secret." Looking over at Tim, his eyes were red and puffy. "I already broke his trust… It can't get any worse than that, *right*?"

Tim sighed, wiping away his tears, giving Sam a handkerchief so he could blow his nose. "I won't tell anyone what you just told me. *I promise*. But I need you to talk to Seb. If you don't, and he finds out on his own, I think with what you just told me… it'll worsen. If you tell him honestly, about the fears you hold inside when it comes to him knowing the truth, he might see how much you care for him and his well-being."

Sam zoned out for a bit, unbeknownst to Tim.

Sam walked home from Henry's office after they had discussed a new set of laws for the city. As he passed the lake, he noticed a figure sitting near the edge. Recognising Seb's clothing from behind, he sneaked over to him, smiling to himself as he loved scaring Seb.

As he got closer, he tried to make as little sound as possible, but each inch he neared him, he *swore* he heard Seb cry.

He stood frozen once he saw the blood dripping down Seb's wrist, pooling beneath the cuts. Rushing forward, he tore off his shirt, ripping it in half to cover the gashes. Using the fabric as a pressure bandage, Sam was almost too stunned to speak. He wanted to yell at Seb, to scream his disappointment, to demand why he had done something so drastic—but *none* of it came out.

He knew Seb had cut deep with the amount of blood that gushed out, crying softly. "Squeeze my hand," he begged Seb. "Can you hear me? Are you good?" Seb didn't respond, he barely blinked. Feeling the faintest squeeze, Sam huffed silently. "Just keep squeezing my fingers, yeah?"

He took off his belt, making a makeshift tourniquet, then took Seb's belt to do the same with the other arm. Looking at him, he noticed how quickly Seb's breathing was. He grabbed Seb and yanked him into a fierce embrace. Seb's breath hitched as Sam gripped him even tighter.

"We need to do it together, okay? Just you and me." He hugged him even tighter, crying softly into Seb's neck. "You're gonna be all right, okay? I'm here. *I'm right here.* Just take a deep breath for me, okay? Let's take one together," he begged Seb, "I need you to breathe." He let go of him, turning Seb's face towards him. "Look at me. A *big* breath, can you do that for me?" Seb slowly inhaled, then exhaled. *"And again."* Seb repeated Sam's order. "You're doing amazing," he reassured Seb, rubbing his arm.

"I'm sorry," Seb said, crying softly. *"I'm so sorry."*

"Shut up," Sam replied in turn, "don't be silly. *Don't be.*" He took a deep breath himself, stuttering through his tears. He tried to stop his body from trembling with fear. "Why didn't you say anything to me? I didn't know it had gotten *this* bad. I'm so sorry for failing you like I fail every other thing I've ever cared about."

*"It's not your fault..."* Seb said softly, almost like a whisper.

"I should've seen *something*, I'm so sorry I didn't see you were so unhappy and struggling. You know that you can talk to me about *anything*, right?" he asked with concern, his face creased with worry. "So, please, *talk* to me. I'm not mad. *I'm not.*"

The flashback slowly faded away as Sam heard Tim speak in the background. He refocused his eyes on Tim, who hadn't noticed Sam had been zoned out for quite some time.
"It's better to break his heart and be honest than find out the consequences of your lies later."
"I can't find him on the brink of death again, Tim. *I can't.*" He turned around to lie on his good arm, hugging himself as he curled up into a ball, sniffling softly.
Tim sighed deeply and patted Sam's back in a comforting way. Walking over to the door, he stopped and turned around. "Just think about it, okay?" With that, Tim left, closing the door to Sam's bedroom behind him.
Once Tim had left, Sam broke down, sorrow pulsed through his veins with every rushed beat of his heart. Eventually, he cried himself back to sleep.

# CHAPTER THIRTY-FIVE

Maddie woke up as she was being dragged across the floor, her feet scraping along. On the way to Henry's office, the two men dragging her were accosted by a man who stopped his conversation with a Trooper to step into their path.

They dragged her after they received the clear to enter, throwing her onto the floor. Her wounds split open; blood gushed out in more ways than one as she coughed up blood. The end of a sword pricked her chin, forced her to look up at the four robed figures that awaited her.

They looked down on her from behind their imposing, ornate masks. Looking over to her left side, she saw Henry on display, his chest carved with a symbol she didn't recognise. She gasped in horror at the sight, looking away from the gruesome scene. But the end of the sword found her chin again, forcing her to look.

"Welcome, Madeline," one of the masked men spoke, "it's my pleasure to present you to the Harbingers of Yeho. The High Council that presides over Zacropolis since the death of its president."

She sniffled softly, trying to look just past Henry at the wall to avoid having to take in his tormented body.

"You've made quite the impression as the Second Lady. Your lofty and benevolent ideal can be a very useful tool, if in the *right* hands, of course." He chuckled softly. "But where are my manners. I'm the emissary of Yeho, and the one lavishly decorated with decadent gold embellishments, is our diplomat. *The One.*"

She spit blood onto the floor, casting him a tentative glance. Then she felt a profound amount of confidence flare up. "How fun, this *boring* banter you have."

He chuckled loudly, shaking his head. "Feisty. I like it. Samuel *really* won the lottery." He walked a little closer to her. "The herald shall announce you to step up and fulfil your duty."

"*Duty*? You made me lose my child! I owe you *nothing*!"

He let out a hum, then stepped back towards his position. "Only the most savvy, magnanimous, and charismatic of individuals could ever hope to stand here in front of us, to behold, to hold any title given... and you're making *fun* of us. Don't you see what happens to people who do that?" He pointed at Henry, making her stomach churn. "I'd pick your next words *very* carefully."

One of the masked men scoffed, scanning with a discerning eye before he returned his gaze to Henry's body.

"I see... a room of undeserving so-called leaders and whatnots who are bumbling around unguided and unchecked!" She spit blood directly towards one of them, the mixture of her saliva and blood landed right in front of their polished shoes. "I'll *never* betray this city, nor will I *ever* give up Sam's location! You can all go to bloody hell!"

The masked men looked down at the spit, then up at her. "Don't make us torture the *little* one."

She watched as they left the room one by one, then tried to break free from the grasp of the two men who had been holding her the entire time. "Don't you *dare* lay a finger on him! You're dead, you hear me! *You're dead!*"

They dragged her away from the office as she kept screaming, until her echoes slowly faded away into nothingness.

She looked at the leg irons that were strapped tight around her ankles, crying softly as the blood slowly seeped down to the floor. The little spikes that were attached to her flesh were somehow less painful than the thought of them touching her baby boy.

She was wearing an electric shock vest, a camera pointed at her to find the perfect opportunity to shock her, but she refused to give them anything. She refused to show her defeat.

She looked over at Abby who sat gagged against the wall, her eyes barely open.

*Maybe it's for the better that our unborn baby's dead. I don't wanna think about how he, or she, would've entered this world with all they've done to me. But Zack... Zack...*

She tried to hold back her tears. Each time a tear rolled down her cheek, she would be shocked, and each time, it went up a level. Each time she was hit, it hurt just a little more.

She noticed the spot where Percy's lifeless body had been lying before, now nothing but a reddish-purple discolouration. As if the floor had suffered torment too, a *bruise* being the result.

She looked at her shrivelled and desiccated skin and her emaciated body. She couldn't even remember *how long* she had been down there. She hit the floor with her fist, no longer caring about the fact that they could see and hear everything.

She then moved her hand towards her ginger hair, pulling a pocketknife from it. Something they clearly hadn't checked for.

She unlocked the blade, and as the shock hit her, trying to stop her from going through with it, she turned her back to the camera and swiftly moved the knife past her neck.

"I'm coming, son. I'm *coming*."

She fell to the floor, her eyes wide open as she stared at the wall where Abby was propped against. A pool of blood formed near her head, and she slowly closed her eyes as she breathed her last breath.

"No! Get in there and *save* her!" the emissary yelled, hitting the emergency button to open the door, which would otherwise have to be opened with several key cards and codes.

Two Troopers rushed inside, relieving her from the electric shock vest she was wearing. They turned her on her back, then noticed her neck was fine. Looking at each other in confusion, she opened her eyes, yelling as she plunged the pocketknife straight into one of the Troopers' necks. Blood spurted out, covering both her and the other Trooper within a matter of seconds. She then took the gun from the dying Trooper, shooting both the Trooper in front of her and the camera.

As the screen went black, the emissary hit the keyboard, yelling loudly. "Get!"

The remaining two Troopers rushed towards the cell where both Abby and Maddie were being held. Upon arriving, they found nothing but their fellow Troopers lying dead on the floor. No sign of Abby nor Maddie anywhere.

Maddie dragged Abby through the president's underground tunnels, trying to find a way out. Abby was barely conscious, slowing both significantly down as Maddie had to pull Abby back up to regain her hold on her.

"Hold on, okay? I'll find us a spot to lay low."

Her hand—which she had cut to deceive the looming eyes—was still bleeding. She ignored the blood that stained both her and Abby's clothes, summoning all her strength to keep going. She broke into an awkward, shuffling run, trying to get Abby to keep up.

She heard voices nearby and hid in a dark corner, covering Abby's mouth who grunted upon the impact. She watched as an unknown figure burst out of his own hiding place, making a beeline for both her and Abby.

"In 'ere!"

He forced Abby's arm around his neck, Maddie followed suit. Whoever it was, he was just as badly injured as both of them were. Having no time to question the unknown man's intentions, she followed him hastily towards a grill that would lead to a small underground tunnel, akin to a hiding spot.

He put Abby against the wall, then moved to remove the grill, telling Maddie to get down first so she could take Abby's legs from him and get her down safely. As they worked together as fast as they could, they heard the voices coming closer.

Having secured Abby, the unknown man jumped down after both, closing the grill just in time before boots appeared above them. A tiny bit of mud left on the boot's sole fell down the grill's openings, hitting the man in the eye. He stayed quiet as he moved out of the grill's tiny bit of light, disappearing into the shadows along with Abby and Maddie, driving them back.

"They're not here," they heard the Trooper say, then watched and listened as his footsteps retreated.

Both Maddie and the man let out a sigh of relief. She looked at the man who was applying pressure to his gaping wound, slumping against the wall. She dropped to her knees beside him, gasping at the sight of the deep wound. She could see the blood pulsing from the hole that was torn in his flesh.

"What the bloody hell happened to you?" she asked him, tearing off a piece of her shirt to force against his wound.

He winced as the piece of fabric touched it, chuckling wearily. "Courtesy of *those* arseholes down 'ere," he replied, his Scottish accent thick. "Albie's the name."

"*Albus?*" she asked softly, almost a whisper. "Alfie and Percy's…?"

"Long-lost brathair? Tha's me."

She chuckled, then shook her head. "I forgot you were adopted."

"Oi, tha's jus' on paper."

She looked him in the eyes, her eyes watering. "You won't make it. This wound… it's *fatal*."

He nodded slowly as she took in the oozing scrapes all across his body. She noticed his hands were red, his knuckles heavily swollen. Blood trickled from a gash on his cheek.

"You've been fighting?" she asked, as he wiped the blood from his nose and lips.

"Wha' can I say, I don' back away from a lil' scuffle."

She shook her head, watching as he wiped away another trickle of blood. "We need to tend to those wounds," she said.

"Yeh said it yerself, *fatal*. Why bother?"

"Don't be absurd," she replied, "if we don't get it treated, it could fester. Make it even *worse*."

He slammed his hand against the wall, then winched. He rubbed his sore knuckles as he gave her the ghost of a smile. "Yeh 'aven' changed a bit, 'ave yeh?"

She shook her head. "Not a bit."

He looked her in the eyes. "I remember teh day I saw yeh firs'. I introduced yeh to my parents to babysit my brathairs. Teh ones who were biological." He looked sullen. "They always loved 'em more."

"Don't be silly," she said, shaking her head. "They adopted you for a *reason*. Your brothers came *after* you were in their life for a long time. And as twins, no less."

"If yer sayin' tha' to make me feel better, I 'ate to tell yeh it's no' really workin'."

She hit his shoulder playfully, allowing him to touch her cheek. "I still remember the day you went missing."

He shushed her. "Don'. We don' need to talk 'bout that righ' now." He made her look into his eyes. "Teh lonelies' people are—"

"Those who are the kindest, the saddest—"

"People are those who smile teh brightest. Teh—"

"Most damaged people are those who are the wisest—"

"All 'cause they don' wish to watch anyone else—"

"Suffer the way they did." She smiled. "I *remember*."

He wiped away a tear that rolled down her cheek. "Yer a good friend, Madeline. Do this feller a favour, 'kay?" She nodded, then leaned in as he motioned her closer. "Tell 'em I love 'em."

She nodded solemnly, hearing him breathe his last breath as one last tear rolled down his cheek. His head fell forward onto her shoulder. Her hand moved up to the back of his head, cradling it as she sobbed.

She still held onto him as she heard the footsteps returning, swiftly moving him away from her shoulder. She looked at his still opened eyes, closing them for him before she heard Abby letting out a terrified whimper.

She rushed over to her, cupping her hand over Abby's mouth. Both held their breath as they listened.

The look of pain that crossed Maddie's face said it all. *They found us.*

She struggled to move as acrid smoke filled her nose. It felt as if something was holding her down, pressing on her chest. With all her might she tried to fight against it, but her eyesight went blessedly black.

# CHAPTER THIRTY-SIX

The Kite hovered above the fourth island. Alex and Stan prepared themselves to head down to the island along with Ray and Val, but then Andrew came forward, even though he had promised Phil to stay behind. His injuries had significantly reduced to a mere annoyance, and he felt good enough to help. Cal had promised to stay behind to avoid being killed off.

"Pray for the best, prepare for the worst," Ray told him.

Before Andrew could respond, he watched as they lowered themselves via the rope one by one. He took a deep breath, looking over his shoulder one last time at where he left Phil. *"The ones who mind, don't matter. Those who do matter, don't mind."* With that in the back of his mind, he descended with the others.

Tim and Alfie monitored them from above, the Kite stood on stand-by. Tim looked over at Alfie, crossing his arms.

"I've this... *inexplicable feeling* that you're not being totally honest with us. Are you?" Alfie remained silent, staring ahead at the screen. Tim knew it was best to err on the side of caution. "Look, you *clearly* know more than we do. Why can't you spill it?"

"They might be listening," Alfie replied, not having moved his eyes. "I can't take the risk. They've got bugs that transmit *everything* you can just about imagine."

Tim opened his laptop. "You *do* know who you're talking to, *right?*" He typed in a few codes. "I can scan for short and long-wave signals. And then..." He typed a new type of code. "With this code I've just created, I can transmit on wave bands that no one else has the capability to scan for. In other words," he said, closing his laptop again, "their bug will not be of *any* use, and *ours* won't be found."

Alfie chuckled, even though he had been trying not to. He took a deep breath, and for a second Tim thought he might speak up, but he remained mute.

"I know you feel guilt. I know you hate leaving your brother behind." Alfie swallowed. By observation, Tim knew he was on the right path. "It's like a parasite, *that guilt*, eating at your soul until there's nothing left to devour, *nothing* but emptiness." He watched as Alfie cracked his knuckles, close to breaking him. "Bottling something up, there's honestly *nothing* worse than that. You can't let such a thing eat at you, Alf. You know it feels just like you're being shot, and that bullet stays inside you forever which causes your wound to never heal. Don't let it become a wound like that."

"You do what you must to get the job done," he replied, grabbing his flask, taking comfort from the content.

Tim sighed deeply. Looking back at the screen, he gasped in shock. "Lads, am I seeing this correctly?"

His earpiece roared to life. *"If by that you mean that we're surrounded by desert, then yes,"* Stan answered.

"How the bloody hell's such a thing even possible?" Tim asked, "there's *no way* an island could become a desert. An island is surrounded by water and water seeps into the core of the earth which—"

*"No time for biology,"* Val interrupted him, *"or ecology, or whatever."*

"You don't have enough water on you."

*"We'll make do,"* Stan replied.

The scale of the island, and thus the desert, shocked Tim. From his humble abode, he saw nothing but endless sand, with no sources of water except for the vast ocean. There was no shade, no caves, and no refuge from the harsh sun. He had never seen anything so big and unnatural. "I hate to be the bearer of bad news, but from where I'm sitting, I can't see *any* spots where you can get some shelter from either heat or *bad things*."

*"How can you see this island's blueprints, but not the other ones?"* Stan questioned him.

"Well, 'cause those other islands were natural, with roots scattered everywhere—across the surface *and* beneath—making it nearly impossible to see *anything*. It's almost like they *want* us to see this one."

*"If they do that on purpose, that can't be a good sign,"* Andrew replied.

"No, so be extra *careful* down there."

*"Will do."*

Tim leaned back, sighing once more. *"They're gonna die."*

They began their trek through the sand, though it didn't take long for Andrew to feel his legs aching, clearly having misjudged his condition. He trudged stubbornly along behind the others until they crested a dune that would provide a view of the landscape.

"Nothing but a long expanse of sand," Stan complained, crossing his arms. "You know, there's *no way* anyone survives here. I bet those three are long dead."

"Don't be so sure," Val replied, "look over there." He pointed at rubble stretching out before them, representing a broken civilisation. A smattering of dilapidated ruins met their gazes.

"Stone ruins? In a *desert*? This has gotta be a joke," Stan continued his relentless whining.

As if to annoy him further, the sun climbed higher into the sky, shining relentlessly down on them. They trekked onward, eventually reaching the site of the next stone rift—a scattered mess of abandoned, broken ruins.

"We should split up," Val suggested. "To have the area scoured quicker." He looked at Andrew. "You go with those two."

Before Andrew or Stan could protest, Val and Ray had set off, trudging through the sand. Stan sighed as he walked ahead. Alex patted Andrew's shoulder, and together they followed Stan towards the chunks of stone that used to make up a city. The three of them set off through the sand until they reached the chunks.

"Here's an opening," Andrew said, observing the small room of the dilapidated building.

He ducked under a collapsed stone pillar, hearing Stan behind him remark that "if the place caves in, I won't bother digging you out."

"Ya seeing any of this up there?" Alex asked through the earpiece, ignoring his boyfriend. "Earth to Tim?"

"Whatever this place is, it must block our signal," Andrew said, observing the walls as he ventured deeper into the building. "You see any of this?"

Faded murals and etchings covered the walls, showcasing images of humanoid, monstrous, and unnatural figures. Though the surface was mostly worn, Andrew, squinting his eyes, could make out some colours emerging from the walls' maelstrom. However, the remnants of the vibrant colouring were long gone.

"This isn't new," Andrew observed. "It's... *ancient*."

"In Val's wise words, we *don't* have time for a history lesson," Stan replied, arms crossed, "we should keep moving."

"Wait," Andrew said, touching one of the murals. "There's gotta be more to this."

"Like what? A *nuance*? Something the carvings themselves can't convey... Bloody hell, Tim's nerdiness is rubbing off on you."

"Stan!" Alex yelled, "what the bloody hell's gotten into ya?"

Stan stood tall as he turned around sharply, his eyes filled with fury. "If we had *never* gone to *any* of these bloody islands, Sam would still be whole! *Literally!*"

He stormed away. Alex wanted to follow him, but Andrew stopped him. "He needs space." He turned his attention back to the murals. "It's almost as if someone warned us about what would happen..."

"What? Like a *future prophecy*?"

Andrew's eyes widened. "My *mum*... this is her. These are *her* drawings."

"What?" He walked closer to Andrew. "How do ya know?"

Andrew sighed. "Don't tell Stan this, but I've got... not just *one* set of powers. I think I've got two of 'em. I can... I *think* I can see future occurrences. And touching this, I can feel a connection, and I see vague memories of my mum popping up in my head."

"Which means yer... one of yer powers are *hereditary*?"

"Seems like it." He touched the mural with both of his hands, "they're premonitions. She predicted this, *all of this*. Look." He pointed at a mural depicting a monstrous figure fighting a humanoid figure, ripping its head off. "Those are the experiments, the *virus-caring humans*."

"That means this island was once part of a normal city before Ashwell and his entourage destroyed it." Alex touched his chin as if he was thinking long and deep. "So, this isn't just an island, none of 'em are."

"They were all part of a city once. *My city*." A tear rolled down his cheek. "Val, Ray... we're from *this city*."

Alex observed the place further. "How come there's no technology here then? That doesn't make sense, does it? In the days of yer parents, there was already a lot of technology. This looks to be from hundreds if not thousands of years ago."

Andrew's voice cracked slightly as he answered Alex, clearing his throat in the middle of his sentence. "That's the *only thing* that's not making sense to me either. But it's plausible that this was the only stone building in the city, and my mum knew it'd be preserved."

"Lads, how long are you gonna take?"

Alex and Andrew eyed each other, then headed back out to meet up with Stan, who was hopping foot to foot on the sand.

Alex couldn't help but laugh at the sight. "Yer panting like we had a good night."

"Not in front of the *kid*," Stan said sarcastically, "what did you find in there?"

"Something that's best shared with *everyone* present," Andrew said. He walked away from Stan, who rolled his eyes at him.

They followed the footprints Val and Ray left behind across the swirling sands.

After an intolerable long trek, they arrived at the mouth of a tunnel, sunken directly into the dune's side.

"I thought Tim said there were *no* tunnels?" Stan said, wiping the sweat off his forehead.

"Only one way to find out where it leads, *right*? Val and Ray came through here," Andrew replied.

"I thought you weren't so brave," Stan said mockingly, taking his hood off.

"Guess we all got things to learn about one another," Andrew replied, giving him a wink.

He passed through the entrance, entering nothing but darkness. His eyes adjusted gradually as he slowly followed the downward-sloping path. It didn't take long before Andrew found himself tackled to the floor, the gleaming point of a makeshift spear only an inch away from his neck.

"State of business," a stern, female voice spoke.

Before Andrew could answer, Val laughed. "They're with us. *Completely* harmless. Well, you might wanna hurl that sharp weapon of yours at *him*," he said, pointing at Stan, "he's kinda an arsehole."

Stan gave him a nasty look, one that could've killed Val right then and there if Stan had the ability to. The woman moved the spear away from Andrew, offering her hand to help him up. Andrew took it, grunting softly as he found his footing, his legs aching and throbbing.

"Sit," she said, pointing to makeshift wooden chairs, two of which were occupied by Val and Ray.

The three of them sat down. Andrew let out a sigh of relief as the pressure of his legs was released. He observed the woman whose facial features finally came to light when she set another torch aflame. Hit by an array of memories, Andrew gasped at the sight of her eyes.

"Are you okay?" she asked as she turned around. "You look like you've seen a ghost." She poured him and everyone else a drink, though he didn't take the wooden cup from her.

"Mate, rude," Val said, nudging his side. "She's offerin' you a *real* drink here, not those fake beverages you lads haul around."

A far-off look clouded Andrew's eyes, appalling him.

Ignoring Andrew's strange look towards her, she directed her attention towards Val and Ray. "So, don't feel obliged to divulge *everything*, but what brings you to this place?"

"Beats me," Val replied casually, "we're rescuin' people off islands from a virus intended to destroy life as we know it."

"Which isn't even *close* to what happened two years ago," Stan added, "back *then,* they just wanted a strong army to fight off what they saw as a threat, and *now* they wanna destroy *all* of humanity."

"These geniuses have angered 'em," Val said, slurping his drink. "That's why they took it a step further, experimenting on us to awaken powers and make us superhuman, so we could aid the infected in the destruction of the world."

Stan turned around sharply to look Val dead in the eye. "You *never* spoke of that when we questioned you. You're *withholding* information from us?" He walked up to him, grabbing him by his collar to haul him off his seat. "What *else* aren't you telling us?"

Val looked over at Andrew who grew more pale by the minute. "Look, I didn't know if you could be trusted. I *still* don't. But I've come to realise that by meeting people like Imogen over here, we might stand a chance."

"What do you mean?" Stan asked.

"*Imogen...*" Andrew murmured under his breath, barely audible.

"Sorry, what was that?" she asked. "You need to speak up, *son*, I can barely—"

"*Mum...*" Tears welled up in his eyes. "You're my *mum.*"

# CHAPTER THIRTY-SEVEN

Gathering all his strength, Sam pushed his legs over the side of his bed, grunting upon the effort. He looked at the stump covered with bandages, sighing deeply to himself. *This is my new life now; there's no denying it. I'm so happy Zach won't see me like this. But Zack... Maddie... How will I ever explain any of this to 'em? Bloody hell, I've been so busy being afraid of Seb's reaction, I never even thought about my family. What if she stops loving me? What if Zack thinks I'm a monster?*

A knock on the door startled him, yelping softly.

"Oi, I thought *I* was the blind guy here," Seb said, laughing softly. He strolled inside. "I wanted to check up on you. It's unlike you to stay cooped up in here all day."

He sat down on the side of Sam's bed, on the side of the arm that was no longer there. Sam tried to move away from Seb unnoticeably, but Seb, now relying on every other sense he possessed, noticed it.

"I'm not *contagious*," he said, chuckling. "Unless you know something I don't?"

Reaching for Sam's arm, Sam tried to pull away, falling off the bed in the process. Landing straight on his buttocks, he let out a soft cry.

"Sam! Are you okay?" Seb asked, finding Sam on the floor with outstretched hands. Helping him up, Seb staggered backwards, gasping in shock. "Why's... what's... where's... *where's your arm?*" His breathing accelerated, the anxiety he felt started to feel palpable for Sam. "What happened?" he asked, a cry of panic heard in his voice.

Sam's face turned red and scrunched up, tears rolled down his cheeks as he heaved while crying. His voice cracked as he spoke, stuttering with every heave he made. "I, I wanted to, to tell you, Seb but how, how could I? After, after everything you've, you've been through I, I couldn't—"

"So, you just straight up *lied* to me?" he yelled, his saliva reaching Sam's legs. "How could you *lie* to me about this? You were there for me during my blindness! So, what? You thought I wouldn't do the same for you? *Me?*"

"It's not like that," Sam said, rasping. "I—"

"Then what?" Sam said nothing. "What, Sam?" Seb insisted. "*What?*"

"I didn't wanna see you try to kill yourself *again*!" he yelled, louder than he anticipated. "I couldn't watch you try to throw in the towel a second time! I was scared! I was scared outta my wits you'd do it *again*!"

"I'm not that weak!" Seb yelled. "That was… *a mistake*! That's what it was, an honest mistake!"

"You don't make *honest* mistakes like that, Seb! It was a deliberate choice at the time and if I hadn't shown up, then—" His heart pounded against his rib cage, his breathing an unrelenting rhythm of fear. A bead of sweat formed at his temples, gripping the bedding.

Seb immediately kneeled next to Sam, embracing him. It had worked the first time Sam shocked Seb with a panic attack not too long ago, but this time, it didn't. Sam was engulfed in an avalanche of panic, tightening around his chest. He let go of the bedding and gripped his heart.

Seb noticed and placed his hand gently over Sam's. He could feel the pulsating heartbeat beneath Sam's palm. He knew Sam was spiralling back to the day he had found him. Sam trembled uncontrollably against Seb, his tears and sweat dampening his skin.

Sam gripped the collar of his shirt, tugging it away from his neck, thinking it might give him more room to breathe. He had already pulled his hand free from Seb's grip. His fingers then moved to the side of his neck, checking his own heartbeat.

"You're okay," Seb said, moving his hand up to find Sam's, he gently pulled it away. "Don't do any of that. Just focus on me, on my *voice*, and on my breathing, okay?" He breathed in slowly, then exhaled slowly, but Sam wasn't cooperating. "You're *safe*, Sam, you'll get through this with me by your side." He felt Sam's hand moving back up to his chest, then pulled it back down to Sam's lap. "Tell me five things you can see."

Sam looked at him warily. "*What?*" he managed to say.

"Five things you can see. Tell me *five* things."

Sam's breathing was uneven, gasping for breath each time he tried to inhale. He squeezed his eyes shut, his muscles tensing.

"Sam, *five* things, okay? Focus on your breathing and tell me five things you see."

"Okay… okay." He looked around the room. "Bed… you… wall… door… ceiling…"

"Good that, now tell me *four* things you can touch." Sam felt himself getting dizzy, slumping a bit against Seb, who knew it was now or never to slow Sam's breathing. "Four things you can touch, Sam. Tell me *four* things you can touch with your hand."

"Bed... you... wall..."

"Now tell me *three* things you can hear."

"You... me... Kite..."

"*Two* things you can smell."

His breathing slowly dissipated as he spoke. "You... and blood."

Ignoring the mention of blood, Seb nodded. "Good that. Now, *one* thing you can taste."

"Blood."

Seb grew worried about Sam's mention of blood. His hand moved up to Sam's lips, using his finger to indicate if blood was present. Feeling some kind of liquid, he pulled his hand back, smelling it. "Did you bite your lip?"

"I think so," Sam replied, which made him chuckle slightly. "*I bit my bloody lip.*"

Seb chuckled nervously but relieved, shaking his head softly. "You're intolerable."

Sam playfully pushed Seb away a bit, his breathing now back to normal. He took a deep breath, grunting softly as he gripped his chest. "I don't wanna keep having these..." He sighed, looking over at Seb. "But I guess it doesn't matter what I don't want or want."

"It does," Seb reassured him, "I'm so sorry that what I did triggered this. I'm so sorry you couldn't be honest with me."

Sam put his hand on Seb's, squeezing it. "I just don't wanna lose the only *real* brother I've got left. After Zach... I can't bear the thought of losing *you*. And I was afraid that by telling you the truth, you'd spiral outta control."

Seb put his other hand on top of Sam's, shaking his head. "I don't *ever* want you having these thoughts again, thinking that you can't tell me *anything* that's wrong or what's on your mind. What happened back then was a moment of weakness, and I've *always* hated myself for how worried I made you. I'll never forget how you slowly sobbed yourself to sleep when you watched over me the first week."

Sam looked at him in disbelief. "You... heard *all* of that?"

Seb nodded. "Enhanced senses that aren't sight, remember?"

"Right." Sam shook his head.

"A wise man once told me that darkness can sometimes show you the light. My *darkness*, my *sight* taken from me, revealed the light I thought I'd never see again." He stopped to grip Sam's shoulder. "*You.*"

They put their foreheads against one another, conveying their sincere regard and acknowledgement of each other's presence. As an intimate form of nonverbal communication, it exuded warmth. Pure appreciation and trust, a sign of respect that exceeded everything else.

"Back then," Seb continued, "I've never stopped feeling like an idiot about so many things I've done. I've been stuck trying to fix that past and I completely forgot about you. I've been so focused on my *own* feelings that I neglected yours." Their foreheads still touching, Seb let out a shaky breath. "You're the most important thing in the world to me, Sam, and I promise you I'm gonna do even better from here on out. I'll *never* make you go back to that trauma again."

Sam chuckled softly, nodding with his forehead still connected with Seb's. "I'm sorry I ever doubted you."

They slowly moved away from one another. "Now, *please*, tell me what happened." Seb then laughed to himself. "But before you do, we should probably visit a second-hand store so you can shop for a new one."

"Bloody hell," Sam replied, hitting Seb in the chest, "that's *cruel*."

"Made you laugh though, didn't it?"

"You're insufferable."

"You love it."

Before Sam could explain to Seb what had happened to his amputated arm, Tim stormed inside. Not even questioning why they were on the floor huddled together, he jerked his thumb over his shoulder, clicking his tongue. "We got an issue."

Tim pointed at the screen. "So, whoever this *Mister X* is that we're dealing with, he appears to be a Cambridge grad." He pulled up some documents. "He's been developing war technology in the form of bioweapons, and instead of selling it to the highest bidder, he's been keeping it to himself." He enlarged a cheque. "People have tried to pay top notch for this, but he's *refused* all offers."

Cal whistled as he looked over his shoulder. "I'd take that money. Imagine what you can do with that." Receiving looks from all the boys present, he raised his hands dismissively in the air.

"I've managed to hack his latest creation, though it's just a partial schematic."

Pulling it up, Sam tried to concentrate on figuring out what he saw, trying his hardest to make sense of the jargon he couldn't understand. "Enlighten us, *please*."

"Right." Tim typed away. "So, if he completes this newest bioweapon virus of his, he'll be able to *expose* humans to a catastrophic insomnia—one that'll withstand any attempts by family members to break the *curse* on their infected loved ones. As Andrew explained, he managed to get to his sister multiple times, *despite* her constant desire to kill him." He began to type. "With *this* virus, their memory will deteriorate completely, causing their brain to cease functioning altogether *and* leading to organ failure. This'll allow unnatural organic growths to form, resulting in even *worse* virus-caring creatures—creatures that *can't* be defeated." He sighed. "They'll be *unstoppable*. They'll take weapons—guns, knives—and turn 'em into body parts. They'll become walking murder machines, not just with *any* unnatural bodily modifications, but with the *deadliest* weapons we use every day, integrated into their *very* flesh."

"What's it called?" was all Sam managed to ask.

"*Serum X.*"

# CHAPTER THIRTY-EIGHT

It was dark. *Pitch black.*

Maddie grunted as she woke up, blinking a few times to try and render her sight back, fearful she had gone blind like Seb. Unable to see anything, she could only hear herself breathing. There were no other sounds present, only *silence*. Though she could swear she heard the faintest sound somewhere in the distance, but if there was any, it was unrecognisable. Unless it was just her mind playing tricks on her.

"Hello?" she tried carefully.

It took her a while to realise she was encased after attempting to sit up, only to bang her head against the wood. The only way to confirm she was truly where she thought she might be was to feel around. She ran her hands over the wood above, below, and all around her. Chances were she had lost consciousness from the impact of being thrown in, her back aching as she tried to shift to her side, feeling the dried blood in her hair and on her forehead. On top of that, the injuries she had sustained earlier still troubled her.

It was terribly warm, her breathing laboured as she tried to find non-present fresh air.

She heard something being dumped onto the box from above, the sound echoing in the confined space. She didn't have time to wonder what it was as small grains of sand trickled through the wood. At first, she thought it was dust, but when she tasted it, she realised it was *dirt*.

"Oi! No! Stop!" She began to pound on the wood, trying everything she could to get the person's attention.

"I wouldn't scream if I were you," she heard faintly from above, "you've got limited air down there and you'd be *wasting* it with your screams."

"Let me go!" she yelled, ignoring the man's unsolicited advice.

"Suit yourself. Die *quicker*. I don't care."

"Where's my *son*? Where's my son you *freak*!" she yelled. "If you've hurt him, if you've buried him too I swear to—"

"Shut up!" She felt more dirt thrown down, way more than the first scoop. "Do us a favour and just shut the bloody hell up!"

She continued to bang her hands against the box, unaware that she was bleeding from the impact. The blood seeped from the top of the box where her rested, landing on her face.

She heard the echoes of her breath and pounding coming back to her from the darkness, her chest tightening as she struggled for air. She knew the man who was burying her alive was right—she *had* to conserve air. She stopped screaming but kept banging.

Sweat cascaded down the side of her neck, dripping from her dampened brow. The heat inside the confines of the box became stifling, and unbearable. "Please, let me out! I'll do anything!" she yelled desperately but realised the dirt-coverage had stopped. "Hello?" She banged again. "Oi! Are you still there?" She kept on banging. *"Somebody? Anybody? Please, help me!"*

She began her futile effort to pry off the top, but it was thoroughly reinforced by the earth. She tried to calm herself, struggling to catch her breath. It took her some time, but eventually, she managed to find a semblance of calm. She coughed, the lack of oxygen making it harder to breathe.

The heat slowly became unbearable. She stripped off her shirt, leaving herself in her bra. Her body fought against the wooden enclosure with every movement. She tossed her shirt, drenched in sweat, down by her feet—though they felt miles away, even though they were only a body length from her.

She shifted her body, pressing her feet against the top of the wooden box, trying to use her weak leg strength to push it off. But it didn't budge—not even an inch. After several failed attempts, she gave up. Her exhausted legs dropped back down. Laying still in pure silence, an outburst of crying escaped her mouth.

She fumbled in her pocket and found her phone. Surprised that it was buried with her, she held onto a tiny spark of hope that whoever put her down there wasn't the smartest. However, looking at the barely one bar of signal strength and half of the battery life remaining, she knew it would be worthless.

"The safe number... *that's it!* I can send a *distress call!*" With her fingers hovering over the dial pad, she struggled to recall the number. "Bloody hell! He concussed me good." She typed in only the first two digits before locking the phone, unable to remember any more. *"Guess he's smart after all."*

She shifted her body, trying to reach her back pocket and retrieve her wallet. But when she opened it, there was nothing inside. No money, no cards, *nothing*. Most importantly, the piece of paper with the safe number written on it was gone too. She screamed in frustration, then immediately tried to calm herself, trying to regain the breath she had just expelled. Desperation setting in, she attempted to call the Troopers' emergency number.

"*This is the Trooper Headquarters. Please hold.*"

"No, wait!" But she was already put on hold. "Son of a—" She slammed the ceiling out of frustration, shaking her head. "This can't be happening, this can literally not—"

"*What's your emergency?*"

She let out a soft scream, not having expected the Trooper to return so quickly. Collecting herself, she tried to be as coherent as she possibly could. "I'm Madeline, the vice-president's *girlfriend*. I'm currently buried, and you gotta *help* me. I can barely breathe, and they've got my *son*, Zack."

"*Ma'am—*"

"I'm buried in a wooden box, and I *need* you to send somebody to my location to help me."

"*Ma'am, slow down. What did you say your name was?*"

"Madeline. I'm the girlfriend of the vice-president of Zacropolis."

"*Okay, Madeline, can you tell me your location?*"

"No, I *can't*. I was taken somewhere underground before this, and they've tortured me in a dungeon along with three others. Their names are Abigail, Percival, and Albus. The two men are *dead*, but I dunno if Abigail's still alive."

"*When you say wooden box, do you mean you're in a coffin?*"

She sighed but decided to remain civil. "I think so. It's made from *wood*... and it *smells* like old wood."

She heard some typing on the other end of the line. "*Madeline, how are you calling me right now? If you're buried in a coffin?*"

She let out an agitated sigh. "I'm calling from my cell phone."

"*And you decided to climb into a coffin with your cell phone?*"

"What? No, that's—" Her voice raised slightly, and she had to stop herself from screaming at the man. "I was *put* here."

"*Okay, how's your breathing?*"

"It's... It's hot in here. I can *barely* breathe, and I haven't even been here that long." She quickly checked the battery life on her phone. With it still holding steady at two bars, she held onto the idea that this lengthy conversation wouldn't end up being useless.

"*Can you remember anything from your previous location? The dungeon? Anything specific?*"

She was surprised at how seriously the Trooper took the situation. Given how the Troopers had been stationed lately, she knew they wouldn't even consider helping her. Before answering his question, she needed to know. "What's your name?"

"You're dying, and you wanna know my name?"

"Yes. I wanna remember the guy who took me *seriously*."

It was silent on the other end of the call, and for a second, she was afraid she had lost the connection. *"Harry."*

"Harry, nice to meet you." She swallowed, finding it harder to breathe with every word she spoke. "Listen, I'm running outta oxygen real fast. Can you omit the coordinates attached to the tracker?"

*"I can try."* She heard frantic typing on the other end of the line, her nails tapping impatiently against the wooden bottom. *"I can see a vague global signal, but it's gonna take hours to find the exact location. You don't have that long."*

She chuckled softly, coughing. "You better get going then."

*"I'm on it."* She heard shouting in the background as the Trooper ordered some of his fellow Troopers to find one of their own, careful not to mention that it was a woman who was trapped. *"They're on their way."*

"Thank you. Why didn't you rat me out?"

*"Well, there are still some good ones out here. I know the Troopers haven't been exactly helpful to you and your family."*

"You know the story... Guess news like that travels fast."

*"Least I can do is try to help Sam's girl, who's the reason I'm alive today."*

She checked her phone—yet another bar was gone. "Listen, I'm running outta battery. If you wanna keep tracking my phone, I gotta end the call."

*"I understand. We'll find you, Madeline, I promise. Hold on for me, okay?"*

"No promises, Harry. But I'll do my *best*."

She ended the call and closed her eyes, humming to herself to slow her breathing. *Zack... mummy is so sorry, my love. I hope we'll reunite in a better place.*

# CHAPTER THIRTY-NINE

Imogen stared Andrew up and down, then let out a mirthless laugh. Her expression hardened when she came closer to Andrew, her lips only inches away from his ear. "Say something like that again, and I'll break your neck. My son died during childbirth, and you don't get to mock me like that."

"You're sorely mistaken," Andrew said, "and I'm *not* mocking you. I'm—"

Val cupped his hand over Andrew's mouth, pulling him with him. "Sorry, he sometimes blurts stuff out. He hit his head a few days ago, still in recovery and all that."

Before Andrew could protest, Val had dragged him away from Imogen. "What the bloody—" Val shushed him.

"She's been *injected*." He pointed at his own neck. "I saw the entry point of a needle. I dunno with *what*, but we need to be careful. Any emotion can set her off. And I *highly* doubt you wanna kill your mum."

Andrew swallowed the bile in his throat as the unwanted images assaulted him—his mother shouting for him to run as the Troopers arrived, knocking her out with the stock of one of their guns. He couldn't believe the lies they must've fed her as they erased her memory.

"She's been sayin' that she's down here to conduct her own experiments for an antidote. She *knows* she's been injected." He pointed at a tent. "She's been here a while."

Andrew looked across the camp she had created until his eyes landed on the wide tent in the far back.

"I'm about to do my newest experiment," they heard behind them. "You boys care to help me out?"

Before Andrew could say anything, or Stan could deny her offer, Val nodded. "Yes, ma'am! We're interested!"

He pulled Andrew along, following her into the tent. Andrew stared in disbelief at the monitors in front of him that all displayed information he couldn't understand. *If only Tim was here...* He tripped over a wire, falling through a curtain. Landing on an operating table with a corpse lying on it, he let out a scream. Looking to the side, he noticed multiple bodies wrapped in body bags.

The others came looking what made him scream, though Imogen plastered a thinly veiled smile onto her face. She brusquely escorted Andrew away from the bodies. "You're a curious one. Just like *me*."

He knew Val warned him, but he couldn't help himself. "That's 'cause I—"

She let out an annoyed sigh, shoving him out of the way before he could finish his sentence.

"I don't want you to force me to dredge up memories I've tried so *hard* to forget. For your sake, *don't* mention it again."

"What's that?" Ray quickly asked, pointing at the humanoid figure suspended in a liquid cocoon.

"That's a pod membrane." She walked away from Andrew. "This person was recently infected with a new serum that I've yet to discover. And that's where you come in." She purposefully ignored Andrew's presence as she addressed the others. "Who wants to play doctor?"

Dressed in lab coats, all of them stood next to her to observe the creature. She gave each a pair of gloves. Andrew stared at the creature as he put his gloves on, making out its unmistakable claws. But something about it looked strange. Its body seemed swollen, and unlike what he had seen before with Minnie, this creature's lower jaw contained sprouting tendril-like pieces of flesh.

"What's that glowing green liquid?" Alex asked. "And those vein-like appendages?"

"Nutrients, probably." She took a scalpel to open the membrane. "I think it's a signalling protein."

"Which is supposed to do *what*, exactly?" Stan asked, his arms crossed.

"Well, I *think* it's meant to trigger the development of the special characteristics you see on display here. But," she said, splitting the membrane along the edge, stepping aside to let the green liquid pour down onto the floor, "that's just a *theory*. Research will have to tell me if I'm right, *or* wrong."

The liquid splashed loudly onto the floor, drops landing on their shoes. Since they were underground, Tim couldn't hear what was being said, though Andrew was sure Tim would be mortified if he knew he was missing out on a potential scientific discovery.

He felt a poke in his side, looking over at Val who passed a scalpel to him. "So, is it like a parasite that they inject 'em with?"

Imogen looked at Val. "Something like that. I've noticed that, even though the serum formulas are slightly different, they share a genetically identical aspect—an environmentally controlled one called phenotypic polymorphism."

"Can you translate that to *English*, please?" Stan asked.

She rolled her eyes at him. "The different genes and environmental influences within the quality or state of existing of, say, a specific species." She passed a couple of test tubes around. "But as you'll see, *touching* it isn't such a good idea." She poked at the outer layer with her scalpel. The sickening sound made Andrew almost gag.

"Why *not*?" Ray asked.

"Well, I've established that it can't pass through our outer skin's membrane, but I'm still unsure about any other things it's capable of. So, don't take *any* unnecessary and stupid risks." She looked at Andrew. *"You*, hold the membrane tight so I can cut it open."

"I thought you said I shouldn't touch—"

"Not unsupervised. Just hold it right here, *and* here, and you'll be *just* fine."

Pointing at the specific spots, Andrew did as he was told, looking over at her as she would collect samples. She took a hunting knife out of her boot as the others kept the test tubes ready. Andrew pinched the two edges of the skin between his fingers, stretching it out as he gagged loudly.

Val scoffed at him. *"Don't be such a wuss. Show her that you're her real son without telling her."*

His whispering made Andrew mad, but only for a split second. He was *right.* If he wanted her attention and to be on her good side, he had to act like her son.

Meanwhile, she leaned in close to get a good look at the membrane. "See this? This fluid line? It stops about three-quarters of the way down the pod, which leaves the top full of air." She carefully cut into the thin layer of sickly flesh on the outside, peeling a piece back to reach the body. Making another incision in the body itself, she waved Val over with his test tube. "Press it."

He carefully pressed it against the incision as she ordered, watching as a small amount of black liquid oozed up and out of the body, dripping into the test tube.

"Good job," she told him, then turning to face Stan. *"You*, take a blood sample, and *you*," she said, pointing at Alex, *"you* go for the tissue sample."

Without anyone refusing, they went to work on their assigned tasks. Ray, having nothing to do, pressed up close to the body. The smell was horrendous. "It smells like a mixture of... sweat..." He sniffed again. "Spoiled milk..." And again. "And the meat that's spoiled from being left out in the sun for too long, to the point of being beyond saving." Everyone eyed him, and he shrugged. "What? Just describing it."

Stan held its arm, drawing blood with a syringe given to him by Imogen, while Alex tore off a chunk of its skin with the hunting knife.

"Wonderful, good work everyone." She grabbed a body bag, urging Ray to help her stuff the body inside while everyone else stepped back to secure the evidence.

A couple of hours had passed as Imogen used the microscope to conduct her research, humming every now and then when she found something, scribbling it down in a small notepad.

Andrew observed her in silence, unable to grapple with the fact that his mother was alive and well. He knew it was a rare commodity for anyone's parents to still be alive. From Sam, he knew only Zach's father to be alive.

"*Kid*, if you keep staring at me like that, *one* of us is going to drop dead." She turned her chair around to face Andrew, who tried to pretend he hadn't been staring at her. She noticed his shapeshifting abilities taking over. "You're one of those *ORPHANS*."

He looked up at her in utter confusion. "The *who?*"

"*ORPHANS*, the boys experimented on to awaken *superpowers* residing within them." She pulled a document out of her notepad. "I've conducted research on one of them since I found them dead in the desert out here."

He took the document from her, reading out loud. "Observing Reinforcements Prioritising Humanitarianism and Non-Biological Species." He stared at her in disbelief. "I'm a *reinforcement?*"

"To prioritise humans, *yes.*" She took the document back. "You were essentially *created* to withstand any threat, to become a bioweapon without claws or tendrils. You're non-biological because you were made from tiny fragments and pigments."

"No," he said, "I'm not. I'm a *real* human."

"No, *kid*, you're not. If you were, you—"

"Would only have *one* superpower instead of two?" She looked at him hazily. "Yeah, I've got prophetic powers, so I can kinda see the future. *Surprise.*"

She got up from her chair, kneeling in front of him. "If that's true, you're *very* special. And *not* in a good sense." She grabbed his hands, squeezing them harshly so he would understand the brevity of her words. "You're the *ultimate* bioweapon. Part creation, part human, you'll be *unstoppable*. You'll be the *world's destruction.*"

He pulled his hands away, shaking his head. "No, I... I *won't* let that happen!" Out of nowhere, thunder was heard, lightning striking one of her monitors.

She stared at it in disbelief, then turned to face him. "I think you've just discovered your third power."

"*What?*" he managed to let out before tears rolled down his cheeks.

"Your powers only unlock when you're close to someone you fully trust. When did your other powers develop?" He stared at her as she wiped a tear away from his cheek. "When my sister Minnie was close to me."

He swore a hint of recognition crossed her face when he said his sister's name out loud, but she dismissed the possibility just as quickly when she took his hands in hers, *kindly* this time. "This power is called *atmokinesis*. I've seen it before in one of the bodies I've studied."

"What does it do?"

"Essentially, you can manipulate the *weather*. It's a type of psychokinesis that requires a lot of your energy and focus. You need to practice keeping it under control." She pointed at her ruined monitor. "Or else *real* people can get hurt." She looked back at him. "You can control storms, such as thunderstorms, rain, wind patterns, and *much* more."

He looked down at their intertwined hands, shaking from fear. "I don't wanna hurt *anybody*..."

"And you *won't*," she said, getting up. "The desert is completely deserted, so there's plenty of space to practice."

"I don't have the time," he said, "we're trying to save people like me from the islands surrounding yours. We've travelled to three so far and we thought this was number four but clearly it wasn't, so now we still have three to go and—"

She shushed him. "I know, Val and Ray filled me before you arrived. And it seems like only those with superpowers are the ones who survive. Or, *must* be the only survivors."

"Yeah, we kinda ruined that twice already," he said, laughing through his tears. He looked straight into her eyes, his voice soft and low. "Your *son*... what did you name him, or what did you wanna name *him*?"

She chuckled softly, the first genuine chuckle he had heard of her. And it sounded just like he remembered. "*Drew.*"

"But then you might've decided to change it to Andrew, 'cause—"

"Because that was my—*your*—best friend's name." She looked at him, her eyes widening as they spoke in perfect unison. "I didn't want to steal his spotlight by naming my son Drew, but then I realised Andrew was the only way to *truly* honour him." She shook her head. "What are the odds someone named Andrew finds his way to *this* island? It must be a sign from above. A sign that my son *never* truly left me."

For a second, Andrew thought he had her back, that he had managed to reawaken her memory. He needed a visceral recollection, but he knew he couldn't just give someone recognition *that* easily.

"Do you have eidetic memory?" he asked her.

"No, not that I know of."

*Of course, she doesn't. That'd be too easy for me and in my world, easy doesn't exist anymore... I'm not even sure it ever did.*

"Why do you ask, *son?*" she asked.

Each time she said *son*, a flare of pain shot up in him. Thinking he had her back, only to realise that was just a nickname she seemed to use alongside *kid*.

"Never mind. It's nothing."

She nodded slowly, sighing deeply. "If you *must* know, I've never stopped respecting and revering his memory, even though he barely lived a minute. Nor have I stopped honouring hers."

"*Hers?*" He looked up at her. "You had a daughter too?"

She nodded solemnly. "Yes, she was taken from me at a very young age, a few days before I was supposed to give birth to her brother."

*No, that's not right either. I was three when I was taken, and Minnie was ten. She told me she had to watch me play in the yard and then the next minute I had just disappeared.* Then he remembered his baby brother who died of polio only two days after his disappearance. Was she perhaps confused with his *brother's* death? That still didn't fully add up, but it was a lot closer to what she believed.

He was never given a name before he died, him being only three days old. Minnie said so, and that was why she was asked to babysit Andrew while their mother recovered from the birth.

"What *other* name would you have given your son, if not Drew?"

She thought long and hard, then smiled. "I've always quite liked Finnley, or Finn, for short."

He smiled softly. "That would've been a lovely name."

She nodded solemnly, a tear forming in her eye. "Sadly, I could never give him that name because… because he died of polio."

"Wait, you said he died *during* childbirth, didn't you?"

She looked somewhat confused at him. "Yes, I did…" She wiped away the tear that slowly rolled down her cheek. *"There's no way…"* She moved her hand up to his cheek. Andrew leaned into the touch of her hand. *"Drew…?"* He nodded and she smiled with joy. *"It's really you."*

Then she let out an agonising scream, gripping her head as she fell to the floor.

"Mum?" He rushed to her side. "Mum? What's wrong?"

She mumbled an incoherent phrase to what he asked. She convulsed.

"Mum? Talk to me!"

She looked down at the floor, jerking in pain.

The others had gathered around them, watching as Andrew helplessly tried to help his mother. But when she finally stopped moving, he put both of his hands on her shoulders.

"Mum?"

She slowly lifted her head towards him, her eyes pitch-black. With a guttural growl, she lunged at Andrew, sending him crashing to the floor, his head slamming against the floor.

# CHAPTER FORTY

Phil strolled into the main room, looking at Tim and Cal observing the monitors. "Has any of you seen Andy?" he asked, "Seb and Sam haven't seen him either."

Before any of the two could respond, an emergency call came in. "*Mayday! Mayday!*"

Tim put his earpiece in so Phil couldn't listen along. "Tim here. What's your status?"

"*We're in big trouble! We've got multiple hostiles, I repeat, we've got multiple hostiles!*"

Tim pulled up their exact location, having put trackers on each of them just in case something like this would happen. "Okay, air support inbound!" he yelled, looking over at Cal. "Man the turret and shoot at *anything* that doesn't look remotely close to *any* of us."

"Copy." Cal rushed off, brushing past Phil who almost lost his footing.

"What the bloody hell's going on?" Phil demanded, but Tim was too busy handling the situation.

"*Package in hand! We've got some test tubes that could potentially house the virus!*"

Due to all the noise in the background, Tim couldn't make out who he had been speaking with. "Copy. We're three klicks away from you. Hold on!" He began to type furiously on his keyboard. "Go east!" he commanded Alfie, who nodded. The Kite soared in the air towards the hostile situation.

"Drew! *Wake up!*" Stan yelled, trying to hold off one of the corpses that had come to life.

Andrew's mother opened her mouth, tendrils sprouting out like tiny veins. As she screamed to awaken the dead, the tendrils vibrated along with her voice. Grabbing a pair of tongs from a nearby tray, Alex pinned one of the creatures' necks to the floor, holding it steady while Ray burned him with his pyrokinesis powers. Its flesh crackled, splitting from the creature's face. Its eyeballs burst open, melting down the sides of its head before it went limp.

Val focused his attention on the wall of tools and makeshift weapons. With his telekinesis, he pulled a deadly-looking machete from the wall, directing its jagged saw blade towards a creature about to munch on Andrew. The machete split the creature's skull in two, leaving a sickly slice of flesh where its head was supposed to be.

Stan looked over at the array of tools, picking up a hefty metal pipe and swinging it to hit a creature straight in the jaw.

Imogen moved towards Andrew as the others were distracted, leaning over him. She opened her mouth as slimy, black saliva found its way towards Andrew's nose, who gasped awake. She moved back, eyeing him confusedly.

"Mum?" he said with a weak voice, his head pounding. "What's... going on...?"

She opened her mouth again, screeching straight in his face. Val looked over at where the sound came from, watching as she lifted Andrew up with ease, slamming him into the wall. Val could swear he heard something break within Andrew's body.

"Drew!" he yelled, rushing towards him, only to be swept out of the way by Imogen's arm. But he managed to soften his landing by using his telekinesis, forcing a pile of rubbish to break his fall.

She moved swiftly back towards Andrew, putting her massive claw on top of his chest, growling in his face.

"*Drew, you've got three broken ribs, and there's internal bleeding,*" he heard through his earpiece.

Unable to question how Tim knew the information, he looked over at the machete sliding his way. He took it in his hand, looking at his mother. Tears rolled down his cheeks. "I'm pushing through it," he told Tim, "for *everyone's* sake." He cut off one of her tendrils, causing her sickly chant to soften.

Some of the newly resurrected bodies were confused, having lost their sense of direction. They made for an easy target, allowing Ray and Alex to kill a few more by burning them.

Andrew watched as one of them flailed wildly, its skin bubbling up into nasty pustules. As they melted, ooze came out that made Andrew want to throw up.

"*That right lung is filling up with blood,*" Tim said, "*your oxygen levels are running low.*"

Imogen's claw was still perched onto Andrew, relentlessly crushing his organs.

"*And you're also concussed.*"

"Do you have *any* good news?" Andrew asked, barely managing to speak the words aloud.

"*We're about to roll in with weapons hot. Hold tight just a little longer.*"

"On your six!" he heard Alex yell to Stan, who barely managed to hold it off considering he had given Andrew the machete he had found.

"Gotta hustle!" Val yelled, heading back over to Andrew to help him. He circled a creature coming towards him, barely dodging its withered grasp when it tried to lunge for him. He stopped in his tracks as he looked over at Imogen.

A series of nauseatingly wet cracks reached both his and Andrew's ears as they watched the tendrils erupt from her back. The serrated tendrils sprang towards Val, who jumped over them. But then, one of the jagged tendrils grabbed Andrew, tossing him against the wall once more.

*"Drew, your blood pressure's dropping rapidly. You're haemostatic."*

Stan grabbed another machete from the wall during the few seconds he had an opening, rushing towards Andrew. Darting forward, the blade flashing, Imogen's torso twisted unnaturally to meet his approach. Two of her back's whip-like growths snatched Stan, lifting him into the air.

"No!" Alex yelled, rushing to Stan's aid.

Ray tried to set her on fire, forcing her to fling her arms wide. Her tendrils writhed and twitched, dropping Stan onto the floor. Alex quickly dragged Stan out of harm's way.

A flurry of tendrils snatched up Andrew, closing around his throat. The blood and lack of oxygen in his throat and lungs caused him to pass out quickly, blood slowly seeping down the side of his mouth.

"Let him go!" Val yelled, throwing a rope around one of her twitching appendages. He pulled at the rope, pinning one of them against her back.

*"Can you reach the extraction point? We're two kicks north to the clearing."*

"We're workin' on it!" Val yelled in annoyance.

Imogen dropped Andrew's lifeless body onto the floor, snarling loudly. All her creatures were dead, and she was the only one left standing. Realising she was in the minority, she fled, leaving *nothing* but destruction in her wake.

With a makeshift gurney, they carried Andrew towards the north, where the Kite had managed to land. They quickly carried Andrew inside, then took off. Phil gasped in horror at the state Andrew was brought in. With his medical background, he was the only one capable of operating on Andrew. But how could he, with Andrew being the love of his life?

"I know what he means to you, but if you keep standin' there, there's nothin' left to care for," Val told him, gripping his shoulder tightly. "You *gotta* fix him. It's your *only* shot at saving him."

"I'll assist," Tim said, nodding at him. "We've got a very special pod on board that can help us determine what he needs without causing *more* damage. It's quite new and it's still a prototype, but with internal bleeding, it's our *safest* bet."

Phil nodded slowly, following Andrew as Val and Ray carried the gurney with him on it, trailing behind Tim.

They reached the pod and carefully lifted him inside. The pod sealed shut as Val stayed behind in the room, watching Ray leave.

*"Stabilising vitals... Scanning vital signs... and suspend,"* a robotic voice spoke as a blue light scanned over Andrew's body. *"Telomere reset."*

"What the bloody hell does that mean?" Phil asked worriedly.

"Resetting his DNA, standard procedure."

*"Alpha wave supply and stimulation activated. Stand-by for metabolic stasis."*

Phil watched helplessly as all kinds of lights flashed inside the pod, biting his fingernails.

*"Stop all metabolic activity, cardiac cessation."*

"What?" Phil began to pound on the pod. "No! You can't just *stop* his heart!"

Tim pulled him back. "They found something that can only be repaired by doing so. You gotta do the surgery. *Now.*" Tim pressed the surgical procedures button, staring at it. "We could technically let the pod do it, but it hasn't been tested yet."

Phil stared at the list of things wrong with Andrew. He took a deep breath. *"Do it.* Put it in command mode."

"As you wish."

Tim pressed the button. The three of them stared at the screen, watching all the things the pod was doing to Andrew. *"Stem cell replication. Thermoregulation. Tissue regeneration. Nanite repair."*

None of the words made sense to Phil, and he began to wonder if the pod was performing *all of that*, or just listing the various subjects it could address during the surgery.

"Oxygenation. Exsanguination."

"What the bloody hell's—"

"It means it's stopping the blood flow *entirely*."

"What? First his heart, then *this*? It's gonna kill him!"

Phil began to once more pound on the pod to try and get it open, but Val pulled him back. "He's gonna die regardless. Either he dies *while* you cut him open and work on him, or he dies *in there*. At least *in there*, your hands aren't doin' the killin'."

"*Vasopressor.*"

Before Phil could ask what that meant, Tim smiled. "It's constricting the blood vessels now... raising his blood pressure... It's *working*."

"*Thoracentesis, neurotransmission.*"

Phil believed he was in reverse neuropathy himself. He felt his nerves damaged to the point that his feet and hands began to tingle.

"*Pericardiocentesis.*"

Luckily, the pod had formed a fog during the entire surgery, shielding all three from any potential nightmares or trauma—even though it was already too late for Phil, who was *clearly* traumatised. He fidgeted with his fingers, continuously biting his nails.

"*Resuscitation process initiated. Defibrillation activated.*"

Phil could see Andrew's body jerking from the shock, burying his head in Tim's shoulder as Tim awkwardly patted his back. The only good thing about the situation was that they never heard a flatline, nor the beeping of a failing heart, when the pod announced his heartbeat was restored.

Phil let out the longest sigh of relief he had ever felt, the tension flooding out of him like a wave. The pod slowly opened, and Andrew lay there peacefully, his chest bare and covered in stitches. His chest rose softly, his breathing even.

"If I ever hear *any* of those fancy words again," Val said, his arms crossed, "I'm cuttin' my ears off. Who the bloody hell programmed that thing anyway? That voice... it's *truly* awful."

Tim ignored him, taking the gurney back out of the hallway. "Let's get him comfortable in his *own* bed."

Phil nodded slowly, buttoning Andrew's shirt before he helped Tim positioning Andrew on the gurney. Val watched them leave the room, giving the pod one final look before turning around, closing the door behind him.

# CHAPTER FORTY-ONE

Cal skimmed through a few of the documents Alex had managed to steal from Imogen, writing down as much information as he could before heading over to Tim, who had just returned from Andrew's room.

"Look at this."

Tim looked at the paper, his brows shooting up. "*Curselings*? *That's* what they're called?"

He sighed softly, looking over at Alex who looked through the cabinet of vials and bottles, holding gauze in his hands. Wanting to keep himself busy, he wanted to help Stan see to his wound. Unable to find any disinfectant, he prepared a washcloth soaked with whiskey. Setting the other materials aside, he perched next to Stan, who lifted his sleeve.

"Only a few of us remain to visit the other three islands," Cal said.

Tim shook his head, walking away from the others. "And what? Lose *more* people? Have *more* hurt and traumatised? We almost lost Drew today. I honestly can't believe he survived."

"So, what, you wanna just give up and go home?"

"Maybe we should." Tim eyed him. "We've sacrificed *enough*."

He proceeded to walk away, but Cal stopped him in his tracks. "Oi, you say that 'cause you believe there's a good chance they'll call our bluff."

Tim gave him a confused look, shaking his head. "No, I'm *serious*."

"You can't just give the bad people the means to control *and* outnumber us... to *destroy* us."

Tim pushed the papers against his chest, not waiting before Cal accepted them as they crashed to the floor. "It's not like these *Curselings* will live forever."

"We dunno that," Cal said, "there's no research known about potential killing methods. They were already dead *before* they were brought to her and that *wasn't* death. They were revived." He stopped himself from talking. "Why am I explaining this to you? *You're* the nerd here."

"None of this can be found in a manual," Tim continued. "If I had known it'd mean choosing *which* lives to save and *which* to sacrifice 'cause our leader is unable to... I can't help but wonder what the *true* cost is. Sam lost an arm, Seb's blind, Drew almost lost his life, and we've got *a lot* of wounded people on board. So, tell me *honestly*, Cal, what's all this worth?"

Cal put his big hand on Tim's shoulder, squeezing it. "We're gonna keep showing up to those islands and we'll keep fighting for those people stuck on 'em. It's worth fighting for."

"Why? To keep Sam's legacy alive? A *hero's* legacy? I don't think so. I'm not fit for that 'cause I haven't *tried* hard enough!"

Proceeding to walk away again, Cal stood firmly, not allowing Tim to do so. "Oi, *what* did you just say? I can relate to the feeling you've not really tried your best, but you *don't* get to say that. You've saved Drew. You planted trackers on 'em, and you *knew* about the pod. Don't sell yourself short, Tim. *I mean it.*"

Tim managed to loosen Cal's grip and moved past him. "Our world is difficult to live in 'cause there's *so* much wrong that I thought was fixed. I know it's not my fault those things are wrong, but it's *my* fault I haven't made 'em better. What good have I *truly* done, other than saving people from their doom?"

"Stop. That's a stupid amount of pressure that's not real and *super* unfair."

Tim scoffed softly. "Yeah, well, I haven't made things as good as I could've, *period*. I could've at least scaled it down, you know? Just a *little* bit."

Before Cal could say anything else to change Tim's mind, he had entered his room, locking the door behind him. Cal remained behind, sighing loudly to himself before walking away.

Tim sank to the floor at the other end of the door and whimpered softly. A large volume of tears flowed steadily down his cheeks as he buried his face in his arms, wrapping them around his raised knees. "I just wanna go *home*..."

Alfie flew them to the next island, hearing a loud sigh behind him as Cal joined him. Before Cal could ask it officially, Alfie nodded. "I'll go down there. *Alone*."

"What?" Cal joined him in the co-pilot seat. "You can't *possibly* think that that's a good idea."

Alfie shrugged. "Don't see another choice. Unless you and Tim wanna join me."

Cal sighed. "I'm not allowed to go, and Tim—"

"Isn't a fighter. I've *noticed*." Alfie looked away from Cal for a second, fiddling with his hair. Then he looked back as the Kite soared peacefully on the autopilot. "I'll be fine. Besides, who's to say the three people on that island aren't still alive and kicking. I might be able to recruit 'em."

Cal looked over at the island they were approaching, noticing someone lying on the beach surrounded by a sea of red. "That doesn't look good."

Alfie let the Kite fly above the body, getting up from his seat. "Last chance to join me. Drew broke protocol too so, who's to say *you* can't either?"

Cal laughed hoarsely, shaking his head. "You're a people reader, *aren't* you?" He sighed. "I just *hate* sitting still and watching helplessly."

The two of them walked towards the back of the Kite, rolling down the ladder until it reached low enough for them to jump off and keep their bones intact.

Before they could descend, Val caught up with them. "I'm comin' with. You need at least *one* person with powers."

"You sure you're up for it after what you just went through?" Cal asked him. "We haven't been away from that place for even an hour."

Val nodded. "Positive, *chief.*"

Cal descended after Alfie, watching as Val followed closely. Not telling anyone they were going down there was a huge risk, but Cal chose to deal with it rather than face any potential embarrassment or a harassing lecture.

Approaching the body, Cal stopped in his tracks. He fell to his knees while Alfie looked for any signs of life, though he knew it was pointless. The deep chasm that was cut into Charlie's chest where his heart ought to be, was a clear indication of what went down before they arrived. Cal had seen some grisly scenes in the past, but his stomach turned at the sight of his friend's body. The gaping, bloody hole in the centre of Charlie's chest made him throw up.

Val seethed quietly, stepping away from the body to stand a few feet away from them.

Alfie approached him. "You know something *we* don't?"

"That cut is made by a claw that's so gigantic, that I don't believe *any* creature made it. It's gotta be *Drew's mum.*"

"That's not even humanly possible, let alone monster—ly. Unless she can levitate or something, and then to the point where she's faster than a Kite with two hundred miles per hour. There's just *no way* she could've beat us to it."

"Unless she can swim!" Cal yelled, having stopped crying as he took out his gun.

Alfie turned around slowly, staring into the dark eyes of Imogen, who snarled at him while dripping sea water. Her mangled hand clamped around Alfie's ankle, dragging him towards the ocean. Once they hit the water, her grip tightened, her dagger-like claws digging deep into his flesh.

"Tim? Tim, can you hear me?" Cal tried desperately, hoping Tim had his earpiece nearby so he would hear the frantic screams. *"Tim!"*

Alfie thrashed, trying to break free from her grasp. With the effort it took him to try, all he succeeded in doing was losing some of the air that was stationed in his lungs. Imogen released her grip on his ankle, seizing him around his waist. Her jaw stretched wide as she bit his shoulder.

Screaming in pain, he forced himself to ignore his further burning lungs, jabbing his fingers directly into her sickly dark eyes. Imogen reeled back, covering her eyes to stop the dark and bloody ooze seeping out of her eyes into the water. Alfie kicked towards the surface, breaking through the water to suck in a desperate breath of air.

"Alfie!" Cal yelled, running towards the shore to try and help Alfie, but he was too late.

All Alfie got before he was dragged back down was one breath. He looked at a Curseling darting out of the weeds, though it looked less terrifying.

*I've had enough of this bloody virus!* He took out his blaster gun. *I'm gonna jam this bloody thing with a well-placed shot, blast the other hunk of junk to pieces.*

The blaster energised to life, activating its target acquisition sensor. Alfie pulled the trigger, ejecting an incendiary bullet through the port. Touching the ammo selector display, he fired a plasmatic blob of pure thermal heat.

She hissed angrily at him while his blaster recharged, ordering the other Curseling to slam into his side. He grunted upon impact, the fear of drowning choking him as it burned in his chest, his lungs desperate for air.

He kicked out at the Curseling, going for the surface once more. She called for more of her Curselings to arise, crowding above him with waiting claws and jaws. He struggled to move away; his limbs felt as heavy as lead.

*I dunno if the darkness is my vision fading... or those things descending on me. But I guess this it. This is where I die.*

Little fireballs exploded around him, causing the Curselings to recoil and hiss as if they were in pain. A chain snaked towards him. He desperately reached out, both of his hands clamping around it, watching as the water reacted with the volatile metal. Once he grabbed hold, it jerked back rapidly, dragging him to the surface.

Air flooded his aching lungs once it whisked him to the shore, collapsing onto the sand. Miraculously, neither Imogen nor her Curselings followed him.

Alfie expelled the water from his lungs, coughing loudly.

He looked up at Ray who had joined them, patting Alfie's back. "You're bloody lucky I heard Cal's desperate cry through Tim's earpiece."

"*Thanks*," he barely managed to say, his body in a state of inertia as he couldn't stop coughing.

Val noticed Alfie's blaster, whistling at the sight of it. "That's a sick lookin' thing you got there, mate. Never knew you carried such a thing with you."

"Perhaps it'd be better to interrogate him about it later," Ray said, helping Alfie to his feet. "He should save his breath."

"*I'm fine*," Alfie murmured, pushing Ray slightly away from him. "Let's just go."

He pushed forward, walking unsteadily as his lungs burned in his chest. Ray and Val exchanged a look before following him, dragging Cal along with them. Cal hadn't been given the chance to bury Charlie, due to the danger of Imogen emerging again.

It was nearing dawn as Alfie and Cal slogged wearily behind Val and Ray. Cal was still reeling from the loss of Charlie when they stumbled upon torches casting a soft, hazy glow over the rainforest. Expecting them to belong to one or two of the guys still stuck on the island, they walked towards them as night faded into day.

"Hello?" Ray tried carefully, not wanting to startle anyone. The camp looked abandoned, pieces of wood and other tools scattered everywhere. "Looks like they left in a hurry."

"But recent," Val said, pointing at the meat coated in dirt, "it's still lukewarm."

Alfie took a deep breath to steady himself, surveying the camp. He noticed a worn path in the nearby vegetation, pointing at it. "They must've gone that way." He gripped his shoulder, staggering back. For the first time, the others noticed how soaked his shoulder was, all the way down to his chest.

"Why didn't you say anything?" Ray said, forcing Alfie to sit down so he could take a proper look.

The long gash stretching from Alfie's shoulder to his chest looked bad. His Trooper armour was damaged, exposing the torn and bloodied shirt beneath it where he had been slashed.

"If *that thing* can damage real and sturdy armour like that, we're *doomed*," Cal said depressingly.

"Would you shush," Val commanded, "now's *not* the time." Alfie didn't look good; his forehead felt dangerously hot as Val touched it. "He's runnin' a fever."

"You don't think that her claws were imbued with virus extracts? What if he's *exposed* to it?" Cal continued, ignoring Val.

"I've never heard of such a thing before," Ray replied, "it's only done by injection. I *highly* doubt it's transmittable."

"Maybe he has antibodies, and it's just a normal fever caused by blood loss and exposure to water," Val added, "Sam's got antibodies, *right*? Who's to say Alfie here doesn't *either*?"

"He needs to return to the Kite," Ray said. "It's not safe for him to be out here like this."

"And then what? Admit to Tim we failed? *Again*? No, he'll come with us," Cal said determinedly. "He'll be better by the time we get back."

Val scoffed. "Look at you hurdlin' from doom scenario to *nothing's wrong at all.* You must be real *fun* at parties."

Before a fight between them could break out, Alfie pointed at the bushes rustling violently. *"Someone's coming…"*

"Or *something*," Ray finished his sentence.

## CHAPTER FORTY-TWO

"Wake up, Andy!"

Hearing Minnie's voice, his eyes opened, blinking against the glow of the sunset he saw the silhouette of his sister standing in. He glanced at the ocean waves, which lapped gently at her feet. It was eerily quiet, and it seemed as if the two of them were the only living things at that moment. No one else seemed present on Earth.

"Is this *Komo beach*?"

She nodded at him, smiling as she grabbed a stick to draw figures in the sand. "I can't believe you remember the name of the beach you've only been to *once* as a toddler."

"It's my *happiest* memory of you," he said, watching as her smile brightened, though she seemed momentarily taken aback. He could feel her sudden wariness, her expression betraying it. She sipped some ocean water before looking at him earnestly. "Did I say something wrong?"

She shook her head. "No, but I need to have a serious conversation with you, Andy."

"Can't we do that *after* reminiscing the beauty of this day? Where's the harm in that?"

She walked over to him, placing both of her hands on his shoulders. "There's not much time." Before he could ask her what she meant, she turned back towards the ocean. "A Trooper can have a hundred names, people like you a hundred identities, enemies like Mister X a hundred faces. But *you*, my little brother," she said, her voice soft but heavy with meaning, "you only get *one* soul."

He grabbed a shell, turning it over in his hand. " I need to protect my friends at all costs—the way I *couldn't* protect you. *You* told me that."

"Maybe not in those exact words, but you need to ask yourself—who's gonna protect *you*?"

He shook his head lightly. "Don't worry about me."

"I worry," she said, forcing him to look at her. *Really* look at her. "Out there, in the *real* world, you're dying," she explained to him.

"*What*? No, I'm sure I'd feel it if I was."

She pushed her hand straight through his abdomen as those words spilled slowly off his tongue, realising he *was* in fact dreaming. He saw himself being put into the pod, lights flashing all around his body. "Bloody hell... I'm following my past self."

She nodded, patting his back. "You're an out-of-body observer right now, akin to a time traveller, but it feels more like a drunken dream."

"*Crazy* dream, is honestly the term I'd use to describe it."

"The truth has revealed itself to you, and it must trigger within you the means to travel back to the waking world. If you don't find that path fast, you'll *die*."

He looked straight at her, grabbing her hands. "Who's to say I can't stay? With you? I miss you like crazy, Minnie."

"I know you do," she said, squeezing both of his hands, "but it's *not* your time yet."

"Neither was it *yours*."

She sighed. "I don't have a purpose on Earth, but *you* do."

He snapped between dream to reality, shaking his head as he struggled to breathe. He felt his head going fuzzy.

"Feel the strength you need, feel the *determination* to stay alive," she said, almost in a hypnotising manner, "have *one last good deed* to your name."

"*Last*? Are you saying that I'll die after I try to help save Zacropolis *and* the world? You're sending me back only for me to die a second time?"

She began to fade, and he desperately tried to hold onto her. "No, don't you *dare* do this to me. *Don't* be selfish!"

She smiled one last time, and when she was gone, he stood alone in the shifting dream—now nothing more than a dark, empty place. The ocean was no longer bright and alive. But then, a bridge began to form. He knew he had to find a way to across, so he put one foot in front of the other. *If she had written me to pass through this place, then I shall follow the idea of that path. I owe her that much, even if I don't like it.*

The ocean emerged once more, realising it now blocked his way, yet the bridge to the light beyond remained ever present. The thought of the real world flickered within the surrounding darkness. He willed it to be real—and it *was*. His dream had already faded by the time his eyes shot open.

Andrew was extensively bandaged around the torso, a breathing tube in his trachea, and an IV drip attached to his arm. He noticed Phil sleeping on the side of his bed, his arm touching Andrew's left leg. Tapping Phil's shoulder, he tried his best not to choke on the tube in his throat.

Phil shot up, staring at Andrew in disbelief. "You're *already* awake? How's that—"

Realising Andrew was choking, he quickly rushed out to get Tim. When they both ran back in, Tim was just as surprised as Phil to see Andrew already awake. With no time to question it, he grabbed the suction device to remove any lingering bodily fluids or objects from Andrew's mouth and airway.

Andrew forced himself not to swallow, watching helplessly, unable to communicate, as Tim ordered Phil to remove the strap holding the tube in place. Tim then proceeded to disconnect the tub from the ventilator.

"Can you take a deep breath for me?" he asked Andrew, pulling the tube out of his throat.

Andrew coughed immediately, gasping loudly as he sucked the air into his lungs. Tim tapped his back to relieve his airways even further, watching Phil who exhaled with great relief.

"I dunno how you're already awake with the injuries you've sustained, but—"

Andrew cut Tim off, breathing heavily as he spoke. *"Sam... need... talk..."*

Having recovered from the miraculous awakening and taken a few sips of water, Sam stared at Andrew as he sat next to his bed.

"So, you're telling me that your sister revived you only to *use you* as a sacrifice?"

"Looks like it," Andrew replied calmly, his arms crossed. "And I think I know why." Sam eyed him questioningly. "I'd give my life for the people of Zacropolis—*and* for Phil—if it meant he'd stay alive, and I know you'd do the same for your girlfriend and son. But Phil will be fine without me, and I know your family *wouldn't*."

"I hope it doesn't come to that, Drew, no matter *what* you think. Did your sister fill your head with that nonsense?" he said, shaking his head. "Look, if you're claiming that I'm indispensable and you're not, you've got it *wrong*. *Everyone* is—every *single soul* on our team and in the city."

Andrew chuckled softly. "Right, 'cause *I've* got the superpowers that'll come in handy for exploitation purposes."

"That's not—"

"No, save it. Dying for a city is *one thing*—that's *my* choice, *my* destiny. But dying for no good reason, like those lads on the islands? That *doesn't* sit right with me. At least this way, something good can come outta it. My life can mean something instead of being nothing but experimental material."

Sam gripped his collar tightly, ignoring the fact that Andrew just woke up from a near-death experience, hanging by a thread. "It almost sounds like you're insulting Zach—he died for *far* more than you can ever imagine. Don't you think *we're* not experiments? For *ten years*, we were. So, don't be a petty little arsehole claiming you've had it tougher than us just 'cause you got *special* treatment." He clutched Andrew's collar more firmly. "Dying how he did is the *last* way you'd wanna go—*trust me*. People like us *never* get a say in how we die or why—that's just how it goes. And you don't get a say in whether *that's* what's gonna happen to you. You can't just lie down and die, *you hear me?* I won't let *anyone* else hold their head high in false bravado."

Andrew took a big breath. "Perhaps you should've just let me die, spare us all from my *false bravado.*"

"Stop!" Phil yelled, who had clearly been listening in this entire time. "For crying out loud, stop! If you wouldn't mind not putting a lid on your life that'd be great! I'm sick of people dying around here or close to dying and us having to do *everything* we can to save 'em! Look at Sam and how *close* he was to dying! Look at *yourself!*"

"I didn't ask *anyone* to save me," Andrew replied.

"You don't *have* to ask that!" Phil yelled, spitting. "That's the point of having friends and people who *care* about you! If you wanna push me away with your idiotic thinking, make stupid choices, lie to our faces, or outright sacrifice yourself? Fine, I clearly *can't* stop you, but I'm *not* abandoning you! If you go, *I* go! And when that day comes and it gets *me* killed—maybe even before you do—maybe *then* you'll realise how much you *matter* to me, 'cause I bloody love you!" Phil grew angrier as Andrew lay there, momentarily perplexed, unsure how to react or respond. Phil headed to the door in a daze, fiddling with the handle before turning back around. "I see that feeling's *not* mutual."

He stormed out of the room, slamming the door shut behind him, leaving Andrew speechless.

Phil entered his room and punched the mirror. He ripped a painting off the wall and threw a monitor to the floor, relentlessly trashing his room until he collapsed, breathing heavily. Anguished, he buried his head in his hands as he sank to the floor, tears stung his eyes like shards of glass. The weight of his unrequited need for validation and love hit him like a ton of bricks. He felt betrayed and misunderstood, as if he had misread Andrew's intentions all along.

Consumed by love for Andrew and rage at his indifference, he was unravelling.

    Andrew stared at the now closed door, looking over at Sam who was just as perplexed. Before either could say anything to each other, Tim knocked on the door. "We've got a problem. There are a few missing and I'm guessing they went down to the next island."
    "*What?*" Sam said, jumping up. "What the bloody hell are they thinking?" He stormed out of the room with Tim following suit, leaving Andrew alone with his guilt.

    "Do we have contact with any of 'em?" Sam asked, sitting next to Tim who put the earpiece in his ear.
    "Negative. I've been calling out to 'em, but the signal's gone."
    "Bloody hell!" Sam yelled, hitting the table. "Who do we've got left to go down there and rescue 'em?"
    Tim eyed him nervously, taking a deep breath. "*Me.* I'm the only one."
    "No." Sam shook his head determinedly. "*Everyone* but you."
    "You don't trust me? You don't think I'm capable?"
    "No, it's not that," he said, sighing. "Seb is my brother, but *you're* my best friend. If *anything* happens to you, I'd watch the world go up in flames."
    Tim put a comforting hand on Sam's shoulder. "Don't think for a second that I haven't felt the same way every time you went out there risking your life. I let you go, *didn't I?* I *never* stopped you, 'cause I know it's not in you to give up on people when you can help 'em. That's not who you're meant to be, and it *never* has been. You've *always* been a helper, delivering speeches and advocating for peace. You remind us that the world only makes sense when we force it to. You're not just brave, Sam—*men* are brave. And you're a *man* through and through." Tim looked straight into Sam's eyes. "This is my way of thanking you for helping me, for showing me the path to bravery. I'll be in good hands besides yours—*my own.*"
    "Tim, I—"
    "No, listen. I see in you several strengths I've always aspired to gain—wisdom being the first, and the ferocity you show *only* when those you love and care for are in danger. In this situation, I can clearly see how that wise part of you shines. I know hard it's been for you lately to manage your emotions and express 'em, and *that's* why every time you do, it makes my day. It highlights

what's truly authentic about you—both as a person *and* as a leader."

"You *really* need to stop," Sam said, "this sounds like a hidden goodbye, like you know you're *not* coming back from going down there." A cold, dark abyss of pure sadness swallowed him whole. "You *don't* get to say goodbye, *you hear me?*"

"Loud and clear." Tim hugged Sam carefully. "This *whole* time, you've been taking the wheel and calling the shots, and I've *trusted you* 'cause you're my best friend. But now, I'm asking you—*just this once*—to trust *me*. I can do this."

Sam heaved a weary sigh, shaking off his unruly thoughts until he regained a semblance of order. "*Go.*"

Tim grabbed his shotgun, glanced at Sam, who gave him a confirming nod, and descended the ladder.

# CHAPTER FORTY-THREE

They sat frozen, eyes locked on the bushes. An ear-splitting shriek tore through the trees, and in the next breath, Imogen charged at them, her dagger-like claws slicing through the earth as more Curselings swarmed to her side.

Cal threw his arms up to shield his face, feeling the wicked talons of Imogen scrape harmlessly against the metal bracers on his arms. She paused, confused—unable to wound him the way she had Alfie. With a vicious swipe, she knocked the gun from his grip, sending it flying out of reach, too far for anyone to try and retrieve.

He scanned the area quickly, spotting a large pole beside the torches. Imogen advanced, slavering at the mouth. He rolled away and sprang to his feet, grabbing one of the posts anchored to the ground. It snapped free in his hand as he used all his strength to tear it loose. Once she charged, he jammed the splintered end of the post straight through her eye socket. Blood and gore sprayed across his face.

She growled in fury, slashing wildly in her rage, striking at anyone within reach. Before they could react, the ground beneath them gave way. Cal watched in horror as Alfie, Ray, and Val vanished. His eyes locked onto a wooden hatch, and before it could slam shut, he leapt through, landing hard on top of Val—who quickly shoved him off.

"Thanks for breaking my fall," he said.

"Don't mention it, *tosser*," Val said, dusting his clothes.

"Alfie's *not* so lucky," Ray replied.

Bright, crimson blood gushed from Alfie's wound. It soaked his clothes, forming a pool in the dirt at his feet. Cal rushed forward, blocking out the creaking of the hatch closing above him, his gun now out of reach. His hands shook from adrenaline as he pressed down on the wound.

"Anyone got a dressin' on 'em?" Val asked, checking his empty pockets.

"Use this," a voice called from behind them, its owner hidden in the shadows.

A makeshift dressing, along with makeshift bandages, was thrown at them. Cal didn't question the material, moving quickly to prevent Alfie from bleeding out. His hands shook uncontrollably, but he used every bit of strength to hold it in place long enough for Ray to help secure the dressing.

"Who goes there?" Val demanded, grabbing Alfie's blaster for self-defence, though he had no clue how it worked or how to use it.

"Relax, Valentine," he heard, looking up at the light blond faux hawk that came into view as the boy stepped into the radius of the torch Val held, along with the blaster. His kind, grey eyes drew attention away from his high forehead and floppy ears.

"Bloody hell," Val said, slowly lowering the blaster, "Reggie?"

Both yelled in happiness, hugging each other roughly but excitedly.

"Keep your bloody voices down," Ray said annoyedly, pointing at the hatch. "She's still up there."

"*She?*" Reggie asked.

"Long story," Val replied, tapping his shoulder. "You alone down here?"

Reggie shook his head. "Nope, Mac, or whatever his name is, he's somewhere in the back."

Cal smiled despite the dire situation. "You're telling me Malcolm's down here?"

Reggie let out a low whistle. "You know the guy? He's a *weirdo first class*. Keeps talking about a Kite or whatever, *anything that flies*, really."

"Yeah, that's Mac for you," Cal said, "he was a pilot."

"Figures." Reggie walked over to Cal and Ray as they worked on Alfie. "Raymond, good to see *you* too."

Ray scoffed, clearly not liking Reggie as much as Val did. "*Reginald.*"

Cal realised that if they knew each other, Reggie was another ORPHAN. "What's *your* superpower?"

Reggie laughed and disappeared. Cal was confused, for he didn't hear any retracting footsteps. But then Reggie appeared again, right behind Cal, and he had to stop himself from screaming.

"I can turn invisible whenever I want, unlike another guy like me who can shapeshift into anything—*except* invisibility."

"You're talking about Drew," Ray said, "we've met him."

Reggie nodded slowly. "So, that means you haven't found the other two?"

Val shook his head. "Not yet, but we'll find 'em eventually."

"Good that, 'cause you're gonna need to brief me further on all this crap. Both me *and* Mac."

Val nodded and watched as Reggie went to fetch Mac, who had been hiding the whole time. When Cal saw him, he quickly made sure Ray could handle Alfie's wound, then threw his arms around Mac. "It's good to see you, mate."

The brown-haired boy with a Viking-inspired beard smiled as they embraced, patting his back. "Likewise."

"You grew a *full* beard? A moustache, even. *Impressive.* Did you get implants? Wait, no you didn't, 'cause you're still missing your front tooth."

"Ha. Ha. *Very* funny."

They teased each other for a while before joining the others, settling down to listen as they began explaining everything.

"So, let me get this straight," Mac said, spinning the tiny makeshift dagger in his hand, "only those *with* superpowers are allowed to survive these islands, so *they* can fight the bioweapons—only to become bioweapons themselves? How does that make *any* sense?"

Val, who had taken over from Cal to tend to Alfie's wound, nodded slowly. "Basically, they need *us* to fight the *Serum X* injection they give to people like Imogen up there—Drew's mum. The family and friends who attack you? They've been injected with *Serum C*."

"But seeing as we've rescued two *regular* people from those islands—despite their better judgement—I think they've started developing it much more hastily. Imogen's the first Serum X creation, and what she can do... it's unlike *anything* I've ever seen," Cal added.

"So, what you're saying is that we destroyed their original '*let's take it slow*' plans and forced them to move it up? How's *that* good news, *exactly*?" Mac asked, sharpening his blade.

"It means there's gotta be a flaw in the formula, somethin' they couldn't test at a convenient pace. They straight up injected Imogen with it without testin' it on any other lab rats. As our nerd Tim would say, they didn't have time to perform experimental neurosurgical procedures upon 'em."

As Mac and Reggie let those words sink in, Ray broke the silence. "Does anyone have an earpiece? I don't have mine on me."

"It's no use down here," Cal replied, "*no signal*."

Ray dropped his head in defeat, sighing softly. "Guess we're stuck down here then. We can't warn any of 'em, and if they come looking for us, they'll *die*."

"They're smart," Val said, "none of 'em will come down here without big guns. Don't worry, we'll be outta here in no time and those *things* will be buried six feet under."

Tim, armed only with his shotgun, followed the trail the others had left behind—tracking their footsteps into the depths of the woods, along with the occasional drops of blood Alfie had left as he staggered behind.

A deafening clang rang out, and Tim couldn't tell if it was natural or *not*. He stopped dead in his tracks, shotgun raised.

"Hello?" he called cautiously. "Cal? Alfie?" He moved along the tracks, walking backwards. "Val? Ray?"

He bumped into something, thinking it was a tree. But the relief faded instantly when he felt something dripping onto him. The thick, slimy substance was transparent, with a sickly yellow glow. Slowly, he turned around and looked up, meeting the gaze of the Curseling looming over him, its mouth wide open. Behind him, a throng of Curselings flooded into the clearing, their teeth gnashing.

Tim fired his shotgun at the one in front of him. It left a gaping hole in the Curseling's stomach, but it quickly regenerated, the wound healing itself.

"Oh boy..." Tim smiled wearily at the Curseling before darting between its legs, quickly making his way to the other side to continue down the path.

The Curseling hesitated for a moment, stunned by Tim's move, but it took only five seconds before it gave chase, its fellow Curselings close behind.

"You hear that?" Val said as he heard the gunshots coming closer.

As Tim ran, he kept firing his shotgun to slow them down.

"That's one of our friends," Cal said. "Get me up there."

"What? That's *suicide*," Reggie said, "you'd be mighty dumb going up there to save *whoever's* out there."

Cal ignored Reggie's clear disdain towards the request, looking over at Val. "Give me a boost."

Val sighed, doing as he was told.

Before Cal reached the hatch, Ray handed him Stan's machete, which he had *borrowed.* "Give 'em hell."

Cal tried to hide his disappointment, struggling to come to terms with the fact that no one seemed willing to help. He pushed the thought to the back of his mind as he reached the hatch and opened it. Climbing out, he left it open, just in case anyone decided to follow.

Before he could close it, realising no one else was coming after him, he heard gunshots getting closer, bracing himself for whatever he had stumbled into. He decided to climb the tree, glancing over at Tim, who was running away from three Curselings.

"Tim?" He knew Tim wasn't the strongest in his Trooper training and had always relied on being the backup. Taking a deep breath, he jumped down, intercepting one of them. He plunged the machete through the Curseling's stomach. Before it could heal itself, he sank the machete into its head, gritting his teeth as he watched the sickly blood bile spill across the ground.

He lost his footing as another Curseling slammed into him. His machete skittered beneath a nearby bush as he hit the ground.

"Cal?" Tim said, shooting at the Curseling Cal had wounded severely, finally killing it. "Where did *you* come from?"

Cal scrambled back up. "Long story. Let's talk about it *after* we defeat these two wankers, huh?" He looked at the machete. "I need you to distract 'em and keep 'em busy long enough for me to reach the machete. What we *just* did, we need to do two more times. It seems to work." He noticed Tim checking the ammo. "How many rounds you got?"

"Not that many."

"Better make 'em count then."

Cal moved swiftly towards the bushes, ducking under a Curseling's claw as it tried to strike. He grabbed the machete, gripping it tightly before lunging forward. He sank the tip of it through the Curseling's chest, straight up beneath its collarbone. The adrenaline drained as he ripped the machete free, just as the Curseling's claw came at him.

Tim shot just in time, sparing Cal from the same slash that hurt Alfie. Cal quickly sank the blade into the Curseling's throat, feeling the acid boiling up inside him as black blood poured over his hand. He jerked the machete up and back out through the Curseling's face.

It dropped to the ground, leaving just one Curseling. Tim, out of shotgun shells, spotted a nearby rock. The Curseling seemed to sense his plan, sinking its teeth into his arm. Tim screamed in pain but managed to rip his arm free. He grabbed the Curseling's head and threw it against the rock. He watched in disgust as the skull cracked open, its brain matter dripping onto his shoes.

Cal finished it off by plummeting the machete straight through the Curseling's heart. "You good?" he asked Tim, who glanced at his arm, his expression filled with pain

"Just some bitemarks, no flesh was torn. *I'll live.*"

Cal nodded slowly. "Sorry we didn't listen. Sorry we just up and went without saying anything."

Tim waved him off. "Say no more, I get it." He looked around. "So, where are the others?"

"Down here!" they heard.

Tim stared into the abyss, recognising Val's voice. "We need to move," he said, "Cal and I cleared the way. If we leave *now*, I think we can make it."

"That's great, but we got a problem, *chief*," Val replied, "Alfie's wounded."

Tim sighed, knowing it was too good to be true to find all of them in one piece. "How *bad* are we talking?"

"Sliced chest *bad*. We stopped the bleedin' as best we could, but to be honest, it's lookin' grim."

"We can use the pod on the ship. Now that we know it works, it makes my life a lot easier as a *stepped-up medic—without* a medical license."

Val and Ray worked together to lift Alfie high enough for Tim and Cal to haul him up. While Cal helped the others, Tim examined Alfie's wound. Alfie was slipping in and out of consciousness, more dead than alive—but not as fatally wounded as Andrew had been.

"Can you carry him on your back?" he asked Cal, who nodded.

Cal hurled Alfie onto his back, who grunted softly from the impact.

Mac glanced at Tim's bleeding arm. "You *both* sure you're not gonna end up like those *things*?"

"*Positive*. I know it sounds strange, considering everything we've read in books and such, but this virus isn't contagious unless injected. *That's* how they keep it contained, to avoid what they thought was happening with the Laeries."

"Good that, wasn't necessarily looking forward to killing you *or* him."

"Guess that doesn't make 'em inherently bad," Reggie said as they walked back. "I mean, they *could've* made it infectious from the beginning."

"That's 'cause they need the experiment results. It's still in the test phase with the hosts," Tim said, watching the trees. "Doesn't mean they *won't* make it contagious later and start an apocalypse that way."

"First, it was meant to eliminate the need for a large-scale army," Cal explained. "They injected us with a serum to make us stronger and more resilient, able to withstand any harm while dealing with the Laeries they saw as a threat to humanity. But in the end, they were just trying to erase what they'd accidentally created."

"And now they wanna erase humanity for good, keeping creatures and *superheroes* to conquer the world bit by bit. They'll unleash the creatures, and by showing the strength and tenacity of the survivors, they'll make sure the world knows that only *they*, the creators of superpowers, can change the world and lead it. They'll assert their dominance and create a much bigger arena than the Dome two years ago." Tim looked straight ahead, a single tear rolling down his cheek. "And most likely, they'll make it infectious, claiming to have the *only* cure in the world. We'll become *superheroes*, only good enough for *gladiator spectacles*."

# CHAPTER FORTY-FOUR

A strange rumble echoed across the horizon. They turned towards the ocean ahead, the Kite coming into view. The water began to churn, bubbles breaking the surface in a growing crescendo of disturbance.

"What the—?"

The vibration in the soles of his feet made Tim stop short, his sentence unfinished. The tremor he and the others felt grew more insistent. With a thunderous roar, the island's peak erupted in a fiery plume, shooting skyward. The sky darkened, ash and pumice raining down, blanketing the ground like baleful snow. The serene atmosphere turned into a frothy, chaotic maelstrom.

"Run!" Cal yelled, struggling to keep Alfie—who was draped across his back—in place as he took off.

The others followed suit, the temperature rising as the volcanic activity intensified. Their lungs burned with ash-laden air, the heat from the eruption pressing against their backs, a sharp contrast to the cool breeze they had felt earlier. Tim glanced at the water, now a churning cauldron of molten lava and steam.

They heard a scream behind them and turned to see Imogen leap onto Mac, who struggled desperately to get her off. Ray wanted to turn and help, but Val stopped him. Val's instinct was right—Imogen had clearly grown, her claws much larger than before. She easily stomped on Mac's head, crushing his skull instantly. Pulp was all that remained from where his head was supposed to be. They stared in horror as her mouth split open with an abhorrently wet cracking sound. Revealing her gaping insectoid mouth, she began to munch on Mac.

But Tim wanted to have a go at her. He grabbed the haft of the machete from Cal's sheath and surged forward. He stabbed the point through the roof of her mouth and watched as the bright, silver tip pierced the top of her skull. For a second, it seemed to have worked, for Imogen stood eerily still. The razor-keen edge slid free with no resistance as he pulled back, covered in black, thick ick.

With a furious roar, she charged straight at him, her eyes blazing. At the last moment, Tim dove aside, watching as she slammed headfirst into a nearby tree. The tree shook from the impact. Imogen staggered back, dazed. With the machete raised high, Tim surged forward once more, slashing her repeatedly.

Bone shattered and tissues tore with each strike, creating a mottled mess of bloody flesh. He lifted the machete above his head, driving the blade clean through her neck. Blood sprayed wildly from the wound, but she seemed unfazed by it. He took a few steps back, watching as she regenerated the damage he had inflicted, becoming whole again as if he had never struck her.

Her claw slashed across his leg and Tim screamed in pain, now bleeding from both his arm *and* leg. Ray stepped in front of him as Tim crumpled to the ground, sweeping his arm to create a wide arc of fire that sliced through Imogen. Val joined in, focusing on the tree beside her. Slowly, the tree loosened from its roots, creaking as it began to fall. It landed on top of Imogen, keeping her trapped only temporarily.

Val hurled Tim to his feet, providing stability as Tim limped beside him. Reggie made himself invisible, sneaking up behind her. While she tried to get free, he got close enough to pull a piece off her skin. She growled in anger, flailing her claws, trying to find the culprit. But Reggie was far away from her by the time he made himself visible again, triumphantly holding a piece of her skin in his hands.

They reached the ladder, yelling that they needed help getting Alfie and Tim up. Stan and Alex were commanded to stay near the door just in case, while Sam made sure the Kite would stay airborne. Stan and Alex lowered the crate they had used on Sam earlier, watching with bated breath as the lava crept dangerously closer.

"Hurry up, lads!" Alex yelled, ready to pull as fast as he could.

Once Tim and Alfie were secured, they began to pull with all their might. Cal and Reggie went second, while Val and Ray waited impatiently for their turn. Val felt something gripping his ankle, and he looked straight into the black eyes of his assailant. He tried to fight back, but she only tightened her grip as she leaned in. Saliva dripped as her jaws stretched unnaturally wide. With his powers, he managed to slacken her grip for a split second, kicking her away from him.

Ray helped Val to his feet, and both jumped into the crate. Imogen lunged for it as it soared through the air, narrowly missing as Sam took off immediately, not daring to waste a second. Val and Ray swung dangerously while Stan and Alex scrambled to pull them up. Cal, who had secured Tim and the unconscious Alfie, rushed to help. It wasn't long before they were all inside the Kite, as the fourth island burned to ashes.

With Alfie gone as the pilot, Sam kept a close eye on the reinstalled autopilot. With his flying expertise, Cal took over while Sam joined Tim in the pod room to observe Alfie receiving medical treatment.

"Show it to me."

Tim looked over at Sam, his eyebrows raised questioningly. He straightened slightly when he realised someone must've told him, revealing fresh red stains blooming across the bandages on his arm and leg.

"They're just *flesh wounds*. Seriously, I'm *okay*." He turned back to the pod. "Besides, shouldn't you question our newest recruit, *Reggie*?"

"Don't change the subject.'

Tim sighed. "I'm not. Have you checked on Josh lately? He hasn't come outta his room since he shot Val. It has me concerned."

"You could've gotten yourself killed down there! You were lucky, but next time you—"

"*Shut up!*" Tim yelled, looking stern at Sam who seemed really irked by the outburst. "You don't get to orchestrate my every move, mate! I make my *own* choices and those are *my* choices. Nobody will tell me what I *can* or *can't* do." The pod opened, and he called for Val and Ray to carry Alfie to his room. As they left, he turned to Sam sharply. "Our past *doesn't* define us, Sam. I'm not a helpless nerd anymore. Our past is but a small part of who we're supposed to be. And the bulk of what we become, that's up to *us*."

Sam looked at him, his gaze softening. "But Zach—"

"I'm *not* Zach, I'm not *anybody* you've lost so far. We've *all* lost people, Sam, and yes—they're a part of you—but only a small piece. Like a little nightmare. One you've gotta be capable of forgetting and burying, 'cause you're destroying yourself. This constant worry isn't good for anyone—not for you, and *not* for me. You gotta *stop* being selfish."

He expected Sam to respond with a quip, but he saw in his deep brown eyes that Sam had gone to a dark place. He *knew* the look. The look you would only ever reach in the very depths of guilt. Tim knew that feeling all too well—just like when he lost Danny forever and blamed himself for his death. Then it hit him that he had likely, if not *at least* twice, treated somebody else the same way Sam treated him.

And then Sam's drinking problem hit him.

Sam walked away, and Tim rushed after him to stop him from taking another swig from the whiskey bottle that he had clearly been drinking from.

"Sam, *don't* you dare—"

"You need to take over." Tim's eyes widened in confusion, then in pure fear. "Take over and exile me. You can make it to the other islands, you've *always* been *way* better at finding covers and exits and whatnot."

Sam pulled the bottle loose from Tim's grip, but Tim stopped him from leaving. "Sam, stop it! *We* need you." He paused. "*I* need you."

"No, you *don't* need me. You've made that perfectly clear."

"You *promised* you wouldn't do this anymore. You said you'd stay and stay sober no matter what'd happen." Sam proceeded towards the door once more, but Tim held onto him firmly. "Aren't Seb and I not worth staying for? You said so yourself!"

Sam exhaled sharply. "You're *everything* to me. *Both* of you. It's not about that."

"Then what's it about?" Tim begged, feeling the guilt flare up in him.

"I've seen the way the world looks without Zach, and I know for certain that losing me would be easier than me losing you, *or* Seb."

Tim shook his head. "It *isn't* better. It'd *never* be better, Sam. I know I've said some things to set you back on your heels, but don't you dare think there's anything—past *or* present—that I'd hold you accountable for or put in front of you for any reason. I'm sorry you can't see that right now 'cause of the stupid things I shouldn't have said earlier, but you *need* to trust me." Sam began to cry. "You did it once before—with Seb, didn't you? You helped him find the light, and you can do it again for yourself. Please. For *me*. For *everyone*." He gently lifted Sam's chin with a finger, forcing him to meet his gaze. "We *all* need you. *Every* single one of us."

Sam shook his head. "You've shown me my greatest sins in just one day, and I keep letting you down by *not* trusting you. I can't do that again. The world needs *you* more than it needs me. *You* should take over as leader."

"Then save me," Tim pleaded, "save *us*. But help me save you—help *us* save you. We're a team, and this is a team effort until the end. We started this together, and we'll *finish* it together."

"It's clearly not that easy," Sam continued, "I *can't* promise you that, 'cause the evidence proofs it never sticks."

Tim hugged him carefully, but strong enough to make sure Sam couldn't wriggle his way out. "All I ask of you—try to make it stick. Just for today, okay? Then we'll try again tomorrow."

Sam moved away from Tim's embrace, his teary eyes looked straight into Tim's soul, showing a broken and small man. "How do I do that?"

"Just let it go," Tim said, grabbing Sam once more to pull him in for a tight hug. "You saved Seb from depression, now it's *my* turn to save *you*."

Sam could hear Tim's heartbeat as they hugged, and despite the tension, Tim's heart allowed for a soothing rhythm, which calmed Sam's nerves. Each understood the other's sorrow in that unspoken moment.

*"We need each other to do the things we can't do for ourselves,"* Tim whispered. Then, in his normal voice, he continued, "that includes looking out for one another when our world feels dull and grey. We gotta lead each other towards the light at the end of the tunnel."

*"You're safe now too,"* Sam managed to say—and Tim hadn't realised how much he needed to hear that in that moment.

Despite acting tough to get Sam to loosen up, he was still shaken by what had happened and needed the reassurance Sam gave him. Their hug lingered a little longer.

A knock on his door startled Josh, jolting him awake from a slumber that had lasted too long, drawn out by the heavy dose of sleeping pills he had taken. He glanced at empty bottle on the floor and kicked it away. Sleep had been elusive since he was freed, and only in deep slumber was he safe—from his memories, rom *them*. But this time, he had taken one too many pills and had been out for far too long.

He quickly opened the door after making sure the empty pill bottle couldn't be found, revealing Stan and Alex standing on the other side of the door.

"Sam asked us to check up on ya," Alex said, casually strolling inside. "Haven't seen ya in a few days."

"Yeah, sorry, I was uh... honestly surprised it took everyone so long to realise I was here. Kinda felt as if I was *forgotten*."

Neither Stan nor Alex dared to say that it was, in a way, exactly what had happened. A lot had happened since Sam's amputation, leaving them completely desolate.

"We wanted to give you your space," Stan said, "but now we've grown worried."

Josh nodded. "Let's just forgive and forget. Tell me what has happened lately."

Alex and Stan didn't question Josh further, which gave him a small sense of relief. He had managed to maintain the façade that nothing was terribly wrong. Yet, as they explained, a flutter of butterflies stirred in his stomach, accompanied by a deep-seated anxiety lodged in his throat—an unease triggered by something in their words, though he couldn't quite tell what. It wasn't a visceral fear, but it lingered all the same.

Once they explained how Alfie had gotten injured, Josh zoned out.

He heard the water rushing past his ears, felt its icy embrace pressing against every inch of his body. Desperately, he fought to keep his head above the surface of the transparent box he was trapped in, gasping for air each time his legs gave out and he slipped under.

"Where are the Laeries?" The voice was shrill yet precise, every word clearly articulated. In the background, he could make out a familiar voice, though not clearly enough to be sure he truly recognised it. "I promise you that we just wanna talk to 'em."

Josh's head went under again as the water poured in faster than before, rising so rapidly that he barely had time to take a deep breath before he was completely submerged. He pounded against the glass, screaming soundlessly at the Trooper who watched him in silence.

"What was that? I can't *quite* hear you in there," the man said, putting his ear against the glass. "Could you repeat that?"

Josh began to mouth words, but it didn't seem coherent enough for the man to let him out.

"Where are the Laeries?" he asked a second time. Not getting much from what Josh was mouthing, he sighed. "Give me a thumbs up if you wanna talk, 'kay?"

Josh, on the verge of passing out, managed to do as the Trooper ordered, though he felt himself slipping in and out of consciousness. The last thing he felt before the world went dark was a pair of hands hoisting him out of the box, water flooding behind him as he was dragged away.

Someone slammed their fists into his chest, jolting him awake in agony, the force instantly breaking a rib and trapping the water in his lungs. He couldn't breathe—it felt even worse than drowning. Desperate, he flailed his arms, gesturing frantically towards his throat, trying to signal that the only way to save him was to insert a needle and drain the excess fluid trapped between his chest and lungs—something he had learned from Will.

He felt immediate relief when the Trooper drained the fluid from his lungs, gasping loudly as he coughed. Each cough hurt more than the previous one, and he began to wish he had let the fluid stay. This was *way* more painful.

"Now, *talk*."

Josh had a hard time collecting his thoughts to find the right words, and each time he tried to speak, nothing came out.

"I've had *enough* of this fake stalling of yours." The Trooper took out his stun gun, shocking Josh. His wet body added an extra layer for the electrons to build up rapidly. He grunted in pain, unable to scream with his sore throat. "If you don't start talking *real* soon, I'll cut off your limbs *one by one* and let you stay awake during the whole thing."

"*Wouson...*" he managed to say.

"I've heard of it," the other Trooper with the familiar voice said. Josh was now certain he recognised the voice. *Jonathan.*

*But that's impossible. Jonathan's dead—has been for years. There's no way it's him.*

Another Trooper began to pound on Josh while the other two Troopers walked away, ignoring Josh's cries to be put back in his cell.

"Josh!" Alex yelled.

His voice jolted him back to the present, and Josh stared at Alex and Stan whose faces were etched with worry. Josh noticed he was no longer seated in his chair but was huddled against the wall in a foetus position.

"What did they do to ya?" Alex asked, placing a gentle hand on his arm. "They tortured ya, didn't they? That's where all those scars come from. Ya lied to us." Josh stared at the floor, unable to meet their eyes. But Alex lifted a gentle finger beneath his chin, raising his head to meet his gaze. "Josh, why did ya carry that *burden* alone? Why didn't ya talk to us?"

Josh couldn't answer. Though he was angry at himself for letting them find out, a part of him felt relieved. His his body hunched over as he began to cry, the weight of his unspoken grief pressing down on him. Alex placed a hand over Josh's clenched fists—a clear sign of his silent struggle—before pulling him into an embrace. Josh gripped Alex's shirt tightly, his strong façade finally crumbling. Stan hesitated, unsure how to comfort the usually stoic Josh. *But Alex knew. He had known all along.*

# CHAPTER FORTY-FIVE

After gathering everyone, Alex stayed by Josh's side to help him recount the torture he had endured. Everyone—except for Andrew and Alfie—listened with bated breath, a poignant silence settling over the room.

"Each time I close my eyes; I see it all happen right in front of me. Each bite I take reminds me of what I couldn't eat as they starved me. Each tiny touch prompts a panic attack. I was too scared to admit how broken I was, 'cause I needed people to keep seeing the Trooper leader I signed up to be. I couldn't show weakness, 'cause I taught my students that weakness will get you killed. Turns out I was *wrong*." He took a deep breath. "It's *strength* that can be the death of you. Overconfidence is your biggest enemy. And I'm sorry I kept this from you for so long. I didn't know how to deal with it, and I assumed *none* of you would either."

Sam shuffled closer to Josh, taking his hand. "We're *all* in this together, Josh. It's okay to be honest with us about *anything*. It's *okay* to ask for help." He rubbed Josh's hand. "It's *okay* to say that you're stuck in your trauma, or that you're haunted by it, that you can't even begin to let it go. Every one of us can relate to that. Maybe not with everything you've endured, but we can still help you cope—on your own terms and at your own pace."

Val chuckled slightly, shaking his head. "It explains why you shot me tryin' to help Sam. You thought I was torturtin' him the same way they tortured you. I get it." He gave Josh a confirmative nod. "You had *every* right to shoot me."

"You all think I'm *weak* now, don't you?" Josh said. "You'll treat me differently, like a broken doll that with *one more* touch will break beyond repair."

"No, *screw* that stigma," Sam said, "*screw* the taboo that says otherwise. You broke that silence, and now you need to break that cycle. And we're here to help you through that. You're more than just that pain, Josh. It doesn't make you less of a leader than you signed up for. But most importantly, you're *not* alone, 'cause people need other people. And you need *us*."

Seb strolled over to them, and with some effort, placed a hand on Sam's and Josh's shoulders. "Furniture doesn't make a home—"

"Home is the place where you feel less alone," Sam finished his sentence. "*We're* your home, Josh, and you're *ours*."

Josh pulled his hand back, only to carefully throw his arms around Sam and Seb, crying softly in their embrace. *"Thank you,"* he whispered. *"I owe you both my life."*

Sam shook his head as he pulled away. "No, you don't. We're your *family.*"

The room filled with incessant beeping and trilling of multiple alarms going off, one of which led to Andrew, the other to dangerous weather approaching.

"Find a safe place to set the Kite down," Sam commanded Cal, who nodded. "We'll have to find cover until the storm blows over." He looked at Phil, but his chair was empty. "Go with him and help, if necessary," he told Alex and Stan, who both nodded, running after Phil.

"He's coding!" Phil yelled.

Alex yanked Phil away, keeping him from witnessing the grisly sight, while Stan started chest compressions. There was no time to get Andrew into the pod.

"Andy!" Phil yelled; his piercing scream echoed throughout the Kite. His scream started sudden, its initial duration short, but the long-sustained sound that followed made Alex's eyes tear up.

Stan's hands pressed rhythmically against Andrew's lifeless chest. Alex's stomach twisted into a knot as he watched, unable to look away while shielding Phil. The tension grew as the compressions continued, each thump echoing in the quiet room.

"Come on!" Stan yelled. *"Come! On!"* He refused to give up. "You don't get to die without saying you love him! I know you do, you wanker! *Wake! Up!*" He pounded fiercely on his chest, and for a second, he thought he saw movement. He kept pounding on Andrew, each hit landing more determined than the previous one. "*Wake! Up!*" he yelled, his voice reverberating around the room.

The final pound he delivered made Andrew jerk upwards, gasping for air. He coughed and wheezed; the colour slowly returned to his cheeks. It was instant relief for everyone in the room, but the gravity of the situation lingered like a thick fog.

Phil tore himself free from Alex's embrace, rushing over to Andrew as if his life depended on it. His chest tightened, and for a moment, he thought he was about to go into cardiac arrest—but nothing happened.

He gripped Andrew's face, bringing it closer to his own to give him a searing kiss. The air crackled with tension as their lips met; the world around them blurred into insignificance. It was like a striking flint against steel when fire erupted, a searing blaze that consumed reason and left only desire in its wake. Time ceased to exist. They were lost in each other—their past pain, their separation—obliterated by the heat of their kiss.

Andrew tasted salt; the remnants of tears Phil shed during their time apart. But now, those tears were forgotten. All that mattered was *this moment*, their mouths, their breaths, and their shared hunger. When they finally pulled away, gasping for air, their foreheads touched. Andrew's eyes bore into Phil's, dark and stormy. *"I love you too,"* he whispered, his voice raw. *"Don't think for a second that I didn't."* He cleared his throat. "You found rescue in me and loved me back to life more than once. I love you, 'cause the universe schemed to help me find you."

"You're formidable to the world," Phil replied, smiling as tears glistened in his eyes. "But to me? *You're the world.*" He wrapped his arms around Andrew—a little too tight—as if holding Andrew was the only thing keeping him from disappearing.

Alex and Stan had quietly snuck out of the room to let the two lovebirds reconcile. Once they closed the door, Stan pinned Alex against the wall, holding his hands up in the air in a tight grip. *"Take me,"* he whispered in a low voice.

Alex lifted Stan, hands supporting him under his arse, as Stan's legs curled around his waist. Carrying him into their bedroom, Alex closed the door behind them.

Alfie's eyes shut open. His visual disturbance was what he noticed first. Black and grey fuzzy edges receded slowly once he became more aware of his surroundings. His sight was the first thing he fought to restore, and one by one his senses came back to him, as if his brain had been going through a reboot. The buzz of the background voices started to register. He began to piece together what had happened, touching the bandage covering his shoulder. A numbing sensation rushed in. He heard a slight ringing in his ears.

He could swear someone was speaking to him, but he couldn't make out what was being said. It seemed as if the world was underwater, as if he was *still* underwater. It came rushing back to him like a flood. Everything was moving in slow motion; all the sounds were garbled as if he was stuck listening to a damaged recording. A fog descended over him, but it soon cleared once he saw who was talking to him.

*"Sam?"*

Sam smiled, patting Alfie's legs beneath the blanket. "Good to see you awake, *chief.*"

Alfie shifted slightly. "How long was I out for?"

"A couple of hours."

Alfie noticed the Kite was abnormally quiet. "We no longer flying?"

Sam shook his head. "We're in the middle of a storm, had to make an emergency landing nearby to make sure we wouldn't crash. Cal got us down."

He nodded slowly. "You're watching over me?"

"What can I say, *someone's* gotta do the job."

"Altruistic as ever I see."

Sam chuckled. "Yeah, well, some might say that my *gaggle* of friends and I are untouchable—'cause we're so selfless."

"Please, not *all* of us are magnanimous," he said, disappearing behind his stoic veneer.

"At least *some* still vouch for innocence."

Alfie sighed softly. "I honestly don't get why you all just bluntly allowed me to stay with you after *everything* that has happened."

"Well, you could've betrayed us *then*, but you *still* haven't— I'd say that counts for something. Thanks to you, we know that whatever the others did to the mutants on those islands, they made the serum so powerful that they've created their first unbeatable test subject. That means we need to move fast to retrieve 'em and stop further development. You've given us a *fighting chance*."

Alfie clenched his jaw as acceptance and resignation flickered across his face. "I had to put a stop to 'em. Reading their plans, I couldn't sit by and let 'em destroy the world you've so *desperately* sought to form." He sighed. "Normally I wouldn't have condoned invading anyone's privacy, but our *home* was at stake."

Sam nodded softly. "You know, I haven't called Maddie to talk about this harrowing journey we're on. I mean, *how can I?* After learning all those secrets and plans, the emotional catharsis it'd bring... I can't do that to her when I'm not there to protect her."

"I bet they've started mixing their cleverly veiled allusions with everything we've been through now that we've thwarted part of their plan."

"You're saying I should *contact* Maddie?"

Alfie nodded. He plucked a Reacher out of his pocket, pulling up her contact information. "I've managed to get you a safe line that *can't* be traced." Sam didn't take it. Alfie scoffed; his eyebrows shot up to his hairline. "Come on, mate. You said it yourself. If I *wanted* to betray you, I would've done so by now. You can stop keeping your feelers out."

An uncharacteristic crease grew in Sam's brow, his expression almost schooled. "Allow me to apologise for my *oafish* behaviour." He dialled their number, but nothing happened. "It says this line is expunged."

"*What?*" Alfie took the Reacher from him. "That's not possible."

Sam immediately grew worried—he had ordered Percy to erase her existence if they were ever threatened. "*Something's* wrong. I need to go home."

He turned around, but Alfie grabbed his sleeve. "We can sleuth and hypothesise all we want, but I *know* my brother. He got 'em somewhere safe, both Maddie *and* Zack. I know about the order you gave him."

"How can you deduce it so easily then? Try Percy."

Alfie did as Sam told him, dialling Percy's number next. He heard the same words being spoken. "He must've erased his own credentials too. That *still* doesn't mean anything."

"Is there *anyone* we can still trust to check in on 'em?"

"Not that I know of." He sighed. "Look, I get you wanna go back immediately. But we've got two more islands to liberate—*then* we can go home. If we go back *now*, we risk it all."

"If we don't go *right now,* we risk my family *and* yours. You wanna lose Percy *too* after losing Albus? This storm could take days."

"Precisely. We *can't* even fly right now. We gotta wait regardless. If we leave, we'll end up dead. How's that gonna help 'em out?"

Sam let out a low growl, gripping his hair with his hand.

Alfie knew about President Goldlib's death, heard it via his comms right before he landed. He surmised that it might be too much for Sam to handle. He knew it would only stir up more fear and frustration, so he chose to stay silent and make idle conversation instead. "How's your arm?"

Sam looked at his stump, sighing. "Progressing."

"How about we get you one of those *nice hooks*? You'll always have a weapon on you."

Sam chuckled wryly and gave Alfie a lacklustre salute in mockery.

"Lads, you're gonna wanna see this," a voice crackled over the intercom.

Sam looked at Alfie, who gave him a nod. Sam left him be, while Alfie hoped it wasn't a broadcast about Henry's death.

# CHAPTER FORTY-SIX

All the passengers on board, except for Alfie and Andrew, looked out through the window at the island in the distance. It hadn't been visible before due to the dark, stormy clouds, but as the storm briefly parted, the island became visible. As far as they could see, it was completely covered by a thick, amorphous layer of ice. The ice sheets stretched across the vast expanse of the island.

"It looks like it's been there for quite a while," Tim observed. "There's no way *anyone* could've survived that."

"You think they've given up on their plan entirely?" Stan asked. "As in, they were so threatened that they killed off even their *most* prized assets?"

"Looks like it. Survival odds like those take a big nosedive after about twenty-four hours. I'd say it's been there for two days at least."

Val scoffed at him. "How can you even tell? It looks like ice to me, and *all* ice looks the same."

Tim offered him his scanning device, refusing to start an argument. "I can see the layers. It's *relatively* new."

Sam was already prepping to leave, grunting with effort as he tried to pack.

"What the bloody hell do you think you're doing?" Tim asked him, rushing over to him as he ripped the bag from his hands. "Are you outta your mind?"

"I can't reach Maddie, Tim. Her file's *gone*." He paused. "*Something's* wrong, and the quicker we get those lads to safety, the better. We can go home, and I can find my family."

Val scolded him, walking over to him. "Those lads are *dead*. Nerdy over here said so himself. There's nothin' we can do for 'em. I say we cut our losses, head to island number six, and get the bloody hell outta here."

Seb strolled over to Sam and Tim, feeling for Sam's bag and taking it back from Tim. "Look, with everyone who's gone, our city's lucky to have Sam. That's *why* he's gotta go."

"He's lost an arm! He's got no proper way to defend himself! No, I'm not leaving you—!"

Sam eyed him narrowly. "It's not in your power to stop me or save my life. I had to let you go too, *remember*? And from the looks of things around here," he said, gripping Tim's shoulder, "there are *others* you can help save. I decided to trust you to go down there and survive, and it's now time for you to do the same for *me*, trust me the same way you forced me to trust you. You know I'm capable, even with an arm less."

Tears formed in Tim's eyes. "You *won't* survive. You haven't healed properly. The cold could cause even *more* damage."

"It's a risk worth taking. I gotta go *home*."

Tim sighed, trailing off to the emergency cabinet. He walked back to Sam once he grabbed a small plastic cylinder. "In here's a shot of epinephrine, also known as pure adrenaline. If anyone down there's on thin ice, *pun not intended*, this will kick their whole body into overdrive. Allows their chance of survival to be about fifty-fifty." He then tossed Sam a syringe and a small glass bottle full of dark brown liquid. Sam squinted at the label. "It's a bottle of morphine. *Just in case.*"

Sam nodded as he took it from Tim, eyeing the crowd standing in front of him. "Who's coming down with me?"

Jonathan walked around the table on which Henry was prepped. He grew impatient as he tapped with his foot, his arms crossed. His veins were basically bulging out of his skin. *"What's taking so long?"*

A smaller guy emerged from the shadows, holding a syringe filled with a sickly-looking black liquid. "I'm not sure this is a good idea, sir," he said. "This serum hasn't been tested yet, and there's *no* telling what could happen to—"

"I didn't ask you *anything*. Shut your bloody mouth and just do it!"

The guy nodded hastily, walking over to Henry's dead body. "I know he's already succumbed, but if this goes wrong, you'll have, how should I put this... *jacked-up berserk* on your hands, sir."

Jonathan drew a handgun from his belt, pointing it at the guy. *"Do it."*

The guy nodded, popping the cap off the injector. He jabbed the needle into Henry's thigh. They waited a moment. And another. *And another.*

Nothing happened.

Jonathan roared loudly, slamming his fist on the nearby table. "Why's it *not* working?"

The guy took a few steps back, afraid of Jonathan's outburst. "Well, sir, I warned you, it's not been tested—"

Jonathan lifted the guy by his collar, his tiny legs dangling frantically. "You said you had the *T-Serum* ready! You said it'd *work*!"

"No, sir, I never said that! I was very specific that it might *not* have the desired effect!"

Jonathan held the handgun against the guy's throat. "Give me *one* good reason why I shouldn't pull this trigger *right here, right now!*"

Henry jolted straight up, his eyes wide and pupils blown. He thrashed wildly, far stronger than the guy had expected. He stared in disbelief at Henry who ripped off his own arm. Other Troopers tried to grab hold of him to restrain him, but he fought back violently. They watched as his arm grew into a deadly-looking glaive, digging right into one of the Troopers' skins. Spit foamed at his mouth, dripping down his chin as the other Trooper struggled against him.

The guy searched Henry's eyes for any sign of recognition, but he let out a feral snarl instead, lunging towards him.

A single bullet shot called out.

Henry stood frozen mid-lunge as he looked at the hole in his chest. His breaths blew ragged through bared teeth as he focused his intention on Jonathan. His chest readjusted itself and formed a hydraulic-powered *lung* that hung outside the body, much to Jonathan's surprise.

"It's *beautiful*," Jonathan exclaimed. "It's *magnificent!*"

Henry's body was covered in deep gashes—evidence of the surgical enhancements done to him, allowing the T-Serum to take over once injected. His face was distorted and twisted. Some parts of his skin overlapped while some parts were stapled down. The glaive had grown from his pectoral muscle, adjusted with claws and needles that could be retracted at any given time.

Jonathan shot Henry in the back, watching as a row of metallic spikes formed along his spine. He smiled. "With Imogen and now Henry, we'll be *unstoppable*. No matter how many times they'll shoot her, she'll regenerate her limbs. But *him*... he'll *never* stop creating weapons from the sheer number of bodily molecules. He's *perfection!*"

He lifted the guy off his feet, spinning him around the room, laughing maniacally and blissfully.

They set foot on land, embraced by the frigid cold. The stark whiteness of the landscape stretched endlessly before them, a canvas unmarked by colour or warmth.

Sam ambled through the frozen tundra, with Ray following suit, his carefree gait that of the untroubled. With his fire powers, he ignorantly believed he was the hero of heaven on Earth. Sam's breath was visible in the icy air, dancing around him like a ghostly halo.

Stan trailed closely behind the two of them, his eyes ever vigilant for signs of danger or *any kind of sustenance*, should it be necessary. His machete gleamed under the pale sun, pointing the way through the labyrinth of ice and snow.

Alex, Val, and Reggie moved behind them in a unified rhythm, their heavy footsteps muffled by the thick blanket beneath them.

The wind picked up, playing with the snowflakes as if they were the most delicate of leaves, swirling them into mesmerising patterns that danced and shifted endlessly. It was calm. *Almost too calm.*

"We *know* we're walking into a trap, right?" Stan said, eyeing their surroundings like a hawk.

"Most likely," Sam replied, unfazed.

"I bet that boy of yours is a whiz with traps. I bet he can set up plenty of 'em and dismantle many of 'em," Val spoke up.

"If he were here," Stan replied sharply, knowing Val meant Tim, "sure, he can assist us from up there, but that only goes so far. We're mostly on our own, meaning we've gotta watch *every step* we take. Understood?"

Before Val could respond, Alex interrupted. "The storm's picking up again." His teeth were chattering as the biting wind whipped past him. "We should head back or make a fire at least to warm ourselves up. I *don't* wanna turn into an icicle."

Ray touched Alex's shoulder once he fell in line with him, taking a deep breath to radiate warmth at a prudent pace. Alex's exhaled breath misted in the frigid air. The flames danced in Ray's eyes as he lowered his hand. "Don't mention it."

It was deafening quiet, apart from the occasional sound and crunch of their boots on the frozen ground.

Ray stopped abruptly, causing Val to crash into him. "Oi! What the bloody hell are you doin'?"

The air grew colder, and the hair on the back of Ray's neck stood on end. It was as if the very essence of winter had condensed around them. The area faded into a blur as the temperature dropped drastically. Ray made a flame appear in his hand, but it flickered erratically, casting eerie shadows on the trees.

The ice beneath them cracked with an ominous sound. Sam's heart skipped a beat as he felt the ground give way. Before he could scream, they were plunged into an icy abyss, the world around them swallowed by the cold.

The rush of freezing water filled Sam's ears, muffling the sound of the ice shattering. His body went rigid with shock. He clung to Ray who tried his best to warm the water, being the lifeline in the icy embrace.

Ray's grip was firm, his eyes focused and determined as he chanted under his breath. The water grew colder, and Sam could feel the life seeping out of him. Panic set in, his breath coming in ragged gasps. The flame in Ray's hand grew, not flickering but pulsing with a warm, golden light that began to spread through the water, allowing the others to swim to safety and climb out.

But Ray and Sam were still stuck. The ice above them shimmered and thickened, trapping them in a crystalline prison. It felt as if Sam were frozen in time, his heart pounding in unison with the creaking of the ice that echoed through the vast, silent cave. Ray's voice grew stronger, his words clearer. "We've gotta get outta here!"

He focused his gaze on the thickening ice above them, and the flame in his hand roared to life, reaching out like a beacon in the frozen dark. The ice above began to melt, but not fast enough. Despite the others running around, trying to find something for them to grasp onto, the cold was seeping into Sam's bones. He felt his strength waning.

"Ray, I don't think I can hold on much longer," he murmured, his voice barely audible.

With a fierce determination, Ray turned to Sam, his eyes alight with fire. "You can do this, Sam. You've survived a bloody amputation for a reason, and you wanna go home, *don't you*?" He shook Sam slightly as he began to lose consciousness. "I *won't* let you go so easily."

Ray's hand tightened around Sam's, and he felt a surge of warmth flood through him, chasing away the numbness. Sam slowly came to. Together, they stared up at the melting ice, Sam's breath coming in short, painful gasps. But then the light grew brighter, the heat more intense. Just when Sam thought he couldn't bear it anymore, the ice shattered. *We're free.*

Ray swam towards the others, practically dragging Sam along with him. Alex and Stan hauled Sam up, while Val and Reggie assisted Ray. Alex immediately hugged Sam as if his life depended on it, rubbing his back to provide him with whatever warmth he could spare. His breath misted in the cold as he exhaled. Stan folded his hands over Sam's, rubbing his frostbitten hands together.

Reggie offered Sam a flask, and he eagerly sipped from it.

"You good?" Val asked Ray, who nodded.

"My body temperature regenerates based on the environment," Ray said, though he sternly ignored the biting wind that cut through his clothes.

"Oi, lads!"

They all turned towards Reggie, who stared at three bodies frozen solid in the icy wall. However, the ice was different—unnatural in both colour and texture.

"It's not even as cold as real ice," Stan said, who had joined Reggie. "And it's got *way* too much of a white shine to be transparent. What the bloody hell's this contraption?"

A sudden, intense light reflected off the ice, blinding them all. They threw their hands up to shield their eyes, and when the glare subsided, they saw a figure standing before them—tall and unnaturally still. He was a little chubby around the edges, his curly ginger pompadour falling back into place. The ice around the figure began to melt, revealing a human form.

"What the—?"

Stan's voice trailed off as the boy took a step forward, his hazel eyes fluttering open. He looked around, his eyes wide with confusion. His skin was pale, almost translucent, and his clothes were tattered, as if he had been fighting a clawed creature.

They stared in disbelief at the boy whose eyes glowed with fiery intensity. Ray noticed, immediately tensing up. The ice beneath his boots crackled with heat. The frozen air around them grew warmer, and the boy began to move, stumbling. Ray's body erupted in flames—not burning, but glowing—casting an eerie warmth across the other frozen bodies.

Everyone else stumbled back as Ray raised his arms. The ice shattered into a thousand shards, sending the bodies tumbling into the freezing water. He took a deep breath, and with a roar that seemed to come from deep within, he unleashed a torrent of fire, melting the icy water entirely.

The boy took another step forward, his eyes fixed on the group as he lent the two boys a hand to climb out. The frozen lake rumbled with newfound life, as if responding to an ancient call. The two boys were pulled towards the lakeside, while the others watched from afar, their teeth still chattering.

They watched as Ray walked over to the boy, a being of fire and ice that fused as one. Ray left a trail of steam in his wake, while the boy remained like an artistic snowflake. Once they stood in the centre, Ray smiled and hugged the boy, diminishing his flame. "It's good to see you, Vince."

"Likewise, Ray."

Vince's body turned back to a normal colour once Ray embraced him. Looking over at Val and Reggie, he smiled. "You two rascals joined too, huh?"

Reggie hugged him next, but Val stayed put. As Vince approached him, they stared each other down.

"*Vincent.*"

"*Valentine.*"

Then Sam smiled, shaking his head. "As I live and breathe." He walked over to hug Nate and Rick, but Nate stared at him in shock.

"What happened to your arm?"

"Long story. But it's good to see you."

Nate hesitantly hugged Sam, unsure how to react or feel about Sam's missing arm.

"And *you*," Sam said, letting go of Nate, "Tim's gonna be thralled to see you."

Rick hugged him, laughing. "I bet. I kinda missed my sidekick."

"Pretty sure you're *his* sidekick."

"We'll see about that." Rick introduced himself to Val, Ray, and Reggie. "Name's Richard, but I go by Rick mostly."

As Ray cleared a spot free of ice for them to sit and have a chat, Sam let Tim know they had found three more, *alive and well.*

# CHAPTER FORTY-SEVEN

Stan blearily poured coffee into mugs for everyone, passing them out. He remembered the fight he had with Nate before they departed, and the thought of him potentially frozen to death had lingered in his mind. They weren't happy thoughts.

"So," Sam said, allowing a long pause to pass through while he exchanged a loaded glance with Vince, "care to explain how you're *not* dead? Did you turn this place into an ice age?"

"No," Vince answered, sipping his coffee. "I prolonged our lives hoping someone like Ray would stop by to allow me to unfreeze us safely. When the ice came, I only knew of one way to save Nate and Rick. They trusted me to—"

"Didn't have much of a choice otherwise," Rick sharply interrupted him. "It was either trust you and *hope* we'd survive—or die a horrible death."

Vince sighed, nodding reluctantly. "I hadn't tried something like this before, so it was a risk. One I *had* to take."

"Your other powers don't work no more then?" Val asked.

"*Other* powers?" Sam looked back and forth between Val and Vince. "What *other* powers?"

Vince turned away from him, his expression maudlin as he rested his hand on his makeshift baton hooked through his belt. "I can manipulate time."

"*How?*" Stan asked. "Can you look into the future or go back to the past?"

"No. I can accelerate it up to five minutes, slow it for a few seconds, and stop it for a maximum of ten minutes." He got up. "To demonstrate." He focused on Val specifically, slowing his movement to take a sip of his coffee. "If I would've wanted to shoot him, and make sure I aim right where I should, I can slow him down and shoot him straight in the chest. No more misses, *guaranteed*."

Alex clicked his tongue, seemingly impressed by this. "Won't take long until we've got an army to take these rascals down *for good*."

"*Rascals*? You mean those bloody hideous-looking things that are zombified and *fabricated*?" Vince asked.

Sam nodded, aiming at his chest. "One of 'em got you?"

"Yeah, I wasn't paying attention. It was just there. *Poof*, slashed me."

Stan put his empty coffee mug down on the ground, making enough noise for the others to look towards him. "I say we continue this conversation before anyone shows up, and before this island throws any other unnatural disaster at us. We still need to get *all three* of 'em to safety. So far, we've only succeeded twice with just two of 'em."

"I don't like the sound of those odds," Rick exclaimed, touching his acne-covered cheek. "You haven't even told us what's going on yet, 'cause you clearly seem to know more than *we* do."

"I know we owe you many explanations," Sam said, "and I wish I had time to tell 'em all. But I've gotta recuse myself for now."

The serene silence was shattered by a sound that seemed to resonate from the very core of the Earth. A low, ominous rumble grew louder, vibrating the ground beneath their feet.

"And this is proof that they *can* in fact hear us," Stan said, getting up hastily. *"Good job, Sam."*

Before Sam could counter Stan's comment, the rumble grew into a roar, a monstrous crescendo that drowned out the muffled tread of the others already packing their stuff after hearing the first sign of something unusual.

"This your official recusal?" Vince scoffed slightly, though his eyes were a surprising mix of curiosity and fear. He sniffed the air, and his expression grew grave. *"Avalanche."*

The ice beneath them trembled, and the first crack appeared like a lightning bolt cutting through the frozen sea.

"Run!" Alex's alarm echoed through the cave and the others picked up their pace to finish packing. They instinctively moved away from the fissure that grew with alarming speed as they made their way back to the top.

Panic began to set in as the ground around them started to shift and shudder. With Vince's warning, they knew *what* was coming: a force of nature that *no creature*, no matter *how* mutated or transformed, could withstand. Sam looked over his shoulder as they began to run, his heart racing as the crack grew into a gaping maw, threatening to swallow them whole.

The sound grew deafening, a cacophony of breaking ice and thunderous echoes that seemed to come from every direction. A wall of snow and ice, a frozen tsunami, began to rise in the distance, gaining speed and power with every passing second.

Their pace turned into a full sprint; their bodies propelled by pure instinct. Val, less encumbered by fear, took the lead, zigzagging through the tumult, the others following in close pursuit.

His eyes darted around, searching for *any* sign of safety, *any* place to hide from the impending doom.

They surged forward without stopping, lurching and bucking, making every step a battle for balance. Val was steadfast in his movements, his eyes never leaving the path ahead.

The avalanche grew closer, a thundering beast of white and blue, consuming everything in its path. The cold wind grew sharp with ice shards, stinging their eyes and faces. The air grew thick with the scent of fear and the acrid bite of what Vince would've deemed *ancient ice.*

The group's cries grew more desperate as the icy jaws of the avalanche snapped shut on Rick, swallowing him without a trace.

"Rick!" Nate yelled, trying to run back for him, but Reggie dragged him along by his sleeve, knowing Rick was gone.

Sam's heart hammered in his chest like a wild drum. He spotted a towering ice formation ahead, jutting out like a lone sentinel from the otherwise flat landscape. Val steered towards it; his instincts honed by a lifetime of survival that he couldn't recall but knew he possessed. The rest of the group followed; their eyes fixed on the potential shelter.

The ice cracked and groaned around them, the ground tilting and dropping like a ship on a tumultuous sea. As they approached the tower, the avalanche was almost upon them, a relentless force that seemed to have a malicious intent to consume them. With a mighty effort, Sam picked up speed, his muscles straining. Val's eyes remained glued to the ice tower, a beacon of hope amidst the chaos.

The tower grew larger, the cracks in the ice closer, the roar of the avalanche deafening. At the last moment, Val skidded to a stop, his legs digging into the frozen ground. He leaned into the tower, his body acting as a shield between the group and the onrushing torrent. The world around them went whiter than white, the air filled with a blizzard of ice and snow. Sam buried his nose in his shirt to keep the stinging particles at bay. The pressure was immense, pushing against them like a giant hand, threatening to crush them into the frozen earth.

And then, just as quickly as it had begun, the world went still. The roar faded to a distant murmur, the ground beneath them no longer a living, breathing thing. Sam cautiously lifted his head, blinking the snow from his eyes. The avalanche had passed, leaving a wake of destruction that stretched back as far as they could see.

They had made it to the tower, huddled together, their forms indistinct in the swirling snow.

With a tremble, Sam moved, his legs unsteady from the exertion. Val gently nudged Sam to his feet, and they emerged from their icy sanctuary. The world had changed, a fresh layer of snow and ice covering the earlier layer of the island, erasing any trace of their desperate flight.

The group looked around, their eyes filled with relief and weariness. The storm *had passed*, but the ice age *remained*. Indifferent to their struggles, it served as a reminder of the precariousness of their lives.

Yet amidst the silence, a new sound grew, faint but unmistakable. A mournful cry pierced the air, a call of pain and loss. Sam's ears swivelled, and he recognised the voice of Stan in distress. Without hesitation, Sam began to trudge back into the storm, his footsteps leaving the first marks in the fresh snow.

Nate looked at him, his own fear momentarily forgotten in the face of Sam's unwavering bravery. He followed, his determination to help rekindled by the continuing trials of their *never-ending journey*.

As they reached Stan, huddled over something they couldn't see yet, Sam rounded the corner to face him. He noticed how rosy his cheeks were. With the wind nipping at their noses, Stan's turned a shade pinker.

The snow was falling fast, painting the world in an even deeper monochrome hue.

Stan looked up; panic etched across his features. "He got swallowed by a hidden crevice!"

Sam heard a muffled cry for help. A cold knot formed in his stomach, his face a mix of concern and shock. The crisp air grew tense near the edge of the precipice none of them had noticed yet. Sam's breath formed tiny clouds around his mouth, swallowing hard. He braced himself for what he would find.

He knelt to peer into the crevice. The sight that met his eyes was one he would never forget. Through the swirling snow, he could just make out the shape of a person, half-buried in a sea of white. The only colour in the stark scene was the crimson stain spreading across the snow.

His heart raced as he shouted to the others far behind him. "Alex's trapped beneath the snow! We've gotta get him outta there!"

The others, despite having stayed behind, sprang into action, giving each other urgent and clipped commands. They worked together with renewed vigour, their movements swift and efficient despite the biting cold. The weight of the situation settled heavily on Sam's shoulders as he began to dig with one arm.

The snow was dense and heavy, resisting their efforts to uncover Alex. With every dig, he felt the panic rising within him.

The minutes stretched out like hours, each one filled with the desperate rhythm of digging and breathing. Sam's muscles burned with the effort, but he didn't dare stop, despite the pain he felt. The person beneath the snow was his friend, *his family*, and *every second* counted.

As they worked, Sam felt the first stirrings of doubt. *What if we're too late? What if the snow has already claimed him?* The thought was unbearable, and he pushed it aside, focusing on the task at hand.

Finally, a hand reached out from the snowy depths, and Sam grabbed it with a gasp of relief. The others joined in, and together they pulled Alex to the surface. His eyes were closed, and his skin was an alarming shade of blue. Sam felt for a pulse, his own heart pounding in his ears. It was there—*faint but steady*. He was alive. *Barely.*

*We've gotta get him to shelter and warmth, and fast. The Kite is too far away from here, and our comms don't work anymore.*

Sam glanced around, his mind racing. The wind howled around him, but he didn't let it deter him. They had to survive until they could reach the Kite, and that meant protecting Alex from the merciless embrace of the winter storm. His breath puffed out in clouds as he tried to keep his breathing under control.

Then, he heard the sound. *The Kite.* He looked up, and a wave of relief washed over him that was almost too great to bear. He waved at the Kite while the others used their flashlights to attract its attention.

It felt as if they were in a cocoon of safety despite the harsh wilderness surrounding them. The storm raged on, but with the Kite in sight, Sam was determined to conquer it. Then, the world around him fell silent as he heard a faint, gurgling growl. *Please, no.*

He turned around slowly, staring at Imogen, who now had nearly impenetrable armour-like skin. Her legs were digitigrade, and her arms were drastically longer than the last time he had seen her. Her claws, now two fingers shorter, looked sharper, coated in a sickly-looking green liquid.

Her head was now protected by an armour-like plate to stop any of their previously launched head attacks. *We were so close. So close.*

# CHAPTER FORTY-EIGHT

With Alex in a comatose state and in desperate need of warmth, there was no time to fight Imogen. All they could do was hold her off until Alex was safely aboard the Kite, then have someone man the turret to keep Imogen at bay so the rest of them could get to safety too.

A coil of heavy rope unfurled in front of Sam. The box would take too long to lower itself. *"Go,"* he told Stan, who quickly secured his end of the rope around Alex's waist. Meanwhile, up in the Kite, Cal fastened his end to a piece of rebar.

Val ripped the pin from a grenade he had stolen from their last-resort stash, hurling it towards the onrushing Imogen. A moment later, it detonated with an ear-shattering bang.

It triggered the avalanche to continue its destructive wake, coming down the snow-covered slope to their right.

"Position her in front of it so it can trap her!" Val yelled incredulously, watching as the explosion barely ripped through her. The shrapnel that had burst through her flesh didn't leave a fountain of gore and pulverised bones behind, as Val had hoped, but instead began to regenerate.

Stan's machete lay on the ground, dropped as he went up in the air with Alex in his arms. Sam grabbed the machete and gave it a few experimental swings, feeling the heft of the blade as it cut through the air with ease.

Despite the rumbling that should've warned her, Imogen opened her mouth to reveal sharp teeth, saliva dripping down. The snow slammed down on her as she swiped futilely at it, her snarl echoing through the falling snow, which covered her little by little.

*"Now!"* Val yelled, his eyes wide as saucers.

Vince grabbed the metal bar that Cal had dropped from above, freezing it instantly. With a flick of his wrist, Val sent the bar hurtling through the air, skewering her leg with a sickening crunch. The ice found its way past her armour—if only momentarily.

Ray's hand ignited with a fiery glow as he aimed for her other leg. Despite her armour, it began to burn slowly, the acrid smell permeating the air. It turned Sam's stomach, making him gag.

Reggie took a deep breath and focused, his body blending with the snow like a chameleon. Once Imogen was unaware of him sneaking closer, he slashed at her leg with his knife and forced her to the ground.

"*Go*, we'll take it from here," Val told Sam, who stood ready to defend himself if it were to be necessary.

Sam looked at the rope that had lowered again, then stared at the four fighting Imogen. He felt guilty leaving them to fight the battle *he had started*, the battle he *couldn't stop* from happening.

"Go! What are you waitin' for?" Val asked annoyedly, reaching out with his mind to search for anything he could use as a weapon.

Nate took it upon himself to force Sam towards the rope, and together they were pulled up to safety.

Val grabbed a piece of metal from the Kite, one he knew could be spared. He let it hover in the air for a moment before flinging it at her with all his might. It sent her flying.

Ray's flames roared to life, forming a wall of fire between them and Imogen. Vince slowed time around the fire, giving them a brief respite. Once Sam was safely in the Kite, the box made its way to the remaining four. They got in quickly.

Val noticed the fire wouldn't hold her forever. Despite the barricade they had built, his determination to stop her from chasing after them sharpened his focus. With a flick of telekinesis, he sent the same piece of metal he had used against her hurtling towards her head. The blow struck, leaving her temporarily disoriented.

Once they were all safe and sound, the Kite took off.

Stan had wrapped Alex in warm blankets, looking around for anything he could use to start a fire. Luckily, Ray came to the rescue once he had rid himself of his pack, kneeling next to Alex. He formed a warm circle of firelight around him. Along with the blanket and the warmth of Stan's body encompassing him, Alex's eyelids fluttered open. His gaze locked on Stan, and in that instant, the fog cleared.

"Hello, *stranger*."

Stan felt his eyes fill with tears as he leaned down, his heart racing with a mix of fear and joy. He had never been so grateful for a simple, beautiful sight. Alex's grip tightened around Stan's hand, but Stan ignored it, pulling him into a fierce embrace.

Stan's heart raced as Alex pulled back, looking at Stan again whose eyes were brimming with unshed tears. Alex leaned in, his intent unmistaable, and Stan closed the distance. Their lips met in a kiss that was desperate and hungry, a declaration of love and relief that seemed to echo the very beating of their hearts.

Ray lipped away quietly, careful not to intrude on their moment of rare intimacy.

The kiss was a whirlwind of emotion—a reunion of souls torn apart, if only for a moment. Stan's arms wrapped tightly around Alex, holding him as if afraid he might slip away again. Alex felt the wetness of Stan's tears against his cheek, and the sensation jolted him back to reality.

He pulled back, breathless, his eyes searching Stan's for answers. "What happened?"

Stan's smile was tremulous, and he brushed a thumb over Alex's bottom lip. "You almost tried to leave before we got pizza."

Alex chuckled. "That date I still owe ya? How dare I try to leave ya behind in a dark world without promised pizza?"

Stan tried his best to see the humour of it, but he was still shaken up by the incident. "Like the stars need the sky to shine," he said, "I'll *always* need you to make my heart do the same."

"I'm right here," Alex declared, wiping away Stan's tears. "I'm whole, happy, *and* alive, and that's all thanks to ya. With ya, I know what I need to come *home* to." Slowly, he reached into his pocket and pulled out a tiny box.

Stan gasped at the sight of it.

"Stan, I've noticed in these past few weeks that every moment, whether that'd be awake or in my dreams, I find myself yearning for ya. Yer presence is the only thing in the world that makes mine go round." He slowly opened the box, revealing a ring he had forged himself with Tim's help before they set out on this adventure. "Stan, I know we've had our ups and downs, but every moment with ya... it has been worth it. Yer the one I wanna share the rest of my life with." He took Stan's hand in his. "There are many ways that can lead to happiness, but all I need is ya by my side, and my happiness is unbreakable." He stared straight into Stan's eyes, welling up with tears that were on the verge of release. "*Will ya marry me, Stanley?*" he asked, his voice trembling with emotion.

The reality of the moment crashed over Stan. "*Alex,*" he whispered, his voice trembling. He had dreamed of this moment countless times, but the suddenness of it left him breathless— especially after everything they had been through.

Alex took his hand, the warmth of his touch anchoring Stan in the moment. "I know this is unexpected, but I couldn't wait anymore. What happened to me today made me realise that I need ya to know... yer the most important person in my world."

Stan's eyes filled with tears as he searched Alex's earnest gaze. The proposal wasn't the grand, public spectacle he had always envisioned, but here, in this quiet, intimate space, it felt *perfect*.

"*Yes*," he said, his voice barely above a whisper. "*Yes, I'll marry you.*"

Alex slid the ring onto his finger, the cool metal a stark contrast to the heat of his skin. Stan pulled Alex towards him, kissing him as if the world had stopped spinning just for them. His heart felt like it might burst with happiness. And in that moment, Stan *knew* he had made the right choice.

"No way!" Seb yelped enthusiastically, clapping his hands as he heard the news. "We're getting a *wedding*!" He grinned as he knew Tim was standing next to him. "You *lost* the bet. *Pay up!*"

Tim sighed, taking a bill from his pocket, giving it to Seb.

"A *bet*?" Sam asked wearily, the excitement he had felt slowly fading into confusion.

"Yeah, I thought you'd be the one to propose to Maddie before Alex or Stan," Tim answered earnestly. But his words caught in his throat as he watched Sam's face fall. "Sorry, I—"

Sam waved him off, quickly changing the subject. "How are we doing with the coordinates for the last island?"

Tim sighed softly. "I've tried a simple triangulation of radio waves, but that was a little imprecise. So, I've tried the pseudo-range multilateration to get us something specific." He sat down behind his laptop. "Once I've identified the correct frequency, I can run it through my self-developed program to pinpoint those coordinates."

"*Radio frequency*? You're tellin' me they've been talkin' about 'em?" Val asked, entering the room.

"Not quite, it's a frequency I've intercepted from Alfie, per his request and allowance." He pointed at the screen. "Alfie told us they *most likely* control the crew behind this, and so we know *how* important Alfie's connection is to their very existence. They've been asking for minute-to-minute updates on his progress, but he hasn't responded all that much." He typed as Alfie entered the room, assisted by Ray. "And so, if Alfie seeks contact with 'em, I can isolate *their* incoming and *our* outgoing frequency signal. I can triangulate that to a nearby ground-based—or well—*air-based* detection facility. That in turn should allow me to geolocate their longitude and latitude, which would lead us to the last island."

"You're thinking the last island is their *homebase*?" Reggie asked.

"Not quite their homebase, more like *ground zero*. The easiest island to reach, in a sense."

Val paced in circles. "So, you're sayin' that the island with Imogen's mum was just a distraction? To keep anyone from findin' the last island—the only places they can do their research?"

"Precisely."

A loud crackle drew their attention to Alfie's radio. A chilling but familiar voice droned from the small speaker.

*"I see you've been trying to hack us."*

"Jonathan," Sam whispered under his breath.

*"I can assure you, you don't wanna travel to that last island. You might not like what you'll find there."*

"Screw you," Val said, "we're done with you toyin' with us. Give us the last three boys and we *might* consider lettin' you walk away."

For a moment, there was an incredulous silence, then Jonathan laughed. *"The offer I'm about to make you... it's more than fair, trust me. If you're not interested, go ahead and head to the island. But don't say I didn't warn you."*

"Please," Val scoffed, "next you're gonna tell us this moment of reprieve is meant to give us some perspective."

*"You're way smarter than you led us believe, Valentine."*

Tim pushed Val away from the radio. "Look, we just wanna get a full picture of this research you've been doing, and what the *true* purpose is. You're not exactly forthcoming, you know."

Sam knew what Tim was doing, since it was clear that these coordinates wouldn't lead to the island, but to Jonathan's whereabouts. They had to keep him online for as long as they could while Tim figured out his exact location.

*"How about you drop this suit of yours—with prejudice? I'll offer you a ten year's salary in one go as severance. On top of that, I'll add a sterling reference to all your resumes so you can seek work elsewhere."*

"And if we *don't* accept?" Sam asked, eyeing Tim.

*"If you accept this offer, I promise we won't need to bring up pesky little felonies to the TI6."*

Sam gasped audibly. "You *wouldn't*."

*"Oh, trust me, I most definitely would. See, here's another thing I, as your unofficial superior, have to offer... secrets. The kinda information that ranges from politically priceless to... personally interesting. Like, say, the location of your loved ones."*

Tim gave Sam a thumbs up, but Sam was sucked into Jonathan's scheme. "*Which* loved ones?"

Jonathan laughed uproariously. *"I'll tell if you turn around."*

Before Sam could answer, Val smashed the radio to pieces with a fire extinguisher. "He's playin' with you to throw you off your game. And he *did*." Val grabbed Sam by the shoulders, forcing him to meet his eyes. "Whoever he's talkin' about, he's *lyin'. No one's* in danger. Bloody wankers like him love makin' their enemies suffer. And that's what we've always been to him—*enemies.* Don't fall for it, Sam."

Sam nodded slowly, hoping Val was right. But his gut feeling told him otherwise. He *knew* Jonathan wasn't lying. He *knew* something was off. And Val robbed him of the chance to learn the exact details.

# CHAPTER FORTY-NINE

Having intercepted Jonathan's coordinates, Tim pinpointed the location a few miles from Zacropolis, in what appeared to be an industrial neighbourhood on the outskirts of a small town.

"That place looks awesome," Reggie said, looking over Tim's shoulder at the image he pulled up. "Like a big echo-y space with piles of metal crap that can be handy for us to win a fight with. It's like they've located themselves there to be knocked over by us." He cracked his knuckles.

"Oi, not so fast, *fangirl*," Val said, "that's *precisely* what they want. They *know* we can use that place to our advantage. There'll be boobytraps literally *everywhere*."

"Val's right," Tim said, "it smells like a trap. We need to lure 'em out."

Ray crossed his arms. "And *how* do you intend on doing that?"

"I know a way," Andrew said, back in his wheelchair with Phil pushing him. "I can shapeshift into one of 'em, sneak inside and blow the joint to bits. They'll be forced to retreat elsewhere. We'll follow 'em to their new base, and strike there."

"And what if that *new place* is just as guarded as a trap?" Seb asked him.

"Then we go for *plan c*."

Ray scoffed at him. "*Which is?*"

Andrew sighed softly, bracing himself for all the reactions he would get. "We drop a bomb on it."

"And what, trade hundreds of lives for the one we need to kill? *No, thanks*," Tim replied.

"There are two of 'em," Alfie said, "Mister X *and* Jonathan. We still dunno *where* Mister X's hiding place is. If we were to drop a bomb on Jonathan, we'd still need to find Mister X before he can flee."

Vince stepped forward. "He might be onto something though. We could reverse-engineer their current location so we can backtrack."

Tim smiled. "We could essentially arm the *mother bomb* to disarm 'em. 'Cause if there was ever a right time for a little lamb to walk into the lion's den—"

"We must do it when the lion isn't home," Vince finished his sentence.

The others stared at the two of them in disbelief. *"Great, as if we didn't have enough nerd talk already,"* Val whispered under his breath, though loud enough for everyone to hear.

Tim ignored him. "I'll have to clear that area unit by unit."

"Get on with it," Sam told him, "we'll round up the last boys on the island so we can plan our attack."

"I'm coming with you," Nate said.

"Me too," Cal replied.

Sam nodded, looking at the others. Val, Reggie and Ray decided to join them while Vince would stay behind with Tim.

*Just one more island. Just one more. It's only one more,* Sam kept telling himself to maintain his sanity. *One more.*

The moment they set foot on the island; Sam noticed something different about the silence. There was no sound of any wind, even the ocean was soundless. The sky turned dark within a matter of seconds, though they had landed in the middle of the day.

"That's not normal, *right?*" Nate said quietly, holding his shotgun ready.

"No, *definitely* not," Sam replied. "Keep your eyes peeled. I think they've already begun to set the destruction of this place in motion."

In the distance, Ray noticed two crosses that were erected, stopping the group to point at them. *"Over there."*

They warily headed over to the crosses, finding a shovel lying right next to one of them. It was all a bit too coincidental. They all knew what they had to do next, but none of them were sure if they were ready to face the truth buried beneath the earth.

*"You don't wanna travel to that last island. You might not like what you'll find there."* Jonathan's words echoed in Sam's mind.

The shovel felt heavier than Nate expected as he grabbed it. Rain poured down, making the handle slick in his grip. He took a deep breath, steeling himself for the task ahead while the others watched in tense silence. Each plunge into the sodden ground sent a wave of unease through them all. The rain intensified, plastering Nate's hair to his face and soaking through his clothes. *But he didn't stop.*

The rhythmic thud of metal against soil formed a grim symphony, muffling the whispers of doubt growing in Sam's mind.

The first shovelful of earth was a mix of rich, black soil and rainwater, the scent of decaying leaves mingling with the faint metallic tang of the shovel.

"These graves have been here for a long time already," Reggie observed. "That a good or... *bad* sign?"

Nate worked methodically; his movements driven by a newfound determination. Each clump of dirt he lifted made his limbs feel heavier. The rain intensified into a downpour, turning his grave-digging into a battle against nature itself, yet his resolve remained unshaken.

After what felt like hours, a leg emerged from the dirt. Nate paused, his breath ragged and his muscles screaming in protest. With trembling hands, he brushed away more of the soil. Slowly, the body of Dave came into view—one of Nate's friends and fellow REBELS. Tears slid down Nate's cheeks as Cal rubbed his back, sharing in the grief of losing their friend.

As they sat mourning Dave, who had clearly died from blood loss due to the enormous gash across his stomach, Reggie began to dig up the other grave. What he uncovered was a girl dressed in ragged clothing. The smell hit them all at once, like a bucket of raw sewage dumped nearby. Her bloated, purple body looked like a carcass, left out by hunters for their pray. She had been dead for a long time.

"Recognise her?" Reggie asked Sam, who stared a little too long at her face.

"Yeah, she... I think *Maddie* knew her. I dunno her name but, I think I've seen her with Maddie once or twice."

He almost hated himself for not remembering the girl's name. Whoever buried Dave next to her had either buried her as well or placed him beside an already existing grave.

They reburied the bodies, heading towards the woods. They heard someone dig, crouching so they could sneak up on the person. From behind, they could see the boy had a honey brown short mullet. His skin was covered in dirt and cuts as if he had just been through the worst fight of his life.

Reggie accidentally stepped on a branch, the snap startling the boy. His amber eyes darted back and forth, wide with panic. The long stubble on his beard hinted that he had been there for quite some time. "Who's there?" he demanded, aiming the shovel towards the source of the sound. *"Who's there!"* he repeated, his voice sharper this time.

Val slowly rose up, his hands in the air. "Oi, easy there, lad, we come in peace."

The others followed suit, holding their hands in the air. The boy lowered the shovel, shaking his head. "Screw you, Val. You scared the shit outta me."

"You know my name?" The closer Val came, the more he began to recognise the boy whose beard threw him off guard. "Toby?" He smiled. "*Tobias*, is that *really* you?"

The boy nodded, and he threw his arms around Val, sobbing. "I *tried* to save 'em, I *really* tried. I've been trying to communicate with their spirits but they're *too* fresh. I can't find 'em."

Val comforted him, rubbing his back softly. "It's okay, we're here now. You're safe."

Toby looked over Val's shoulder at Ray and Reggie, who came over to them to join the hug. As Sam, Nate, and Cal watched them, Nate poked Sam in his side. "*So, if he's alive, and he's burying a body, does that mean he's the only survivor?*"

"*I'm afraid it looks like it. Which means one more island we couldn't thwart.*"

The boys in the group hug pulled away from one another, and Toby's eyes landed on the three boys he didn't recognise. He waved awkwardly at them, and Sam gave a small wave in return

"Tell 'em about your power," Val encouraged him, "they're cool. They know of ours."

Toby sighed softly. "Well, I uh... I've got something called *neuroelectric interfacing*, which basically means I can communicate with the dead and see and manifest 'em, and I can read thoughts to target people with walking nightmares."

"Oh. That's... that's uh... *creepy*," Nate replied softly. "*Really* creepy."

Sam wasn't even remotely grossed out by it, pointing instead at the grave. "Who are you burying?"

Toby looked at the grave, then pointed towards the woods. "His name was Stephen; said he was an alien in a previous life?"

"Steve," Sam said, sighing softly. "Yeah, he's... he *was* a good man, and a great cook." He jabbed his thumb over his shoulder. "Did you bury Dave? And the *girl*?"

"*Girl*? What *girl*?" he asked. "You lads dug up the other grave?"

Val nodded slowly. "We had to. But seein' as you dunno her, I'm assumin' that grave was already there?"

Toby nodded. "Steve and I buried Dave there yesterday. We camped nearby and decided to head someplace else, but then they came back."

"*They*? Who's *they*?"

"The ones who killed both Steve and Dave. Those... those *things*. They slashed Dave's stomach—he bled out in seconds. And

Steve... they tore out his heart like it was nothing. I've never seen anything like it."

Sam shook his head, simmering as guilt clawed at him. He hated himself for wasting so much time talking to Jonathan when they could've been here already. If they had arrived sooner, maybe they could've saved Steve.

"Let's get him and bury him," Ray said, "it's the *least* we can do."

He and Reggie set out with Toby to collect Steve's body. Once again, an eerie silence overshadowed the island. A silence that whispered of an impending crescendo. Sam didn't know what to think of the grave that already existed before Toby buried Dave. *Someone was here before Toby to bury that girl's body. There's no way Jonathan was here to do it. But perhaps there are other graves. Perhaps this is what he meant.*

The uneasiness of it all seemed to slow his heart until it almost stopped. He felt as if he had swallowed a lump of cotton. He couldn't get the picture of the girl's body out of his mind. Just the thought of her made an all too familiar tickle of revulsion reappear, filling his stomach with a sickening speed. It triggered his gag reflex. He forced himself to shut his eyes, to focus on *anything* else but her body. Anything to will his stomach to settle down.

"Sam! Sam, *come quick*!"

Sam got up so quickly, he got a kick from the orthostatic hypotension. Shaking the dizziness away from his vision, he raced towards Nate.

Upon arriving, Sam looked at Nate's face, a look of horror that Sam knew all too well. He noticed them standing over a freshly dug grave, but it *wasn't* empty. As Sam got closer, his head spun again. His face was a full shade paler as he stared at Percy's lifeless body.

"*Percy*..." he said, his voice breaking. "No..." His knees gave out, and he sank into the dirt.

Val's face twisted in disgust as the stench hit him. Percy had been dead for quite some time too.

"Isn't that Alfie's brother?" Cal asked Sam. "Didn't you mention he was with your girlfriend and son?"

Sam couldn't speak. He couldn't blink. He couldn't even breathe. Terror froze him in place, his eyes locked on the sight before him. His thoughts were tangled, as if a million spiders had spun cobwebs in his mind. Percy's lifeless eyes stared back at him, unblinking. The fear that gripped him moments ago dissolved into a crushing wave of sadness.

"I bloody hate to say this, but Alfie needs to come down here," Cal said, realising he wouldn't get any real answers to his questions. "He *needs* to see this."

Sam's eyes stayed fixed on Percy, his body frozen in place, unmoving. Cal sighed, patted Sam's back, and hurried towards the Kite to fetch Alfie.

Reggie circled the grave, his steps careful, when a torrential downpour began to fill it with water. Ray attempted to evaporate the rising water with his flames, but the relentless rain kept pouring, and he could feel his energy draining at an alarming rate.

The more Sam thought about his girlfriend and son being in potential danger, the more he tried to picture what had happened to them. His mind became fuzzier by the minute with all the doom scenarios that filled his brain. He heard an alarm go off in his head, not knowing it was Toby who tried to reach him.

He tinkered with Sam's mind, attempting to alter his thoughts—perhaps even erase something that would bring Sam back to himself. He knew Sam was the leader, and without its leader, the group would fall apart.

Sam buried his face in his hands, leaning so far forward in the mud that only the edge of his arse rested on dry ground.

"No!" An icy, piercing scream reverberated through the desolate woods, chilling the air and sending shivers down every spine. It was as if the very essence of fear had materialised into sound, cutting through the silence like a jagged blade. The trees seemed to recoil, their branches trembling in the response, while the moon—though it wasn't meant to rise yet—hid behind a thick veil of clouds, unwilling to witness the source of such anguish.

Alfie's scream had unleashed a primal force, leaving an indelible mark on all their psyches. As he drew closer to Percy, the guttural cry that erupted from him transformed into hysterical sobs, each one ripping through the group like a raw, unrelenting wave.

His legs gave out as he collapsed next to Percy. "No, no, no," he chanted, his voice a broken record of denial. He reached out to touch him, but his hand hovered just above his cold, still body. He couldn't bear the finality of his absence. His sobs grew louder, filling the woods with grief so raw and primal that it once more seemed to shake the very foundation.

Sam had been sucked back to reality by Alfie's screams, knowing all too well the kind of pain he was experiencing. When

Zach died, Sam felt a pain he had never felt before. It was as if someone had reached inside his chest and ripped his heart out, leaving him hollow and aching. Alfie's screams made those feelings rise to the surface of his very being.

"Why?" Alfie yelled, "*why?*"

The realisation hit Sam like a ton of bricks: Percy would never be able to share what had happened, never seek his brother's comfort or advice—or even Sam's. The weight of it was unbearable. He buried his face in his hands once more, while Alfie's body convulsed under the sheer force of his grief.

The moment stretched into an eternity as they sat in heavy silence. Toby could see Alfie's mind racing with thoughts of what *could've been*—what *should've been*. The weight of his guilt bore down on him, an unrelenting burden he would carry forever.

"Even if you hadn't left," Toby said, resting a hand on Alfie's shoulder, "there's no guarantee he'd still be here. Don't blame yourself for something you might never have been able to prevent."

Alfie was too consumed by his emotions to notice that Toby was a stranger to him—let alone that Toby could read his thoughts word for word. But it didn't matter. He screamed again, the sound rising so loudly that even those in the Kite could hear it. Yet Alfie no longer cared, lost in the ruins of his shattered world.

Val looked up at the sky, desperate to drown out Alfie's deafening screams. The first star of the night began to glimmer, but it grew brighter and faster than any star he had ever seen. His heart skipped a beat as it expanded, swelling from a pinprick of light to a fiery ember streaking across the sky—a blazing messenger of doom. The island, already far from tranquil, felt even more fragile and exposed, as though the heavens themselves were preparing to unleash their wrath upon it.

His gaze remained fixed on the approaching celestial body. The meteor loomed larger by the second, the air around it was crackling with electricity, its fiery aura bathing the night in ominous shades of orange and red. Val stood frozen, awestruck, unable to fully grasp the magnitude of the catastrophe hurtling towards them.

Only Tim, with his years of experience and knowledge, understood the gravity of the situation. Watching from the Kite, he shouted through their earpieces, urging everyone to seek shelter—to find the strongest places they could. But his words were nearly swallowed by the meteor's thunderous roar as it tore through the atmosphere, descending with terrifying speed.

The ground trembled violently, the trees lurching as the deafening roar grew louder. The waves churned in a chaotic symphony of destruction. Ray followed Val's gaze; his eyes now locked on the meteor as if silently communicating with the fiery spectre. But his energy was too drained to intervene before the moment of impact.

The meteor struck the island with the force of several atomic bombs, the explosion igniting the night like a newborn sun. The shockwave unleashed a towering tsunami, racing towards them and swallowing the moon in a wall of white-hot devastation.

# CHAPTER FIFTY

The screams were drowned in the raucousness of what Sam could only call *apocalypse*. His heart shattered as he glanced at Nate's body, torn apart piece by piece, by the relentless force of unnatural nature.

The heat was unbearable, and the ocean's saltwater began to boil, sending plumes of steam hissing into the air and forcing the Kite to divert. Nate's clothes—or what little remained of them—were already singeing.

Sam's eyes burned with tears, stung by the acrid smoke thickening the air.

A thunderous boom reverberated through the woods, louder than any thunder they had ever heard. The ground beneath them shook even more violently before, leaving behind a massive, fiery-red monolith fossil embedded in the earth.

Another meteor fragmented in a shower of sparks, the largest piece slamming into the ground just feet away. The resulting shockwave tore through the air, its force so immense that it knocked Sam off his feet, even as he scrambled to rise.

The sky blazed with an eerie, red-orange glow, transforming into a harbinger of catastrophe. In the heart of the woods, where Percy's body lay, the latest meteor had left a smouldering crater.

Val hauled Sam back to his feet while Ray did the same for Alfie, dragging both away from Nate's and Percy's bodies—away from ground zero. As they reached the ocean, they watched in horror as the sea before them receded, the pulling back faster than any tide they had ever seen. A massive tidal wave formed in its wake, growing into a hundred-foot-high monster poised to devour *everything* in its path.

Val knew they had mere seconds. His eyes darted along the shoreline until they locked on a solitary tree, its roots a gnarled, tangled knot of wood. "Hold on!" he bellowed over the deafening roar of meteors slamming into the earth. Without hesitation, he began climbing the tree, motioning for the others to follow. "Come on!"

Reggie and Ray hoisted Sam and Alfie up the tree as Toby climbed higher to help Val, pulling him up with all his strength. Looking down, Toby saw Cal offering them a hand, but his gaze shifted to the wave—an unstoppable, roaring beast barrelling towards them without mercy. "Hurry up!" he shouted.

Ray and Reggie began climbing next, gripping the tree tightly to help Cal up. But it was too late. The wall of water struck with brutal force, slamming Cal into the tree. A sicking crunch echoed through the chaos, sharp and brittle like fibreglass, following by a spray of fiery foam. The others clung to the tree for dear life, their knuckles turning white as they watched the ocean's fury claim Cal. His body was pulled away, disappearing into the relentless current. The tree groaned under the immense pressure, its trunk bending dangerously close to snapping, yet it held firm—a solitary sentinel defying the tsunami's wrath.

The water surged up around them, an unnatural torrent that felt endless, ripping and tearing at the tree and filling their lungs with salty dread. They all knew—no natural phenomenon could make the water raise so high on this island. *That much they all knew.*

The world fell into an eerie silence, broken only by the deafening rush of retreating water, as though the ocean, having unleashed its wrath, was now fleeing back to the horizon to bury its fury.

When the water finally receded, leaving them coughing and gasping for air, the island was unrecognisable. It had become a moonscape of fire and ash, the once-lush woods now charred skeletons, and the sand scorched to brittle glass. The only thing left standing was the tree they had clung to—a blackened silhouette against the smouldering backdrop.

They climbed down slowly, their legs trembling on the scorched earth. The heat was overwhelming, and the air was thick with the stench of burning vegetation and seared flesh. Dazed, they scanned the devastation, desperate to find anything familiar amidst the ruins to help them relocate the Kite.

Sam's world had crumbled, replaced by a nightmare landscape that pulsed with malevolent energy. They had lost Nate *and* Cal—two lives they had fought to save from Mister X's grasp. And yet, *somehow*, he had still managed to tip the scales back in his favour.

*It was deliberate, there's no doubt about it. I'll make 'em pay for what they've done. I'll avenge every life they've stolen from me, the ones I fought so hard to save, both then and now. I'll make 'em suffer the way they've made me suffer.*

Hatred coursed through his veins, and revenge was the only balm for his guilt he could imagine.

Amidst the wreckage, he heard it—a faint beeping, a rhythmic pulse that grew louder with each passing second. It was coming from his earpiece. His eyes, alight with a mix of terror and anger, locked onto the others'.

"We gotta go!" he yelled; his voice hoarse from screaming. "The meteor! It brought something with it!"

The tension thickened as they realised the horror wasn't over. The island had become a battleground for forces far beyond the smouldering ruins. The beeping grew louder, escalating into a frantic staccato, as if urging them to move faster. Whatever Tim had seen from the Kite was threatening enough to trigger the only alarm loud enough to reach them on the ground.

Sam stumbled through the devastation, smoke stinging his eyes and every muscle in his body aching from the effort of staying upright.

*Why can't those fragments from meteors and meteorites be made of mineral alloys? The kind with healing properties?* Sam thought as he ran. *Just small doses—something we could put in a back molar to release those properties over time and extend our lifespans. Why does everything around here have to be murderous?*

His earpiece crackled to life, and he knew Tim was about to deliver the ballistics of the situation. *Quite literally.*

"Lads, I managed to do some forensics from up here—long story how. Anyway, I've got positive results for incendiary residue. There are traces of something called nitroglycerine, which is—"

"Bloody English please, mate!" Val yelled.

"Bomb-making materials, the kind you can only find in barrels. When you lads were booked, I noticed there are two mercury tilt switches on the island—"

"English!"

"You can't impound on those switches, nor can you deactivate 'em 'cause they'll blow."

"So why the bloody hell are you tellin' us this while we're runnin' for our lives?" Val grew so annoyed that if Tim had been running alongside them, he had tripped him and left him for dead.

"There's a cell phone detonator linked to 'em. I traced the frequency back to its point of origin—that signal's connected to all the other bombs." He paused. "The mother bomb."

"So?" Reggie now asked. "What about 'em?"

"They're trying to erase every trace of what they've done, every piece of evidence hidden on this island. This was their base of operations—there's no denying it. We've gotta stop those bombs from going off and prevent 'em from starting over with a clean slate."

"Aren't you evacuatin' us for that *specific* reason?" Val asked. "If we don't vacate the area *right now*, the perimeter will be filled with our blood!"

Sam came to an abrupt stop, causing Val to collide with him and hit the ground hard. "If you don't shut up right now, I'll *leave* you behind!"

Val scrambled back up, shoving Sam backwards. "I'm sorry for tryin' to get us all away from here! Have you forgotten that two people died? Apparently, *we* can't die," he said, pointing to his fellow superpowered peers, "but *you* can. You wanna hate me for havin' changed my mind and grown fond of some of you? Be my *guest*!"

Sam stood perplexed. If he expected anything to come out of Val's mouth, *it wasn't this.*

"Lads, I've found the mother bomb. If you can get to it, I can teach you how to dismantle it."

"What about Mother Nature trying to swallow us whole?" Ray asked.

"It's right below you."

Sam's eyes locked onto a faint red flashing light beneath the thin layer of earth. Dropping to his knees, he began to dig, ignoring the meteors crashing around him with deafening force. When he uncovered the bomb, its sheer size didn't even faze him.

"*If you can hook your tether to it—the one on your belt—I can calibrate it to extract the data and map out the circuitry of its network.*"

Sam didn't bother questioning why he had such a device attached to his belt; he simply did as he was told.

"Okay, based on the wire configuration... In theory, since this is the trigger for all the others scattered across the island, disarming this one should disarm the rest too."

"Nerd to the rescue," Reggie said, his arms crossed. "Is he gonna use his giddy tech voice next?"

Sam ignored the empty comments, focusing on the task at hand. He was on a clock after all.

"Okay, start by finding the red wire, and the purple one. Those are the power chargers."

As Sam held the wires between his fingers, he already knew what Tim was going to say next. He glanced at Ray, who had pulled out his small blade, ready to slice through them.

"*Wait!*" Ray moved the blade away from the wires. "*Looking at the programming a bit deeper, there's no way out. The way they're linked causes all the other bombs to detonate if you try to disarm this one.*"

"Were you seriously tryin' to set us up as patsies? Have us blow up and take the fall while you flee?" Val snapped, fury in his voice. "I'm riskin' my life down here, and you try to—"

Sam struck a precise spot on Val's neck, causing him to slump to the ground, unconscious. The others stared in stunned silence, but no one said a word. "Go on," Sam said to Tim.

"*Okay, the mother bomb is now untethered. Once the timer on my end hits zero, all the other bombs will be neutralised. You've got five minutes to throw it into the ocean.*"

"Wait," Toby said, "we'd cause *another* tsunami. There's gotta be another way."

"*There isn't. I've found a way outta this that has disarmed the others, though not the mother bomb. You should be thanking me for changing the plans in the blink of an eye.*"

"I'll thank you when we survive this and *aren't* chained to a ticking time bomb," Toby replied sarcastically.

"Technically, we're strapped to one," Ray said, though the looks he got made him look down embarrassed.

He and Reggie lifted the bomb from the sand and rushed towards the ocean. Swinging it back and forth a couple of times, they hurled the bomb into the water.

"*Three minutes on the clock. Get outta there!*"

"Wait, won't the evidence be blown to smithereens regardless of whether the bomb goes off?" Toby asked. "There are meteors everywhere, not to mention the tsunami we barely escaped."

"*I've managed to impound some evidence, and we'll get to that once you're safe and sound. I'm not just a nerd. I'm a justice seeker too.*"

Sam laughed softly. "That, you most certainly are."

A meteor cast an elongated shadow right where Sam stood, just as Toby tackled him to the ground. Sam nodded his thanks, then ran towards the kite as it came into view. Val's arms dangled limply as Reggie carried him towards their escape plan.

"*Two minutes!*"

As if the ocean knew what had been done to it, the waves grew more insistent, the water creeping further up the beach. The earth trembled beneath their feet once more, a low rumble that swelled into a roar. Then, with alarming speed, the ocean retreated, pulling away from the shore.

The meteors ceased, and the beach fell silent. The only sound was the retreating hiss of the water, leaving a trail of bubbles and foam.

"One minute!"

In the distance, a towering wall of water rose from the horizon. The first droplets of spray reached them, a harbinger of the monstrous wave approaching with unstoppable force.

*They must've triggered another tsunami. When that bomb goes off... we'll all die. They made us.*

As if on cue, the bomb exploded. A 90-foot tidal wave raced towards them, followed closely by the tsunami itself. The earth beneath them shuddered more violently with *each step*, urging them to flee faster.

The wave rose taller, a towering beast of water and power that seemed to swallow the very sky when it collided with the bomb's shockwave. The kite hovered above the island, near a steep incline; the ladder barely reached it, having lost a huge chunk in the earlier tsunami.

"Up there!" Ray yelled, leading the way.

They scrambled up the slope, gripping branches and vines, ignoring the cuts and scrapes that marked their ascent. The wave had become a living creature, a force of nature bearing down upon them with the fury of a thousand storms. The canopy above swayed with the oncoming rush of air, its leaves producing sounds that mimicked screams, adding to the screeching prelude of the tsunami.

The wave was almost upon them now, a towering leviathan reaching for the stars. The ground trembled violently beneath their feet, and the first rush of water reached the slope they were climbing, a frothy, white tongue that licked the earth greedily.

Val slipped from Reggie's back

"No!" Sam yelled, knowing it was his fault for knocking him out cold. His heart pounded with the rhythm of approaching doom as he let go, crashing into the chaos. The water nipped at his heels, a cold, unyielding force that seemed to chase him as he fought to reach Val.

The wave was a monster, but Sam was human—and humans are capable of great things when driven by empathy, care, and the desire to save others. The world had narrowed to this one, desperate act of necessary kindness in the face of overwhelming terror.

The wave pursued relentlessly, trying to stop Sam with every step as the water swelled around him. He reached Val, slapping his cheek hard. Val stirred, staring at Sam with confusion.

"We gotta go! Can you move?"

Val nodded, moving his ankle. "I think so. It's just my ankle."

They climbed back up, their grip slipping on the wet foliage, muscles screaming with exhaustion. The wave had become a living entity, a ravenous maw that devoured everything in its path, including the very slope they were scaling.

Like a wall of churning destruction, it cracked the slope, separating Sam and Val from the others. With a roar that seemed to shake the earth's very foundations, the wave crashed over them, burying them under a deluge of saltwater.

Val felt the force of the water rip him from the slope, his body tumbling through the dark, turbulent sea. His thoughts were a chaotic mess, a jumble of fear and regret. *Find Sam. Save him. He did it for me.*

His head went under the water once more, struggling against the current and the darkness.

Breaking the surface, he coughed up saltwater and gasped for air. His legs felt heavy with fatigue, his heart weighed down with sorrow as he searched for Sam, but he couldn't find him anywhere. "Sam!" he yelled desperately. *"Sam!'*

Seconds turned into minutes, and minutes felt like hours when he saw a figure struggling against the current—arms flailing, mouth open in a silent scream for help. The water churned around them, the current growing stronger by the second. He swam towards Sam as fast as he could, while Sam desperately fought to keep himself above the water.

Val reached for Sam's outstretched hand. Sam clung to him with the desperation of someone who knew he was drowning, with only one arm to pull himself to safety—if that was even possible. Val kicked hard against the water's relentless pull, his muscles burning with the effort, but he *didn't* let go of Sam.

Surfacing, he hauled Sam up onto what was left of the slope. Sam's head lolled back, revealing the blue tinge to his lips. He gasped for air, coughing up water as Val dragged him closer to the gap. Val knew Sam hadn't swallowed enough water to die from it, but there had to be a lot still lodged in his lungs.

He scooped Sam into his arms and carried him to the top of the remaining slope. Sam was limp, his eyes closed, and Val feared the worst. With trembling hands, he began chest compressions, the training from a long-forgotten first-aid class rushing back to him.

The others watched with bated breath as Val worked on Sam, each compression sending a jolt through his body.

Val didn't stop. *He couldn't.*

Time seemed to stand still as Val worked tirelessly, willing life back into the waterlogged body before him.

A cough, a gasp, and a shuddering breath. Sam stirred, and Val stopped, releasing the longest sigh of relief he had been holding in. Sam's eyes fluttered open, locking onto Val's. *"Thank you."*

Val nodded, clapping his back softly. "We gotta go! *Now!*"

Ray's voice brought Val back to reality. All this time, they had waited for Val and Sam to return safely. They could've gone to safety, but none of them had moved. It was a prime example of what Sam's saviour complex had led to—even Toby, who had known Sam for less than an hour.

One by one, they reached for the ladder, climbing up. Val was the last to go before the Kite left the final island of their rescue mission.

# CHAPTER FIFTY-ONE

They sat in a circle, studying the schematics Tim had printed out. Despite the grim situation and all the deaths that had occurred, there was no time to mourn. Jonathan knew they were onto him, and if they found *Jonathan*, they would find *Mister X*.

Tim pointed at the map, indicating a specific location that seemed to be nothing more than the middle of nowhere.

"Here's a secret tech lab that they've got going on, at the top floor of a radio tower. We won't be able to fly towards it, they'll track us from miles away. We'll have to trek towards it and sneak inside. The case with the serum is in their lab. That's our *last* objective before we can go home. If we get the serum, we get full proof." He pointed at the printed documents. "I've found someone named Subject 15, a male in his late thirties who was previously a member of the Trooper perimeter security force. According to several reports provided by the superior officers, he was taken during one of his occasional patrols a few months ago. He claimed to have escaped, holding important information within his body. The exact date of his injection is unknown, 'cause he concealed any subsequent symptoms." He flipped the page. "However, they soon noticed visible injuries, including a partially healed puncture site where the needle had entered, along with severe necrosis at the extremities of the skin. He then attacked his superior officers, resulting in two casualties."

He revealed the photograph which pictured a grotesque image of a half-eaten officer, all his organs exposed with bites taken out of them. Sam turned away, sick to his stomach from the water that had filled his lungs, the bodies he had found in the graves, and now *this*. It was all *too much*.

"The officer he attacked died, and the Subject itself died too. But that wasn't a normal death." He flipped the page, concealing the photograph. "Multiple gunshot wounds were necessary to eliminate the threat—one to the torso and one to the head. As stated here, 'The damage to its chest should've been fatal, but the Trooper who shot Subject 15 reported that the Subject continued to fight until the Trooper shot him, his bullet piercing the Subject's skull.' That's where *my* research comes in." He took his laptop from the table and opened it in front of them. "We... *you've* killed a couple of 'em by causing severe head trauma, so can confirm that this is indeed true, and that this is the only effective means of exterminating these... *individuals*. With *our* data, along with the data from the experiment site and the officer's official report, we can infer that whatever's inside this serum controls its host by connecting to the brain. If we fail, we can delegate our work to the proper authorities, who can take over from us."

"But we *won't* fail," Val asserted, "we've come this far. No, *you've* come this far." He got up from his seat. "I didn't realise how much you've all sacrificed two years ago. I speak for everyone who's like me that we were oblivious to any of your actions. And now, seein' just how much you've collected back then and added now, it's clear that *you're* the experts, and we're just the means to an end. If *anyone* can see this through, if anyone can get us justice and stop this madness once and for all, it's *all of you*. We're just simply here to offer whatever kinda help we can."

Reggie got up, nodding. "We'll do whatever it takes. We're *with you*."

Ray joined him, followed by Vince. Toby stared at them for a few seconds before getting up himself, determination clearly written across his face.

Everyone turned to Sam, who had been awfully silent through the meeting. He slowly looked up from where he was seated, shaking his head. "I'm *not* risking more of us. We're *done*." He paused. "We've *lost*."

"What happened to our valiant and altruistic leader? We *haven't* lost. We're so close to finishing this that we can bring peace. *Real* peace," Alfie said.

"Really? And who's to say we won't face another threat in the future?" Sam got up from his seat. "Why's it *our* job to save people? To save *our* city? Why do we have to be *heroes,* with or without superpowers? Why do *I* need to sacrifice *everything*—and *everyone*—I love?"

Alex, feeling much better, walked over to Sam and cupped his face in his hands. "That's 'cause we're stronger together than apart. We *started* this as a team, and we'll *finish* it as a team—come what may."

Sam shook his head. "It's gonna end *in blood*. Imogen's still out there, for crying out loud!"

"But that doesn't mean we *shouldn't* at least fight," Stan said, standing next to Alex. "We've got choices—and *you've* taught us that. Two years ago, you showed us that no matter what, we *always* have a choice. And we're crazy bastards, so we choose *not* to go down without a fight. We *choose* to go down swinging. We keep fighting for the things we believe in, for the people who *can't* defend themselves. Don't stop repeating your own words just 'cause you feel beaten down. You lifted us up during our darkest days—and Seb especially. *You know that.*"

It was the first time Stan had given such a speech, leaving Sam so perplexed that he was unable to give him a counterargument.

"We're gonna give those bastards a *'give 'em bloody hell'* attitude. They'll regret ever messin' with us," Val asserted. He made Sam look at him, pulling his gaze away from Alex. "I know life's short, and ours seems to be shorter than most people's, but come on, *Samuel*. Don't tell me you're gonna spend it wringin' your hands."

"*Sam*," he hissed softly, "my name's Sam."

"Atta boy." Val clapped him on his back. *"That's* the Sam we know and love."

Sam shook his head slightly as he stared into Val's eyes. "If you think it matters who you *were*, you've got it wrong. What stands in front of me right now, it's about what you decide to do. And you chose to do the right thing. I'm sorry I ever doubted you or left you adrift."

"Forgive and forget," Val said, extending his hand. "As long as we shake on it."

Sam chuckled, shaking Val's hand.

"We need a motto," Seb said, who got up from his seat. "And I know the *perfect* one." He extended his hand, and while everyone hesitated at first, Sam was the first to follow Seb's gesture. "Our peace is helping people. And our powers? Our history of experiments? That doesn't control us. *We* control *it. We* control *our* destiny. We might be a little weird, sure."

"Would rather call us *wacky*," Val added, but Seb ignored him.

"Some of us more than others." He turned towards where he heard Val's voice coming from, giving him a look. "But it works 'cause we're *a team*—a team that knows what to expect from each other and how to keep each other safe. Maybe that part of us that's gonna win this war will be our own powerful force. And we can get better, 'cause we've been getting better every day. And if there's *one thing* that we've all learned, it's that heroes are *never* perfect. So, let's bring this win *home*."

They all cheered in unison, a battle cry that resounded far beyond the Kite. The world knew its heroes would come to liberate it.

Three days later, the Kite neared its destination—the end of all ends, lurking in the shadows. Tim sat behind his laptop, and everyone had gathered around him, including Phil, Andrew, and Josh.

Not all the injuries of those who had sustained them had fully healed, but most were close enough. Sam knew no better than to rely on every bit of manpower he had to spare, as the others had made it *abundantly clear*.

"Okay, I've hacked into their server and added all our biometrics under Trooper aliases to their backdoor security system." He typed quickly on his keyboard. "I've decrypted most of the locks standing in your way, so you should be able to get in and out smoothly." He pointed at the screen. "I've got some backup en route, just in case. It's not much, but they're vigilant citizens who've been on Josh's radar for quite some time."

Josh nodded. "Some of those I trust with my life, but they never made it past Trooper bootcamp 'cause they always kept an eye on me. It was *never* my team to begin with."

Sam patted Josh's back apologetically.

"You need to head to the second level first, there's a door there that will have six key blocks. I've already disarmed four from here, but the last two need to be disarmed manually."

"Is Jonathan on-site?" Sam asked, his fist clenched.

"Negative, haven't spotted him yet." He typed again. "We're with fourteen people, so I suggest we split up." He turned his chair around. "We've got six people with *special* gifts, which leaves eight of us. I suggest we divide into two groups of four and two of three. One group of four will go up to gather more evidence, so they need to consist of *at least* two gifted people. One group of three will go with 'em in case things go awry and they need cover. One will be gifted too, so we'll have a total of three going up to assist with gathering the information." He pointed at the map's two entrances. "The other group of four and three will stay outside on lookout, distracting any guards at the perimeter long enough for the ones inside to get the job done. If we find Jonathan, we don't kill him— we arrest him. He's our *only* key to finding Mister X, so we need him alive. *Understood*?"

Everyone nodded, and Tim began distributing the weapons they might need. It made their packs heavy, but with the uncertainty of not knowing what creatures—besides Imogen— might lie in wait for them, every weapon imaginable was necessary to have on hand.

"Andrew, Sam, Val, and Seb, you'll be the group of four to gather evidence. For cover, you'll be accompanied by Ray, Alfie, and Josh." He distributed their gear and then pointed to the rest of the group. "Stan, Vince, Reggie, and Alex will handle the distractions. Phil, Toby, and I will provide backup and keep a close eye on things from the technical side. Everyone clear on their roles?" After receiving affirmative nods and grunts, Tim gave a nod of his own. "Then let me debrief our mission once more. We're gonna infiltrate the facility and seize any bio-research evidence pertaining to the experiments and the viral attacks on our friends." They nodded in agreement, confirming everything was clear. "Get some shut-eye, 'cause tonight, it's time to end this *once and for all*."

With the cover of night, they sneaked towards the facility. Sam donned the modified glasses, equipped with an upgraded infrared compartment, and used them to scan the area. Tim had outfitted everyone with his self-developed stealth technology. Sam knew it was the best-in-class, for he trusted Tim's skills blindly after all the projects he had successfully created—projects that had saved countless lives, both in the past *and* present.

"*We're making our depth right now, going one-five feet.*"

"Copy that," Sam replied to Tim. "Make sure you keep that ten-degree down."

"*Roger.*"

"Oi," Val said, "what'll happen to the tech genius that's fated to carry the world on his back?"

Sam swore he could hear Tim chuckling on the other end of the earpiece. "*He'll take a nice, long, hot bath when this is all over.*"

"With a rubber duck as company, I hope."

"Shut up."

Seb chuckled softly, shaking his head. "You're insufferable."

Val clapped him on the back. "Given my solidly *middle-class* position, I can only air these thoughts by cloakin' 'em in a dose of humour."

"Middle-class position?" Sam said, "that's rather dismal."

Val barked a laugh. "Careful now, can't break your reputation for being as silent as the shadows themselves."

"That so?"

Val shrugged. "Rumours."

Sam sighed, his eyes scanning the area with the precision of a hawk searching for prey. Their attire—blends of black and grey, with a bulletproof vest—clung to his body like a second skin. The moon hung as little more than a silver sliver in the sky, offering little light but enough for Sam to make out the outline of their destination: a towering steel facility surrounded by a high concrete wall. The place was a fortress, a bastion of secrets they were tasked to breach.

Sam's breathing remained steady as he led his group towards the perimeter. The facility hummed with a low frequency, a subtle reminder of the activity within its walls. The Troopers patrolled with a predictable rhythm, their footsteps echoing through the stillness. Sam waited patiently, timing their movements to coincide with his group's. When the moment was right, he signalled Val, who scaled the wall with the grace of a spider. The others followed suit, helping Sam up. Their gloves—courtesy of yet another of Tim's inventions—enabled them to find their grip on the cold, unforgiving surface. Sam's heartbeat remained steady as he reached the top, the result of outstanding teamwork. Their training, and the success of previous missions, allowed them to keep their nerves in check.

Once over the wall, they dropped into a crouch, surveying the landscape before them. The grounds were well-managed, with neatly trimmed bushes and a meticulously paved path leading to the main entrance. Occasional spotlights swept the area, but it was the Troopers themselves that posed the biggest threat. Armed and vigilant, their eyes scanned the perimeter for any sign of trouble.

"We gotta be extra careful; they upped their security it seems. A single misstep means discover and failure," Sam whispered. "Stay low, stay quiet, and follow me."

He waited for the next sweep of the lights before making his move. As the beam passed over him, he quickly rolled into the shadows of a large bush, feeling the thorns bite into his clothing and landing on his stump. He had to bite his tongue to stop himself from screaming.

Once the light had moved on, he was up again, and the others followed his every move. They sprinted across the open space with the speed of a ghost. Their destination was a side door, one Tim had observed to be less frequently monitored. As they reached it, Sam motioned for Seb to move forward so he could listen. Seb could hear the faint sound of muffled voices and the tap of a keyboard from within, but nothing that suggested anyone was on the other side of the door.

"Clear."

With a gentle touch, he tested the handle. It was *unlocked*. He allowed himself a brief smile as they had crossed the first hurdle with relative ease. Slipping inside, they found themselves in a narrow corridor, the air thick with the scent of industrial cleaner.

"You think they killed someone?" Andrew asked, whispering. "It smells as if they covered up a crime scene."

"With these people, everythin's possible," Val replied. "Keep your eyes peeled."

Andrew nodded as they moved further. The walls were lined with pipes and wires, hinting at the complexity of the machinery that lay beyond.

"We're heading in your direction," Josh said, "once we get the go."

"Go, stay safe."

"Copy."

With Josh, Alfie, and Ray moving in to join them, Sam pulled the blueprints Tim had printed out from his pack and unfolded them. Despite having studied them all night, it wasn't enough to memorise the layout by heart. *"Okay, we're close. Stay on me."* He tucked the blueprints away, each step now bringing them closer to the heart of the facility, where the secrets were supposedly kept. The stakes were high, and failure wasn't an option. *Infiltrate, acquire the intel, and get out without leaving a trace. Easy-peasy, lemon squeezy.*

As they moved deeper into the belly of the beast, Sam couldn't shake the feeling that something was waiting for them— *something that would test their skills to the limit.*

# CHAPTER FIFTY-TWO

The first Trooper came into view, his back turned as he inspected a wall-mounted camera. Sam took a deep breath, centring himself. Speed and precision were key, and with only one arm, he knew he was at a disadvantage.

He nodded at Val, who, with one swift motion, emerged from their hiding spot. Val's hand covered the Trooper's mouth before he could register his presence. A quick twist of his neck, and the Trooper crumpled to the floor—unconscious but alive. Val paused, listening for any signs of alarm, but all remained quiet. He dragged the Trooper into a nearby room and secured him with zip ties.

The corridor split at a T-junction. To the left, the sound of distant footsteps grew louder, signalling the approach of more Troopers. To the right, the path was clear, leading to the server room where the intel was likely stored. Sam weighed their options. The element of surprise was crucial, but so was speed. He opted for the right, knowing they could deal with the Troopers later if needed.

The server room was a stark contrast to the industrial corridors. The air was cooler here, filled with the soft hum of computer fans and the occasional beep of a machine. Rows of metal racks lined the walls, their LED lights blinking in a rhythmic pattern. Sam quickly located the server they needed, its panel glowing with a soft blue light.

"We're in," Sam told Tim through the earpiece.

*"Insert the USB drive into the access port to begin the data transfer."*

**Data processing… Data monitoring…**

Sam stared at the download bar, each second stretching out like an eternity. He could feel the tension building in his shoulders, the weight of knowing this was the most critical part of the mission. If they were caught now, everything would be for nothing.

The sudden sound of footsteps sent a jolt of adrenaline through his body. He spun around, his hand instinctively reaching for the silenced pistol at his side. But it was too late. The door swung open, and a pair of Troopers stepped into the room, their eyes widening in shock at the sight of the intruders. Before they could react, Val had already drawn his weapon and fired two silent shots. The Troopers crumpled to the floor, *dead*.

They paused, listening for any other threats. Sam's pulse pounded in his ears. *This wasn't supposed to happen... we'd try to be non-lethal... Bloody hell.*

The data transfer was almost complete.

"Bloody hell. You lads have no idea what I'm seeing right now," Tim's voice crackled through the earpiece. "It's worse than we thought. They're trying to hack into the entire city's infrastructure—our transit, emergency services, the Trooper army, even our weapons. They're taking the whole bloody country hostage."

"What for?" Sam asked, dreading the answer.

"They're no longer just experimenting with a serum to see who's strong and who can resist it, to control them for whatever purpose within our city. Now, they're planning global domination with mutated slaves. The computational power I'm looking at would require an enormous server farm. We're not just dealing with Mister X and his associates—this is way bigger. This stretches across the entire country."

"That's why the source data we're tryin' to copy involves thousands of those exabytes," Val said, pointing at the screen. "It's not downloadin' *fast enough*, and we're runnin' outta time."

"How safe's our hack?" Sam asked, but his question was already answered when he heard boots thundering down the corridor, growing louder by the second.

"The alarm's been raised," Andrew said.

"Blimey, you think?" Val said somewhat sarcastically, taking his weapon back out.

Sam knew they had to move fast to remain undetected. The USB drive beeped, signalling that its task was complete—much to everyone's surprise. Sam quickly pocketed it and took one last look around the room, ensuring they had left no trace of their presence.

They slipped back into the shadows. Sam's mind racing as he plotted their escape route.

"*How's it coming along?*" Sam asked through the earpiece.

Tim stared at the blinking screen of his laptop, frustration mounting. The code he had been working on for days refused to cooperate. His fingers danced over the keyboard, trying to coax the program into action. The lines of code swam before his eyes, a sea of ones and zeros—each one holding the key to their success. He had to disable the alarm before it went off.

"Attention, a dangerous infiltration has been detected in the serv—"

The alarm died down, going out with a fizzle.

Tim let out a sigh of relief. "*That* was close." He touched his earpiece. "They'll hopefully go check the power room instead of the server room. But be on your guard."

Sam scanned the hallways through his infrared, but when the darkness proved too much for the device, he slipped on his night vision goggles. Through the lens, he saw the toppled furniture and shattered glass littering the room next door. Before he could wonder what had happened, a figure blocked his view. Blinking, Sam pulled off his goggles and stared into the eyes of something he thought had been destroyed: a T-Rooper.

Its tall, sleek form loomed in the dark, the dust hanging around it like a shroud. Everyone froze, the silence suffocating, though Sam knew it was too late. The T-Rooper's eyes glowed with a cold, calculating precision as it scanned them. Its arms ended in semi-automatic weapons, poised to unleash havoc.

"Let *me* talk to it," Val said. Before Sam could stop him, Val had stepped forward.

The T-Rooper's head tilted slightly as it took in the scene.

"We're not a threat," he said, "we belong here. We're interns."

The T-Rooper's eyes narrowed, a silent analysis. Then, with a whir of gears, it spoke. *"Your identity hasn't been verified. Please provide clearance."*

"We don't have clearance; we left our papers in the boss' office. Stupid, am I right?" Val said, patting the T-Rooper's chest.

The T-Rooper stared down at his chest, then at Val's hand who slowly pulled it back. *"Access denied,"* it said, its voice cold and emotionless. *"Compliance is mandatory."* It raised its arms, the weapons glinting menacingly in the dim light.

"We're *not* the enemy!" Andrew yelled, his voice cracking with panic.

The T-Rooper's response was swift and calculated. *"All humans are potential threats."*

Sam quickly slipped his night vision goggles back on, scanning for anything he could use as a weapon. Guns and blades wouldn't be enough against the T-Rooper, but something else might work. His eyes landed on a metal baseball bat leaning against the wall. He didn't question why it was there—his instincts took over.

With a split-second decision, he whispered, *"When I say go, run,"* forcing the USB drive into Andrew's hands.

Without waiting for a response, Sam sprinted towards the T-Rooper, gripping the bat with all the strength his one arm could muster. The T-Rooper's reflexes were quick, but it hadn't expected the human element of surprise. The first hit glanced off its fireproof armour, but the second connected with a satisfying clang. The T-Rooper staggered, giving the others enough time to reach the far end of the hallway. With a blood-curdling roar, it regained its footing, its weapons now trained on Sam.

Val dove in, grabbing a chair and hurling it at the T-Rooper's legs. It crashed to the floor, shattering the chair into pieces. "We've gotta bring it down! It's the *only* way!"

The T-Rooper's eyes narrowed; its target locked on Sam. *"You'll be neutralised,"* it said, raising an arm to fire.

But before it could act, Andrew reached into his pocket, retrieving the USB drive Sam had given him—hoping he wouldn't have to use it this way. Now, there was no choice. Partly shapeshifting into an owl to take advantage of its keen eyesight, he spotted a port on the T-Rooper's side and inserted the drive. Its eyes flickered, and for a moment, it hesitated.

*"Run!"* Val yelled, pulling Seb along.

Sam yanked the USB drive out and sprinted after the others, knowing it was only a matter of time before the T-Rooper was back on their trail.

The hallway was a maze of shadows and flickering lights. Behind them, the distant thuds of the T-Rooper rising to its feet echoed through the corridors.

"Where are we going?" Andrew panted.

"The stairs," Sam said. "We gotta get to the roof."

They climbed as fast as they could, their hearts pounding with every step. The T-Rooper's footsteps grew louder, reverberating through the stairwell. Reaching the top floor, Sam glanced back. The T-Rooper was ascending with eerie grace, its magnetic feet clinging effortlessly to the metal.

*It's clearly been updated. That's not good. I can't predict its movements anymore.*

The door to the roof swung open, and the cool night air rushed in. They stepped out, the T-Rooper's eyes tracking them—glowing like twin embers in the dark.

On the rooftop, the din of the facility was a stark reminder of the warzone they had stumbled into. Helicopters hovered overhead, their spotlights sweeping in erratic patterns, searching. For something. For someone. *For them.*

Distant pops of gunfire and the rumble of explosions painted a grim picture of the battle raging below—one the others were most likely caught in.

"We need to get to the other side of the building," Sam said. *"Now!"*

They sprinted across the rooftop, their footsteps hammering against the concrete. Behind them, the T-Rooper burst from the stairwell, unfazed by the height or the obstacles in its path. With inhuman grace, it vaulted over the building's edge, landing on the neighbouring rooftop with a thud that sent tremors through the concrete beneath their feet.

"It's *still* following us!" Andrew said, his breath ragged.

*"Keep moving,"* Sam urged, his eyes on the T-Rooper as it approached.

They reached the edge of the building, and Sam hesitated, his heart in his throat. He stepped onto the bridge of planks and cables stretching to the next rooftop. Without a second thought, he leaped across, the planks groaning under his weight. The others followed close behind, their eyes locked on the T-Rooper's unwavering gaze. As Sam reached the middle of the bridge, the T-Rooper took a step back, calculating the distance.

*Then, it leaped.*

Time seemed to slow as Sam watched the T-Rooper soar through the air, weapons poised to strike. But before it could reach them, a figure burst from the shadows—a blur of motion that sent the T-Rooper, and all of them, tumbling off the edge of the roof.

Sam hit the ground hard, the impact knocking him out for a moment. Groaning, he gripped his head, hearing the others stirring around him. He looked towards the T-Rooper—its eyes dark.

*Had the fall broken its programming?* Relief washed over him as he slowly got to his feet.

Then his gaze fell on a grave.

As he read the marker, his breath caught. His heart stopped.

### Madeline

# CHAPTER FIFTY-THREE

The rustling of leaves was the only sound that broke the stillness of Sam's discovery. He stared at the unassuming marker, the name *Madeline* etched into the cold marble. A peculiar feeling stirred in his gut, a mix of dread and disbelief. He approached the grave, his legs growing heavier with every step. The name was hers, but it made *no sense*.

*She's at home... she's not supposed to be here... she's supposed to be alive, waiting for me back at our home with our son. It must be a joke to distract me. Jonathan's playing games with me.*

The earth around the grave appeared disturbed, as though something had been buried hastily. Without a second thought, he dropped to his knees and began to dig, his hand trembling with a mix of fear and determination. He had to know *why* her name was here, why this *couldn't* be real. The scent of fresh soil filled his nostrils as he dug deeper, his breaths coming in shallow gasps.

Val began to dig alongside him, and so did Andrew, until they hit something solid. Something that *shouldn't* have been there.

With a trembling hand, Sam brushed the dirt away, revealing a wooden coffin. His heart pounded in his chest as he pried it open with Andrew's machete. The smell of decay hit him like a punch to the gut, but he didn't flinch.

Inside lay *his* Madeline, her once-beautiful face now a mask of horror and agony. She was dressed in her favourite blue dress, the one she had worn on their first real date. Her eyes were open, staring blankly at the sky. There was no blood pool around her head, and Sam knew what that meant.

His world shattered into a million pieces. He yanked her out of the coffin, refusing to believe she had flatlined, clinging to the hope that she was merely brain-dead. He remembered what Tim had once told him: the brainstem can still tell the lungs to cough. He listened, though his own heartbeat shattered the fragile hope. He began to try and resuscitate her, but Val tried to pull him away. Sam shoved Val back hard, refusing to give up on her.

Her lifeless eyes stared at him as he slammed his hands against her chest. He screamed, saliva dripping in a long line from his mouth onto her body. "No! No! Wake up, Maddie! *Wake up!*"

Andrew moved to look inside the box, pulling out a photograph. Turning it over in his hands, he gasped. "Sam." When he didn't get his attention, he yelled louder. "*Sam!*"

Sam stopped, turning around sharply. When his eyes landed on the photograph, he shook his head violently. "No, no, no, no, no, no." He stared at the ultrasound, his tears falling onto her lifeless body like a waterfall. "No, she wasn't... no, no, no... *this isn't true*..." He slammed his hands against her chest again, holding the photograph in his grip. "Maddie! No!" His scream was so loud, so piercing, that the others had to cover their ears. It was an agonising scream, so painful that it reverberated through their own hearts as though they were being stabbed.

Sam dropped the photograph onto the ground, cradling her cold body in his arms. He screamed her name until his voice was reduced to a hoarse whisper, his tears mixing with the soil that clung to her lifeless skin. Her entire body slumped forward as he desperately tried to hold her with one arm, rocking her back and forth as he cried relentlessly. He gathered her head to his chest, holding her tightly as he sobbed heart-wrenching sobs that echoed through the open space. The reality of her death was too much to bear.

He laid her back on the cold ground, climbing into the open grave beside her, curling his body around hers, desperate to feel some semblance of warmth. The grief consumed him, a ravenous beast that devoured every inch of his soul. He couldn't imagine a world without her in it, without her laugh, her touch, her gentle voice. She had been his *protector*, his *confidante*, his *rock*. He whispered his love to her, his voice cracking with every word. "*One last time, I'll be the one who takes you home.*" He sobbed, almost unable to speak further. Though he knew that even if he took her home, their house—once filled with the echoes of their laughter—would now hold only the sound of Sam's anguish. And *their son...*

*I haven't even thought about our son...*

The chill of the earth seeped into his bones, but he didn't care. This was where he belonged now, *with her*. The darkness closed in around him, and he closed his eyes, ready to join her in the quiet embrace of the afterlife.

But as he lay there, feeling the cold seep through his clothes and into his skin, unaware that the others hadn't disturbed him due to the threat that had awakened, something strange happened.

He felt a faint fluttering in his chest, a warmth that grew with every beat of his heart. It was as if Maddie's spirit was trying to reach out to him, to tell him that this wasn't the end. He didn't understand it, but he knew he couldn't give up, no matter how much he wanted to. He had to find out who had done this to her, *why* she was buried here, in this forsaken place.

With a newfound resolve, he climbed out of the grave, his body stiff from the cold and the effort of digging.

He looked up at the others, desperately trying to continue escaping across the rooftops, having left him behind.

The T-Rooper was relentless, its heat vision cutting through the night as it searched for them.

"What do we do?" Andrew asked, his voice strained with exertion. "What about Sam and Seb?"

"Sam's safe down there, as much as I hate to say it," Val said. "As for Seb, I dunno where he went." He looked around. "We need to lead it into a trap, somewhere we can use *its own power* against it."

Understanding dawned on Andrew's face as he looked around too. "There!" he said, pointing at a switch.

Val nodded, and together they sprinted to the edge of the roof, their hearts in their throats as they stared down at the ground below. The T-Rooper was gaining on them, its magnetic feet clanging against the rooftop. With a leap of faith, they jumped, catching the fire escape ladder just in time. The T-Rooper's footsteps grew louder, its heavy breathing a constant reminder of the danger pursuing them.

As they reached the bottom, Val looked up and saw the T-Rooper hovering above, its magnetic feet keeping it suspended in midair. "*Now!*" he shouted, and Andrew flipped the switch.

The alley was flooded with blinding light, and the T-Rooper let out a screech of pain as it was momentarily blinded. They didn't wait for a second invitation, sprinting into the light. Their eyes stung, but at least the T-Rooper's heat vision was useless.

Hearts racing, they reached the safety of a trailer, the T-Rooper's screeches fading into the distance.

"Should've named ourselves the *Resistance*," Val said, catching his breath.

"We gotta reach the command centre," they heard Tim say. "I know what's after you, and the only way to bring it down, destroy its network."

"Then I'm countin' on you to guide us there."

"Sam can see it with his glasses. I've added the directions to—"

"Sam's not comin' no more."

"What do you mean?"

Val sighed. "Does the name Madeline ring a bell?"

"Yeah, that's Sam's girlfriend and the mother of his child. Why?"

Val didn't know that piece of information, realising he never had a chance to sit down and chat with Sam. He almost felt guilty about it. "She's *dead*. We found her buried alive in a grave." There was silence on the other end of the line. "Tim?" Still nothing. "Tim!"

"Sorry. I..." Val heard a shaky sigh. *"She was like a sister to me. I can't leave Sam alone. Sent me the location."*

"You're *not* gonna risk your bloody life for this. We need to bring this to an end so we can give her the justice she deserves. You *know* the only way outta this is by endin' this once and for all. So, where's this command centre at?"

Another shaky sigh escaped. *"Straight ahead—you're practically standing right in front of it. The USB drive will be the key. If you insert the other side into the T-Rooper, it'll—"*

"I *kinda* already did that," Andrew said. "It didn't do much though."

*"That's 'cause I didn't have time to activate the virus I worked on, just in case we ever had to eradicate 'em. If you can get it back into its mainframe, we might stand a chance."*

"Copy that," Val replied. "Come on, let's get past the backup."

They ventured across the darkened alley, the air thick with the scent of burning metal. They approached the command centre's entrance, and Val checked his weapons. He nodded at Andrew who did the same.

"You okay to kill your first enemies?"

Andrew nodded slowly, sighing deeply. "As ready as I'll ever be, *I guess*."

Val kicked the door open, stepping into a room buzzing with activity. People with various skills and backgrounds were working together, operating and hacking the city's systems. All eyes turned to Val and Andrew.

*"The command centre's a floor below you, but it's heavily guarded,"* Tim said.

"Then what the bloody hell are we lookin' at here?" Val asked.

*"The end."*

Val knew it wasn't their objective, as they had a different plan laid out, but they were in the thick of it now. As he scanned the area, his eyes landed on the fire hydrant just outside the door. He rushed back outside, and before anyone could react, he opened the hydrant, flooding the room.

Water gushed out, filling the space and creating a rushing barricade that destroyed their equipment and forced everyone to flee to avoid electrocution. The T-Rooper's footsteps grew fainter as it rushed to investigate.

Seizing their chance, they slipped back into the building and took the lift down to the command centre. The door slid open to reveal a room thick with tension. Screens flickered with data, and a group of people, surrounded by Troopers, huddled around a central computer.

"*You made it. We need that virus, now.*"

Val nodded to himself, glancing up at the sky for a moment. "Please forgive me for tryin' to save the world, don't let me end up in *hell*, blah blah blah." He opened fire on the Troopers, taking careful aim as he did. The bullets streaked through the air, tearing through the clothes of the front-most Troopers. One of them pulled the trigger of their pistol, the bullet ripping across Val's chest. The impact sent him flying backwards, but the bulletproof vest absorbed the force, preventing any lasting damage.

As Val was locked in the gunfight, Andrew quickly stepped forward, his hand shaking as he inserted the USB drive into the computer. The screens flickered, and the T-Rooper's movements on the monitors grew erratic.

"*Good job, it's working.*"

A glimmer of hope formed in Andrew's eyes. *We can do this. Together.*

Once Val dealt with the Troopers inside, they heard the battle outside intensifying—the clang of metal on metal and the whine of lasers piercing the air.

"You gotta hold out until the virus spreads through the T-Rooper's network," Val said, staring at the download bar as it inched from left to right—far too slowly for his liking.

"*We'll do our best,*" they heard Josh murmur through the earpiece. "*How nice of you to deliver him as a package to us.*"

"Can't have *all* the fun to ourselves, right?" Val chuckled softly.

Andrew's eyes were wide with fear and admiration for Tim's programming. "You're gonna save us all."

"*Don't jinx us.*"

The room was thick with the tense silence of anticipation as they watched the screens. The T-Rooper's movements grew more erratic, then it dropped to the floor. The screens went black.

Val cheered, clapping a hand against Andrew's shoulder with a burst of enthusiasm. "We did it!"

But the victory was short-lived. The doors to the command centre flew backwards, and a squad of Troopers stormed in, weapons raised. Gunfire erupted—the air trembling with each deafening shot. A hail of bullets tore across Andrew's back, agony flaring through him at every impact. His fury crackled through the room as he shapeshifted, his form warping with raw power. The Troopers collapsed, their bodies flattening in a ripple that surged outwards from Andrew like an unrelenting tide.

Val whistled, eyeing Andrew's phoenix form. "And here I thought Ray was the *only* fire-head we had. Bloody hell."

Andrew shifted back to human form with a deep sigh. "Let's just leave."

"You don't need a minute to, *you know*, clear your head before you *confront* our friends?"

Andrew gazed towards the dim glow ahead, emanating from the door left ajar. With no one standing between him and Val, he smiled. "Nah, I'm good. Better than ever, trust me."

Together, they departed the command centre, setting off to reunite with Ray, Alfie, and Josh—and to search for Sam and Seb.

# CHAPTER FIFTY-FOUR

Once they found them, Alfie wiped his nose and turned away, unwilling to let Val see him cry.

"What's up with *him*?" Val asked, though it was clear he had already noticed Alfie's state.

"He found his adoptive brother," Ray said, arms crossed. "We came across his twin, Percy, on the island, but his other brother... we found buried not far away from where you lot found Maddie.

"Bloody hell," Val muttered, casting a glance towards Alfie. He stepped forward, and then—what no one had thought possible—he embraced him. A part of him wished he had done the same for Sam earlier. He would've loathed the idea of going soft on any of them, had he never been exposed to the power of friendship. But as Alfie melted into his embrace, Val realised just how much he had missed out on all those years.

"What's that *smell*?" Andrew asked, wrinkling his nose in distaste.

"Ray's with us," Josh replied, "otherwise I would've said he was *burning* something."

The scent thickened with each passing minute as they struggled to place it. It was faintly sweet—like overripe berries—but laced with an unsettling metallic tang. Whatever it was, it wasn't natural.

They quickened their pace, heading towards the meeting point where the other two groups were supposed to be. Yet as they arrived, an eerie silence greeted them. The dim glow of Tim's laptop flickered, casting warped shadows along the walls. Then, the quiet fractured—a distant thump echoed through the space. *Then another*. It was the sound of bodies hitting the floor. They exchanged a wary glance before following the noise.

They found several of their friends strewn across the ground, caught in various stages of collapse. Some slumped forward, while others had fallen mid-stride, limbs twisted at unnatural angles.

The scent became overpowering as they moved closer, a thick, suffocating fog clinging to the air. It seeped from a diesel-spewing van parked just around the corner. Then, from the mist, a Trooper emerged—a hulking figure clad in a gas mask, his gloved hand gripping the handle of a gas blaster. He didn't spare them a glance, just kept moving, dragging something heavy behind him. As he passed, they caught a glimpse inside the van—where their unconscious friends lay in a heap, piled like discarded ragdolls.

Andrew gasped, his hand flying to his mouth. *"We've to do something!"*

Josh's eyes narrowed. *"Yeah,"* he said. *"We do."*

The Trooper gave no sign of acknowledging them, his footsteps echoing through the silence as he carried out his grim task. The thumps grew more frequent, each one tightening the coil of tension. The gas was spreading, creeping into their lungs—a subtle, insidious pull at the edges of their consciousness.

*"Let's go,"* Val said, his voice edged with urgency. *"We need to find out where they're takin' 'em."*

Andrew nodded, swiping at the drowsiness threatening to drag him under. They had to act fast. Turning the corner, their eyes burned from the acrid air as they spotted the source of the gas—a large canister, hissing as it spewed noxious fumes into the night. And then, before they could react, Tim crumpled to the floor, swallowed by the dark embrace of an unnatural slumber.

*"We gotta turn it off!"* Andrew hissed; his voice strained as lethargy weight heavy on his tongue.

Though the Trooper clutched his gas blaster, ready to finish what he had started, it was the canister that kept their friends locked in unnatural slumber. A mix of dread and urgency propelled them forward, but the closer they got, the stronger the pull of exhaustion became—dragging at their limbs, lulling them towards unconsciousness.

Val snatched up a nearby stick and fumbled with the valve. His movements were sluggish, each second a battle against the creeping haze, but he managed to twist it shut. The hissing ceased abruptly, leaving the air dense with its lingering stench.

*"Boo,"* they heard behind them.

As they turned, a second Trooper had joined the first. With a swift blast from his gas weapon, the last of their group succumbed to the fumes, collapsing one by one before being hauled into the van like the others.

Through heavy-lidded eyes, Val watched groggily as the van doors slammed shut. Summoning the last of his strength, he hit the alarm Tim had installed—a final warning, a desperate signal for Sam and Seb, who were still out there. They were the *only* hope left now.

Sam and Seb emerged from their hiding spot. After leaving Maddie's grave, Sam had stumbled upon Seb, concealed in plain sight as gunfire erupted around them. Now, the gunfire had ceased, and here they stood—on the grounds of a facility ruled by a man who was once their friend but had long since turned cold. In a place like this, hope was a rare and powerful weapon.

*And Sam had hope. Hope* that the silence meant their friends had prevailed. *Hope* that the battle was over. But as they neared the rendezvous point, Sam's heart stuttered. The scene before them was a wasteland of destruction. Sections of the facility lay in ruins, flames devoured what remained, and the air hung thick with the acrid stench of burning rubber and scorched metal.

"What's wrong?" Seb asked, noticing that Sam had stopped leading him forward.

"Nothing. Just... stay *close* to me."

They moved cautiously through the area, keeping to the shadows to avoid any patrolling Troopers that might still be lurking. Up ahead, a group of Troopers had formed a tight perimeter around the building, their weapons raised—holding several of their own at gunpoint.

They crept towards a stack of nearby crates, pressing themselves against the shadows as they blended in. At the front, the Troopers' scanning eyes swept over the area, passing right over them.

"What's happening?" Seb asked.

Sam quickly shushed him by putting his hand over Seb's mouth. *"Quiet."*

"What's going on?" Seb tried again.

Sam observed the group. *"What do you hear?"*

Seb's enhanced hearing proved invaluable as he leaned in closer to the crate, listening intently. *"They're saying these rebels tried to make a stand... and that they should stop resisting against the relentless onslaught."*

*"They're gonna be executed?"* Sam swallowed. If he still had both of his arms, they could've made a move. But they were both disabled now and had to be *extra* careful. *"What else are they saying?"*

*"That they'll soon join the others."*

Sam signalled for them to move, pressing a hand to Seb's shoulder. They slipped into a nearby alleyway, keeping low. *"We need to find a way to help 'em without being seen,"* Sam murmured, his mind racing as his eyes swept the area for anything that could give them an advantage.

And then he saw it—a miniature construction site meant to expand the facility, abandoned in the chaos of the rebel uprising. The cranes and bulldozers sat idle, forgotten in the rush, but they held potential. Sam grabbed Seb and pulled him along, weaving through rubble and shadows. The cranes loomed over the battlefield; their long arms poised like sleeping giants. Without hesitation, Sam began scaling the nearest one, motioning for Seb to stay hidden below.

The climb took longer than it should have, his muscles straining as he hauled himself up. With a final grunt of effort, he reached the controls and activated the crane. The sudden movement snapped the Troopers' attention upwards, but before they could react, the heavy metal arm swung into motion. It struck with devastating force. Troopers were sent hurtling through the air like ragdolls, crashing into the wreckage below.

The sight reignited the rebels' spirit. Those who had been forced to their knees found their footing, pushing back with renewed determination. The tide was turning. Sam leapt from the crane, landing hard before throwing himself into the fight. One arm gone, yet he moved with lethal precision, his machete an extension of his body.

Seb followed, relying on his bat-like sensors to weave through the fray, striking with a desperation that turned into ruthless efficiency. Through it all, Sam's heart thundered in his chest. The battle was fierce, but he knew—they had the upper hand now. The Troopers had power, but no heart. No soul. And that made them *beatable*.

As the last non-rebel Trooper collapsed, one of the rebels turned to Sam, his eyes glinting with newfound respect. "You must be *Sam*. We've heard *a lot* about you."

Sam brushed off the remark. "Have you seen our friends? The ones dressed like me and Seb here?"

"No," said a red-haired rebel, shaking his head. "We were brought out here after the gunfire up ahead died down. No clue who was involved or what happened to *either* side of that fight."

Sam nodded. "And Jonathan? Any idea where he's at?"

"No, but—'"

The Trooper's words died in his throat as Imogen materialised behind him. Her claw drove clean through his chest, ripping out his heart. For a fleeting moment, it throbbed in her grasp before falling still. Panic erupted. The remaining Troopers stumbled backwards, scrambling to escape, but she was relentless—tearing through them one by one with terrifying precision.

Sam's gaze snapped to a semi-automatic rifle lying discarded on the ground. Without hesitation, he grabbed it. 'Help me with this!' he ordered Seb.

They positioned themselves behind the rifle, Seb holding it steady as Sam took aim. His eyes locked onto Imogen—she knew. Somehow, she sensed what was coming. Without hesitation, she bolted towards the nearest entrance.

It didn't make sense. Why was she running *now*, and not *before*?

Sam fired. The rifle rattled in his grip as the bullets tore through her. Pustules along her skin ruptured, spraying foul fluid. But she didn't stop. Imogen scaled a nearby wall, her claws sinking deep into the metal framework. Sam's line of sight wavered—he couldn't get a clear shot. *Then she leapt.*

Her body hurtled towards a nearby platform—straight for the entrance operator's booth. A sickening crunch of metal filled the air, twisting Sam's stomach. He watched, wide-eyed, as she slammed headfirst into the booth, crashing through it as if it were paper.

Imogen's blazing eyes locked onto Sam. Thick saliva dripped from her pincers, while her forked tongue flicked back and forth, tasting the air. Then, without hesitation, she lunged—straight for Maddie's grave. Sam dropped the rifle in an instant, nearly knocking Seb down with it. Sam didn't hesitate. He tore after Imogen.

His steps faltered, horror rooting him in place as he watched her crash to the ground—right beside Maddie's grave. She descended into a frenzy, tearing into Maddie's remains with wickedly sharp teeth. Blood pooled fast, dark and glistening beneath her as she feasted.

"No!" Sam shouted, but the cry caught in his throat as she rose from the shadow of Maddie's grave. Her eyes burned like embers in the darkness.

His gaze dropped to the blood pooling at her feet. His hand lifted, hovering near his mouth—And then, *he snapped.*

His gaze landed on a skewer. Without hesitation, he grabbed it and charged. Slamming into her with full force, he drove her back against a nearby wooden box. He didn't stop until the metal pierced through flesh and wood, pinning her hand in place.

"Good luck eating my girlfriend with a *jacked-up hand*!" he yelled in her face, his breath ragged. She snarled back, low and guttural, her fury burning in her eyes.

The sound of slow, deliberate clapping echoed behind him. He turned sharply, his breath hitching as Jonathan stepped out of the shadows. "Well, well," Jonathan drawled, a smirk tugging at his lips. "Never thought you had it in you to hurt a *lady*. If I recall correctly, you *adored* Jo."

Sam glared at him, his eyes burning with fury.

"You know I *hate* tardiness, don't you? *Always* hated it." He walked closer to Sam. "I was wondering *where* my missing party member was."

He looked over at Seb, slumped over a Trooper's shoulder, being carried towards a van. He knew he couldn't help Seb if he was captured too. Without another thought, he turned and sprinted back towards the woods.

Branches whipped at his face as he crashed through the woods. He clutched his pistol tightly, forcing himself forward, trying not to stumble.

As he raced away, a tiny shape emerged from behind a tree. His instincts screamed at him to change course. He tried to veer left, but before he could, his foot snagged on something hidden beneath a bush. A trap. The snare snapped shut. Agony ripped through him as the metal wire cinched tight, biting deep into his skin. A strangled scream tore from his throat as he hit the ground, pain blinding him.

His vision blurred, eyes watering from the sheer intensity of it. And then—footsteps. *Slow. Purposeful.*

*Jonathan.* Closing in, his presence looming, his walk nothing short of predatory.

"I can get you outta there—but you gotta promise to be a *good boy* first."

Sam studied the well-crafted snare, designed to trap an animal. He understood the simple mechanics of it—a loop of wire, anchored to a sturdy tree branch, set at ankle height to catch unsuspecting prey. His brow creased with worry. Losing an arm had been bad enough—he couldn't afford to lose a foot too.

"You know that it can cut off circulation, *right*? Or break your bones if you don't remove it carefully?"

He shifted lower, pretending to search for the right spot to release the tension. The wire was cold beneath his fingertips, biting into his skin. A sharp wince escaped him as Jonathan, with deliberate cruelty, tightened the trap further, forcing the wire deeper into his flesh.

"Just say you'll be a *good boy*, and I'll get you outta there."

"Why should I believe *anything* you say? You *killed* my girlfriend, didn't you? *Where's* my son? Did you *kill* him too?" His voice was taut with fury.

"I'll take you to your son—who's *very* much alive—if you *promise* to behave. So, will you?"

Sam couldn't tell if he was lying, but the possibility gnawed at him. If Jonathan planned to use his son as leverage, then he *might* still be alive. Slowly—reluctantly—he nodded.

At last, with a metallic click, the wire loosened. Sam gasped in relief as he wrenched his foot free. The gash around his ankle was raw and bleeding, but he forced himself upright. A Trooper seized him, slinging him over their shoulder. He didn't resist—for now. His blood dripped steadily to the ground, leaving a faint trail in his wake.

## CHAPTER FIFTY-FIVE

Sam hit the floor hard, a grunt of pain escaping him.

"Sam!" Tim yelled, jolting awake from the gas's effects. Around him, the others were slowly stirring, emerging from their forced slumber.

Jonathan tossed a first-aid kit towards Tim. "Clean it up."

Tim pulled a relatively clean strip of cloth from the kit and wrapped it tightly around Sam's ankle. The pressure slowed the bleeding, and the cool fabric offered a sliver of relief, but each touch still drew a sharp grunt from Sam. His ankle throbbed relentlessly. He gritted his teeth, eyes burning with unshed tears.

Before he could react, a Trooper slammed the butt of a rifle against Tim's head. He crumpled with a groan, rolling weakly from side to side on the floor. Sam's hand shot to his mouth, stifling a yell. Making noise wouldn't help *any* of them now.

Jonathan smirked mirthlessly, kneeling in front of Sam. "I see you're learning. Guess you remembered I *hate* loud noises."

"*Sam*? That you?" He heard movement in the cell next to him as Stan stirred, waking up groggily.

"Don't worry, *all* your friends are here in the dungeon." He patted the floor beside Sam. "I'll have you know that the exact spot you're sitting was where I kept your girlfriend captive. And those brothers of that *traitor*." He snapped his head to the left, confirming that Alfie was in the other cell beside Sam. "And that maid of hers. I kept 'em *all* here."

"Why?" Sam asked. "Why do *any* of this? Why do you work for Mister X?"

Jonathan got up, leaning against the wall. "Well, I guess I owe you an explanation, hm? *His* plans? *Your* purpose?" He took out a piece of paper, unfolding it. He cleared his throat. "Let me explain the implementation of phase two, as written by Mister X himself."

"*Dear Subjects of OSU,*

*As you are aware, you were part of an experiment two years ago, conducted by my associates, Duncan Ashwell and Wesley Lawrence, during phase one. The reason you are still alive right now is due to a vexatious and uncanny will to survive, despite all the odds we have thrown at you. You have thwarted our phase two, but I shall still explain what this was supposed to entail, so you might understand the brevity of what you have done. Eighteen people were sent to survive on the islands, with only one supposed to leave alive. Out of all those people, you have managed to save three souls who were not meant to survive. You were all part of phase one's experimentation to implement test results, and our ORPHANS were supposed to be phase two. With those two combined, we would have initiated phase three, in which you would have been exposed to a variety of threats—the very kind you have already fought against. Natural disasters and bioweapons, to be exact. This was not meant to occur until phase three, where the island survivors would have been forced to endure the ultimate test—either to kill their family members and fellow stranded islanders or be killed themselves. With our ORPHANS present, we were to gather results on who could potentially defeat them, along with their mutated family members, and who could not. Phases two and three would have taken place solely for my purpose of judging and analysing your responses. Sadly, our meticulously constructed blueprint, our carefully conducted experiment, was ruined by your derelict desire to be a hero. We, therefore, had to accelerate the kill zones to collect the phase two and three resultant patterns simultaneously. This, too, you painfully thwarted. I was supposed to orchestrate this to achieve the greatest breakthrough in the history of warfare—and of science, of course. For centuries, we have been exposed to wars, to citizens who disobey their laws and president, to soldiers who refuse to risk their lives for the greater good. You may have disrupted phase one, but not to the extent that you have sabotaged phase two."*

Tim groaned, clutching his head as he shot a glare at Jonathan. "So, what, everything was just a meticulously planned variable? 'Cause if it was, a bunch of *delinquents* like us wouldn't have been able to destroy the experiments you—"

A Trooper struck him in the back of the head, cutting him off. Sam tensed, instinctively moving to help, but another Trooper raised a gun, forcing him to stay put.

Jonathan carried on as if he had never been interrupted.

*"You would have saved humanity—and yourselves—had you not foiled phase two."* Jonathan paused for effect. "OSU stands for Operation Safeguard Unit, an organisation that exists for one purpose and one purpose only; to rid the world of sinners, to create a society of obedience, to produce a species fit to be controlled. We would have unleashed our bioweapons, allowed the ORPHANS to destroy them, and demonstrated to the citizens that only by abiding the law could

*they be granted protection. If they refused, they would be forced to join the cause—fuelling our progress in the advancement of humanity. We would have injected them with the new serum, refined through the results of phase one and two, to create outstanding bioweapons. Those who chose to ignore our warning would witness the sin of disobedience—and the beauty of order and oppression. We would have eradicated catastrophe, forging a world of followers, purified by divine intervention. We would have kept the cities in tow—"*

"As slaves," Val called from across the dungeon. "You would've forced *everyone* into servitude, strippin' 'em of free will. Turnin' 'em into greenhouse plants without the capacity to think. Trappin' 'em in their *own* bodies like prisoners."

Sam heard Val grunt—no doubt receiving the same treatment as Tim.

Jonathan pressed on, though his agitation was beginning to show.

*"We would have kept het cities in tow by demonstrating our unlimited technology and human capital—advancements beyond anyone's understanding or knowledge—ensuring that only we could help them. That only we could liberate them. They would cease to trust what their own eyes and mind perceived and place their faith in us, their sole saviours. We would operate their brains—"*

"*Manipulation*, that's the word you're lookin' for there!"

Another grunt followed from Val, and Jonathan's foot began tapping against the cold floor.

*"We would operate their brains and nerve receptacles to ensure total obedience, to make them forget their transgressions and become absolved. They would be allowed to live on as bioweapons, aiding us in converting more people to our cause. They would never truly die, instead receiving the unparalleled gift of science—one no other would ever attain. They would be chosen. They would be special. And they would embody a new hope when the OPRHANS defeated them. Because the ORPHANS are our special experiments, the citizens would obey. Everything that has been thrown at you, my dear subjects, served a purpose in our collection of patterns. But your escapes did not. You will be punished for that—by receiving the gift of all gifts. You will be placed before the ORPHANS as an example, to*

*show the citizens what happens when one dares to disobey and derail our absolutism."*

"I won't do your biddin'!" Val shouted. "You can torture me *all* you want, but they're *my* friends! Whatever kinda programmin' you had installed for us—it's failed. Andrew fell in love, and I've gone soft! You've *already* lost, you bloody stupid, dumb, worthless, brainless losers!" Another blow landed. Then another. *And another.*

Sam knew they wouldn't kill any of the so-called ORPHANS. They were too valuable—key to manipulating Zacropolis and the neighbouring cities. Besides, they were practically unkillable. Only *they* had the power to destroy the bioweapons, but nothing, as far as anyone knew, could destroy *them.*

*"We are still dangerously short of what we need, so we must up the ante. You will all remain here while we continue our experiments. Soon, you will be sent to one final island—one we have kept hidden. There, you will be forced to kill each other until a single survivor remains, allowing us to retrieve what we so desperately lack. We will create new ORPHANS using our specially designed Serum X, for we have no other choice. You will become part of phase two-point-zero, enabling us to advance into phase three. It is time for things to be rectified. And do not worry—you have already been exposed to a virus we developed specifically for you. A very special, private concoction that you should feel honoured to receive. For if you disobey, you will die the worst death fathomable, leaving you with every incentive to—"*

"Something close to *Zach's death*?" Sam finally spoke up. "It's close to what *we* were exposed to before, isn't it? Only it's more advanced, and it'll be even slower and more excruciating than what he went through. It'll no longer be just symptoms; it'll be close to debilitating effects that'll force us to succumb painfully *and* slowly."

Jonathan's eyes met Sam's, and Sam could swear he saw the tiniest hint of guilt. Then, *it clicked.*

*"You're* Mister X. It was you *all this time."*

Jonathan sighed, lowering the paper before folding it. "Took you this long to figure it out, huh?"

*"How could you*? How could you *kill* Zach after you made him believe you were *dead*?" Sam screamed.

"He wasn't supposed to die!" Jonathan took a deep breath, steadying himself. "Ashwell forced me to stage my death—had Jo be an accomplice too. I was told that Zach had antibodies in his body, the kind that could potentially lead to a cure for the serum he had administered to *all* of you. At that point, Ashwell had become so reliant on his serum that he couldn't risk a cure being found. But then he told me he could use the antibodies to enhance the serum, to make it even more potent. Jo killed herself 'cause Ashwell ordered her to. If she refused, he would've killed you *and* Zach—the two boys she loved more than *anything*... More than *me*..." Jonathan blinked away his tears, snorting as he hissed softly. "Turns out, it was both of your blood combined, along with a binding agent, that would've created the *cure*. But you... you didn't *just* have antibodies. You were *immune*. Like *me*. Or so I thought." He sighed. "My so-called immunity caused Zach's death. My antibodies should've *never* entered his system. Antibodies clash with antibodies. Only a combination of immunity and antibodies was safe. Not even immunity and immunity—just *one* of each. Ashwell lied to me. Lied to *all* of us." He shook his head. "Zach was an experiment *within* the experiment. And I'll *never* forgive myself for the price he paid for it."

"Jo *knew* Ashwell was lying, didn't she? She tried to warn us."

Jonathan nodded solemnly, doing his utmost to hide his tears. "She knew Ashwell would've tortured her, so she chose her own way out. Can't say I blame her."

"Then why the bloody hell do you wanna torture people yourself? Why do you want world dominance?"

Jonathan barked a laugh, the few tears that had welled up vanishing as if they had never existed. "You *really* think I want world dominance? You didn't listen to a single thing I just read aloud, did you? I'm *sick* of lies and betrayals. *Sick* of people disobeying others for their own gain. *Sick* of people like Ashwell, who think they know better and end up hurting others in the process. *I* wanna control who the bioweapons hurt. I wanna reward those who, like me, are *obedient to a fault*—so that *nothing* like what happened to Zach ever happens again. That's why those experiments and island trials were so important. But you—" he shoved his face closer to Sam, voice rising—"you had to go and *ruin* it! And now I'm forced to sterilise, as it were, to wipe everything clean and start over from scratch. I gotta destroy Zacropolis, erase all traces of the past—both then and now—to make sure we *all* begin equally. I'll build a new city, one shaped in my image—one better than yours. 'Cause Goldlib was dirty too. He *knew* what was happening when Josh was taken. He *initiated* the whole ordeal—to toughen 'em up, to prepare 'em for the worst."

"He prepared us for *you*," Josh spoke up from the cell to Sam's left, "now it all makes sense. He *knew* what you were up to, the things you'd expose us to. He prepared us to go *against* you."

Jonathan slammed his hand against Sam's cell door. "And *he* committed the first sin by doing so!" He let out a menacing chuckle, his bloodshot eyes wild—like a man teetering on the edge of madness. With a heavy sigh, he forced himself to calm. "And with *everything* that has gone awry, I'm left with no choice but to disperse a gasified version over the city—coating *everyone* in the new serum I'm developing. That way, I can round up those who disobey me and inject 'em with *Serum C* afterwards."

"It's no longer a serum, though, is it?" Tim grunted. "It'll be a virus. Can't you see that?"

"I do what's *necessary*! I *never* said I liked it!" He strode towards the cell door, pressing both hands against it. "I'm *forced* to cleans this world of its sins—the very sins birthed by people like Ashwell and Goldlib, who was a terrible father."

"Hold up," Sam said, his eyes widening. "*Was*? What do you mean by *was*? Is he *dead*?"

"You'll see," Jonathan said.

"And Maddie? *Why* did you kill her?"

Jonathan shook his head. "I can't have another immune baby walking around on this earth. Having you and your son was already trouble enough."

Tim shook his head. "But you killed her baby first, didn't you? She had a miscarriage. I could see there was no baby inside her womb when Sam stared at her lifeless body. She didn't *have* to die, but you were afraid they'd try again. That's the *only* reason you had her killed—even though you *knew* you've just threatened 'em *not* to have another child."

Sam knew he should've been shocked, but he couldn't afford to let it sink in. Too much was happening at once for the weight of it to fully reach him. "*Where's* my son?" he finally dared to ask. "If you killed her *and* my unborn baby, and you're gonna kill *me* too, then what do you plan on doing with him? Kill him as well? Or is he *already dead*?"

Jonathan sighed. "If I tell you, what difference does it make? You'll die whether you know or not, and even if you die knowing, you won't remember it wherever you go. It *doesn't* work like that."

"Where's my son?" Sam shouted. His voice was sharp with demand. "*Where*?"

"*Quiet!*" Jonathan roared, slamming a kick into Sam's stomach. "Or I'll take that other arm before I kill you!" Sam crumpled to the floor, gasping in pain as Jonathan stepped back, already turning away. "Enjoy your last night together, Sam, 'cause tomorrow is your last day. And your friends? They're going someplace else." With that, Jonathan strode out of the dungeon, leaving nothing but silence in his wake.

# CHAPTER FIFTY-SIX

Sam sighed softly, glancing over at Tim as he spat a mouthful of blood into the corner of the cell.

"Are you okay?" Sam asked him, to which Tim shook his head.

"No. I can't believe I was so *stupid* to fall for this."

"For what?"

"This location. I should've seen more, but he used a virtual location tool." Seeing Sam's furrowed brows, he sighed softly. "It's basically a masking system—especially useful during calls and other forms of tracking. It lets you manually choose any desired location and obscure everything else."

Sam scooted closer to him. "None of this is your fault. We shouldn't have all gone in at once. We were all so focused on the evidence that we forgot to think smart. I think those islands messed with our ability to think."

"Right. There's a study on that—the possibility of a *serious* decline in the brain's ability to process and retain information, especially after a prolonged period of intense focus."

Sam smiled as Tim slipped back into his occasional nerd talk. No matter how many times they had been broken before, that part of Tim could never be shattered.

Sam leaned back against the wall as Tim continued talking about the study, his mind racing to latch onto any clue buried within Jonathan's words. He fixated on Jonathan's mention of immunity and the threat of a possible cure. The chances of finding Zack were slipping away by the minute.

"Sam?"

Tim's voice jolted Sam from his thoughts. "Yeah?"

"Are you *scared* of death?"

Sam looked over at him, slumped against the wall, his usual nerd talk was silenced. Scooting closer until he was right next to him, Sam draped an arm around his neck. "I'll have peace knowing I'll see my girlfriend again. *And* Zack. And if my son's up there, I'll see *him* too."

"What about *us*?" Tim asked. "We'll *never* find a sanctuary like you again."

"A what?"

Tim chuckled. "Sanctuary? Come on, you can't seriously be telling me you dunno the meaning of that word?"

Sam shook his head, but he *did* know the definition. He just wanted Tim to feel special.

"It's basically a place that you visit to find peace. It's a *safe place.*"

"Ah, of course. Thanks for explaining that to me."

Tim nodded, but his face quickly fell, his expression turning sullen again. "But I'm serious. What will we do when you're... *gone?*" Tears welled in his eyes as he searched Sam's, looking small and afraid. "Don't leave me, Sam. *Please.* I *can't* do this alone."

Sam chuckled sincerely, shaking his head. "Yes, you can, 'cause you've proven again and again that you're more than capable. If there's *anyone*, I trust to continue our mission, it's *you.*"

"Who says I wanna continue? I *don't* want you to leave 'cause I'm scared—I'm scared I'll ruin everything you fought for, everything you've done for us and the citizens. What if I mess it up so badly that we all end up dying on the very islands we so desperately tried to escape?"

Sam touched his chest, right where his heart ought to be. "I'm *not* leaving you, Tim, *ever.* I'm gonna be with you and everyone else." He clenched his hand into a fist and tapped it against Tim's chest. "I'll be right here. *Every day.*"

Tim shook his head. "You can't promise that. Zach isn't here either, *is he?*"

Sam refused to answer, refused to believe there was truly nothing after death—that he would be stuck in some kind of limbo, appearing only when necessary. He *wouldn't* let that happen. "I'll be with you every step of the way, okay? But you gotta promise me you'll keep fighting. You *never* give up fighting. You fight the good fight—every minute, every day—'cause it's the *only* way."

Tim wanted to argue, wanted to shout at Sam that there was no will to live if he was gone—but he stayed quiet. He was tired. Tired of fighting, tired of trying. "*I promise,*" he said eventually, his voice soft but just loud enough for Sam to hear. He whispered, "*We all need someone who gets us like nobody else does.*" Then, a little louder, he added, "*Especially* when we need it the most. I need a soul to rely on, a shoulder to cry on. I need *my best friend* to get me through the highs and lows."

Tim leaned against Sam, who didn't know how to respond to any of it. All he could think to do was take Tim's hand, squeeze it, and nod. As they sat there together, they waited for morning to come.

The sun slowly rose the next morning, casting light over the dawn. Sam was escorted out of the cell, his friends trailing behind him, their heads hung low, hands bound behind their backs. Daylight filtered through the trees as they left the dungeon, illuminating the small structure ahead of them.

Nestled in the heart of the facility stood the gallows, a rope swaying from it.

"Please, you *don't* have to do this," Tim tried, his voice desperate and pleading. "We'll do *anything*."

Jonathan forced Sam to stop walking, then turned around sharply. "Listen, I don't grant mercy to those who've betrayed me and done me wrong. Even if they weren't aware of their betrayal towards me, it's betrayal *all* the same. Now, be a *good boy* and shut up." He slapped the back of Tim's head, then moved to join Sam at the front.

Jonathan brandished his knife as they walked, gripping it with expert precision. Sam knew he would cut him loose with that same knife once life had left his body. Somehow, the sight of Jonathan holding the blade felt more real to him than the impending doom of the gallows.

To his left, Sam saw an older structure resembling the gallows, its wooden beam teetering on the verge of collapse. As they moved forward, a ray of sunshine broke through the trees above, glinting off something metallic. He noticed it came from the thicket of vines just outside the facility's walls, but he dismissed it as a mere coincidence.

As they reached the gallows, Jonathan led Sam up the few steps while the Troopers forced his friends to sit and await the *show*.

"Any last words?" Jonathan asked, his voice thick with a mix of anger and delight as he tightened the rope around Sam's neck.

The tension was palpable, the kind that made the air feel like it was holding its breath.

"No." Sam's eyes were fixed on the horizon, where the sun played a game of hide and seek with the clouds of dawn. His voice was eerily calm, a stark contrast to the storm of emotions raging inside him. "Just make sure it's *quick*."

The gallows creaked in the wind, a morbid reminder of the fate that awaited him. The wooden structure stood tall and proud, a silent sentinel over the dusty facility square. He saw his friends' faces, a canvas of various emotions—pity, anger, anticipation, and a few droplets of genuine sadness. No, not just *a few* droplets. *Full-on, raw sadness*, accompanied by tears and sniffling noses.

Jonathan grabbed a stool, his gaze shifting to Sam's forehead, which was beading with sweat despite the chilly breeze.

"Wait," Sam said, his voice cracking slightly. "I *do* have a few last words." Jonathan let out an annoyed sigh but gave Sam the go-ahead to speak. Sam took a deep breath, his eyes never leaving the horizon. "Just tell my son I'm *sorry*," he murmured, his voice barely audible over the rustling of leaves in the nearby trees.

He let Sam step onto the tiny stool, his toes barely brushing the top. Jonathan kicked the stool away, and the sickening snap of what sounded like his neck was all his friends heard. Sam's body jerked once, twice, then hung still. The finality of death settled in as his eyes remained wide open, slowly glazing over.

Then, a trapdoor beneath Sam's feet swung open with a thud that echoed through the square. There was only a moment of weightlessness before the rope grew taut and snapped. The trapdoor slammed shut with a deafening roar, and Sam plummeted into darkness.

His friends screamed, a racket of horror and disbelief. Some gasped collectively, their eyes wide with shock. As the dust settled, all that remained was a part of the rope, its grim purpose unfulfilled.

"*No!*" Jonathan yelled, rushing to the trapdoor in a frantic attempt to pry it open. "No, no, no, *no!*" He ordered his men to check beneath it, but for some reason, they couldn't find any door or opening. "He was supposed to be *lifeless!*" Jonathan shouted. "His soul was supposed to be sent to meet its maker!"

His voice echoed around the facility. Sam's friends stared in shock, unable to believe what they had just witnessed. If was as if the very earth had decided to swallow Sam whole, but they weren't certain if Sam was truly alive. The sound that had come towards them sounded as if his neck had been snapped, but perhaps he was spared from the noose's cruel embrace.

Jonathan's face went ashen as he called for his Troopers. "Start digging! We *need* to get to him!" he bellowed, his voice cracking with urgency. "Whoever did this *must* be found! I want 'em *both* to be found!"

He exchanged bewildered glances with his right-hand Trooper, who was unsure whether to escort Sam's friends back to the dungeons or leave them to join the search. But Jonathan commanded him to take them back, and the Trooper screamed in frustration, a yell so loud it sent nearby birds scattering in a frenzy.

Sam lay motionless, his eyes wide open. His chest was still, his lungs having shut down. The hanging hadn't taken long to send him to the other side, considering the rope had been secured tightly around his neck. Plus, by the sound of it, he had likely broken a nerve in his neck.

"*Sam?*" He looked up, seeing his girlfriend on the other side of the room. She rushed towards him, crashing into his arms as he hugged her tightly. "*My love,*" she whispered in his ear. "*I missed you.*"

Sam, unsure whether this was real or not, hugged her back with everything he had, almost squeezing her. "*I can't believe I'm holding you, Maddie.*"

She slowly pulled away from him, still sitting in his lap. Gently, she moved a stray strand of hair from his forehead, touching his lips with her finger before leaning in to kiss him. He kissed her back with all his might, inhaling the moment.

He broke the kiss, the questions weighing too heavily on his mind. "*Am I dead?*"

She shook her head slowly, her finger brushing his chin. "You're in a state called *liminality*."

"Which means?"

"Which means that you're neither here, nor up there." He looked at the trapdoor he had fallen through, then back at her.

"But *you're* dead."

"No one's ever *truly* dead, my love." She rubbed his chin and smiled.

"Zack? Where's our son?"

She shook her head. "He's not here, my love. It's just me."

"Zach's not here either?"

She shrugged. "I dunno who *Zach's* supposed to be, and he doesn't know who *I'm* supposed to be. I've been trying to find him—*anyone really*—but I can't find anybody."

"What does that mean?" Sam asked, though a bright, white light forced him to cover his eyes. As he tried to look at her one last time, he watched her fade away. Desperately reaching out for her, he felt himself being pulled away, despite his desperate attempt to stay with her.

He sucked in a huge breath of air, coughing loudly as his eyes shut open. His hands shut up to his neck, feeling the remnants of the rope's prints etched into his skin. He touched his chest, feeling his heartbeat, his lungs filling with oxygen, and emptying it all the same. His chest rose and fell in a panicked rhythm, realising he was very much alive.

As he moved his head to assess his surroundings, he groaned, touching it. The nerve he had broken felt more like a pinched one, sending a wave of pins and needles through him. The pain extended into his arm.

"How the bloody hell am I alive?" he wondered out loud. "It's *impossible*."

"No, it's *not*." He noticed a shadowy figure standing on the other side of the dark hole he had fallen into. "I shot a dart in yer neck tha made it feel as if yeh snapped yer neck, softenin' yer nerves, recreatin' the sound of a snapped neck. Yeh simply passed out, but yeh were nowhere close to death."

It was a female voice, kind but laced with a soft accent he couldn't quite place. Then again, had he heard Albus speak, he would've recognised it. As she stepped out of the shadows and lit a torch, Sam gasped when he saw her face.

"Joanna?"

# CHAPTER FIFTY-SEVEN

She chuckled softly, then let out a sigh. "No, but I get tha a lot. Perks of bein' identical twins." She extended her hand to help Sam to his feet. "Name's Agatha, Aggie fer short."

Her stared at her in disbelief. The resemblance she had to Joanna was uncanny.

"Why did Jo *never* mention you?"

"To ensure she 'ad a back-up plan in case things would go awry. An' awry they went." She cut Sam's bindings. "Sorry 'bout yer arm."

"Yeah, thanks." But then he realised that when he saw Maddie just now, she hadn't noticed he had lost his arm. Or was his arm restored in that moment of being trapped in the veil?

"We need to get yeh outta 'ere," she said, "can you walk?" Sam nodded, taking a few steps forward as she walked towards yet another trapdoor, this one leading outside the facility. But as she turned to glance at Sam, she sighed. "Yer thinking o' goin' back to rescue 'em, don't yeh?"

He nodded slowly. "I can't leave 'em. I'd never forgive myself. Plus, my son's still out there. He's *not* dead, and I *can't* leave him."

She exhaled loudly, letting out a low whistle. "I knew yeh were gonna say somethin' along those lines." She held a set of keys in front of his eyes. "Let's go rescue those nitwits of yers."

Four Troopers guarded the cells in the dungeon, holding their weapons at the ready to shoot any intruders. Tim sat alone in his cell, throwing a tiny stone against the wall to pass the time. He was unsure whether he should cry or not, for he didn't know Sam's fate. It was way worse than the guarantee of death.

Out of the corner of his eye, he saw movement, and before he could fathom who or what it was, he saw Sam slam a foot down on a nearby silver serving tray that had borne the food of the night before. He kicked it up so he could catch it with his hand. In one seamless motion, he swung it in an arc, the edge of it hitting the wrist of a Trooper.

The Trooper spun around, perplexed at who stood in front of him. A bullet from a silenced pistol pierced straight through his brain, and he dropped dead to the floor.

One of the other Troopers planted his arm around Sam's neck. Sam's neck bumped roughly against the Trooper's torso, surprised by how hard his muscles were. With a growl, Sam twisted in the Trooper's grip, grabbing his arm. He planted his feet against him, pushing hard until the Trooper slammed into the wall.

Yet again, a silenced pistol bullet found its way into the brain, and Sam recovered quickly, scrambling back up from the floor. He settled into a low fighting stance as the third Trooper charged him. The Trooper unleashed a flurry of punches, tightly controlled and relentless. Sam deflected his blows barely, giving ground as their fight pushed them closer to Tim's cell, who was so astonished to see Sam alive and in the flesh that he stood frozen by the cell door.

Sam feinted an attack from the left, and the Trooper's fist landed squarely in Tim's stomach, causing him to crumple to the floor. Sam swooped right, leaping at the Trooper and tackling him to the ground. Sam pinned him on his back with his knees as the Trooper's voice turned low and husky, almost a growl. His gaze shifted from Sam to the weapon Agatha held. "You can *kill* us, but you *won't* get outta here alive."

"We'll jus' 'ave to see 'bout tha," she replied, shooting him point-blank. Then, she shot the last remaining Trooper before he could shoot Sam and smiled. "Good work, especially with one arm."

"Thanks," he said, taking the keys from one of the Troopers, he unlocked his friends' cell doors.

"Yer not from around here, are ya?" Alex asked her. "I can hear yer accent's a lot thicker than mine."

"Born an' raised elsewhere. Joanna an' I were separated after birth, but tha never stopped us from stayin' in touch in secret." She looked over at Alfie. "Yer brathair was my husband. I'm sorry fer yer loss."

Alfie walked over to her, and despite knowing her for only a few seconds, he hugged her tightly. "I'm just glad I've found family after losing 'em all."

She smiled, patting his back somewhat awkwardly. "Don' worry kid, I'm not goin' anywhere. Can' miss out on gettin' to know yeh. Albus spoke highly o' yeh an' Percy, said he missed both o' yeh a lot. An' he regretted teh way things 'ad gone."

"*Me too,*" Alfie said, slowly letting go of her. "I'm sorry too."

She nodded, wiping away a tear that rolled down his cheek. "C'mon, let's get teh bloody hell outta 'ere." She wrapped an arm around his neck and escorted him outside, with everyone else following in tow.

As they ascended from the dungeon, they quickly hid under nearby undergrowth, watching as Imogen descended on several Troopers who seemed helpless despite their weapons. She tore into them with her teeth and claws, much to everyone's surprise.

"I thought Jonathan's injection programmed her to his will?" Andrew asked as he whispered. "Then why the bloody hell does she attack her own people?"

"I think I know why," Josh said, pointing at their Kite. "He's taking off. If we don't stop him, we won't have a way to get home, and he'll be able to destroy everything he's built. He'll have a clean slate, and no one can betray him. We would've gone down with it."

Bile rose in Sam's throat, but he forced himself to watch as the Troopers were devoured. He had memorised each of their faces when he was about to be hanged, so he could haunt them in the afterlife. But now, he just had to watch—for the sake of justice. *Madeline's justice.*

Terrified screams filled the air behind them as Imogen broke into a shambling run after finishing with the first group, her teeth and claws bared as she descended upon her next batch of helpless prey.

"Any plans?" Phil asked. "I know a bunch of us are useless, considering she doesn't react to weapons."

"We'll take care of it," Val said determinedly. "All of you just gotta distract her long enough for us to strike."

They all nodded, and as they separated, Phil pulled Andrew towards him, kissing him passionately. Andrew hummed quietly; his eyes closed. When Phil pulled away, he rubbed Andrew's cheek, causing Andrew to open his eyes. "You come back to me; you hear?"

Andrew nodded slowly, kissing Phil once more. "There's not a bloody thing in this world that can stop me from returning to you."

With one final kiss, they parted, and Phil watched with heartache as his boyfriend walked away from him.

Despite the panic that flickered across Sam's face, he was determined to get everyone home safe and sound. His panic-stricken expression was quickly replaced by steely resolve. He grabbed a shovel that lay nearby. Their confiscated weapons were beyond reach, and not even a machete could be found lying around.

Agatha followed his lead, grabbing a nearby rake. Stan and Alex began devising a distraction as they sneaked closer to Imogen, who was peacefully munching on a Trooper's body.

"Oi! *Fatty!*" Alex yelled, throwing a rock at her.

She turned around sharply, her eyes blazing with fury. Alex dove to the side as she charged, chunks of turf flying as she bore down on him with alarming speed.

Agatha charged at her with the rake, scraping it across her back. Imogen screamed in pain, then sent Agatha flying with her massive arm. Agatha slammed into the wall hard, slumping down against it.

Sam glanced over at Seb, who used his senses to locate Imogen. Sam knew he had to keep Seb out of harm's way, but he also knew Seb wouldn't forgive him if he did. He felt a tap on his shoulder and turned his head towards Alfie.

*"See that?"* Sam followed his finger, pointing at a motorbike. *"I've got an idea. Cover me."*

Before Sam could refuse, he sprinted away. Imogen caught sight of him and charged after him but didn't get very far when Sam aimed the shovel, hitting her straight in the head with it. The shovel clattered to the ground with a loud clang. She turned her attention to where it had come from. Once she had Sam in her crosshairs, she charged again.

Tim pulled Sam out of harm's way just in time as she barrelled past them, crashing into the wall next to Agatha, who quickly scrambled to her feet, limping away from Imogen.

They heard the roaring of the motorbike as Alfie revved the acceleration to get her attention, using it to threaten her. As she turned to face him, he took off. She ran towards Alfie, but he didn't back down. He revved the acceleration further, then used the platform of the gallows as a ramp. Some of her flesh was shredded beneath the tires, chunks of her flying off. She crumbled to the ground, roaring in aggression.

Alfie lost control of the motorbike and crashed hard to the ground, his knees scraping as he slid until he came to a halt in front of Seb. Seb stretched his arms out to feel for Alfie, pulling him towards him for safety.

Imogen got back up, roaring once more, and as she lurched closer, Josh brandished the shovel he had picked up after Sam's throw, his hands trembling slightly. All he saw in front of him was the Trooper who had done him the most harm, and in the rage of his flashback, he swung at Imogen. The shovel connected with a sickening thud. Imogen stumbled back, groaning in pain, but she didn't fall. She fixed her gaze on him, hunger burning in her lifeless eyes.

Val focused his mind, and the shovel began to hover in the air. He sent it straight down into Imogen's back from above, and she howled in pain. From that angle, *no one* could've impaled her that way. She was transfixed by the unexpected movement, as Andrew, having shapeshifted into a cheetah, dashed around her, leaving a trail of afterimages in his wake.

Her head snapped back and forth as she tried to follow Andrew, who nimbly dodged her outstretched arms.

Seb stepped forward, a brick in his hand, and with a grunt, hurled it at her legs. The impact made her trip, and she hit the ground with a thud, sending a plume of dust into the air.

The moment she was down, the others pounced. Val levitated more objects to keep her at bay while Ray set her alight like a tinderbox. Toby summoned the spirits of the dead Troopers surrounding them. They rose to their feet and began attacking Imogen relentlessly, the sound of impacts and snapping bones filling the air.

Reggie, now invisible, crept close enough to plant a makeshift Molotov cocktail beneath her body—courtesy of Ray. Slipping away, he grabbed a rock and hurled it at the bottle they had found nearby. Flames fanned out beneath her, and Ray let out a celebratory whoop as more and more of her skin began to vanish.

They knew she could regenerate her limbs, so they did everything they could to stop her from doing so.

But Imogen was *relentless*, her movements growing more erratic and dangerous as she attempted to rise. Then, as Vince froze her in place with ice, Andrew marched forward as a hybrot. He turned the shovel used earlier into a spear, fusing his biological and electronic elements. Ray gave him an extra boost by sending electricity towards it, charging the shovel.

Andrew yelled as he charged at Imogen, who watched in horror at the crackling spear. She groaned as Andrew drove it straight through her heart. She gasped, slowly falling to the ground, her knees hitting the concrete first. She pulled the spear out, but it was too late. Her body crackled with the intensity of the energised metal.

Her torn clothes came into view, her skin turning a sickly grey. Her vacant eyes shifted into human eyes, her mouth still smeared with blood. Traces of the creature she had been before remained, but she regained a bit of her humanity.

Her eyes met Andrew's as he fell to his knees beside her, having shapeshifted back. He held her, cradling her as she slipped further into his embrace. *"Andy..."* Her hand reached up to his face as tears welled in his eyes. *"I'm so sorry..."* she whispered, her voice barely audible. *"I was trying to protect you... pretending to have forgotten you..."*

"I'm *not* a kid anymore, mum," he said through his tears.

She smiled weakly. *"I know that, but a mother's job... it's never done..."* Her voice went hoarse as she coughed. *"I tried to stop him... that man. He said he'd hurt you... if I didn't cooperate. I let him... transform me 'cause he promised me... you'd be safe."* She noticed a small blade lying near a Trooper's head. She reached for it. *"You must finish it,"* she told him, her voice urgent. *"You must end this before it's too late... and I turn back."*

"No," he said, shaking his head determinedly. "We can change you back, mum. You can become *human* again. Sam here, he made people turn back into humans before. He can do it *again*. I *know* he can do it again, mum. He can do it ag—"

She stopped him, placing a finger on his lips. *"Please."* She put the blade in his hands, closing his fingers around it. *"I can't hurt you again..."*

His hand shook violently. "I *can't*," he choked out, "I *can't* do this. I *can't* lose you too after losing Minnie. I just got you back."

With a heavy heart, she leaned in and kissed him on the forehead. *"I love you,"* she whispered, *"remember that."* She turned her body towards the blade, aiming for her heart. The moment the blade pierced her heart—this time, her human heart—she felt the serum's particles retreat, the hunger for flesh and death dissipating. She gasped for breath, feeling human again. *"Goodbye, my son,"* she managed to say, her eyes filled with love and sorrow.

Andrew watched in disbelief as she took her last breath, the colour returning to her cheeks. He pulled the blade out and dropped it, sobbing uncontrollably as he tried to stop the bleeding. "Mum, please, don't leave me!" he yelled, "please don't go! *Please!*" He applied pressure to her wound, his hands soaked with her blood. "Stay with me! Mum, *please* stay with me!" Phil walked over to Andrew, trying to pull him away from her. "No! Let go of me! *Let me go!*" But Phil refused, cradling Andrew in his arms as he sobbed, wetting Phil's shirt.

The others sank to the ground next to Andrew, and Sam and Alfie, having lost their own family, knew the pain he was experiencing. Both placed a hand on Andrew's back, connecting with him in a way no one else could. All they knew, in that moment, *was loss.*

# CHAPTER FIFTY-EIGHT

The ground beneath them trembled. Sam's eyes widened as he felt the vibration in his chest, a strange and unsettling tremor that grew stronger by the second. The horizon split open, a fissure in the earth snaking towards them. From the depths of the crevice emerged a creature that defied all logic. It was heavily built, but not like anything they had seen before. This monstrosity had a hydraulic-powered lung hanging outside its body, a grotesque parody of Tim's invention.

The lung thrummed and pulsed, a horrific symphony of mechanical and biological sounds that sent chills down Sam's spine.

The creature's face was a twisted mask of agony and rage, distorted beyond recognition. Skin flaps overlapped, as if sewn together by a mad surgeon in a hurry, and staples held other parts in place. But Sam swore he *knew* it.

His gaze was drawn to the glaive that grew from the creature's pectoral muscle, the blade a ghastly extension of bone and sinew, adorned with retractable claws and needles that gleamed in the fading sunlight. As the creature took a step forward, a row of metallic spikes slid from its spine, eliciting a gasp from Sam.

The creature's entrance had the unintended effect of splitting the group into two. Sam watched in horror as the creature, which had once been a man, came into view. Then it hit him, based on Jonathan's earlier comment. *"Henry?"*

The tremor grew into a full-blown earthquake. The ground shook so violently that the very foundations of the facility seemed to tremble.

*"Bravo! You've killed my first, real creation! Didn't think you had it in you."* Sam could swear he heard Jonathan laugh from up there, though his ears still hummed slightly from the impact of Henry's landing. *"I see you've met your beloved President!"* they heard the Kite's megaphone say, looking up at it hovering just above them, the spotlight of its searchlight landing squarely on Henry. *"Isn't it magnificent? This might be my best creation yet."*

"What did you do to him?" Sam asked, "what did you give him?"

Jonathan, who had planted a microphone on Imogen, heard Sam's question loud and clear. He laughed, and Sam rolled his eyes at him. *"What can I say? I somehow knew you'd defeat Imogen, so I advanced the serum against everyone's advice. Those who advised against me are dead. And I've observed you, working together to defeat Imogen, which means she had a flaw. But Henry, he can't be killed. You see, I made his skin so rubbery that nothing can penetrate it. Anything that tries bounces right back. So, please, go ahead and try. I'd love to see one of you die by your own hand."*

"So, what? Not even our *superpowers* can defeat him?" Val asked. "I thought you wanted to use us as superheroes to show the world they could still rely on you to save 'em and be the *ultimate hero*?"

"Well, plans change. As I'm sure you know, Sam was supposed to be dead, and you would've been escorted away, but someone ruined my plans once again. And I'm sick of my plans being ruined!"

A few warning shots from the turret landed right next to Sam, missing him by barely a hair.

"So, let's see how well you'll fare against the masterpiece I call Physicorum, which basically means indestructible. 'Cause Henry is no more."

Hearing his new name, Physicorum launched himself, landing with a thunderous boom. It sent a shockwave that knocked over walls and cracked the pavement. The earthquake had separated the two groups further, leaving six of them exposed, staring down their new nightmare.

Physicorum took a lumbering step towards the group of six, its eyes locked on Sam. Agatha grabbed Sam's hand and sprinted towards the wall, with Josh, Tim, Val, and Alfie following. The heavy thuds of Physicorum's footsteps echoed behind them.

Agatha led them to a hidden entrance. Upon entering, they realised she had been stationed there *in secret* for quite some time. Sam had many questions, but the air was so thick with the smell of oil and metal that he couldn't concentrate enough to form words.

His heart raced as he watched her rummage through some tools. Her eyes scanned the room with the precision of a hawk. "Ah, 'ere," she said, thrusting a handful of spanners and wrenches into their arms. "Use these if it gets too close."

"He just said that *no* objects will work!" Val said, taking one of the tools from her. "Nor will our powers!"

"Jus' trust me!" she yelled.

Physicorum had followed them, the door they had entered hanging off its hinges. Sam's grip tightened around the cold metal, his palms slick with sweat. Physicorum's lung was in overdrive, pumping air in and out with a frantic rhythm that seemed to fuel its rage.

"Remember, aim fer teh joints," she instructed. She picked up a makeshift spear, a piece of rebar sharpened to a fine point. Physicorum lunged, and Sam swung wildly. The tools clanged against its armoured chest. Physicorum roared, a sound that shook the very air they were breathing. It swiped at Sam with the glaive.

Agatha stepped in. The spear flashed through the air, impaling Physicorum's lung. Physicorum stumbled back, the lung hissing and spurting fluid. Sam seized the opportunity, darting around it and heading for the back door, the others in tow.

But Physicorum wasn't so easily deterred. With a snarl, it pulled the spear from its chest and tossed it aside, the lung already repairing itself. The spikes along its spine grew longer, gleaming in the flickering lights. Sam could see the gears turning in Agatha's head as she searched for a new plan, her eyes darting around the room.

"Teh van!" she shouted, pointing to the beat-up van parked in the corner. "We can use it to get away!"

The others heard her idea, and Sam watched as those they had been separated from sprinted for the vehicle. As they took off, Physicorum's footsteps pounded closer. Sam and Val tossed the tools into the back and fumbled with the passenger door as the others climbed in.

Agatha dove into the driver's seat and turned the ignition. The engine roared to life. Physicorum's hand slammed down on the bonnet, but Agatha didn't flinch. She slammed the gas, and the van lurched forward. Agatha glanced in the side mirror as Physicorum was thrown aside, its body crumpling against the wall.

For a moment, they thought they had escaped. But as they tore down the beaten path, the lung fully restored and the spikes on its back quivering with malice, Sam's heart sank. He realised the horror wasn't over. Physicorum was relentless, driven by a hunger they could never comprehend.

With a roar of the engine, Agatha navigated the van through the woods, dodging trees left and right. Physicorum was relentless, its monstrous form closing in with each passing second. Sam clutched the door handle, his knuckles white with fear as he watched Physicorum gain on them. Its lung pumped faster, the sound a horrific symphony that seemed to spur it on. Physicorum leapfrogged over a toppled car once they hit the road, which seemed to appear out of nowhere but had been abandoned for quite some time. It landed with a crunch of metal and glass. Agatha swerved to avoid it, the van's tires screeching as they lost traction.

They could hear the others in the back of the van scream and hit the walls, unable to hold themselves upright.

Physicorum was closing in, its glaive poised to strike.

In a daring move, Agatha slammed on the brakes, sending Physicorum hurtling over the bonnet. The van's momentum carried them forward, and Sam watched in the side mirror as Physicorum slammed onto the pavement.

Physicorum rolled to its feet, unfazed by the impact, and began to give chase once more. Sam's chest tightened as he saw the spikes on its back extend further, each step sending tremors through the ground.

They rounded a corner of a nearby deserted town, and Sam spotted a narrow alleyway. "Take it!" he yelled.

Agatha nodded; her jaw set in determination. The van barrelled down the alley, barely fitting between the brick walls. Sam could feel Physicorum's breath on his neck, the vibrations from its steps shaking the very metal of the van.

But the alley was a trap. The exit was blocked by a collapsed building, and Physicorum was closing in.

Agatha slammed the truck into reverse, but it was too late. Physicorum's glaive sliced through the air, embedding itself into the driver's side door. Sam watched in horror as Physicorum wrenched the door off its hinges, reaching for Agatha.

Her scream was cut short by a deafening crash as the van collided with the alley's entrance. The impact sent them spinning, the world outside becoming a whirlwind of metal and concrete.

Sam felt the crunch of bones as he was thrown against the dashboard, and he knew that Physicorum had made contact. The van's alarm blared. When the world stopped spinning, Sam found himself in a twisted mess of metal and shattered glass. Val groaned beside him, his face a mask of pain, but he was alive. Agatha was nowhere to be found.

Through the windshield, he could see Physicorum, its body crumpled but still moving. The lung had been damaged, its rhythmic pulsing erratic, but it was clear that it wasn't going to stop until it had claimed its prey.

The others in the back of the van let out a mix of moans and whimpers. Sam could see blood seeping from their wounds as the barrier behind him had been broken upon impact. None of them lay still. They had survived the *initial* assault, but they were trapped and vulnerable. Sam *knew* they had to act fast.

"We *need* to get outta here," Tim said, his voice shaky but firm. "We *can't* stay in this death trap."

Sam nodded; his eyes glazed with pain. "We gotta find Agatha first," he murmured. "She'll *know* what to do next."

But Physicorum had other plans. With a roar that seemed to shake the very earth, it began to pull itself towards the wrecked van, the glaive still lodged in the door, dragging a trail of sparks behind it.

Sam knew that their chances of escape were dwindling. They had to move—and move *now*.

Gritting his teeth, he managed to unbuckle his seatbelt and push himself out of the van. His legs wobbled beneath him, but he forced himself to stand. Adrenaline flooded his veins. Physicorum was almost upon them, its twisted face a snarling rictus of hunger and anger. Sam took a deep breath and stepped forward, the tool in his hand feeling surprisingly heavy.

"*Stay back*," he warned, his voice stronger than he felt. Physicorum paused, its eyes narrowing, the lung's hissing growing more erratic. Sam tightened his grip on the tool, raising it like a shield.

Physicorum lunged again, and Sam swung the wrench with all his might, connecting with Physicorum's knee joint. The blow sent a shockwave through his arm, but Physicorum barely flinched. It brought the glaive down in a sweeping arc, and Sam dove out of the way just in time. The blade bit into the pavement, sending up a spray of sparks.

"*Now!*" Val yelled; his voice strained.

Sam turned to see him struggling with the stuck door, his body contorted in pain. Sam stumbled back to the car and yanked the door open, pulling Val out just as Physicorum was about to attack again. Physicorum loomed over them, its twisted face leering down, the lung's rhythm increasing in intensity.

Sam knew they couldn't fight it in the open like this. He scanned the alley for an escape route, his eyes falling on a metal ladder leading up to a fire escape. "The ladder!" he pointed.

Physicorum seemed to know what their plan was, sending the van flying as it used all its strength to do so. Sam and Val watched in horror as the van landed on its roof, the others still inside.

"No!" Sam yelled, but Val pulled him towards the ladder. Both stumbled towards it as Physicorum's steps pounded closer.

Sam climbed first, his muscles screaming with effort as he used only one arm. He pulled Val up after him with *all his might,* but he wasn't fast enough. Physicorum's hand grazed Val's ankle, but he kicked it away, climbing higher. The ladder groaned under their weight but held firm.

As they reached the top, Physicorum's lung gave a final, desperate wheeze before bursting open, showering them with a foul mixture of gore and grease. Sam retched, the smell overwhelming. It burned their skin, resembling a chemical reaction.

Sam's heart raced, causing him to spiral into a panic attack. "I *don't* wanna lose another arm! I don't wanna—"

Val stopped him from spiralling, dragging Sam into the safety of the building.

They collapsed into a second-story apartment, slamming the window shut just as Physicorum reached up. Sam could hear the scraping of metal on brick as it tried to follow them.

Val poured some water from his flask—surprisingly, Jonathan had never taken it from him—over Sam's burns, then over his own.

"We *can't* stay here," Sam panted. "Henry will find a way in."

"That's *not* Henry, so *don't* call him that," Val spat, throwing his empty flask away.

He refused to let Sam tell him otherwise, pulling him along as they stumbled through the darkened room, avoiding the shattered glass and debris. Sam's mind raced, trying to formulate a plan. Their city was miles away, and this town wasn't safe. They *had* to find another way.

"The *basement*," Val said, his voice weak but determined. "We can *barricade* ourselves in until help comes."

"*If* help comes."

Sam knew he meant Agatha, but he wasn't so sure they would get out of this alive.

They made their way down the stairs, the air growing colder and danker with each step. Sam's heart hammered in his chest as they stumbled into the dark, musty space. The sound of Physicorum's claws scraping against the wall grew fainter, but Sam knew it wouldn't be long before it found another way in.

They gathered what they could to block the door—broken furniture, boxes, anything that could potentially help. Sam's hand trembled as he held a crowbar, ready to fend off Physicorum if it breached their makeshift barricade.

The wait was agonising. Each creak and groan from the building above sent a bolt of terror through him. He could feel the weight of Val's gaze on him, his eyes full of fear and hope. They had to survive and find a way to stop Physicorum.

As the hours dragged on, the sounds from outside grew fainter. Sam's arm ached from holding the crowbar, but he didn't dare let go. Physicorum was still out there, waiting, and Sam *knew* it wouldn't give up easily.

Then, a knock on the basement door. *"It's me,"* came the voice.

Hearing Agatha's voice, they moved some furniture away. Sam hugged Agatha, who hugged him back.

"Where's he?" Sam asked her.

She shook her head. "No idea. When I came to, he was gone. Yer friends are severely wounded. We all are." She sighed. "We need to get 'em, 'an ourselves, to a doctor. We should get to tha' city o' yers, lay low. Think o' a plan, find an army, fight back. But not right now. *Right now*, we tend to teh wounded."

Sam nodded, and together with Val, they followed Agatha outside to check up on their friends. Sam dreaded what he would find. Or rather, in which *state* he would find them.

# CHAPTER FIFTY-NINE

Sam never thought about the possibility that Physicorum would simply give up and move back to the crash site. When they arrived, they found Physicorum slicing through a whole pack of wolves like they were paper dolls. He looked over at the van. The doors were still shut, meaning the others had the same idea to hide and hope for the best.

The sun hovered lazily in the sky, casting long shadows across the cracked asphalt. Sam swore he heard a door opening and looked over at the passenger's side. He watched as Seb crawled out, a dust cloud billowing around him as his feet hit the ground. His clothes were torn and bloodstained.

"Seb, no..." Sam said. As he prepared to walk over to Seb, Val stopped him.

"*Don't.* You're too far away to reach him in time. It's *too late.*"

Sam watched helplessly as Seb began to yell. "Oi! Ugly piece of arse! Yeah you, bloody arsehole! I'm *right here!*"

Physicorum turned around sharply, his glaive glinting in the sunlight. His skin was even greyer and more decayed than before. With a sudden burst of speed, Henry swung his glaive at the van while Seb ducked out of the way. The blade sliced through the metal with a high-pitched screech, sending sparks flying. The van's side panel fell away like the peel of an orange, exposing the others inside.

"*Now!*" they heard Alex yell as they dragged Stan outside. His leg was busted, and as Sam observed it from afar, it was clear it had been crushed after the van had been hit. *Seb didn't distract Henry 'cause he had a death wish; he did it to save Stan.* A sense of pride washed over Sam. *That's my boy.*

Physicorum raised his weapon again, the muscles in his unnaturally powerful arm rippling with unnatural strength. Before anyone could fathom what was about to happen, Physicorum's glaive disappeared into a mist of decayed flesh and bone. In its place grew a chainsaw, revving to life with a gruesome metallic growl.

"What the bloody hell's that?" Val managed to croak out.

"That's not possible," Sam said, "that's just *not* possible."

With a flick of its wrist, the chainsaw blade grew longer, extending into a deadly whip. Physicorum grinned wickedly as he lashed out, the teeth of the chainsaw cutting through the air like a serrated blur. He stepped in front of the van, with a few still inside. The chainsaw blade swiped through the air with a deafening screech, slicing through the van's side and splitting it cleanly in two.

The empty half raced down the tiny hill where Alex and Josh had dragged Stan, skidding to a stop in front of them. The two halves of the van stood firm up the hill, smoke billowing from the shattered chassis. The air thickened with the stench of burning rubber and gasoline. Physicorum stepped closer to the wreckage, his chainsaw arm pulsing with sickening vitality.

"It's gonna blow!" they heard Andrew yell. "Quickly! *Get out!*"

Andrew ran towards Seb, grabbing his hand. As they fled from the van, the gas tank ruptured with a deafening boom. The explosion sent a shockwave that knocked them off their feet, their ears ringing. The heat washed over them, setting their clothes alight and searing their skin.

They rolled on the ground, fighting to extinguish the flames that clung to their clothes and hair. Through the smoke, they saw Physicorum staggering away from the blast, his chainsaw arm was a twisted mess of metal and flesh. He roared in frustration, his eyes glowing with malevolent rage.

The boys were scattered around, some on the ground, others crawling away from the inferno. The smell of burning flesh filled the air, making Sam's stomach turn. *They had to move fast.*

Grimacing against the pain, Andrew and Tim stumbled to their feet and saw Sam, Val, and Agatha running towards them. Then, they heard Ray's voice behind them.

*"Help me,"* he choked out, his eyes pleading. *"Alfie...* he's still in there somewhere."

Sam and Andrew exchanged a look. They knew the risks but couldn't leave anyone behind. Val tried to stop them, but they stumbled back into the flaming wreckage, leaving Val, Tim, and Agatha behind, their distress palpable as Agatha supported Tim.

The heat was intense, the smoke thick and choking. The interior of the van was a twisted nightmare of shrapnel and fire. They moved as quickly as they could, their eyes stinging from the acrid smoke. Then, they saw him—a small figure curled up in the back, unconscious. Sam and Andrew didn't hesitate; they grabbed Alfie and dragged him out of the van while Ray kept the flames at bay.

The flames licked at their heels, but didn't reach them.

They emerged into the open, gasping for breath, and laid the unconscious Alfie on the ground, assessing his injuries.

Physicorum had recovered from the blast and was heading straight for them, his ruined chainsaw arm flailing wildly. They had *no choice* but to run.

The sudden boom of a rocket pierced the air, shaking the very foundation of the earth. Sam's eyes widened with a mix of hope and fear. *Is that a rescue? If so, who's left to save us? Is it a new threat?*

He watched as the rocket slammed into Physicorum with the force of a meteor. The explosion was so intense that, for a moment, Physicorum appeared as a silhouette against the blinding light. Yet, when the dust settled, Physicorum remained standing—his body charred and twisted, but not destroyed.

"What does it take to *kill* this thing?" Val asked, his voice dripping with annoyance.

Sam watched in awe as Physicorum staggered back, his chainsaw arm lost in the explosion. The rocket hadn't killed him, but it had weakened him significantly. They took it as their cue to escape. They gathered everyone—Vince carrying the unconscious Alfie on his back—and sprinted away from the outskirts of the facility, putting as much distance between themselves and Physicorum as possible before it regenerated.

The world was a blur of flaming metal from the van and rocket. They darted through the wreckage, their hearts pounding in their chests, careful not to trip over the debris that littered the ground. The smoke from the burning van choked them, making it hard to breathe.

As they got further from the crash site, they stopped. They didn't dare speak, their breaths coming in ragged gasps. They focused on putting one foot in front of the other, their legs burning with exertion. The unconscious Alfie stirred on Vince's back, his eyes fluttering open.

"How are you doin'?" Val asked him.

"*Been better*," he managed to say.

"There, am I seeing that right?" Reggie asked, pointing at a Kite. "Jonathan in there?"

Sam shook his head. "No, that was Henry's." He walked closer to it, finding a note.

**"You're welcome. Both times. Signed, R."**

Sam wanted to question who *R* was, but Tim beat him to it. "We can *finally* go home." He gently lowered Sam's arm, which was holding the note. "So, let's go home. *Please.*"

Sam looked over at the others—broken, bruised, and barely alive. They needed medical attention, and they needed it *now*.

He nodded slowly. "Okay, let's go home."

*We can deal with our mysterious helper later.*

Despite Sam wanting to look for his son, he *knew* he wasn't anywhere in the facility. He just *knew*. It pained him to leave and make it seem as though he hadn't even tried, but he had his friends to take care of. With the confirmation right in front of him that they were still alive, he had to *prioritise* them over his son's *uncertainty*.

They got everyone into the Kite and set off for Zacropolis.

When Agatha landed the Kite and its doors opened, Sam's heart pounded in his throat. They emerged into a Zacropolis that wasn't the one they had left behind.

They stared at the mist-shrouded ruins that had once been homes, the road deserted, with cars scattered everywhere. Wooden frames creaked slightly in the wind. The city, once vibrant with the chatter of bustling families, now echoed with silence. Dust settled on burst furniture, leaving a fine layer that reflected the dim sunlight filtering through the clouds.

Half-eaten food lay strewn about, some slowly browning. A single ant marched across the ground, its antennae twitching as it searched for food. The sun cast a ghostly glow on weeds overtaking the sidewalks. The streetlights flickered sporadically, despite it being daytime. The occasional gust of wind sent a chill down the spine of the empty homes, as if the very air was whispering a secret—a secret it had been holding too long.

A wolf's distant howl pierced the silence, a mournful song that seemed to carry the weight of the abandoned city. The echoes bounced off the desolate buildings, creating a sense of loneliness that was palpable.

One car in particular caught Sam's attention. He walked over to it. It appeared mostly intact; unlike the others he could see around him. It had veered off the road, straight into a nearby tree. The windshield was cracked, and the driver's side door was warped, but there was no other visible damage.

A lonely tune hummed somewhere in the distance; the only sound not silenced by the stillness that had engulfed the remains of the once vibrant city. Sam turned his head towards the source of the sound and noticed another car—this one upside down.

He ran over to the car, and to his astonishment, a young girl was trapped inside. Poppy was small for her age, with curly auburn hair matted to her forehead by sweat and blood. Her clothes were torn, and dirt streaked her pale skin, but there was a spark of defiance in her wide, brown eyes. Sam waved Val and Ray over. Their muscles strained as they yanked open the jammed door. Sam took the girl's arm and helped her out of the severely damaged car.

"Are you hurt?" he asked her, noticing the dried blood on the side of her head. "How long were you stuck in there?"

"I dunno," she said earnestly. "My daddy was with me, but he left to get help. Then the car tumbled over, and I couldn't see what caused it. I heard my daddy yell my name before everything became silent."

"How did you survive so long without food and water?" Val asked her.

"My daddy put a bag filled with food next to me. I lived off it all this time."

"How old are you?" Ray asked.

"Nine. *And a half*," she added with a smirk.

"And what's your name?" Sam asked her.

She looked over at Sam, then noticed he only had one arm. "Are you a *pirate*?"

He couldn't help but chuckle at her innocent question, shaking his head. "No, but that would've been cool. What do you think my pirate's name would've been?"

She stared at him, thinking hard, her eyes scrunched. "*One-armed Buckler*!"

Sam smiled softly. "That's a good name, *kid*."

"Poppy," she said, "my name's *Poppy*."

"Nice to meet you, Poppy," Sam said. "I'm Sam, and these two are Val and Ray." He looked towards the remains of the medical centre, noticing it was the most intact building nearby. "How about we get you checked out, hm? Perhaps your daddy's there too."

He didn't see any bodies lying nearby, so whatever happened here hadn't caused any casualties. Maybe they were warned beforehand, evacuated, and made it out of the city safely. *I gotta hold on to that hope, or else I'll lose my mind.*

They escorted Poppy to the group and continued their trek to the medical centre.

Their boots crackled on the shattered glass that littered the pavement. The buildings they passed were mere skeletons of their former selves, the windows like vacant eyes watching them.

They approached the medical centre, its once-proud façade now scarred by the ravages of time. The lobby door hung off its hinges, a silent sentinel to the decay within.

"No..." Sam said, defeat lacing his voice. "This *can't* be true."

Andrew's hand hovered over the blade at his side as he listened. The building was still, the air thick with the scent of mould and decay.

"Just how long has this been deserted? There's *no way* any of this is recent, but it's also *impossible* for any mould to grow within the short time we were gone," Tim said, observing the area.

"You think whatever happened here was a time warp of some sort?" Reggie asked.

"*What?*" Seb asked, having no idea what that meant.

"Someone manipulating time," he answered. "We... had *another* superpowered lad, but they said the experiments didn't show any promising results. They said *he* was the common denominator of *all* the failures surrounding him. They said *he* was the problem."

Sam sighed. "So, he lashed out? Destroyed our city for no apparent reason?"

"Or does he work for *Jonathan*?" Tim asked.

Reggie shook his head. "I doubt it."

"*Samuel?*"

Sam turned around to stare at the doctor who had delivered his son. The doctor was a tall man with salt-and-pepper hair, slightly tousled at the back, and a prominent scar running down his left cheek—a reminder of the many battles he had fought, both physical and metaphorical. His beard, now peppered with grey, was neatly trimmed, and his sharp green eyes held a mixture of exhaustion and kindness. Without a second thought, Sam rushed towards him and embraced him. The doctor awkwardly patted Sam's back, but then leaned into the touch, sighing contentedly.

"It's so good to see you, *boy*."

Sam pulled away. "Are there any survivors, Mr. Winters?"

The doctor nodded. "About two hundred." He looked at Poppy and smiled gently, reaching out to carefully examine the dried blood on the side of her head. "Your daddy's been worried sick, but I put him on bedrest. So, it's *my* fault he didn't come looking for you sooner, *sweetie*." He gently cleaned the wound, his movements precise and kind, as Poppy winced but didn't pull away.

She nodded slowly. "I *knew* my daddy wouldn't leave me."

He lifted her up. Then, with her balancing on his arm, he escorted everyone else inside to tend to their wounds.

After he reunited Poppy with her father, Mr. Winters guided them to his office.

"He's really trottin' out that welcome wagon, isn't he?" Val whispered.

"He's a good man. We can trust him," Tim added.

Mr. Winters closed the door behind him, pointing to the makeshift examination table. "Put him on there," he said, nodding towards Alfie, who was clearly in the worst shape. "Can you give me that jar with the medicinal plants?"

Tim knew what he meant and hobbled over to it. "I assume the electricity's all gone, and so are any medications?" Tim asked him as he handed him the jar.

"Afraid so. We've been trying to make do with what we've got at our disposal, but so many people died…" He stopped himself, unable to finish the sentence. He sighed. "Forgive me, *as a doctor*, it stings."

Tim nodded and decided to change the subject. "So, do you use the Lavandula Dentate for inflammation?"

Mr. Winters laughed. "Blimey, how I missed your sharpness." He looked over at a beaming Tim. *"Go on."*

"Which makes that," he said, pointing at the yellow-rooted greenish flower, "Hydrastis Canadensis. Goldenseal."

"Fer cleanin' cuts," Agatha said. "Me sister taught me."

Mr. Winters nodded. "I'm going to need *a lot* more when I look at the lot of you. Would you be so kind?" he asked Tim, who nodded.

"On it."

"I'm coming with you," Andrew said.

They left the room.

They walked to the back of the medical centre, where they reached a series of raised flowerbeds full of plants.

"Bloody hell," Andrew said. "This is *impressive*."

"In case of an emergency, such as this," Tim said, settling down on the floor, "we rely on *herbs*." He began to cut the goldenseal's leaves, which were tucked alongside a variety of other plants, including lavender, aloe vera, and yarrow. "*You* cut the lavender." Andrew nodded, following Tim's instructions.

Tim collected some rosemary and yarrow, then looked over at Andrew, who gave a gallant bow as he presented a bundle of purple flowers. "This enough?"

Tim chuckled. "That's plenty. *Good job.*"

Andrew smiled, then looked over at him with a more serious expression. "Is Sam gonna be all right?"

Tim let out a long sigh. "Heavy's the head that wears the crown." He looked over at Andrew. "As long as we keep an eye on him and be there for him, he'll be *fine*." Though he said the last word unconvincingly, getting up. "Let's head back inside."

They gathered the plants and walked back.

They followed Mr. Winters to his makeshift workbench, where he washed the plants before adding them to a mortar and pestle.

Val let out a low whistle. "We've gone back to ancient times, haven't we? Who would've thought we'd have to climb back up from scratch?"

Mr. Winters ground the ingredients into a thick paste, looking over at him. "We'll rebuild. We've done it *before*, and we can do it *again*."

He winked at Sam. "Now, *who's* next to receive my miracle salve?"

One by one, Mr. Winters treated them, and one by one, they felt life returning to their exhausted bodies. After admitting Alfie to an empty bed, the others were treated by one of the survivors who had assumed the role of chef, cooking them a hot, nutritious bowl of soup.

They were finally *safe*. And it was *finally* over.

# CHAPTER SIXTY

Once night fell, and everyone was soundly asleep, Sam stirred awake, sitting straight up in his makeshift bed. He kicked the blanket away and got up. Taking a lantern from the bunch they had stored in the back, he walked outside.

The starry sky above him seemed like a stray thought in his racing mind. He looked up at the cobalt sky. He remembered when he took Zack outside—the night he couldn't sleep and had a nightmare.

They admired the stars stretching as far as their eyes could see. Sam looked at his son with sincerity as he gazed at the stars, his innocent eyes shining brilliantly in the starlight.

"You had a nightmare, didn't you?" Sam asked, his honeyed words just above a whisper to avoid waking Maddie. "Is that why you came into mummy and daddy's room?"

The young boy nodded, burying his head in Sam's clothes.

"I've got nightmares too," he answered honestly, "and someday, when you're older, I'll explain it all to you. What they mean, why they come, why they don't seem to go away no matter *how* hard you try." He sighed softly. "But when you're old enough, I'll tell you *how* you can survive it." He rubbed Zack's head, smiling to himself. "You know what I do? I make a list, right here." He gave Zack's head an extra rub. "That list... it's made up of all the good things in life, even the tiniest things that seem unimportant. *Even those I remember.*"

He gave Zack his bottle of milk, and Zack began to drink it eagerly. "Let's say it's a game, and we both know you love games. Don't you?" Zack nodded, still sipping his milk. "So, when you've got a nightmare again, I want you to think about playing in the backyard with daddy, making biscuits with mummy. And I need you to do that repeatedly. *Can you do that?*"

Zack nodded eagerly, mumbling incoherent words to confirm he understood.

"I know it gets a little tedi—*boring* over time. And we *don't* like boring, do we?"

Zack shook his head, finishing his milk.

"But trust me, this is the *best* game you'll ever play. And there are far worse games out there to play. But not this one, right? 'Cause this one's—"

"Best!" Zack yelled, chuckling.

Sam smiled. "Well said, son. Well said."

Zack leaned his head back against Sam's side and slowly drifted off to sleep. Sam stayed with him like that for a little longer before lifting Zack and bringing him upstairs to his bed.

Sam stood in front of his former home, now a desolate landscape of splintered wood and crumpled metal. The neighbourhood looked as if it had been picked up by a giant hand and shaken until only the most stubborn structures remained standing. Sam's eyes scanned the debris, searching for any trace of the house *he used to call home*. The once lively home was now a graveyard of a forgotten life.

Sam took a deep breath, trying to push down the bile rising in his throat. Each step felt like a struggle, as if the very ground beneath him was fighting to keep his memories buried.

A solitary doorframe leaned precariously against a pile of rubble. Sam's heart lurched as he recognised the spot where he had painted the blue numbers of their address. The door itself was gone, vanished into the chaos around them.

He stepped over the threshold, shards of glass crunched beneath his boot. The house was a gutted shell, filled with the haunting echoes of happier times.

The living room lay in ruins before him: the couch they had spent countless evenings on, the telly that had played Zack's favourite cartoons—both reduced to a tangled mess of fabric and wire. Sam had to clench his fists to keep them from shaking.

The mournful whistle of the wind was all he heard, as he moved through the wreckage. Sam felt as though he was navigating a maze of pain. Every shattered piece of furniture, every scattered photograph, was a reminder of the life that had been torn apart.

His foot caught on something, and he looked down to see a cracked frame with a photograph of Maddie, her smile frozen in time, Zack's tiny hand reaching for hers. Sam's knees buckled, and he sank to the floor, the frame clutched to his chest.

Tears streamed down his face, mixing with the dust as he studied the photograph. *The three of us, so happy, so alive. I can almost hear Maddie's laughter, feel Zack's sticky fingers in my hair.*

The sobs that wracked his body were deep and raw, a testament to the grief that had been bottled up for too long.

Finally, after an hour, and with a trembling hand, Sam pushed himself to his feet. He knew he couldn't stay here, not in this tomb of memories. But he also knew he couldn't leave, not with the sheer possibility that Zack might return home someday.

He took a deep, shuddering breath and whispered to the ghosts of his past. *"I'll find you, my son. I promise."*

Then, he thought to himself that leaving behind evidence was probably better. He found a piece of paper that seemed intact, and a small pencil that would do the trick. He sat back down on the floor, trying to keep his tears from falling onto the paper and destroying it.

*"Dear son,*

*I hope that wherever you are, you are safe and content. A parent's worst nightmare is finding out their child is not happy or is in pain. I do not know if you will ever read this, nor will I know how old you will be, but know this. I have never stopped looking for you, and I will never stop looking for you. That is my promise to you, my boy. One day, we will be reunited—you, me, and mum. And you do not have to be scared, my boy, I promise. You know why you do not have to be scared? Because your daddy is out there looking for you. And you hold onto those good things I taught you to think about whenever you have a nightmare. Whenever you think of a good thing, I will know, and I will find you. I need you to remember those good things so I can find you, my son. I love you, more than you will ever understand. You are the light of my life, and I will do anything to find you and hold you in my arms again. I will see you soon.*

*Your daddy."*

Sam left the note under a rock near the door, where it would be the first thing Zack saw if he walked through the remains of the house. With renewed determination, Sam stepped into the starry night, the photograph clutched tightly in his hand.

The search had only just begun.

Sam gasped awake. The room he found himself in was whiter than white. A white so bright it almost blinded him. He found himself dressed in white clothes, lying on a bed with white covers. *What the bloody hell?*

He heard voices from outside the door and walked over to the hallway, where he found his friends gathered. Some cried uncontrollably.

"I *can't* believe he did this," Tim said, being comforted by Seb, who couldn't contain his own tears either. "If he goes, *I* go. *End of story*," Tim added, his voice cracking.

"No, you *won't*," Val replied. "We *endure* this, and we *survive* this, just like we've endured and survived everythin' else."

"You haven't known him that long! Don't you *dare* tell me how to act or feel!" Tim shoved Val backwards. "After all I've been through with him, with everyone else in this bloody room, everything that we've done *can't* just be for nothing! It *can't*! 'Cause if I lose him, I'll lose *myself*! I lost my best friend Danny two years ago, and if *he* dies too, literally *everyone* I've ever cared about will be dead. And *you*," Tim said, jabbing a finger at Val's chest, "have no *bloody* idea what loss means!"

Val wanted to argue with Tim, scream at him, but Seb's fallen face made him stay silent.

"Everyone except for... *me, right?*" Seb said, even more upset by Tim's words than by whatever was going on, unbeknownst to Sam.

Before Tim could stop Seb from leaving, Seb walked away. Josh immediately followed him to ensure no one else would get hurt.

"*Listen*," Andrew said, walking over to Tim and Val. "Ever since we came back, I've *struggled* with surviving, with forgetting, with processing. But no matter what, I kept finding something I could fight for, and that was *love*." He grabbed Phil's hand. "We moved in together after we had gone our separate ways, but then you notified us that Sam was missing, and everything came rushing back. *Everything* we've been through that has been haunting me. But, if I were given a second chance somehow, I'd do it *all over again*." He paused. "*Everything*."

Tim nodded slowly, taking a deep, shuddering breath. He looked over at Val. "I'm sorry for... what I've said."

"Weirdly enough, I think I'm not the person you need to apologise to." He pointed towards the door Seb had disappeared through. "We'll hold down the fort here. Go talk to him."

Tim gave a confirming nod, then patted Val's shoulder before he left the others alone in pursuit of Seb.

"I know you're lost in the darkness," Sam heard Maddie say, appearing to him for a second time. "But you *need* to promise me that you'll look for the light, *and* our son. You made him a promise in that note, didn't you?"

Sam sighed. "I'm just tired of trying. I've been trying for *weeks*."

"It's only been eight weeks, *my love*. It's not gonna be that easy." She put her hand on his knee. "I just wish you weren't so scared to ask for help. It took everything outta me to have you confide in me so we could handle the problem."

"*Problem*? Which *problem*?"

She looked at him, her eyes wide. "You... dunno what happened?" He shook his head, and she forced a smile. "Well, never mind that then. I know you've broken yourself apart for me and Zack, and I *love you* for that, but I need you to *fix* yourself first."

"But that slows *everything* down. If I focus on myself *now*, the chances of finding Zack alive get slimmer."

"I know that," she said, grabbing his hand. "But you *can't* find him if you're unwell. I *need* you to stop using your old habits to manage your emotions, to escape reality, and as a coping mechanism. You *can't* be the responsible one *all* the time. Sometimes it's okay to *not* be okay, if you ask for help. You don't *have* to suffer alone." She cradled him in her embrace. "I know you think you carry the burden well, but I *know* it's heavy."

"You can only be a star when you burn," Sam said softly, though not soft enough for a whisper.

"You really think *no one* will come to save you when you ask for it?" She pushed him slightly away from her to look him straight in his eyes. "I *need* you to get up and be a *man*. Be *emotional*. Be *vulnerable*. Be *helpless*." She got up, her hands slipping out of his. "Wake up, Sam. *Wake up* and bring our son home. *Wake up!*"

Sam gasped awake, blinking against the harsh fluorescent lights. His eyelids felt sticky and heavy. The world came into focus in fragments—the white walls, the sterile smell mingling with the hum of distant machines. A rhythmic, relentless beeping pierced the silence, and Sam realised it was attached to him. His body felt like a wrung-out sponge, every muscle screaming in protest as he tried to sit up.

"Easy there," a gentle voice said as a firm hand pushed him back onto the pillow. Sam's eyes locked onto Tim, his familiar figure standing beside his bed, a reassuring presence amidst the confusion. "You've had quite the night."

He tried to speak, but his throat was a desert, his tongue thick and clumsy, croaking out only a rasp.

Tim nodded and held a cup of water to his lips. Sam took a tentative sip, the cool liquid soothing his parched throat like a soft balm.

"What... *happened*?" he rasped, his voice barely a whisper.

"You were brought in after an overdose," Tim said, his voice trying to remain calm, though it faltered. "*Alcohol*..." He cleared his throat, taking a sip of water himself. "They said... they said you're *lucky* to be alive."

Sam's heart thudded in his chest, a dull echo of the beeping monitor. "*Lucky*," he murmured, the word tasting bitter on his tongue. He remembered the bottles, the desperate need to escape, and now, realising it, he *hated* himself. "Bloody hell..." he said. "*No... bloody no... What have I done?*"

Tim's eyes searched his, a silent question reflected there. Sam looked away, his gaze settling on the plastic tubes snaking out from under the blankets. He closed his eyes, willing the tears not to come. He couldn't bear to look into Tim's eyes any longer. *I've hurt him and Seb so deeply. Everyone. The ones I've tried to save, the ones who've tried to save me, I've failed 'em. I've failed my son.* The guilt was overwhelming, a crushing weight, but maybe... maybe it was a sliver of hope. *'Cause maybe, just maybe, this means that Zack's still alive and waiting for me. And I'm destined to find him.*

The sound of footsteps grew louder. Sam braced himself for the onslaught of emotions, for the faces that would soon be staring down at him with a mix of relief and disappointment. But as the doors swung open, Seb was the first to race towards Sam's bed, hugging him so tightly that Sam could barely breathe.

"If you *ever* scare me like that again, so help me, I'm gonna *kill* you, bring you back to *life*, and kill you *again*."

"Have you been standing there *all night*?" Josh asked Tim, noticing the chair hadn't been moved from the wall.

"I was tired, but I couldn't sit down. I just *couldn't*. Is that weird?"

Josh shook his head. "That's a perfectly normal reaction."

Alex chuckled, shaking his head. "Trouble always seems to find us, doesn't it?" He eyed Sam. "And I know we all have our reasons for things that happen, but we," he said, holding Sam's hand, "*we're* all in, 'cause there's no *in-between* for us."

"You've saved *everyone*," Stan added, putting his hand on top of Alex's and Sam's, "and while you might wonder who's gonna save *you*, why don't you *let us*?"

Ray walked over too. "I know you think that the responsibility falls on you and *you alone*, but it's *not* true. It falls on *all* of us."

"What we did," Reggie added softly, "we did for *us*. Finding your son belongs to that category."

"For those we love," Josh said, "we sacrifice *everything*. Let *us* sacrifice too."

Vince, Toby, and Alfie walked over as well.

"And one day," Toby began, "we'll have what we prayed for—"

"And what we begged for—," Vince added.

"And what we hoped for," Alfie finished.

Andrew and Phil joined the group of misfits, smiling.

"And we'll have enough time to find him," Andrew said, "for we've gathered information."

"But," Phil said, noticing Sam's immediate change in expression, "we'll *only* share it with you *if*—and only *if*—you take us as your team. *All* of us. We're kinda a package deal."

Tim moved closer to Sam, putting his hand on his shoulder. "I know you think we can't handle it after our *previous adventures*, but we *can*. We can pretend, just like *you*."

That made Sam chuckle, against his better judgement.

"But we can't save someone, nor *help* someone, who's already *dead*," Seb said, his voice shaky and saddened.

"*I'm sorry,*" Sam said, holding Seb's hand and squeezing it. "I'm so sorry, *brother*."

"Don't be sorry," Seb replied, squeezing Sam's hand. "*Be better.*"

Val was the last to step forward, smirking. "You want a battle for your son? I say we give 'em war and bring that little boy back to where he belongs so I can teach him some manners. Make sure he *doesn't* follow his daddy's footsteps in down-tellin' me."

Sam chuckled, shaking his head.

"Ya boys leave nuthin' fer me to say," Agatha said, appearing in the doorway. "Blimey, what a bunch yeh are."

"But we're *your* bunch, aren't we?" Tim said, gazing at Sam. "*Right, Sam?*"

Sam looked at every one of them, his eyes welling up with tears. He let out a long, deep sigh, then smiled the brightest he had ever smiled since their return. "What would I be without you lads? *Come here.*"

They all moved in for a group hug. Val tried to move away to avoid having to hug all of them, but Ray pulled him back in. And as much as Val hated it, he had to admit, though he would never say so out loud, that the hug felt nice.

*It felt like home.*

Two weeks passed before Sam was dismissed from the medical centre. He dreaded going back to his home, the one he was trying to rebuild but felt lost within. As it came into view, he braced himself for what he would find inside.

As his foot stepped over the threshold, the other remained outside, weighed down as if filled with lead. He noticed bottles and cans scattered across the room, blueprints for the T-Roopers and Kite strewn about, and notes littering the floor. He closed the door behind him, sinking to his knees as he stared at the wreckage—and the sheer amount of alcohol he had been drinking.

He crawled over to a nearby plastic bag and began collecting the empty bottles and cans, *one by one*.

His gaze drifted to the vials of the serum they had recreated from the evidence they had gathered, and to the microscope he had stolen from the collapsed library for more thorough research.

He dropped the last can into the bag. As he moved towards the microscope, a knock on the door made him turn. Wondering who it could be—he hadn't told any of his friends he had been dismissed—he walked over and opened it.

Seb and Tim stood in front of him, both carrying bags. They dropped them onto the floor and threw their arms around Sam's neck, who could barely brace the weight of their embrace.

"What the bloody hell's this?" he asked, chuckling slightly.

Tim and Seb moved away from him and smiled. "Well, you used to live with three people in one home, and we thought, let's make that happen again."

Sam stared from Seb to Tim, shaking his head slowly. "You're not serious…"

"*Very*," Tim said. "Stan and Alex have fixed up their home, Andrew and Phil have found a place of their own, the other superpowered friends are sharing an apartment, and Josh and Alfie are roommates now."

"And Agatha has moved into *our* room," Seb added.

"So, you gotta take us in," Tim said, "or else we'll be *homeless*."

Sam was perplexed, too stunned to speak.

"No, but we're *serious*," Seb said, noticing the quietness. "We *wanna* be with you, Sam. We *wanna* be the help you can rely on, the help you can ask for and instantly receive. You're *not* alone in this anymore, 'cause we'll be right next to you through it all. We might not be able to make things perfect, but we can try to make 'em a little better at least. So, if you need a hug, need to vent, wanna laugh, feel insecure, can't sleep, need to cry, we'll be here. *Always.*"

Sam's cheeks wetted, and he nodded. "I don't deserve you two."

"Yes, *you do*," Tim said, "just as much as *we* deserve *you*."

Sam's heart skipped a beat, and they hugged each other as if tomorrow wouldn't come.

*My son's still out there. And despite the bad choices I've made in the end, my friends have helped me find the important things when I thought I had lost 'em.*

*My smile.*
*My hope.*
*And my courage.*
*I'm gonna find you, Zack, my dear boy. That's my vow to you.*
*With some help, I'm gonna bring you home.*
*You're coming home.*

# EPILOGUE

"Oi, little lad, wanna play?" a man's voice called out.

Zack looked up from his scattered pile of toys, blinking sleepily. The room was bright, the light from the single bulb above casting eerie shadows on the walls. Two figures loomed in the doorway, one human, the other *not*.

The robot was a newly advanced T-Rooper; the human was Jonathan, smiling with a face that seemed painted on. He held out a shiny, new toy car, and Zack's eyes lit up. It was just like the one he had lost months ago.

He toddled over, his chubby fingers reaching for the metal wheels.

"Your name's Zack, *right*?" Jonathan asked, his smile never wavering.

"*Zack*," he said shyly, taking the car from Jonathan. It felt cold and heavy in his small hand.

"Well, Zack, I'm *Jonathan*. I brought you some more friends to play with," he said, gesturing to the floor behind him.

Zack craned his neck to see what new toys had arrived, his heart racing with excitement.

The room was indeed filled with toys. There were action figures and robots, a plastic castle with tiny soldiers, a train set that snaked around the edges, and a mountain of stuffed, programmed animals. It looked like a toy store had vomited into the small, square space.

The walls were painted a cheerful blue, with clouds, birds, and a Kite to give the illusion of the outdoors. But Zack *knew* it wasn't the outdoors. The outdoors had grass and trees, and the sky didn't have a switch that could be turned off.

Jonathan crouched down, his knees popping. "Aren't you *lucky?* You've got *everything* a boy could *ever* want!" His eyes searched Zack's, looking for a spark of happiness. But Zack just stared at the toys, his mind elsewhere.

He didn't know *why* he was here or *why* he had so many toys. All he knew was that he *wasn't* home. He *wasn't* with mummy or daddy, and that made his tummy feel funny.

"You see, *Zack*," Jonathan began, his voice smooth and calm, "I've got *a big job* to do. And *you're* gonna help me."

Zack's eyes grew wide, and he took a step back, clutching his new car tightly. "*Home*," he whimpered.

Jonathan's smile remained plastered on his face, but his eyes darkened. "Not yet. First, we need to make sure *nobody* can *ever* take you away from me."

The tension in the room thickened, a palpable silence that seemed to suck the air out of the space. Zack looked around, the toys now seeming less like friends and more like a prison. He didn't understand what was happening, but he *knew* he didn't like it.

"You see," Jonathan continued, his voice low and serious, "I've got a plan. A big plan that *nobody* can stop. And I need you here, safe and sound, while *I* make it all come true."

Zack's bottom lip quivered, and he squeezed his eyes shut. He didn't want to listen to this man's plan.

*"I'm gonna make the whole world our playground,"* Jonathan whispered, his breath hot against Zack's ear. *"But we can't have anyone messing it up, can we?"*

Zack's heart raced faster, and he felt a tear slip down his cheek. He didn't want the world to change. He just wanted to go *home*.

*"Don't worry,"* Jonathan said, patting Zack's head. "You won't remember *any* of this. You're just a little kid. You'll forget all about it by tomorrow."

But Zack *knew* he wouldn't forget. He *knew* this room wasn't where he belonged, and he *knew* he had to find a way out— *no matter what it took.*

Days turned into weeks, and the toys lost their shine. The paint on the soldiers' faces chipped, the stuffing of the animals grew matted with his tears, and the tracks of the train set collected dust from disuse. Jonathan would come in occasionally, bringing more toys and telling him more about his plan. Zack would listen, nod, and play along, hoping that one day he'd find a way to escape.

One evening, Jonathan brought in a toy that was different from the rest. It was a small, plastic remote control with a single button. *"This,"* he said, his eyes gleaming, "is a *very* special toy. It's gonna help us with our little *project.*"

Henry appeared beside Jonathan, causing Zack to crawl away.

"Don't be scared," Jonathan reassured, "he's an example of what you're about to see. And he's *friendly*. You know *why*? 'Cause *I* control him." He held the remote out again. *"Take it."*

Zack took the remote with trembling hands. It felt cold and unfamiliar, unlike the soft, comforting toys he'd grown used to. He pressed the button, and a strange buzzing filled the room. The toys around them began to twitch and writhe, their plastic eyes rolling back in their heads. They grew larger, their limbs stretching and distorting into grotesque shapes. The robots' faces melted into snarling monsters; the soldiers' bodies elongated into creeping horrors. The room was alive with a nightmare only Zack could see.

Panic surged through him, and he dropped the remote. The buzzing stopped, and the toys collapsed, lifeless, onto the floor.

Zack stared at Jonathan in horror, his two-year-old mind struggling to process the madness. Every time he saw the door; it was always locked. And every time he heard footsteps approaching, he had to pretend to be the happy, oblivious child Jonathan wanted him to be.

Jonathan left the room, his laughter echoing for minutes until it finally disappeared, followed by Henry's heavy footsteps.

Zack crawled to the corner, curling up with his legs pulled to his chest. He began to cry silently, rocking himself back and forth. Looking up at the sky, he remembered how his daddy used to fly high above. His tiny heart clung to the hope that one day his daddy would appear.

*Daddy? Home?*

# END OF BOOK TWO

TURN THE PAGE TO START READING THE EXCLUSIVE PREVIEW AND TEASER OF THE THREEQUEL TO THE DOME CODE AND THE ISLAND TRIALS

# CHAPTER ONE

Seated in a stark, white chair, a young man thrashed about, desperately trying to escape his bindings. His grunts echoed hollowly in the vast, sterile room around him. The chair was cold and unyielding, its steel frame biting into his skin despite the thick padding that had been placed there. His wrists and ankles were bound tightly with rubbery straps that smelled faintly of antiseptic and fear.

His heart thudded in his chest like a drum that had lost its rhythm, each beat a staccato reminder of his racing thoughts. His eyes darted around the room, taking in the labyrinth of pipes and tubes that snaked along the ceiling, the gleaming metal surfaces of the counters, and the myriad instruments that hummed and beeped with a life of their own. The air was stale, recycled through vents that whirred and clicked. The walls were lined with cabinets filled with bottles and vials of every size and colour, their contents a mystery to him, though the promise of pain was unmistakable.

The doctor, a stern-faced man with short black hair and glasses that concealed eyes never quite meeting the young man's, bustled around the room. His lab coat billowed behind him like a cape. His movements were precise, almost *choreographed*, as he checked dials and made notes on a clipboard.

The doctor's name was Ralph Darach, a former associate of Duncan Ashwell. But the young man had come to think of him as *The Maestro*, conducting his twisted orchestra of science with a cold detachment that sent shivers down his spine. Ralph's voice was the only sound that pierced the quiet, a low murmur of words and numbers that seemed to dance in the air before dissipating into the void.

The last thing the young man remembered before waking up here was the sharp prick of a needle and the sensation of his world spiralling away from him like water down a drain.

The door to the lab swung open with a hiss, and a young man in a lab coat entered. He had green eyes that seemed out of place in this dystopian chamber of horrors. *He seemed kind.* His spiky brown hair, combed to the side, gave a trustworthy feeling. Though the tiny piece missing from the top of his right ear made the young man wonder what had happened to him.

The lab-coated man approached the young man cautiously, as if he were a wild animal he didn't want to startle. His voice was soft, almost a whisper. "I'm Jonathan, Dr. Darach's assistant. And I know this all seems a bit scary, but you're *in good hands*." He tapped a nearby screen. "We're about to begin the first phase of the experiment."

His voice was so sturdy and harsh that the words barely registered in the young man's mind as he focused on the voice, a hint of inhumanity showing through.

The chair began to recline, the restraint around his forehead tightening as the room tilted backwards. The lights above grew brighter, then dimmer, and his vision swam with spots. He felt a coldness spread through his body, starting at his toes and creeping upwards like a shadow.

"Just relax, *it'll all be over soon*." Jonathan's voice grew distant, the words turning into a comforting lullaby as the world around him blurred and faded into something fuzzy and indistinct.

The coldness reached his chest, wrapping around his heart and squeezing until he could hardly breathe. His eyes snapped open, and he saw Ralph standing over him, a syringe in his hand. The liquid within swirled in vibrant colours, pulsing with a life of its own.

Ralph's eyes were intense, filled with a mix of excitement and something else—was it *hatred?*

As the needle descended towards the young man's arm, the room around him began to spin. He tried to scream, but his voice was choked in his throat, a silent cry that reverberated through his mind as the world faded to black.

When the young man awoke, the pain was searing. His muscles contracted, and his bones twisted as though being reshaped into forms that defied nature. His skin itched and burned, as if a thousand ants marched beneath it, rearranging his very essence. He could feel his body changing—growing, stretching beyond human limits.

The room remained the same, but his perception of it had shifted. The edges of everything blurred and sharpened in dizzying contrast. The familiar smells of antiseptic and fear were now overwhelmed by the coppery tang of his own blood and the sickly-sweet scent of something *foreign*.

The restraints held him in place, a cruel reminder of his captivity, as his body fought the transformation. His skin stretched tight over the shifting bones, and his teeth ached as they lengthened, pushing painfully against his gums. He felt his nails thicken, turning into claws that scraped against the armrests. The agony was so intense, he thought he might *go mad*, but the thought passed quickly, swallowed by the overwhelming tide of pain.

When the change was complete, the young man felt a strange sense of *relief*. The pain had subsided, leaving behind a heavy ache that pulsed through his body like a second heartbeat. He tried to sit up, but his new form was unwieldy, his movements jerky and uncoordinated. Looking down, he saw that his hands were no longer hands at all, but grotesque appendages ending in sharp, hooked claws. His eyes had transformed, the pupils now dilated into black voids that saw everything in harsh, unrelenting contrast. His body was covered in a patchwork of decaying flesh and torn clothing, his veins now pitch black, crawling beneath his skin like creeping shadows.

"How do you feel, *Rory*?" he heard Jonathan ask.

"*Reborn*," Rory hissed, his voice rasping through his new, jagged teeth.

"Good that," Jonathan replied. "Your vitals are stable. Tell me what—"

Rory began to struggle against the straps, desperation flooding through him. His breathing grew ragged, and just as he was about to let out a scream, his body convulsed violently.

The first flicker of fire ignited deep in his chest, a tiny spark that flared up into an inferno in an instant. His skin blistered, the smell of burning flesh overwhelming his senses. The chair beneath him began to smoulder, its plastic and fabric warping and cracking under the intense heat radiating from within him. He watched, horrified, as his hands turned to ash before his very eyes, the flames crawling up his arms, licking towards his face.

The agony was beyond description—an all-consuming, searing heat that burned away every part of him. His screams were swallowed by the deafening roar of the flames, which now consumed his entire body. The pain was a chaotic symphony of sensation, tearing through his mind and body. His consciousness began to slip away, the room around him dissolving into a haze of heat and light.

Through the haze, he caught sight of Jonathan's face—a mixture of devilish delight and disheartened frustration. Jonathan seemed pleased with the results, but there was a flicker of something else, something dark and unresolved, in his eyes.

Then, a child was escorted into the room by a creature far larger than Rory had become. The child's eyes were wide with terror, and he tried to shield his face with his hands, unable to look at Rory's burning body. The creature—massive, imposing—bent down, its gigantic hand pressing against the child's, forcing him to look at Rory with a cruel, unrelenting grip.

And then, the fire was gone. In its place, an unbearable cold seeped through his body, a chilling void that seemed to devour him whole. Rory's muscles locked in place, rigid and unyielding, as the last of the flames flickered out. For a brief, suspended moment, there was absolute stillness. Then, with a final, pathetic groan, the chair beneath him gave way. Rory crashed to the floor, his body now reduced to a charred, smouldering husk, the remnants of his former self barely recognisable.

The lab fell into an eerie silence, the faint hiss of cooling embers the only sound breaking the stillness. The air was thick with the stench of burnt flesh and plastic, mingling into a nauseating fog that clung to the walls.

Zack, a three-year-old with a mop of unruly hair, wandered the halls of the facility. His small hand trailed along the wall, fingers exploring the cold, unyielding surface. His bare feet made no sound as he padded through the sterile corridors, unaware of the horrors that lurked behind the closed doors he passed.

As he turned a corner, the acrid scent of burning filled the air, sharp and unsettling. He stopped, his nose wrinkling in confusion. The door to the lab where Rory had been transformed was slightly ajar, and through the crack, he could see the room beyond—something no child should ever have to witness.

Rory lay on the floor, his body a twisted mess of blackened flesh and bone. The flames had long since ceased, but the stench of charred remains lingered in the air.

Zack took a tentative step forward, curiosity overcoming his fear. He had never seen anything like this before, and part of him wanted to understand—to make sense of the creature that had been created. His eyes widened as he looked at Rory's body, the smouldering embers of what had once been his flesh, layers of fine ash left behind. But it was the *sound* that truly terrified him—the crackling of bones as they calcified, turning from living tissue to something more akin to stone.

The horror washed over him in waves, each more powerful than the last. Tears filled his eyes, and his lower lip quivered as the weight of the situation settled in. The room around him seemed to close in, the walls pressing against him, and the floor grew unsteady beneath his feet. He stumbled backwards, slapping his hand against the doorframe.

A piercing scream escaped him when Rory's hand grabbed his leg. He kicked desperately, but Rory's hand remained unmoving, frozen in place.

"*Help!*" Zack cried, voice cracking. "JJ, *help!*"

The lights flickered, and the room grew darker. Zack's sobs echoed through the corridors as he stumbled and fell, scraping his knees on the unforgiving floor. He tried to turn and run as fast as his little legs could carry him, but Rory's hand, now a grotesque mass of bone and tissue, clung to him.

"*Push the button, Zack,*" Jonathan's voice came over the speaker, cold and measured. "*Go on, I know how much talent you possess when it comes to pushing buttons. Remember what I showed you four months ago? Only you can push the button. Only you can stop this.*"

Zack felt the same pressure Jonathan had placed on him back then, shaking his head repeatedly. "No! *Don't wanna!*"

Jonathan let out a loud sigh through the speaker. "*Don't make me hurt your daddy.*"

Zack cried louder, his tiny face scrunching up. "*Mean man!*"

"*I can be way meaner if you don't do what I say. Push. The. Button.*"

Zack's hand hovered above the button, hesitating. He looked at Rory, whose eyes met his. Zack couldn't tell what his eyes were trying to say, but the thought of Jonathan hurting his daddy was more terrifying than anything else. With trembling hands, Zack pressed the button.

A large stone, suspended from the ceiling by cables, came crashing down, pulverising what remained of Rory. A cloud of white dust settled over Zack instantly, his tiny foot trapped beneath the rock.

He screamed in pain, tears streaming down his face so fast that his trousers were soaked.

Jonathan finally emerged from his hiding spot, walking over to Zack, who struggled desperately to free himself. "*Make pain stop!*" he whimpered.

Jonathan loomed over him. "You continue to *defy* me as your caretaker. This is *precisely* where you belong right now. See it as a little loophole that'll grant you your freedom if you listen and do what *I* say."

"Please," Zack begged, "*I pain!*"

Jonathan sighed, looking over at Henry. He waved him over, and as Henry lifted the rock from Zack's foot, Jonathan smiled. "Like

I said, *earn it."* He motioned for Henry to drop it, crushing Zack's foot a second time.

Rory's half-decayed bones littered the floor, turning to dust once the stone hit them again.

Jonathan stood before Zack, bending down to his level. "Listen, *kid.* I've *already* killed your mummy, and I can kill your *daddy* too. Don't make this any harder than it needs to be." He slipped his finger under Zack's chin, forcing the boy to meet his gaze. "So, next time I ask you to *push* the button, what's the *one* thing you gotta do?"

"Push..."

"Good boy."

Jonathan turned on his heel, walking away without saying another word.

The pain in Zack's foot was unbearable, a white-hot agony that shot up his leg, searing through his very soul. He could feel his bones grinding together, the pressure unrelenting as his sobs filled the small room. He screamed again, his cries echoing off the walls. The tears streamed down his face, mixing with the dust and grime that coated his cheeks. His breath came in ragged gasps, each inhale a battle against the pain that threatened to swallow him whole.

The world around him turned into a blur of shadows, morphing into a jagged tomb of twisted metal and broken glass. The only light came from the flickering emergency lights above, casting eerie patterns on the floor as they danced in their death throes.

*"Zack? Can you hear me?"*

Zack heard an unknown voice reach him in his head, panic-stricken by how clear it sounded.

*"Don't be afraid of me. I'm a friend of your daddy. My name's Andy, and I'm here to help you. I've seen what you're capable of. You're a special one. And I'm special too. Now, listen to my voice, okay?"*

Zack nodded slowly. The voice was far kinder than Jonathan's had ever been, and something inside him told him he could trust this person named *Andy.*

*"Concentrate on my voice. Let it in."*

Zack didn't understand what Andy meant, shaking his head. "No, *not know."*

*"It's already in you, Zack, it just needs to come out. Think about daddy, okay? He's right here next to me and he loves and misses you so much. If you do this, you'll come home, I promise you that. But you gotta listen to yourself. Let it in. Set it free."*

"Daddy?" Zack said, his heart lifting with hope.

"Yes, daddy's right here. And daddy needs you to be a good, strong boy. Can you do that?"

Zack nodded determinedly, feeling a strange warmth spread through his body. It began in his chest, a gentle glow that grew stronger with each beat of his heart. The pain in his foot lessened, replaced by a tingling sensation that spread up his leg and into his torso. He looked down, and to his amazement, he saw his skin knitting itself back together, the bones beneath realigning with a sickening crack. The rock that had held him captive began to shift; the weight lifted as if by some unseen hand.

With a final, desperate push, Zack managed to wiggle his foot free from the rock's grip. He rolled onto his back, panting heavily, his eyes wide with shock and disbelief.

The warmth grew stronger, the glow now visible to his own eyes, pulsing in time with his heartbeat. It was as if a switch had been flipped, and now, instead of fear, he felt something else—*something powerful and fierce.*

He stood, his legs shaking, and took a tentative step. The pain was gone, replaced by an unfamiliar strength that surged through his veins.

"Good lad. Now, don't tell the bad man about this, okay? It'll be our little secret."

"Okay."

It was the last thing Andrew was able to tell Zack before the world fell apart.

# ABOUT THE AUTHOR

Skye Lewis, born February 21, 1997, is the author of *Raven's Phoenix*, the first book in a planned YA fantasy trilogy, and the *Life of Emotion* series, published between 2015 and 2017. Skye is currently working on multiple books across genres such as war, thriller, horror, sci-fi, and fantasy.

A writer and blogger since the age of fourteen, Skye has devoured hundreds of sci-fi and fantasy books and films. With a background in teaching, marking, and communication (with a diploma), journalism (with papers), English language and culture (with a future diploma), and archaeology, Skye chose to debut as a fantasy and sci-fi author under their current pen name.

The *Life of Emotion* series (2012-2017) follows a young woman as she chases her dreams, unaware of the consequences her choices will have on those around her—and her future. This five-book series chronicles her journey through friendship, heartache, and strength.

*Raven's Phoenix*, published in February 2021, is the first book in a planned trilogy about mythical creatures, dark secrets, and magical powers. The story follows a group of strangers who become friends and fight together to rid the world of evil. Books two and three are set to be published at an unspecified date.

*The Dome Code*, the first book in a planned sci-fi and dystopian trilogy, was published in May 2022. *The Island Trials*, the second book in the trilogy, was published in February 2025, with the third book set for release in early 2026.

# ABOUT THE ART

The book cover was designed and illustrated by Coach K.

The cover of this book is inspired by key elements from the story. It depicts a burning island, its trees and small huts still smouldering amidst the destruction. The dark, smoky skies reflect the perilous journey the characters face. In the foreground, a few boys walk towards the island, their figures silhouetted against the fiery chaos. This scene represents the Troopers' struggle to escape the islands, while also confronting the devastation and tyranny they must overcome. The island's landscape and the dramatic colouring are directly inspired by the environment described in the book. The references used were non-copyrighted designs by Coach K.

The cover was made using Adobe Photoshop and Adobe InDesign.

The book title and author's name were both sketched based on a reference image. The font for the book title is an Adobe font, Battery Park, and is licensed for commercial use. The author's name is a standard Adobe font, also licensed for commercial use.

Printed in Great Britain
by Amazon